CECIL COUNTY
PUBLIC LIBRARY

FEB 0 4 2014

301 Newark Ave
Elkton, MD 21921

**But my attacker wasn't interested in sex. He was aroused by something else altogether—blood. My blood.**
My fear.

The next instant, his teeth clamped over the bleeding wound. Pain blasted up my arm like lightning. Sickening sucking sounds filled the night air. Fear burst like a blinding light in my brain. "Fuck!"

The perp pulled me toward the ground and pinned me. The impact knocked the weapon from my hand, but it only lay a couple feet away. I reached for it with my left hand. But fingers can stretch only so far no matter how much you yearn and curse and pray.

The pain was like needles stabbing my vein. My vision swam. If I didn't stop him soon, I'd pass out. If that happened he'd drag me into those tunnels and no one would see me again.

Fortunately, elbows make excellent motivators. Especially when they're rammed into soft temples. At least they usually are. In this case, my bloodthirsty opponent was too busy feasting on my flesh and blood to react. Finally, in a desperate move, I bucked my hips like a wild thing. He lost contact with my arm just long enough for me to roll a few centimeters closer to my target.

I reared up, grabbed the gun, and pivoted.

The pistol's mouth kissed his cheek a split second before it removed his face.

Backup arrived thirty seconds too late.

CECIL COUNTY
PUBLIC LIBRARY

# BY JAYE WELLS

## PROSPERO'S WAR

*Dirty Magic*

*Cursed Moon*

## SABINA KANE

*Red-Headed Stepchild*

*The Mage in Black*

*Green-Eyed Demon*

*Silver-Tongued Devil*

*Blue-Blooded Vamp*

## SABINA KANE SHORT FICTION

*Violet Tendencies*

*Rusted Veins*

# JAYE WELLS

www.orbitbooks.net

Copyright © 2014 by Jaye Wells
Excerpt from *Strange Fates* copyright © 2013 by Marlene Perez

All rights reserved. In accordance with the U.S. Copyright Act of 1976, the scanning, uploading, and electronic sharing of any part of this book without the permission of the publisher is unlawful piracy and theft of the author's intellectual property. If you would like to use material from the book (other than for review purposes), prior written permission must be obtained by contacting the publisher at permissions@hbgusa.com. Thank you for your support of the author's rights.

Orbit
Hachette Book Group
237 Park Avenue, New York, NY 10017
HachetteBookGroup.com

First Edition: January 2014

Orbit is an imprint of Hachette Book Group, Inc. The Orbit name and logo are trademarks of Little, Brown Book Group Limited.

The Hachette Speakers Bureau provides a wide range of authors for speaking events. To find out more, go to www.hachettespeakersbureau.com or call (866) 376-6591.

The publisher is not responsible for websites (or their content) that are not owned by the publisher.

The characters and events in this book are fictitious. Any similarity to real persons, living or dead, is coincidental and not intended by the author.

Library of Congress Cataloging-in-Publication Data
Wells, Jaye.
    Dirty Magic / Jaye Wells. — First edition.
        pages cm
    ISBN 978-0-316-22843-5 (trade pbk.) — ISBN 978-0-316-22844-2 (ebook)   1. Werewolves—Fiction.   2. Fantasy fiction.   I. Title.
    PS3623.E46898D57 2014
    813'.6—dc23

                                                        2013018997

10  9  8  7  6  5  4  3  2  1

RRD-C

Printed in the United States of America

*For Mom, the original kick-ass chick.*

# Chapter One

It was just another fucked-up night in the Cauldron. Potion junkies huddled in shadowy corners with their ampoules and pipes and needles. The occasional flick of a lighter's flame illuminated their dirty, desperate faces, and the air sizzled with the ozone scent of spent magic.

I considered stopping to harass them. Arrest them for loitering and possession of illegal arcane substances. But they'd just be back on the street in a couple of days or be replaced by other dirty, desperate faces looking to escape the Mundane world.

Besides, these hard cases weren't my real targets. To make a dent, you had to go after the runners and stash boys, the potion cookers—the moneymen. The way I figured, better to hunt the vipers instead of the 'hood rats who craved the bite of their fangs. But for the last couple of weeks, the corner thugs had been laying low, staying off the streets after dark. My instincts were tingling, though, so I kept walking the beat, hoping to find a prize.

Near Canal Street, growls rolled out of a pitch-black alley.

I stilled and listened with my hand on my hawthorn-wood nightstick. The sounds were like a feral dog protecting a particularly juicy bone. The hairs on the back of my neck prickled, and my nostrils twitched from the coppery bite of blood.

Approaching slowly, I removed the flashlight from my belt. The light illuminated about ten feet into the alley's dark throat. On the nearest wall, a graffitied dragon marked the spot as the Sanguinarian Coven's turf. But I already knew the east side of town belonged to the Sangs. That's one of the reasons I'd requested it for patrol. I didn't dare show my face on the Votary Coven's west-side territory.

Something moved in the shadows, just outside of the light's halo. A loud slurping sound. A wet moan.

"Babylon PD!" I called, taking a few cautious steps forward. The stink of blood intensified. "Come out with your hands up!"

The scuttling sound of feet against trash. Another growl, but no response to my order.

Three more steps expanded my field of vision. The light flared on the source of the horrible sounds and the unsettling scents.

A gaunt figure huddled over the prone form of a woman. Wet, stringy hair shielded her face, and every inch of her exposed skin glistened red with blood. My gun was in my hand faster than I could yell, "Freeze!"

Still partially in shadow, the attacker—male, judging from the size—swung around. I had the impression of glinty, yellow eyes and shaggy hair matted with blood.

"Step away with your hands up," I commanded, my voice projected to make it a demand instead of a suggestion.

"Fuck you, bitch," the male barked. And then he bolted.

"Shit!" I ran to the woman and felt for a pulse. I shouldn't have been relieved not to find one, but it meant I was free to pursue the asshole who'd killed her.

My leg muscles burned and my heart raced. Through the radio on my shoulder I called Dispatch.

"Go ahead, Officer Prospero," the dispatcher's voice crackled through the radio.

"Be advised I need an ambulance sent to the alley off Canal and Elm. Interrupted a code twenty-seven. Victim had no pulse. I'm pursuing the perp on foot bearing east on Canal."

"Ambulance is on its way. Backup unit will be there in five minutes. Keep us advised of your twenty."

"Ten-four." I took my finger off the comm button. "Shit, he's fast." I dug in, my air coming out in puffs of vapor in the cool night air.

He was definitely freaking—a strength or speed potion, probably. But that type of magic wouldn't explain why he mauled that woman in the alley—or those yellow predator's eyes. I tucked that away for the moment and focused on keeping up.

The perp loped through the maze of dark alleys and streets as if he knew the Cauldron well. But no one knew it better than I did, and I planned to be right behind him when he finally made a mistake.

As I ran, my lead cuffs clanked heavily against the wood of my nightstick. The rhythm matched the thumping beats of my heart and the air rasping from my lungs. I had a Glock at my side, but when perps are jacked up on potions, they're almost unstoppable with Mundane weaponry unless you deliver a fatal shot. Killing him wasn't my goal—I wanted the notch on my arrest stats.

"Stop or I'll salt you!" I pulled the salt flare from my left side. The best way to incapacitate a hexhead was to use a little of the old sodium chloride.

A loud snarling grunt echoed back over his shoulder. He

picked up the pace, but he wasn't running blind. No, he was headed someplace specific.

"Prospero," Dispatch called through the walkie. "Backup is on its way."

"Copy. The vic?"

"Ambulance arrived and confirmed death. ME is on his way to make it official."

I looked around to get my bearings. He veered right on Mercury Street. "The suspect appears to be headed for the Arteries," I spoke into the communicator. "I'm pursuing."

"Copy that, Officer Prospero. Be advised you are required to wait for backup before entering the tunnels." She told me their coordinates.

I cursed under my breath. They were still five blocks away and on foot.

A block or so ahead I could see one of the boarded-up gates that led down into the old subway tunnels. The system had been abandoned fifty years earlier, before the project was anywhere close to completion. Now the tunnels served as a rabbit warren for potion addicts wanting to chase the black dragon in the rat-infested, shit-stench darkness.

In front of the gate, a large wooden sign announced the site as the FUTURE HOME OF THE CAULDRON COMMUNITY CENTER. Under those words was the logo for Volos Real Estate Development, which did nothing to improve my mood.

If Speedy made it through that gate, we'd never find him. The tunnels would swallow him in one gulp. My conscience suddenly sounded a lot like Captain Eldritch in my head: *Don't be an idiot, Kate. Wait for backup.*

I hadn't run halfway through the Cauldron only to lose the bastard to the darkness. But I knew better than to enter the tunnels alone. The captain had laid down that policy after a rookie ended up as rat food five years earlier. So I wasn't going to follow him there, but I could still slow him down a little. Buy some time for backup to arrive.

The salt flare's thick double barrel was preloaded with two rock-salt shells. A bite from one of those puppies was rarely lethal, but it was enough to dilute the effects of most potions, as well as cause enough pain to convince perps to lie down and play dead. The only catch was, you had to be within twenty feet for the salt to interrupt the magic. The closer, the better if you wanted the bonus of severe skin abrasions.

The runner was maybe fifteen feet from me and a mere ten from the gate that represented his freedom. Time to make the move. I stopped running and took aim.

*Exhale. Squeeze. Boom!*

Rock salt exploded from the gun in a starburst. Some of the rocks pinged off the gate's boards and metal fittings. The rest embedded in the perp's shirtless back like shrapnel. Small red pockmarks covered the dirty bare skin not covered with tufts of dark hair. He stumbled, but he didn't stay down.

Instead, he leaped up the gate and his hands grasped the top edge. A narrow opening between the gate and the upper concrete stood between him and freedom.

"Shit!" Frustration and indecision made my muscles yearn for action. My only choice was to take him down.

Speedy already had his head and an arm through the opening at the top of the gate. I surged up and grabbed his ankles. Lifted my feet to help gravity do its job. We slammed to the ground and rolled all asses and elbows through the dirt and grass and broken potion vials.

The impact momentarily stunned us both. My arm stung where the glass shards had done their worst, but the pain barely registered through the heady rush of adrenaline.

Speedy exploded off the ground with a growl. I jumped after him, my grip tight on the salt flare. I still had one shell left, not that I expected it to do much good after seeing the first one had barely fazed him. In my other hand, I held a small canister of S&P spray. "BPD! You're under arrest!"

The beast barely looked human. His hair was long and matted in some patches, which alternated with wide swaths of pink scalp—as if he'd been infected with mange. The lower half of his face was covered in a shaggy beard. The pale skin around his yellow eyes and mouth was red and raw. His teeth were crooked and sharp. Too large for his mouth to corral. Hairy shoulders almost touched his ears like a dog with his hackles up.

If he understood my command he didn't show it. That intense yellow gaze focused on my right forearm where a large gash oozed blood. His too-red lips curled back into a snarl.

I aimed the canister of salt-and-pepper spray. The burning mixture of saline and capsicum hit him between the eyes. He blinked, sneezed. Wiped a casual hand across his face. No screaming. No red, watery eyes or swollen mucus glands.

His nostrils flared and he lowered his face to sniff the air closer to me. His yellow eyes stayed focused on my wound. An eager red tongue caressed those sharp teeth in anticipation.

For the first time, actual fear crept like ice tendrils up the back of my neck. What kind of fucked-up potion was this guy on?

I don't remember removing the Glock from my belt. I don't remember pointing it at the perp's snarling face. But I remember shouting, "Stop or I'll shoot!"

One second the world was still except for the pounding of my heart and the cold fear clawing my gut. The next, his wrecking-ball weight punched my body to the ground. My legs flew up and my back crashed into the metal gate. Hot breath escaped my panicked lungs. His body pinned me to the metal bars.

Acrid breath on my face. Body odor and unwashed skin everywhere. An erect penis pressed into my hip. But my attacker wasn't interested in sex. He was aroused by something else altogether—blood. My blood.

My fear.

The next instant, his teeth clamped over the bleeding wound. Pain blasted up my arm like lightning. Sickening sucking sounds filled the night air. Fear burst like a blinding light in my brain. "Fuck!"

The perp pulled me toward the ground and pinned me. The impact knocked the weapon from my hand, but it only lay a couple feet away. I reached for it with my left hand. But fingers can stretch only so far no matter how much you yearn and curse and pray.

The pain was like needles stabbing my vein. My vision swam. If I didn't stop him soon, I'd pass out. If that happened he'd drag me into those tunnels and no one would see me again.

Fortunately, elbows make excellent motivators. Especially when they're rammed into soft temples. At least they usually are. In this case, my bloodthirsty opponent was too busy feasting on my flesh and blood to react. Finally, in a desperate move, I bucked my hips like a wild thing. He lost contact with my arm just long enough for me to roll a few centimeters closer to my target.

I reared up, grabbed the gun, and pivoted.

The pistol's mouth kissed his cheek a split second before it removed his face.

Backup arrived thirty seconds too late.

# Chapter Two

I limped into the precinct a couple hours later. A huge white bandage glared from my right forearm and a black eye throbbed on my face. My blood-soaked uniform had been confiscated by the team that arrived shortly after my tardy backup to investigate the shooting. They'd also taken my service weapon, salt flare, S&P spray canister, and shoes. Which left me feeling naked despite the blue scrubs I'd been issued by the wizard medics.

After sewing up my arm in the back of an ambulance while I'd answered the shoot team's questions, the wizard had slammed a syringe full of saline and antibiotics into my ass. The shoot team had waited until they'd gotten a good eyeful of my rear bumper before they declared me free to go. I knew better than to believe I wouldn't be hearing from them again. Especially after they'd warned me to stay within Babylon city limits.

I'd just dropped by the precinct to grab my things before heading home. I'd called my neighbor, Baba, from the ambulance to let her know I'd be later than usual. She'd said it was no problem staying late to keep an eye on Danny. Luckily, she'd been too wrapped up in the show she'd been watching to question me about the reason for the overtime. If I were even luckier neither she nor my brother would notice the bandage on my arm when they saw me, but it would take a miracle to miss the black eye.

My feet felt like they were encased in lead boots instead of flip-flops as I made my way toward the locker room. I caught my reflection in the glass of one of the interrogation rooms and cringed. My one good eye looked unnaturally blue next to its swollen purple twin. I'd managed to get all the smears off my face, but my brunette hair was still matted in spots with Speedy's blood. I needed a hot shower and a stiff drink— preferably at the same time. But first—

"Prospero, get your ass in here!" Captain Eldritch yelled from his doorway. The entire squad room went silent as cops paused to gape at the unfolding drama.

With a heavy sigh, I dropped my duffel bag at my desk and performed the walk of shame. My colleagues didn't bother to cover their curious stares and smirks. For the next few hours, this scene would be replayed and analyzed around the water-cooler along with the leaked details of the shooting. Cops were worse than housewives when it came to gossip.

"Sit down." Stress lines permanently bracketed Eldritch's mouth. His baldpate glowed dully under the harsh fluorescent lights. The desk hid a paunch that betrayed a lifelong love affair with fried dough, but one would be unwise to mistake his gen-erous midsection for a sign of weakness. He'd maneuvered his way up from patrolman to captain in a criminal justice system rife with political intrigue and bureaucratic red tape. For his efforts, he was rumored to be next in line for chief of the entire BPD. In other words, he was not a man to piss off.

"I won't bother asking if you're all right because I can see you are. Instead, I'll begin by asking what the fuck you thought you were doing?"

"Sir, I—"

He slashed a hand through the air. "Don't bother. You weren't thinking. Not a damned thing. That's the only explanation that makes any sense. Because I know you were trained better than to enter a dangerous confrontation with a hexed-out suspect without backup."

"If I'd waited for backup that bastard would be running free through the Arteries."

"Thanks to you he's not going to be running anywhere ever again."

I leaned forward, my hands up in a pleading gesture. "It was a clean kill, sir." If you could call blowing someone's face off "clean."

He sat back and crossed his arms over his gut. He hit me with his best cop glare—the same one I used on suspects until they broke under the oppressive weight of silence. But I wasn't a criminal—not anymore, anyway—and I knew I'd done the right thing. In fact, if I had to do it over again I would have made the same call.

"Even if I'd waited for backup the outcome would have been the same." I looked right in his eyes. "He was immune to every defensive charm I tried. There was no stopping him without lethal force."

The captain scrubbed a hand over his face and sat up. His chair creaked in protest. "Christ, Prospero. Damned if I wouldn't have done the same thing." I opened my mouth to ask why I was getting the riot act if that was the case, but he held up a hand to stall my arguments. "Be that as it may, since this case involved deadly force, the rules dictate that I put you on suspension pending an investigation of the incident."

My mouth dropped open. "But—"

"There's not a damned thing I can do about it, so don't waste your breath. We got bigger issues to discuss."

I shook my head at him. Forcing a cop to take leave after the use of deadly force was standard procedure, but I wasn't about to sit on the sidelines with a new lethal potion on the streets. Still, the look in his eyes told me arguing would only prolong the suspension.

"The ME identified your perp." The lightning-fast change in topic nearly gave me whiplash.

"And?" I frowned.

"His name was Ferris Harkins." The female voice surprised me from the doorway.

I swiveled to see a tall woman in a smart navy pantsuit. Her brown hair was cut in a no-nonsense bob. The lines between her brows told me they were used to frowning, and the steel in her gaze hinted at a razor-blade tongue. She wore her watch on her right wrist and her briefcase was clutched in that same hand. Whoever she was, she was definitely a Lefty—just like me.

I glanced back at Eldritch. He didn't look surprised by the new arrival so much as resigned to it. He pasted his best politician smile on his lips and rose to shake her hand. "I was about to inform Officer Prospero of your interest in the case."

"That's a diplomatic way to phrase it, Captain." She turned to me. "Special Agent Miranda Gardner."

I frowned at her. "Which agency?"

She smiled tightly. "MEA."

Something heavy bounced off the base of my stomach. If the Magic Enforcement Agency was involved, things were about to get...complicated.

After a moment's hesitation, I rose and offered her my left

hand. I usually offered my right to Mundanes to avoid awkwardness, but she offered me her left, which confirmed she was an Adept.

Her handclasp was brief but firm enough to tell me she meant business. When I looked down at our hands, I noticed a cabochon ring on her middle finger.

"Nice ring," I said. "Tigereye?"

She nodded and pulled her hand away. "The stone of truth and logic."

And she wore it on her Saturn finger—the finger of responsibility and security—which meant she wanted a boost in those areas. Interesting.

She tipped her chin at my wrist. "And your tattoo—Ouroboros?"

I placed my right hand over my wrist, as if the snake might jump off my skin otherwise. "A youthful transgression," I said in a flippant tone that disguised the massive understatement it really was.

Eldritch cleared his throat. I looked up to see Gardner watching me with a too-wise gaze. Either she already knew the snake swallowing its own tail was the emblem of the Votary Coven or she merely smelled the lie on me. Time to change the subject.

"Why is the MEA interested in Ferris Harkins?" I glanced at Eldritch, but he looked away.

"What your captain was about to tell you before I interrupted," Gardner said, "is that the man you killed tonight was an MEA informant."

I closed my eyes. "Fuck. Me."

"Funny, that's exactly what I said when his name popped up on ACD two hours ago as deceased."

ACD stood for the Arcane Crime Database, a federal clearinghouse of all magic-related criminal activity in the country.

Actually, that's not entirely true. ACD just kept track of the illegal dirty magic. The corporate labs that produced legal, "clean" magical products, aka Big Magic, bought their legitimacy through lobbyist bribes and the generous tax revenue they generated for Uncle Sam.

I opened my eyes. "Were you aware when you recruited him that he was a hexhead with a hard-on for murder?"

"He wasn't a hexhead when we recruited him." She handed over a picture of a male. Mid-twenties, scruffy with a hardness to his gaze that hinted at life on the street, but no noticeable signs of magic use—dilated pupils, scabs, etc. A far cry from the gaunt, savage creature I'd killed. A scribbled date at the bottom told me the picture had been taken a week earlier.

"Are you sure we're talking about the same guy?"

"Positive. I've just come from IDing the body."

Usually potions took several months—sometimes years—of heavy use to transform normal people into freaks and monsters. "You expect me to believe a potion turned this guy"—I held up the picture—"into the beast I shot in less than a week?"

She removed her cell from her briefcase and flashed another picture. This one was taken at the morgue. There wasn't enough face left to compare so it was impossible to use that to verify whether the identity matched the first shot. But then Gardner tapped the image to indicate a tattoo of a skull with the words *Et in Arcadia ego* underneath on the dead man's left wrist.

Frowning, I lifted the old picture again. Sure enough, the same tattoo was on Ferris Harkins's "before" picture. "The tattoo's the same. But that's hardly conclusive."

"True. However, as you'll see in the file, the identity was also confirmed through fingerprints."

I blew out a deep sigh. "Okay, so how did this guy"—I held

up the first shot—"end up like this?" I held up a screen shot from the file that had been taken from my vest cam. In it Harkins looked like something from hell: a wild-eyed hellhound with bloodstained teeth.

"Four days ago, we sent Harkins to do a buy," explained Gardner. "He was supposed to meet up with one of my agents an hour later but never showed. We've been looking for him since. At first we figured he ran off with the buy money, but then this." She motioned vaguely at me as if I was the *this* in question.

My mouth fell open. "You gave a CI cash and then set him loose in the Cauldron? What the fuck did you think was going to happen?"

"Prospero," Eldritch warned.

"Sorry," I grumbled. "But what was the MEA doing setting up a buy in the Cauldron to begin with? And why didn't we know about it?"

"Forgive me, Officer," Gardner said, laughing. "I wasn't aware the federal government had to ask your permission to run investigations in Babylon."

I crossed my arms and sucked at my teeth to prevent more expletives from escaping. Eldritch wouldn't meet my eyes at all—so much for support from that quarter.

"Your actions tonight have complicated the shit out of my case," Gardner continued.

"Seems like you complicated it yourself when you lost your snitch, Special Agent."

Her eyes narrowed, but she didn't rise to the bait. "A few weeks ago, one of our agents working undercover in Canada reported that an illegal shipment of antimony was being sent to Babylon."

Antimony is a common metalloid used in everything from

cosmetics to the treatment of constipation to the manufacturing of ceramics. Gardner's mention of a shipment was notable, however, because the element was also used in a lot of potions. In fact, it was so commonly used in alchemy that the government had started regulating its sale a decade earlier to try to limit street wizes' access to it.

"I don't suppose they gave you a delivery address?" I asked in a dry tone.

Gardner's lips pressed together. Guess she wasn't a fan of sarcasm. "No, but we got our team in place shortly after and have been watching things since. About a week ago, Captain Eldritch called to tell us there had been a couple of unusual assaults."

"Nothing like what happened tonight, but pretty violent," Eldritch said. "The victims had each been bitten multiple times."

"Why didn't you put it in the debriefing reports?" I demanded.

His face hardened at my challenge. "I didn't want to alarm anyone unnecessarily."

I swallowed my retort. If I had to bet, Eldritch hadn't made the report official because then his precinct would have gotten some unwanted attention from the chief and the mayor, who was up for reelection. "So you told the MEA instead?"

"Ever since Abraxas went to Crowley, the MEA has been keeping an eye on Babylon," Eldritch offered, "waiting to see who would step up to fill the power vacuum."

I snorted. "No one would be dumb enough to do that while Uncle Abe's still alive." As I spoke I kept a careful eye on Gardner to see her reaction to my casually claiming Abraxas Prospero as kin. She didn't even blink, which meant she'd known who I was before she walked into that room. Part of me was relieved not to have to explain the connection or how I'd walked away from Uncle Abe and his coven a decade earlier. In fact, the last time I'd seen him was when I watched his trial on TV with the rest of the city. During the testimony, he'd smiled at the camera like he'd been savoring a juicy secret. I shivered, shaking off the memory.

"So you figure whoever ordered that antimony is trying at least to consolidate the Votaries." I crossed my arms and tried to sort through all the angles.

*Votary* is another name for wizards who specialize in an alchemical form of dirty magic. In the dirty magic food chain, Votaries are at the top, followed by the Os, who specialize in sex magic, and the Sanguinarians, who deal in dirty blood potions.

"That's one of our theories." Gardner was watching me carefully now that she knew I had criminal blood in my veins.

It had been five years since Abe earned his all-expenses-paid trip to Crowley Penitentiary. Before his downfall, he'd been the grand wizard of the Votary Coven and the godfather who'd kept all the other covens in line. Once he was behind bars, no one had the balls to come forward and declare themselves the new kings of the Cauldron, so the covens splintered, which resulted in lots of turf battles. If Eldritch and Gardner were right about someone's trying to make a power play, we were looking at a lot more dead bodies piling up before this was all said and done. But that was a pretty huge *if.*

"Antimony has lots of uses besides alchemy, Special Agent."

She crossed her arms and smirked at me. "That's true, I suppose. But we've checked the official shipment manifests of every freighter that's come into Babylon in the last month. No shipments of antimony showed up. That means whoever received it was trying to keep it off the record."

"Look, even if you're right and the antimony was used in the potion Harkins was on," I countered, "it doesn't mean we're looking at consolidation of power. It could just be a new wiz who wants to make his mark."

"You could be right." She nodded. "That's one of the reasons we sent Harkins to make a buy. We were hoping that once we knew who was dealing the potion we could convince them to flip on the distributor."

"But he got hooked before he could report back to you," I said.

She nodded.

"What's the potion called?"

Gardner exchanged a tense glance with Eldritch, who'd remained tellingly silent during the exchange. No doubt about it. Special Agent Gardner was in charge. "The street name is Gray Wolf."

"Clever," I said.

"Why?" Eldritch asked. He'd worked the Arcane beat for years, but he was still a Mundane. Sometimes the intricacies of the craft eluded him.

"The gray wolf is the alchemical symbol for antimony," Gardner explained.

"Shit," I said. "If this stuff takes off, we're toast." From what I'd seen, Gray Wolf created both immunity to defensive magic and a ravenous craving for human flesh. Plus it acted incredibly fast on the user's body chemistry.

"And now that Harkins is dead, we're back at square one," Gardner said.

My stomach dipped. I didn't regret killing Harkins, but I was sorry my actions made getting the potion off the streets more difficult. "How can I help?"

"Nothing beyond a detailed report on your altercation with Harkins. Maybe you saw something we can use."

I nodded absently. "You mentioned that you thought Gray

Wolf was alchemical. Does that mean you had a wizard analyze the ingredients?"

"Yes, off a blood sample we gathered at one of the crime scenes. But our team's wizard has only had a chance to do preliminary tests."

I chewed on my lip. I'd love to get my hands on that sample to figure out what made Harkins change so quickly. A new thought arrived hot on the heels of that one. "Wait, do you have any BPD officers on your task force?"

Since the 1980s, the MEA had been partnering with local police agencies by bringing local cops in on cases. It benefited the agency because it got access to locals who understood the dynamics of their cities, and the cops benefited because the MEA paid generous overtime. In other words, if they were hiring, I wanted in.

Gardner frowned at the change of subject. Then she exchanged a glance with Eldritch.

"I'm putting together a list of candidates," he said, not meeting my eyes. Translation: I wasn't on it.

"Look, I know you don't know me from Adam," I said. "But I'd love a chance to consult on this case."

Her eyebrows rose at my audacity. When she didn't laugh, I forged ahead.

"I was the last one to see Harkins alive"—I counted the reasons off on my fingers—"I grew up in the Cauldron, and, as we've already covered, I was raised in the Votary Coven."

She glanced at Eldritch, who suddenly looked very uncomfortable. "Officer Prospero, I wouldn't need extra bodies on my team at all if you hadn't killed my star CI tonight."

I snapped my mouth shut.

"She's right, though," Eldritch said, shocking the hell out of me. "She knows these streets. Plus, when you asked for that list you said you wanted Adepts. There are only a handful on the force." Usually Adepts in law enforcement went the CSI route because of the lab work.

Gardner raised a brow. "So why wasn't she on the list already?"

Eldritch glanced at me with an expression that put me on edge. "Leave us."

"Sir, I—"

"Go." His voice was quiet but held a thin edge of steel.

Gardner didn't smile or send me any other sign of encouragement. "We'll call you back."

I shot Eldritch a pleading glance before I walked out the door. I was pretty sure Eldritch wanted me to leave so he could tell her I wasn't ready for MEA-level work. After all, I was just a beat cop. Usually detectives and officers already members of special Arcane units got the sweet gigs on MEA task forces.

The other officers in the bull pen were doing a minimally convincing job of looking busy. But the instant I exited the office, the energy in the room shifted.

I crossed my arms and leaned against a metal desk. Inside the office, Eldritch was talking. Gardner listened with her arms crossed. Every muscle in my neck was so tight it cramped. The more I thought about my idea to join the team, the more I wanted it to happen.

Promotions were rare and incredibly competitive in the department. Thus far, I'd been told that my background in the covens wasn't a factor in being passed up. Instead, the excuses were always that I fell a hair short of the top score on the test or that someone else was just more qualified. But with each missed opportunity, I grew more restless. After five years, busting hexheads and the occasional corner kid felt like playing Whac-a-Mole. But being on a task force would let me be where

19

the real action was happening. I'd be going after the supply side of things—potion cookers and the coven wizards.

"Yo, Prospero?" A deep voice called from behind me. Guess the other cops got tired of watching and had decided to drum up some drama by shit-talking.

I ignored them and started chewing on my right thumbnail. Was Eldritch arguing for or against me? I couldn't tell from Gardner's body language, which hadn't shifted at all.

"I heard you shot a guy in the dick," another baritone called. "That true?"

"Why?" I didn't turn around. "You want a demonstration?"

Male chortles echoed from the break room nearby. The swoosh and thump from the potion vending machine hinted that one of my colleagues was helping himself to a late-night energy potion. I always found it ironic how many cops justified using clean magic to fight the dirty kind. Then again, most cops weren't Adept, so it was easier to compartmentalize magic into a good camp and an evil one. Black versus white, legal versus illegal. Hell, the Big Magic corporations claimed their government-sanctioned potions weren't even addictive, which they "proved" using studies they themselves had funded. But anyone who cooked potions could tell you the line between the two was little more than vapor. Whether you used it with good intentions or ill, magic was magic, and instead of being black or white, most of it was smoke-screen gray.

Just then, Gardner's head swiveled and she stared right at me through the window. I met her gaze without flinching. Whatever Eldritch had just told her put that speculative gleam in her eyes.

Movement behind me. One of the knuckleheads decided he'd bring the bullshit to me instead of yelling across the room.

"Did you really chase the guy into the Arteries?"

I turned to see Officer Michael Hanson. He was nice-enough-looking for an idiot. While I got a lot of BS from my colleagues for being an Adept, most grudgingly accepted that I was decent at my job; Hanson always found a way to remind me that magic made me an outsider. Ironic since his utility belt was weighed down by enough protection amulets to choke a dragon.

"No," I snapped.

"That's too bad." He took a too-casual sip from his can of Excalibur, the most popular brand of energy potion.

I frowned up at him. "What's that supposed to mean?"

He shrugged. "Just figured you'd feel at home down there with all the other Sinisters."

*Sinister* was derogatory slang for someone born with a genetic predisposition to do magic. A lot of cops didn't trust any Adepts, period, because they didn't believe anyone could wield magic without being corrupted by its power. Plus, since laws made any evidence gathered through arcane means inadmissible in court, a lot of cops didn't want any Adepts on their teams because they didn't trust us to do things by the book. Therefore, as an Adept cop who had grown up in a coven led by a known criminal mastermind, I was doubly damned in the eyes of bigots like Hanson. So I'd gotten used to being called everything from "Lefty" to the middle-of-the-road "Gauche" to my personal favorite, "Freakshow."

I pinned him with a pitying glare. "That the best you got?"

His eye flared at the challenge. "No, this is." His hand cupped his balls.

"According to Alice in Dispatch"—I lowered my gaze to his crotch and winced—"there ain't much magical about that wand."

In addition to being a prejudiced dick, Hanson also had a fetish for Adept chicks like Alice. He'd never hit on me, which told me he had either some sort of intelligence or at least a healthy sense of self-preservation.

His face went pale and then flared red. Heavy silence loomed in the background where the peanut gallery looked on.

"Now if you'll excuse me, I'm kind of in the middle of something." I turned back to the window and dismissed him altogether.

"Bitch," he muttered and stormed away.

Inside the office, Gardner was standing with her back to the window. Her shoulders and head obscured my view of the captain's face. Whatever was being said, it was clear they were wrapping up.

A loud racket behind me sounded like Hanson kicking a chair. I was saved from having to turn and face the disapproving looks of my colleagues when Gardner opened the door. She walked out without sparing me a glance. I rose slowly, watching her go. I wanted to call out and ask what was going on, but pride prevented it. I did, however, notice a thick folder tucked under her arm.

Eldritch came to the door. "Prosper—" The yell cut off when he saw me standing ten feet away. He shot me a look dripping in annoyance. "Come on."

When I walked in, Eldritch's expression gave me nothing to go on.

"Well?" I demanded, watching him for any hint of what was coming.

He blew out a breath and tossed a pen on his desktop. "She said she'd be in touch."

My mouth fell open. "That's it?"

He nodded and dropped into his chair. The overtaxed vinyl sighed in resignation.

"Was that my file she had?" I asked.

"I gave her the down and dirty, but she wanted time to review your performance records."

I chewed on my lip. My record was pretty good despite the lack of promotions, so that wasn't my concern. Instead, it was the background search she'd also find in there. "You told her about…everything?"

He took a sip of cold coffee and nodded. "Yep," he said after he swallowed.

"And?"

He looked up with a warning glance. "And what, Officer?"

I relaxed my tense shoulders and tried to look contrite. "I'm sorry, sir. I'm just trying to figure out if I have a chance at the task force."

He grimaced and sat back in his chair. "If it makes you feel better, she didn't seem scandalized that you're related to half the coven members in the Cauldron."

I let out a relieved breath.

"But," he continued, "I also told her you're a pain in the ass."

I tilted my head but didn't take the bait. "I doubt that scandalized her, either."

"True enough." Eldritch chuckled, but then he blew out a deep breath. "You want my advice?"

I didn't but nodded anyway.

"Go home and get some rest. You look like hell."

# Chapter Three

Tinny music and rapid beeping greeted me the next morning when I stumbled into the kitchen. The morning news droned from the small countertop TV near the fridge. Danny didn't look up from his battle against zombies or mutant ninjas or whatever foe the kids were killing these days. A snack cake hung from his lips and an open soda on the table revealed his idea of a nutritious breakfast.

"We're out of milk," he murmured around the mouthful of refined sugar.

"Good morning to you, too, Sunshine." Opening the fridge, I removed the carton of milk I'd grabbed on my way home from the precinct the night before. My hand slammed it on the table next to his soda, and my hip shoved his dirty gym shoes to the floor. "And how many times have I told you shoes don't belong on the table?"

He looked up then. "Hey! What happened to your eye?"

I cringed. After sleeping like the undead, I'd totally forgotten about the shiner. I chuckled and shrugged it off. "It's nothing."

"Right," he snorted. "If I came home with a black eye like that you'd call out the National Guard."

I paused because he was right. A lot of my overprotectiveness was a hangover from the violence I'd seen as a kid, but Danny's fears for me were justified given that my job required me to wear weaponry. He deserved some sort of explanation.

"No biggie. Got it from a perp who didn't want to be arrested."

He eyed me suspiciously and I was suddenly thankful the long sleeves of my ratty, green chenille robe hid the bandage. "Well, did you get to use the salt-cannon on him?" Danny was always fascinated by the salt charms I used in the line of duty.

"I did," I said, leaving out the bullet I'd also used. I rummaged in the fridge for breakfast but came up uninspired. Eyeing the box of snack cakes, I decided they weren't so bad. Cake had eggs and milk, right? Plus they went really well with coffee.

Luckily, the perky news anchor's voice covered the damning crinkle of cellophane.

"Last night Mayor Owens hosted a fund-raiser for his reelection campaign." The TV flashed a shot of the mayor's five-hundred-watt politician smile and polished suit. His eyes were too bright and his skin had the too-smooth texture that could be achieved only through expensive, clean magic elixirs. "Babylon real estate developer and major contributor to the mayor's campaign, John Volos was also in attendance at the event." The image jump-cut to one of the mayor glad-handing a disgustingly handsome man in a tux that cost more than most people made in a month.

I tried not to choke on the suddenly dry mouthful of cake.

Unlike Mayor Owens's elector-granted influence and potion-bought looks, the charisma and power radiating from John Volos existed on a chromosomal level. Even when we'd been kids, he'd been a force of nature.

The screen switched to tape of Volos smoldering into the camera, a perky redhead on his arm. "I'm proud to put my support behind Mayor Owens. He's done so much to encourage the redevelopment of the Cauldron, which is an issue close to my heart."

"What heart?" I snorted.

"Huh?" Danny murmured.

"Nothing."

He looked up and saw the TV screen. "Hey! It's John."

I slapped the off button with more power than I'd intended. The TV jumped and the screen went black.

"Jeez, what crawled up your butt today?"

"Finish your breakfast."

He rolled his eyes and pulled the earphones down. I glared at the screen for a few seconds behind Danny's back, but a honk from the curb outside tore me away from my foul mood.

I nudged Danny. "Move it, kid."

He grimaced and looked up like I'd just interrupted him performing important surgery.

"Pen's out front," I added.

Penelope Griffin was my best friend. When we'd met we'd both been waitresses at a crappy chain restaurant while we worked our ways through college. I'd been earning my night-school degree in criminal justice while she worked toward her master's in school counseling. Now she was a counselor at Meadowlake, the exclusive prep school Danny attended. Without her recommendation to the school board, I never would have gotten him away from Babylon's public prison-yard schools. Luckily, Pen also had worked a favor from the finance office for a small discount on the astronomical tuition.

Danny nodded and jumped out of his chair. While I went to the back door and waved at Pen, he scrambled to shove his books into his knapsack.

"What's up with the eye?" she called, leaning across the passenger seat.

"Long story."

"I'll come over tonight for a beer and you can fill me in, okay?"

I nodded just as Danny brushed by me. "Have a good day!" I called in my best impersonation of June Cleaver.

This earned me a grunt. After Danny was in the car with his face buried in the game again, Pen pulled away.

I was turning to go back inside when a "Yoo-hoo" caught my attention. Glancing toward the house next door, I saw Baba limping across her front yard. Her long, gray hair flowed around her angular face and all the way down to her rear end, which was covered in the world's ugliest housecoat. Her last name was Nowiki, but her real first name was kind of a neighborhood mystery since she insisted we all call her "Baba." Depending on whom you asked, the Polish word meant either "grandmother" or "witch." I'd never seen any kids running around her house, but I had seen Baba dancing around her backyard under a full moon. Naked.

Witches are members of the Mundane pagan religions who use the rituals of magic to worship deities. Their magic could be strong—especially in groups—but not nearly as powerful or useful as the magic used by well-trained Adepts, who are able to harness energies that Mundanes can't access. It's kind of how a housewife uses ingredients in her kitchen to create a decent meal. The same items in the hands of a trained chef become culinary art.

I crossed the yard to meet Baba halfway.

"What the hell have you done to yourself? Look at ya!" she said by way of greeting. "Is that a black eye? And what's with the bandage?" She reached for the edge of my sleeve to see more, but I shied away.

"Just had a little run-in with a reluctant criminal." I shrugged. "No biggie."

She crossed her arms over her flat chest. "Did ya throw the book at the bastard?"

I bit my lip to hide the smile. "Something like that."

Cops shows were Baba's favorite things in the world. That's why it was always so easy to convince her to babysit Danny when I had the late shift. Her meager retirement income meant luxuries like cable television weren't an option. So she hung out at my place most nights watching TV cops strut around saying things like, "This time it's personal," and "I'll have your badge for that!"

"Thanks for keeping an eye on Danny last night until I got home." When I'd arrived the night before, she had been snoring on the couch. I'd gently woken her up and helped her home, but we hadn't talked much since she was only half-awake. "Happy to." She waved a gnarled hand. "The crime channel was having a marathon of *Blue Devils* anyway."

*Blue Devils* was her favorite show. It was about a ragtag team of vice cops who alternately killed and fucked their way through every investigation while narrowly dodging Internal Affairs. I'd never admit it out loud, but I'd watched a late-night episode or twelve and it was pretty good in a totally inaccurate and trashy way.

"Still," I said, "I appreciate it."

"Look, Kate, I am happy to help out and all—you know that." She lowered her beer and squinted at me. "Hanging out with the kid is nice and I enjoying being able to watch my stories."

I nodded, bracing myself for the *but*.

"But don't you think it's about time you let Danny stay here alone?"

My stomach clenched. "No."

"Kate," she began in a patient tone, "he's old enough not to need a sitter. He's what? Fifteen?"

"Sixteen on Thursday," I corrected.

"Old enough not to need an old biddy like me hanging around. Hell, if something happened he'd be taking care of me!"

That was a lie and we both knew it. Baba might be old, but she could be meaner than a polecat when crossed. I'd seen her wield that cane at everyone from the mailman for running over her petunias to a Jehovah's Witness who tried to save her soul. "Regardless, I feel better knowing he's not alone here at night."

She pursed her lips, which made the wrinkles around her mouth accordion like an air filter. Baba's second favorite thing in the world was smoking, and the habit had left its marks on her face and in her raspy voice. "Suit yourself," she said. "But don't be surprised if he comes to you saying the same thing."

I sighed. "Did he say something to you?"

She shook her head. "He's too polite to, you know that. But I can see it in his eyes every time I show up."

"Annoyance?"

"Disappointment. Like he's waiting for you to trust him."

Well, if that wasn't a sucker punch. I knew Baba meant well, but after the night I'd had this was the last discussion I wanted to have. "I'll think about it," I lied.

"All right," she said softly. The woman hadn't lived to the ripe age of seventy-two without picking up a thing or two about dealing with people. She knew I was lying, but she also knew pressing me about it wouldn't convince me to see her side. "Anyways, I brought ya something." She dug a gnarled, arthritic hand into the large pocket of her housecoat. From it she lifted a glass jar—the kind used to pickle vegetables—and shook it. The liquid inside was disconcertingly red, like fruit punch, and kind of oozed inside the glass instead of sloshing.

"What is it?"

"It's that tea I was telling you about."

I shook my head. Baba talked about a lot of stuff and I found sometimes it was best to zone out a little. "Which one?"

She sighed. "Remember? The other day you complained that you hadn't had a date since that horrible one with the mortician."

I nodded. Barry Finkleman had been nice-enough-looking, but his idea of a fun time was taking a girl to the funeral trade show to check out the latest in embalming equipment. Not exactly the recipe for romance. "What about it?"

"I said you were attracting the wrong kind of men because you had lost touch with your feminine side."

That brought me up short. If Baba had ever said that to me, I would have remembered it. "Baba, are you sure we had this conversation, or did you just make that snarky comment to yourself?"

"Doesn't matter." She waved an impatient hand as if I'd mentioned an insignificant detail. "Anyway, when I was a young girl, my mama made me this special tea on my wedding night. I think I'd told you that Mr. Nowiki was a little light in his loafers?"

Mr. Nowiki was Baba's deceased husband, whom she loved more than cop shows and smoking combined. I spoke carefully to make sure I understood her correctly. "Baba, are you saying Mr. Nowiki was gay?"

She reared back. "Bite your tongue, girl!"

"But you just said—" At her horrified look, I raised a conciliatory hand. "Forgive me, I misunderstood."

She cleared her throat. "As I was saying, Mr. Nowiki was very shy when we got married. When we started dating it took him two months just to hold my hand. I swear I tried to rip the man's pants off more than once, but he said we had to wait until our wedding night."

The image of Baba trying to seduce Mr. Nowiki made my skin break out in hives, so I decided to hurry her along. "Where does the tea come in to all this?"

"Oh, so I told my mama I was worried my loving husband might be too nervous to do the deed. She said sometimes men are intimidated by strong women so they need a little help." Baba lifted the mason jar. "So she made up a batch of this tea for me to drink before the ceremony."

I decided not to mention that the stuff didn't look like any tea I'd ever seen. Instead it looked more like red slime. "Did it work?" I asked instead.

"Did it ever!" She threw back her head and laughed. "Right after the ceremony, he threw up my skirts and took me in the rectory!"

"Um." I blinked at her. Cleared my throat. "What's in it?"

"A little rosemary, coriander, rose petals, some cinnamon for spice." She waggled her snow-white brows at me. "The rest is a family secret, but I brewed it with water collected from a full-moon rain shower for extra potency." She held the jar up to the light as if she could see her past inside it. "Mama called it her 'Love Brew,' but I prefer to call it 'Sexy Juice.'"

"Baba—"

"Hmm?"

She was always trying to press this stuff on me. She came from a long line of kitchen witches who brewed home remedies from things in their gardens and passed their folksy wisdom down through the generations. I'd tried a million times to explain to her that I didn't use any sort of magic—folk or otherwise. She always blustered and explained that her teas and tinctures weren't the same as "the devil's handiwork" I chased down in the Cauldron.

But that morning, I couldn't muster up the energy for another discussion about respecting my boundaries.

"I—" She looked so excited about the prospect of helping me end my romantic dry spell that I couldn't hurt her feelings. I sighed and accepted the jar she pressed in my hands. "Thanks, Baba."

She beamed, showing off her slightly crooked front tooth and the gold crown that adorned her left incisor. "My pleasure, doll. Just remember to heat it up first. It also wouldn't hurt to mix in a little nip of bourbon. If you don't have any"—she reached into the collar of her housecoat and removed a flask from inside, presumably from her bra—"you can borrow some of mine."

I definitely drew the line at drinking another woman's bra hooch. "That's all right." I held up a hand and tried to look grateful. "I'm sure I can manage."

She nodded decisively, like her work here was done. "On that note, I gotta go get ready for bingo at the senior center. If I don't get there early enough that bitch Harriet Krauss steals all the good dotters."

I nodded as if this were a problem I often dealt with myself. "Good luck, Baba. And thanks for the tea."

She winked saucily and said, "You can thank me after some hot stud gives you a ride on his spitting kielbasa."

After that gem, I quickly extracted myself to go enjoy some quality time with junkie snitches, who were much less disturbing to be around than horny septuagenarians.

# Chapter Four

A lot of people believe police work is all shoot-outs and high-speed chases. Truth is most of our hours are filled with paperwork or sitting on our asses in shitty city-issued cars waiting for something suspicious to investigate. That day, however, I was in my own shitty Jeep, since Eldritch's suspension meant I wasn't officially on duty.

However, if Gardner let me on the task force, I wanted to arm myself with as much information as I could find about this new potion. That's where the third part of police work came in—working informants.

As usual, I found Mary in the park near the empty playground that was originally built for the kids of factory workers at Babylon Steel. The area used to have green grass and bushy trees and lots of colorful monkey bars and swing sets. Back then, America was still the capital of the steel empire begun by Carnegie and his cronies. But starting in the 1960s, the steel manufacturers' hubris caught up to them when some Chinese alchemists revolutionized steel processes and took advantage of the deregulation of foreign imports. It wasn't long before the steel industry here collapsed completely and ushered in a more dubious threat to the fabric of America: the magic industry.

Sure, magic had existed throughout our history books, but mostly it had been framed as the superstitions of less educated societies. However, after an alchemist changed the economy of America, modern scholars and scientists took the old wives' tales and studied them for the first time using scientific methods. Turned out all the witches who were burned in the Middle Ages hadn't been just the innocent victims of the Catholic Church's war on women. Sure, magic had always existed, it's just no one really understood how it worked. That was until a scientist named Ezra Green discovered the genetic marker for magic was tied to left-handedness.

Now, five decades later, everyone and their mothers used "clean" magic to wash their clothes and add zip to their sex lives. Instead of steel and iron funding America's power, magic was the currency that kept us going. But the damage to Babylon and the rest of the Rust Belt towns couldn't be undone. Especially since the illegal dirty magic industry had set down its black roots in our soil.

The park I stood in had once been a symbol of Babylon's bright future, but now it was nothing more than a barren scrub lot filled with bent, rusted sculptures exploring the theme of urban decay.

I continued to make my way toward Mary. Her back was to me, but the alto of her lullaby floated to me on the breeze. Her hunched shoulders curved protectively around the burden strapped to her flat chest.

I hesitated, worried I might be interrupting nap time. Little Man was always so grumpy when he hadn't had his morning rest.

My footsteps on the gravel path gave me away and she turned, ready to defend her precious burden. Mary's misshapen head reminded me of old-timey illustrations of Humpty Dumpty, except covered with random tufts of long brunette hair. Despite the deceptively large cranium, her brain had the mental capacity of a toddler.

Speaking of toddlers, the baby carrier strapped to her chest was custom-made and filled with alternating bands of salt slabs and body armor. From his perch on Mary's chest, Little Man watched my approach through drooping lids. A blue knit cap perched on top of his small bald head. His tiny mouth opened into a yawn before he spoke.

"The fuck you want, Prospero?"

I looked into the homunculus's eyes and said, "How's it hangin', LM?"

His mouth twisted into a jaded grin too mature for his chubby-cheeked profile. "Low and to the left, as usual. Wanna see?" His chubby hand made for the waistband of his diaper.

To the passerby, the pair probably looked like a hulk of a woman with questionable personal hygiene carrying a creepy baby doll. Instead, Little Man and Mary were actually conjoined twins. Their mutations were the result of their mother's addiction to fertility elixirs. Unfortunately, she hadn't survived pushing out the twenty-pound baby Mary.

On the other hand, Little Man started as what appeared to be a mole on his sister's chest, but eventually he grew into the homunculus she carried everywhere. Any advantage Mary had over Little Man in size was mitigated by the fact that he got all the brains.

I grimaced and shook my head. "Got a few questions for you."

"Come back later." His infant-sized lips pursed into a pouty moue. "It's almost time for sleepies."

36

I pulled my wallet from my pocket. His eyes widened. That kind of money could buy a large pack of diapers or some special time with a discount whore.

"In that case, let's retire to my office." He motioned his tiny fist at Mary.

She pivoted her large body like an ocean liner executing a wide turn and lumbered toward a nearby bench. Even sitting, the giantess loomed over me, which meant Little's face was even with mine.

"I assume you're here about that junkie you smoked?" he snapped.

I nodded.

"Rough business," LM said, his high-pitched voice a facsimile of sympathy. "Word is you shot his dick off. That true?"

"Thought you knew better than to listen to rumors."

LM shrugged. "Every rumor holds a grain of truth."

"The challenge is finding that one little grain in the pile of bullshit," I said. "Anything you can tell me about a new potion making the rounds?"

He wrinkled the bald skin where his eyebrows would have been if he'd had any hair. "Like you said, I know better than to listen to rumors."

I raised the bills and rubbed them together. "Tell me anyway—just for shits and giggles."

Little raised a hand to indicate Mary should lean closer to me. I paused and then played along, leaning close enough to smell Mary's body odor and the diaper cream on LM's ass. "People been talking about a unique new package."

I kept my expression poker blank. "Who's putting this package out?"

He shook his head. "No one's naming any names. Either way, that new shit? The Wolf? Nasty."

The wound on my arm throbbed. "Tell me about it."

"Hear it makes the user crave human flesh." Little Man ran a speculative glance over my blackened eye and the bandage peeking from under my shirtsleeve. "You know anything about that?"

"Maybe," I evaded and changed tactics. "Back up a sec. You expect me to believe you don't have a theory about who's cooking this potion?" I looked in his heavily lashed blue eyes. "Stinks like shit, LM."

The laugh that came from his mouth was a bizarre, squeaky cackle. "That's why I like you, Prospero. You understand that 80 percent of the Cauldron is illusion."

"So what's the real story?"

"Honestly? If it's a new wiz, he's got titanium balls. Unless..."

"Yeah?"

"The potion's not from a new source at all."

"Preliminary tests say it's alchemical."

"Heard that myself." He shrugged. "Could be a low-level cooker looking to make a name."

"Any of the old Votary boys making noises about stepping into Abe's shoes?"

"No one wants to die that bad, Prospero." He laughed.

Steel bars didn't prevent Uncle Abe from playing puppet master on the streets. None of his loyal guys would dare step up to usurp his power. Which meant whoever was putting this new potion out either had Abe's blessing or was someone who wasn't loyal.

"But," LM continued, "if I were a betting man, I'd say the lead contender would be your old friend Volos."

My stomach dipped. "Just because Volos testified against Uncle Abe doesn't mean he wants to take over the coven." John Volos had been the prosecution's lead witness against Uncle

Abe in exchange for a generous immunity deal. Since that trial, Volos appeared to have turned his life around. He'd started several companies and was a generous contributor to charities and the election campaigns of a few powerful politicians at the state and local levels.

"Maybe he doesn't want to take over the coven," LM said, his face going all soft-focus as if he was imagining a distant possibility. "Maybe he wants to start one of his own."

I frowned. "Why would he want to risk all that legit power to start peddling dirty potions again?"

A voice in my head whispered, Because he missed cooking. Just like you.

I shook off the wayward thought. "It just doesn't add up."

"You asked for theories, right?" LM pursed his lips. "What if Volos has just been biding his time? He's started all these revitalization projects, right? Like the one near the Arteries?"

He was talking about the new community center Volos was building on the abandoned lot where I'd killed Ferris Harkins.

LM continued, "What if he's doing all these projects to gain back territory from the other covens? The one by the Arteries is on Bane's turf. Then there's the one he's starting next year in Aphrodite's sector." Bane was the leader of the Sanguinarian Coven, which specialized in blood magic. Aphrodite Johnson was the priestess and coven leader of the Mystical Coven of the Sacred Orgasm, aka the Os.

"Okay, so he's building community projects on other covens' turf," I said. "Maybe it's a simple 'fuck you' to the other covens."

"But why? I mean, if he's gone legit why bother the covens anyway? Volos has too much power to be threatened by Aphrodite or Bane enough to flip them the double birds."

I sat back and mulled it over. I'd never fully trusted Volos's supposed evolution, but it was hard to believe he'd put a potion as dangerous as Gray Wolf on the streets. "Why would he choose this potion?" I said almost to myself. "What's his angle?"

"Jeez, what? You expect me to do all your work?"

I pressed my lips together and shot him a look. If he was right and Volos was behind this potion, this case was about to become a major shit show. I blew out a long breath. "Christ. What a mess."

"You ask me, things been fucked up round here ever since your uncle got sent to Crowley. Say what you will about the man, but he kept shit in line."

I couldn't share LM's nostalgia for the good old days when Uncle Abe ruled the Cauldron like an unenlightened despot, but he was right about things being in upheaval since Abe left. Nature abhors a vacuum, and Abe's exit left a huge one in Babylon.

LM nudged me with his elbow, breaking me out of my troubling thoughts. "I heard something else."

I raised a brow and waited. He cleared his throat and rubbed his fingertips together. "Jesus, LM. You're bleeding me dry today." Normally I'd file an expense report to be reimbursed for paying off CIs, but in this case I was pretty sure Eldritch would laugh me out of the precinct since I intended to use this information on a MEA case. And I was pretty sure Gardner wouldn't open the coffers for an unauthorized meeting with a CI if I got on the team. Which meant whatever LM was about to tell me better be worth my having to skip lunch that day.

I pulled a five and two ones from the wallet. He shot me a withering look as if I'd insulted him. "It's all I got. But if your tip's good, I'll make sure and visit you next time I have a full wallet and a need for info."

He sniffed and sighed like he was doing me a favor. "All

right, so one of my boys says if you wanna get a piece of the new package, you gotta go through this guy at the Green Faerie."

"The absinthe bar on Exposition?" I frowned. "Who's the connect?"

Little Man shook his head. "Not sure. I guess there's some password or some shit. You know how the wizes are with new customers. Gotta sniff 'em out first, make sure no Arcs"—the slang for Arcane officers—"are poking around."

"What's the password?"

"Beats me." LM shrugged. "But you hang around long enough I bet you'll see something interesting."

"Well, it's a place to start, I guess." If we could catch the dealer maybe he could be flipped into admitting his source. That was a big *if*, though, given we had no idea who the dealer was. It was an even bigger *if* regarding whether there would even be a "we" since I still hadn't heard from Gardner.

My lack of optimism must have telegraphed through my posture because Mary raised a ham-steak paw and awkwardly patted my shoulder. "It's okay, lady."

I forced a smile at her. "Thanks, Mary." With a sigh, I rose.

"Ahem," Little Man said. "There's the small matter of our fee."

I handed the wad of bills to him. He stuck them in his diaper. Before I could continue, my phone buzzed in my pocket. Normally I wouldn't have taken a call during a meeting with an informant, but I was still waiting for word from Gardner.

"Prospero," I said, trying to sound capable and trustworthy.

"It's Gardner."

"Hi—"

"You're in," she barreled ahead. My stomach dipped with excitement, but I kept my features bland for LM's benefit. "Nine a.m. sharp tomorrow." She rattled off an address on Stark Street.

"Thank you so—"

"And Prospero?"

"I—Yeah?"

"Don't make me regret this."

I cleared the bubble of emotion that unexpectedly formed in my throat. "I won't."

"Good. Oh, and you're in the MEA now. Try to dress the part."

My hand went to the frayed collar of the T-shirt I'd thrown on to go meet LM. No doubt she was thinking about the scrubs I'd worn the night before. "Yes, ma'am."

" 'Sir,' Prospero," she snapped. "Call me 'sir.' "

With that the line disconnected. I sat looking down at the phone for a minute, unsure whether to do a victory dance or crap my pants. For a woman offering me good news, she sure didn't sound too happy.

"Ahem." LM stared at me expectantly.

"Sorry," I muttered. He looked curious about the call, but I wasn't ready to show that particular hand to him yet. I needed to change the subject and fast.

"So what are you gonna do?" LM asked.

"What do you mean?" I frowned at the homunculus's impish smile.

LM shrugged and leaned back on his elbow against Mary's chest. "Way I remember it, you and Volos used to be sweet on each other."

I sighed. "Right. Used to be. That was a long time ago, LM. Besides, I'm not convinced he's involved. He's got too much to lose to go back to cooking."

"Still," LM said slowly, "you know what they say, right?"

I raised a brow and waited.

"The wizard can leave the magic, but the magic never leaves him." He winked at me. "Ain't that right, Prospero?"

The insinuation made me want to tell the homunculus to go fuck himself, but I knew better than to react. Betraying any defensiveness about my own relationship—or lack thereof—to dirty magic would be ammunition in his little hands. Especially if any of the lowlifes I was trying to arrest were more generous tippers than I was.

"Thanks for the help." I tipped my chin.

LM nodded back, but a speculative gleam in his eye told me that brain of his was already strategizing the best way to use our conversation to his advantage.

"See you around, Mary."

The giantess smiled, revealing an abundance of sickly white gums and a handful of crooked, decaying teeth. "Be careful, lady."

I smiled and turned away. There was no use telling her that if I'd been the careful sort, I would have moved the hell out of Babylon years ago.

# Chapter Five

I sat in the car for a moment before turning over the ignition. After five years of working my ass off on the beat, I finally had my big break.

I closed my eyes and savored the sugar rush of excitement. Joining the MEA was like making the big leagues. No more blisters on my heels from walking the beat. No more washing my hands twenty times a day to get the sour, junkie stench off my fingers. No more disappointment when the promotion was passed to someone else. Now, I'd finally be able to go after the big dicks. The wizards who orchestrated the covens. The master cookers who developed the potions. The moneymen who made sure cash and magic flowed through Babylon's veins like tainted blood.

My cell shouted in the car's quiet interior. Opening my eyes, I scrambled to grab it. "Prospero."

"Gardner called?" Eldritch said by way of greeting.

"Yes, sir."

"Good. Need you to come in today to sign some paperwork before you start."

"What kind of paperwork?"

"A couple of payroll forms since MEA will be footing the bill for you while you work with them."

I rolled my eyes. The brass was always downplaying the amount of paperwork we needed to fill out. His "couple of forms" were probably more like ten pages filled out in triplicate, signed in blood with the promise of my firstborn. "I'll be there within the hour."

After I'd hung up with the captain, I started the car and pulled away from the curb. Since I had a little time to kill before I hit the precinct, I decided to celebrate the good news with a double-double from the Slaughterhouse. A quick hunt through the cup holder, ashtray, and under the seats of the Jeep netted me four petrified french fries, a Pretenders CD I'd misplaced months earlier, and five dollars and sixty-seven cents in change.

I pointed my car in the direction of the second-best burger joint in the Cauldron. I told myself I wasn't going to the first-best place—Mickey's on Hughes Street—because it was too expensive even though it was only two blocks from the precinct. The Slaughterhouse actually was cheaper, but the real reason I chose it that day was it sat only three blocks from Volos Towers.

I had to admit that when Little Man mentioned John's name in relation to the new potion I hadn't been surprised. From the instant Gardner told me Gray Wolf was alchemical, I'd thought of him. Of course I had. Yet, my stomach dipped anyway because if LM was right, now that I'd made the team, I'd probably cross paths with Volos sooner rather than later.

It had been about a decade since I'd spoken with him. I saw him on the news all the time, but it was a different drama altogether to think about being in the same room with the man.

Complicating matters, too, was the worry that once Gardner

found out about my past relationship with a potential suspect, she'd kick me off the case. Which was the real reason I was praying John wasn't behind this. If I was lucky, some new evidence would surface that pointed the investigation in another wizard's direction. And if I wasn't lucky… Well, I guess I'd leap off that bridge when the time came.

◆ ◆ ◆

Forty minutes later, I pulled Sybil into the parking lot along the Riverwalk. I told myself I chose the spot because it had a lovely view of the Steel River and Bessemer Bridge. But the tall tower looming over the river mocked me. I'd come here because I was horrified yet intrigued about the prospect of investigating the man who owned that tower.

Shoving a few fries in my mouth, I decided all I could do was show up at Gardner's office the next day and see what shook out. After a deep, calming breath, I settled back and lifted the burger. For a few moments, the savory, mustardy, dill-pickle deliciousness distracted me from the prospect of the return of John Volos drama in my life.

Overhead, birds swooped and called as they danced over the surface of the river, looking for a good catch. If this had been a shoreline on another part of the river, I would have laughed at their fruitless attempts. But this stretch of riverbank was part of the renovated Riverwalk District. Just beyond the twenty-story tower, the rust-brown waters of Steel River acted as a moat between the Cauldron and the less shameful sections of Babylon. Used to be this stretch of riverfront property was dotted with shanties and run-down factories, but over the last few years—thanks in big part to Volos's friendships with the city's leaders—the area was on the upswing.

The new Riverwalk boasted boutique stores and upscale restaurants. There were even some luxury condo developments in the works for upwardly mobile Mundanes who wanted to feel edgy and hip by living in the more "colorful" part of town.

In addition, Mundanes flocked across Bessemer Bridge on the weekends to visit the flea markets and artisanal goods stands set up along the water. Naturally, since it was still officially the Cauldron, there was always lots of overtime work available for the BPD at the Riverwalk so that the Mundanes weren't bothered by the magical dregs of the city. And high above all of that was Volos Tower, which had become a symbol in the city for progress and hope for the Cauldron.

I couldn't help but wonder at the irony. John Volos had gone from being Uncle Abe's heir—after I left—for one of the biggest magical crime syndicates in the city to a respected community leader and successful businessman in little more than a decade.

I shook my head and swallowed another delicious bite of my burger. As I chewed, I became aware of a strange rhythmic sound outside the car. I rolled down the window and realized it was the swoop, swoop, swoop of an approaching helicopter. I stopped chewing to stare at the speck of black rapidly approaching the tower.

That's when I realized that the parking lot sat right next to the tower's helipad. Frozen in indecision, I could do nothing but stare, slack jawed, at the approaching aircraft, which had probably a 90 percent chance of containing the very man I'd been worried about seeing.

By the time I realized I was being ridiculous and rolled up the window, the helicopter was lowering itself onto the helipad. Looking around, I saw I was probably five rows back from the border between the pad and the lot. I reached my free hand toward my glove box and removed the binoculars I always kept there.

The helicopter landed and the blades overhead were powering down. The door popped open. A long, slim female leg emerged first, followed by the rest of a statuesque redhead. The winds from the river and the slowing rotors loosened strands of titian hair—probably a vanity potion since no one was born with that shade—from her formerly neat chignon. She wore a black skirt with a cream silk shirt and break-your-neck stilettos. I squinted at her through the binoculars. She looked familiar, and I realized I'd seen her just that morning on TV as she stood next to Volos at the mayor's fund-raiser.

Before I could speculate much about her position in his life, I was distracted by a shadow moving in the helicopter's door. I held my breath. In the next instant, a dark-blond head and tall, trim physique emerged from the shadowy opening. He unfolded up, up, up and scanned the immediate area looking like a god of capitalism surveying his domain.

Awareness skittered up my spine—or maybe it was a warning. All around me, the air tightened with anticipation as I waited for him to spot me. I wasn't sure if I was relieved or disappointed when he simply turned to the chick and said something. She threw back her head and spread her ruby lips into a wide smile that exposed a row of pearly white teeth. A French-manicured left hand rested lightly on his arm as she gazed up with her no doubt witty retort.

Oh yeah. They were fucking all right.

I grabbed a notebook and jotted down that theory. But lots of CEO types screwed the help. That didn't mean Volos was cooking or, worse, dealing potions again.

I took another bite of my rapidly cooling lunch. But now the burger tasted bland and greasy. I was suddenly ashamed at my lack of willpower. I shouldn't have been in that part of town to begin with, much less sitting in that particular parking lot. As much as I liked to think I'd moved on from my past, that decision proved I still enjoyed prodding those old bruises.

I wiped my hands and face clean with a napkin, threw the trash in the bag, and—

*Pound, pound, pound.*

I jerked my head toward the driver's side window and cursed. A dirty, near-toothless man stood at the window, holding up gray rags and a bottle of blue liquid. "Wash your windows, lady?" His voice came muffled through the glass.

I shook my head. "Get out of here."

The toothless smile morphed into a scowl. "You ain't gotta be so cunty about it."

I made a shooing motion with my hands while I glanced toward the helicopter. Volos and the lady were starting to walk away.

*Bang!*

The window washer took issue with my dismissal and banged the bottle against the outside of the window. "Fuck you, bitch!"

With a sigh, I removed my Glock from under my seat. I figured a quick wave of the weapon would end the one-sided discussion.

"Oh really?" He lifted the stained Grateful Dead T-shirt to reveal a potbelly and the frayed waistband of his jeans. Nestled in the matt of grizzled hair covering his abdomen was the stock of a pistol.

I guess he'd wanted my attention, but now that he had it I was pretty sure he wouldn't enjoy it.

I threw open the door and yelled, "Hands on your head!" I flashed my badge as I raised my gun.

"Relax, bitch. I waddn't gonna shoot ya!" He put his hands in the air and stumbled back. "It's just a pellet gun."

I jerked it from his waistband, careful not to touch skin. Sure enough, it was a Merlin Px4, which was a sixteen-shot air pistol. It looked just like a Mundane semiautomatic pistol, but instead of bullets it used BBs or pellets as ammo and had a $CO_2$ cartridge to provide realistic blow-back action. Lots of street toughs used these peashooters or dart guns to deliver nasty potion-filled projectiles at their enemies. The weapons weren't illegal because the pellets and BBs weren't as dangerous as bullets, but they were regulated because they were so commonly used in Arcane crimes.

"You got a permit for that peashooter, ace?"

"Not sure." He thrust his hips up. "Why don't you check my pants?"

I grimaced at his pelvis. "How about we check it down at the station?"

"Ah c'mon. I didn't do nothin'."

I raised a brow. "You flashed a weapon at an officer."

"Ah man! I didn't know you was a cop. Thought you was just an uppity bitch."

"As it happens, I'm both. Do not move." I grabbed his arm. "What's your name?" I spun him around and applied cuffs.

"Bob."

"Bob what?"

"Just Bob." He shrugged.

While I patted him down, I tried to ignore the stench of brimstone coming off his clothes. "Are you on any potions, sir?" I swung him back around and removed his sunglasses. Sure enough, the irises were mottled brown and light blue.

He shook his head. "No, ma'am."

The track marks on his neck told a different story. Probably any profits he made from the window washing went straight into the vein. There was a satchel on the ground that probably represented all his worldly possessions. "You live around here?"

"Over at Saint George's Mission." He shrugged and glanced over my shoulder. "Heeey, isn't that what's-his-name?"

I glanced back to see Volos and the redhead were watching us. My stomach dropped as though it had been thrown off the Bessemer Bridge. In my annoyance over the homeless guy, I'd completely forgotten about Volos. They were a good bit away from us, but I definitely didn't want that kind of attention. I pulled my baseball cap lower over my forehead.

I pushed Bob toward the Jeep. "All right, sir. We're going to head down to the precinct. On the way maybe you'll remember where you left your permit."

Bob reared back like I'd asked him to hold a snake. "I ain't ridin' in that thing."

"Relax, it'll be fine."

"How do I know where you're really taking me? Maybe you got a plan to kidnap me and make me your sex slave."

I scanned a dubious gaze over the man's ratty gray hair, serious dental hygiene crimes, and the dirt caked black under his nails. "It's tempting, but I think I can control myself today."

A quick glance in their direction and I realized Volos was starting toward us. When Bob realized this he said, "Maybe I should ask what's-his-name to be my witness so if you decide to take advantage of my body I got proof."

"I swear on my mother's grave that I will not touch you." Not a hard promise to make to a man who smelled as if he hadn't showered since Nixon was in office. "Now let's go."

Touching him as little as possible, I helped Bob into the car and strapped him in with his hands cuffed behind so he wouldn't bolt. As I jogged around to the passenger side, I saw

Volos and the girl had gotten bored watching us and were getting into a waiting limo with the license plate VOLO$. Just before he got into the car, Volos looked back in our direction. Just in time to see me put the car in drive and peel out of the lot like a woman with the devil on her tail.

"That was who I thought it was, right?" Bob said.

"Yep."

"Too bad you didn't let me say hi. I bet he woulda offered to bail me out on account of me being a victim of the system and all."

I rolled my eyes. "Trust me, Bob. The system's treated you a lot better than that guy would."

# Chapter Six

I escaped processing an hour later after leaving Bob in the capable hands of the intake sergeant. Since Eldritch hadn't officially signed the paperwork that put me on leave yet, no one gave me any hassle about arresting someone, but I didn't get lots of speculative looks. Guess the gossip train had left the station to spread the word about the shooting.

By the time I reached Eldritch's office, I was exhausted.

"You're late," he said without looking up.

"Sorry, sir. I had to arrest someone."

He looked up quickly. "How the hell did you manage that? You said you were on your way to the station."

I shrugged. "Window washer flashed a piece at me."

He shook his head. "What's this world coming to?"

"So you have some paperwork for me?"

He made quick work on explaining the forms I needed to fill out to make the temporary assignment with the MEA official, as well as paperwork regarding overtime—to be paid by the

MEA—and some releases saying that if I got killed in the line of duty the MEA claimed zero fiduciary responsibility.

"Fucking Feds," Eldritch said after I'd filled them all out. Guess he wasn't a fan of their red tape, either.

"Listen—thanks for talking me up."

He waved it off. "Just remember who you really work for."

"Does that mean I'll still be reporting to you?"

"Technically you'll report to Gardner, but I'll want you to keep me up to speed on any major moves in the case."

I opened my mouth to protest, but he shook his head and barreled on. "Shut up and listen, okay? If Gardner thinks she can just stroll into my precinct and swing her dick around"— he paused, as if he caught the incongruity of that statement a second too late—"anyway, I won't have them making moves that could compromise ongoing investigations or put the cops on my command in harm's way."

I nodded. "Understood."

He ignored my tone. "Anyway, good luck with it."

"Sir," I said, bringing up something that had been bothering me ever since I found out the MEA was taking lead, "if Harkins was anything to go by, every foot-patrol officer is at risk as long as that shit's on the streets."

He blew out a breath. "Budgets are tight, so I can't put extra officers on each shift."

"With all due respect, I'm pretty sure once the media gets hold of this, the mayor's going to be asking why something wasn't done."

He pursed his lips as he thought it over. "I suppose I could have foot patrols partner up for the time being. Let's just pray Gardner's team is on the ball. Because if it does get to the mayor, it's going to be a shit storm."

"Plus we don't want any officers harmed, right?"

"Of course," he said too quickly. The phone on his desk buzzed. He punched a button. "What?"

"Sir, you have a visitor."

"Who is it?"

"Ramses Bane." The voice speaking through the intercom sounded as shocked as Eldritch looked and I felt to receive that news. "He said it's regarding Officer Prospero, sir."

My stomach flipped inside out. "What the hell?" I whispered. This day could not get any weirder.

"Send him in," Eldritch said. He disconnected and looked up at me. "Any clue?"

I shook my head. Bane was the grand wizard of the Sang Coven, and I knew him because he'd been allied with Uncle Abe for years. But I had no idea why he was showing up at the station to talk to my boss about me.

"Stick around," Eldritch said. "But play it cool."

I nodded and went to stand behind the captain.

A few minutes later, a guy about my age with long white hair, dark sunglasses, and an ankh tattoo in the center of his forehead strolled through the door. This wasn't Ramses Bane, but his son, Hieronymus.

When he saw me standing behind the captain, his face morphed into a sneer. Harry and I had grown up together in the Cauldron. He was two years younger, but light years ahead of me in the asshole department. Apparently, he didn't have much warmer feelings for me because after making a face, he looked away as if the sight of me made him ill. "You Eldritch?"

The captain didn't rise. "Yes. Where is your father, Mr. Bane?"

Harry looked pleased that the captain knew who he was. "He's out in the car."

Eldritch frowned. "Why was I told Ramses was here to see me?"

Harry shrugged. "Figured you'd be more likely to agree if I said I was him."

"You were correct. Why is he out there while you're in here?"

"My father doesn't do well in the sun," Harry said. I snorted. Ramses Bane had lived down in the Arteries for so long he was basically a mole rat. His addiction to his own blood potions didn't help things since the side effects included severe anemia and rickets. Personally, as much as I didn't like Harry I preferred dealing with him to his father, if for no other reason than Harry was the less creepy-looking of the pair.

He removed a smart phone from his pocket and held it up. "But he'd like to speak with you."

Ramses Bane appeared on the screen, dashing my hopes of avoiding him that day. He was ensconced in a cocoon of black leather from the back of a limo. The dome light overhead glowed dully off his bald scalp and did little to warm up the complexion of his moon-pale skin. But his most distinguishing features were his eyes. Long-lashed, brilliant-blue doll's eyes. On a woman they'd be beautiful, but on his masculine face they were unsettling. When he looked at you, cold dread coated the skin.

"Captain Eldritch." His high voice sent frozen nails skittering down my spine.

"Mr. Bane," Eldritch said, his voice hard. Just like me, he expected this was all bullshit.

"Officer Prospero, it's been far too long."

Not long enough, I thought. "Bane," I said instead.

"What can we do for you?" Eldritch said.

"My son has some footage in his possession I think you'll be very interested in seeing. Hieronymus?"

Harry retrieved a paper sleeve containing a CD from his pocket. "You just need to put this in your computer to watch it."

I crossed my arms and laughed. "Sure, and download a virus that allows you to hack into the BPD servers? Not fucking likely, Harry."

He gritted his teeth at my use of his nickname. "The name's Hieronymus." The "bitch" was silent.

"We assumed you would be suspicious," Bane said. "Harry also brought a laptop."

Harry turned a tight smile on Eldritch. "May I?"

Eldritch glanced back at me, obviously, like me, he suspected Harry might be trying to get close enough to potion us. I nodded quickly, curious to see what the Banes were up to. Harry placed the laptop on the desk, slipped in the disc, and hit Play.

The video that came up on-screen was grainy, as if it had been taken with a security camera. There was no sound, either. I squinted at the screen, trying to figure out what exactly I was seeing. "What is—"

"Shh," Harry said. "It's coming."

A few tense seconds later, Ferris Harkins ran into the frame. I realized then that we were looking at the entrance to the Arteries. Harkins scrambled up the gate, and a split second later, I appeared and jumped at Harkins.

"What the—"

"Quiet, Prospero," Eldritch snapped. I realized then this was the first chance he'd had to see a broader view of what happened the night before instead of just the grainy, chaotic footage from my vest cam. I already knew how the scene was going to play out, so I stopped watching and focused instead on figuring out Bane's angle. Maybe something appeared damning in the footage. Or maybe they'd manipulated the video. I sighed and focused back on the screen. Harkins and I were grappling on the ground now. I was reaching for the gun. The fear and pain on my face made me look away.

I knew the moment the big climax happened on-screen because Eldritch stiffened. Harry stepped in and hit a couple of keys and when I looked back the image was frozen on my bloody face screaming toward the officers who were in the background, running toward the murder scene.

Eldritch's chair squeaked as he leaned back. He didn't say anything. Either he was processing or he wanted to force Bane to explain himself.

"I installed cameras at all the tunnel entrances a couple of years back," Ramses Bane said. "I hoped the added security would help cut down on the crime in the tunnels."

I rolled my eyes. Bane thrived on the crimes in those tunnels. He'd probably installed the cameras so he could see police raids before they arrived.

"It was hard to miss the crews outside our front door last night so I looked at the tapes to see what had transpired. Once I realized what occurred I thought it best to step forward rather than force the BPD to get a subpoena. Especially since it's clear from the footage that Officer Prospero was acting in self-defense."

I squinted at the phone. Why in the hell would Ramses Bane be interested in defending my innocence? Something stunk here and it wasn't just the aftershave Harry doused all over himself.

Eldritch cleared his throat. "I appreciate you coming forward with this. It will be helpful."

Harry nodded with an air of false modesty, even though he was nothing more than an errand boy. Bane leaned forward, filling the screen with his round face. "I consider it my civic duty to help the police in protecting the city from this dangerous new potion."

"We'll take this footage into consideration, sir," Eldritch

said. "If there's anything else you think of, please don't hesitate to contact me directly."

"My son is leaving my personal cell number as well as his own." He blinked at the camera with what I guess he considered an earnest smile. Instead, he looked awkwardly feral with his lips curled back to reveal white gums too large for his tiny, gray teeth. "We'd be happy to aid this investigation in any way possible."

"Mr. Bane—"

"Ramses, please," the bald man purred.

"Yes, sure," Eldritch said. "Pardon me for being suspicious when you've gone out of your way, but why the sudden urge to aid the BPD?"

Bane smiled silkily into the camera. "Let's just say that it's in all of our interests to see the responsible party arrested as soon as possible."

I raised a brow. "Does that mean you have a theory as to who put Gray Wolf on the streets?"

Bane chuckled. "Naturally, but I'll keep my theories to myself for now. Suffice it to say, I pray the responsible party will be caught and punished harshly."

Eldritch stood as though he'd heard enough. "Thank you for your time, Mr. Bane. We'll be in touch if we have any more questions."

"As you wish," Bane said. "Say good-bye, Harry."

"Good-bye," the younger Bane parroted. Then he closed the phone, gathered the laptop, and nodded before exiting. Eldritch and I stood in silence, watching the white-haired wizard make his way back through the station. Finally, once he'd disappeared, Eldritch whistled low.

"What the hell do you think that was about?"

I chewed on my lip. "My best guess? He either believes or

knows one of his enemies is behind this. Ramses Bane doesn't help anyone unless there's something in it for himself."

Eldritch sighed and nodded. "I'll call Gardner and let her know what just happened."

I glanced over at him. "What are you going to do with the footage from last night?"

"Relax, Prospero. I plan on handing it over to the shoot team. It might still take some time to wrap up the red tape, but you'll be cleared." He turned and looked me in the eyes. "Not that I ever doubted," he added quickly.

"Thanks, sir."

He nodded, all magnanimous. "Just remember to keep me in the loop on the MEA's progress."

It hit me then. Eldritch didn't go to bat for me because he thought I was the right candidate. He did it because he knew how much I wanted the job, and he was betting that my gratitude would ensure I'd keep him in the loop on the MEA's movements. Looked like Bane wasn't the only one who only did favors because he expected to reap personal gain.

I sighed. "Sir, I don't exactly love the idea of being a double agent."

He waved away my concern. "Don't think of it that way. Think of it as—helping out the BPD team."

That was the problem, I thought, whose team was I on now, exactly? Eldritch wanted to use me, and Gardner didn't seem too psyched to be saddled with me.

"The team," I said. "Right."

# Chapter Seven

That night, Pen leaned back in the peeling Adirondack chair and took a swig of her beer. "You did what now?"

I shrugged and crossed my ankle over my knee. Danny's light was still on. The throbbing bass line of his music seeped out from the shitty insulation around the basement window. Soon I'd have to go in there and tell him to turn off the music and get to sleep since it was a school night. But for the moment I didn't have that excuse to avoid the interrogation by my best friend. She knew the perfect places to apply pressure until I cried mercy and spilled all the details she wanted to hear.

"I killed a guy and then talked my way onto a task force that's taking on the most powerful wizards in the Cauldron," I said, keeping my tone nonchalant. When I put it that way, I kind of understood the worry creasing her brows. Good thing I hadn't mentioned my little field trip to Volos's office. No doubt she would have put that under the category of psycho-ex-girlfriend behavior, instead of the strategic surveillance I'd convinced myself it was.

She blinked at me.

"What?" I looked away from the anticipation on her face, the one that always preceded a nice, long, tough-love therapy session.

"How did you feel after you shot him?"

I almost rolled my eyes. The problem with having a psychologist for a best friend was she always wanted to know about stupid things...like emotions. "Um," I said, stalling, "I felt... shitty."

It was her turn to roll her eyes. "Jesus, Katie. Way to use your big-girl words."

I sighed and surrendered. The sooner I got this part over with, the sooner we could start gossiping about fun stuff like getting a pelvic exam or a root canal. "At first I was just scared—worried he'd kill me before I could stop him. But then, once it was over, I felt kind of relieved and...numb. I guess." At the last second, I added in a small voice, "Maybe a little proud."

She perked up. "Proud?"

I sighed and leaned forward with my elbows on my knees. "You didn't see the woman he killed, Pen. *Savaged* is more like it. Killing him doesn't bring her back, but it means he can't ever do that to anyone else. I did what needed to be done and I'd do it again."

She pursed her lips and narrowed her eyes as if she was trying to see lies embedded in my pores. I met her stare with a neutral expression. Finally, she blew out a breath. "Well, damn. You actually sound kind of healthy about it."

I shrugged. "Don't get me wrong. It wasn't exactly a party, you know?"

She nodded.

"But in a way, I guess it has a silver lining because if it hadn't happened I never would have gotten a chance to be on this task force."

"Tell me about it."

I eased back in the seat to give myself time to gather my thoughts. "Don't know much yet. They're looking for the wizard who's behind this new potion. Guess I'll find out more tomorrow."

"Wonder if there will be any fine-ass MEA agents on your team." Now a different kind of instinct drove Pen. Not the need of a therapist to analyze behavior, but that of a best friend hot on the trail of juicy drama.

I frowned at her. "Trust me, even if there are I'm not interested. This is my big chance to prove myself and no ass is fine enough to wreck this opportunity."

"Hmm."

I rose to get another beer from the six-pack sitting on the table. The yard was already covered in a light blanket of fall leaves. Soon it would be too chilly to sit out here for our weekly Bitch 'n' Beer sessions. I sighed and handed another cold one to Pen. "But I'm never opposed to a little eye candy."

She tapped her can to mine. "Here's to fine asses and eye candy." She barely made it through the toast before the laughter began.

Pen had one of those laughs that came straight from her soul. She never tittered politely. She always opened up her whole being and shouted her amusement at the world. It got embarrassing in small restaurants, but on that night, with the first of autumn's smoky chill surrounding us and the moon overhead sharing the joke, I grabbed onto the sound of my best friend's laughter like a buoy.

No doubt about it, this case wasn't going to be an easy one. It's one thing to collar street-level potion cookers. You take a batch away and there are always a dozen more waiting in the wings. It's something else entirely to go after the head of the beast. Coven leaders didn't just play to win—they played to punish.

A heavy weight settled into my stomach. Just guessing, but I think it was the realization that I'd jumped into the deep end of shark-infested waters. "Shit, Pen. What have I gotten myself into?"

She pressed her lips together and watched me for a few seconds, as if she was trying to decide how much honesty I could handle. Finally, she gave a little nod as she made her decision. "You could walk away."

My mouth dropped open. "What do you mean?"

"Back off the team and take the suspension." She shrugged too innocently for this to be a spontaneous suggestion. "I can lend you some cash and maybe you can pick up some part-time work to keep things afloat."

I sat back heavily in my seat. "That's crazy."

"Is it?" She raised a brow. "You've been going zero-to-sixty for the last few years. You've barely had any vacation besides a few days you took off when Danny got an ear infection or something. Maybe taking the suspension will give you time to figure out what you really want."

"You think I don't know what I want?"

"I think you thought you knew." She leaned forward and put a hand on my knee to soften the emotional gut punch. "But I sometimes wonder if you actually want what you got. Arresting wizards won't bring your mother back, Kate."

"Jesus, don't pull that shrink shit on me," I said, my voice rising in a combination of anger and panic. "I worked too hard to get where I am—"

"Just because you worked hard to get here doesn't mean this is where you belong."

My stomach dropped. "What the fuck is that supposed to mean?"

She held up her hands. "Settle down, Katie. I'm not attacking you."

"You just told me you think I'm some sort of fraud."

"Is that what I said?" She tilted her head. "Or is that what you heard?"

My mouth snapped shut. Time to regroup before I gave her any further ammunition for the commitment hearing. "Look, I'm not saying things are perfect. You know I've been struggling to get promoted off the beat for a while now with no luck. There's never enough money unless I sign up for a lot of overtime, but then I never see Danny." Saying all that aloud made me short of breath, as if a tide were rising around me. "But if I can prove myself on this task force, everything will be easier. The pay will be better. The schedule a little more flexible so I can be here more."

"He's practically a man now, Katie."

"I know," I snapped. My eyes strayed to the light coming from his bedroom. "Anyway," I continued in a less combative tone, "I know life isn't perfect. But I still love the work and this task force is everything I've been working toward. Plus, if I had to sit around here in my bathrobe while they finish the investigation I'd go batshit."

She raised a brow.

"Well, bat shitt*ier*."

She finally cracked a smile. "Just watch your ass." My best friend raised her bottle and clinked it with mine. "I'd hate to have to kick it if you got hurt."

# Chapter Eight

The next morning, I woke up with a little extra zing in my veins. I'm not usually one for all that today-is-the-first-day-of-the-rest-of-your-life crap, but for the first time in a long time I felt like I might actually make a difference. Not just on the Cauldron's streets, but in our lives—mine and Danny's. My new sense of purpose and pride lasted about as long as it took me to walk into the kitchen.

"What are you wearing that for?" Danny's mouth was screwed up as though his toaster pastry had gone rancid.

My lips pressed into a grimace. Guess I didn't have to ask him how I looked. "Got a meeting this morning."

"At a funeral home?"

I shot him a look but didn't argue. The last time I'd worn the black suit was at my mother's funeral ten years earlier. When I'd pulled it out of the back of my closet that morning, it had been hard to miss that the hem was drooping and the color faded with time. But Gardner had said dress for the job, and I imagined MEA types only wore suits.

Turning to grab the coffee from the cupboard, I reminded myself that I wouldn't be wearing the frumpy suit for long. The minute that sweet MEA overtime kicked in I'd be able to afford some new duds.

I glanced at the holes in the knees of Danny's jeans. Make that new duds for both of us.

"Seriously, though," Danny said, "what kind of meeting?" He paused, his face going squinty and suspicious. "Wait—did Principal Anderson call you?"

"No," I said dragging out the word. "Why would your principal be calling me?"

He forced a laugh and fidgeted with the cord of his headphones. "No reason."

I shot him my best interrogator's glare, but he didn't break. "Anyway, it's about a new assignment."

"Oh." With that he put his headphones back on and tuned me out. So much for that sibling-bonding moment. I shrugged it off for two reasons. First, I wasn't too keen on telling Danny I might be involved in a potentially dangerous assignment. And second, I wasn't sure I'd actually get a permanent spot on the team, so why waste the breath?

I leaned against the counter and eyed the back of Danny's head. His hair was in the style his peers favored—meticulous messiness. I swear the kid took half an hour applying goo to his hair so it could look exactly like it had when he rolled out of bed. Shaking my head, I realized I sounded a lot like a mom. Or what I assumed normal moms sounded like.

A car horn interrupted my ruminations. I went to the door and waved to Pen with the hand not cradling my coffee. She leaned out. "Looking hot!"

"Thanks!" I appreciated the compliment even though we both knew it was a lie.

"Give 'em hell today, okay?"

I smiled and gave her a thumbs-up even though my stomach was churning with nerves. The clock over the stove beeped the half hour. Shit, if I didn't hurry, I'd be late for my first day on the job. I grabbed a snack cake for the road and hopped in Sybil to go meet my destiny.

Unfortunately, destiny had other plans. I stuck the cake in my mouth and the key in the ignition. Sybil made a sound somewhere between a cat coughing up a fur ball and a congested demon. "*Th*it!" I cursed through my mouthful of carbs.

I considered trying to get under the hood and figure out what was going on, but traffic getting into the city was always horrible this time of morning. Any delay on my part would mean being late.

Decision made, I gulped down the mouthful of food, hit a couple of buttons on the cell phone, and ordered up a taxi. Looked like destiny had just decided what I'd be using my first MEA paycheck to cover.

◆ ◆ ◆

The address Gardner had given me led to a decrepit building on the outskirts of the Cauldron. Abandoned train tracks—relics of Babylon's steel empire—lay behind it like rusty veins, and in the distance Lake Erie glowed in the smog-dulled morning sun. The scents of dead fish and a faint chemical odor warred with the acrid exhaust from the freeway a few blocks over.

The cabbie pulled into a trash-strewn lot near two unmarked cop cars that screamed "Nothing to see here." The taxi he'd picked me up in was one of those new potion-fueled jobs. I'd been in such a hurry to get there on time, I hadn't given a second thought to getting inside. I had, however, seen Baba's curtains twitch as we'd glided away from the curb outside my house. Considering I'd just poured the Sexy Juice she'd given me the day before down the drain, I had a little twinge of conscience over my hypocrisy. Still, potion fuels were clean magic and it wasn't as if putting a potion into a car's gas tank was the same as sticking a needle full of dirty magic into someone's neck to help escape reality. Plus, I was pretty sure if I'd been late, Gardner wasn't the type to accept excuses.

Still, I had to admit the taxi was a sweet ride. The potion fuel made cars hover above the streets, so the government had given them special lanes on the roads. Being able to fly literally down the freeways meant we avoided all the gridlock caused by the Mundane vehicles clogging the asphalt. We'd sailed across the Bessemer Bridge with a few minutes to spare before I had to report for my new job.

"We're here," the cabbie snapped as he threw the car in Park. A whirring sound accompanied the tires lowering to the pavement for landing. "Forty bucks, not including tip."

I grimaced. While the ride had been pleasant, the expense of the magic taxi left a lot to be desired. "Do you take credit?"

"I guess." His lips pursed like a schoolmarm's. "There's a service charge, though."

Forget having philosophical qualms about using a magical taxi. The real issue was I couldn't afford to use them. Especially since I'd spent part of the ride over calling in a favor from my neighbor, Joe the Mechanic, who said he'd give me a discount on the labor and parts for the repair, but that he couldn't get around charging me for the tow into the shop.

"Fine." I shoved the card across the seat at the taxi driver. While he ran it through the machine, I glanced out the window and up at the building. Gardner had told me the offices were on the second floor.

"Here," the cabbie said. He passed the receipt over along with a pen. As he did, I saw that his fingertips were green.

I hesitated taking the receipt. "What's that?"

"Oh, this?" He held up his fingers and wiggled them. "It's from the special fuel." He lovingly stroked the headrest of the passenger seat. "Makes this baby fly like a dream, but you get a little on your skin and you're green for days."

"Hmm." People thought clean magic was safe no matter what. They never questioned the weird little side effects that were sometimes worse than the thing they were supposed to fix. I kept my opinion to myself, though. If he wanted to turn green it was his own business.

I took the receipt and prepared to sign it, but when I saw what he'd done, I forgot all about my impending meeting with my new team and his green fingers. "The service charge is five bucks? That's bullshit."

He shrugged. "Convenience is costly, lady. The potion-fuel it took alone cost more than that a gallon."

"And how do you explain the additional ten-dollar tip you added here?" I stabbed a finger at the receipt.

"For service with a smile?" He grinned, exposing crooked front teeth. "Plus seeing how I got you here so quick since ya had your panties in a twist about not being late."

That much was true, but my annoyance didn't reduce any as I signed the receipt. The time I'd gained by taking the stupid special taxi to begin with was burning with each second I sat there arguing with the asshole. "Fine." I threw the receipt over the seat at him.

"Have a nice day," he said in an overly friendly tone that made the back of my teeth itch.

"Whatever." I exited the cab and slammed the door. A muffled "Hey" reached me from inside. I turned my back on the hexed cab and started across the lot. A whoosh of wind flirted with the hem of my skirt as the driver zoomed away.

On my way toward the door, I could feel eyes on me through the cloudy windows. The inspection made me feel self-conscious and I hated that my new colleagues had the benefit of checking me out first. Regardless, I threw my shoulders back and strutted toward the building like I owned the shithole.

The faded sign bolted to the roof told me the second floor used to be an old-fashioned boxing gym. Thugs once worked out their aggression in places like this where they could kick each other's asses with the law's blessing. Now that gyms like this one weren't around anymore, they fought in the streets with guns and potions instead of gloves and fists.

On the ground floor, a small bodega clung to existence by the quicks of its nails. A door next to the one for the grocery had faded gold lettering, which told me the place upstairs used to be called Rooster's Gym. Under that someone had spray-painted the word *cock* with a helpful graphic of a penis for the illiterate. I pushed it open and was faced with a tall set of narrow wooden steps. As I climbed, the scent of old sweat and decayed wood assaulted my nose.

My low heels clomped on each riser and echoed through the space above no matter how much I tried to have a light step. When I reached the top and found my new team waiting for me, I wasn't all that surprised. I'd made enough noise to raise the dead.

The room behind them opened up like a cathedral. The large windows made up two walls. Two doors led off the back, maybe to an office and a john. The old ring still stood in the center. Its ropes were cracked and smelled of old vinyl and even older sweat. The once-white mat was now yellowed with age

71

and boasted some dubious stains. In the center, they'd placed a large table and a whiteboard—a makeshift war room.

To the left of the ring, a couple of desks were pushed in a corner. Each had an ancient laptop chugging away on the surface. Along the opposite brick wall, beneath large metal-framed windows, speed bags, punching bags, a few pairs of cracked gloves, and a couple of jump ropes made up what passed for the workout room. In the front right corner of that same wall, slabs of plywood separated the rest of the space from what appeared to be a lab, if the beakers I spied through the cracks were any indication.

I took in all of that quickly and turned my attention to the agents who were staring me down. Since I was coming onto their turf, I went ahead and spoke first. "Special Agent Gardner around?"

A petite female with the spiky black hair and cocky posture that screamed she had whatever the chick version of a Napoleonic complex was jerked her chin up. "Who wants to know?"

"Officer Kate Prospero, BPD. She's expecting me."

"Hey, Morales," she called over her shoulder.

From further back in the room, I spotted a dark-haired male with his back to us. He sat on a stool reading a paper at a makeshift coffee bar. "What?" He didn't turn around.

"Gardner say anything to you about expecting company?"

One wide shoulder rose toward his ear. "Nope."

"You sure you got the right address, girlie?" This from a tall Asian guy with dreadlocks. Each strand was decorated with beaded charms and small potion amulets, and a pair of lab goggles was perched on the top of his head. The alchemical symbols tattooed up his left arm marked him as a wizard— probably the team's lab wiz. He wore black jeans, a white T-shirt, and a vintage embroidered vest. As he spoke his dark eyes sparkled with mischief and a smile flirted with his lips.

I realized then that I was the only one in the room wearing a suit. The chick wore jeans, a concert T-shirt, and combat boots. Morales, from what I could see from this distance, also wore jeans and an untucked plaid shirt with scuffed motorcycle boots. Looked like I'd misunderstood Gardner's instructions when she'd told me to dress as though I belonged in the MEA. My damned suit couldn't have made me look more like I didn't belong.

I crossed my arms and tried not to let my embarrassment show. Looked like MEA cops liked hazing new recruits as much as the BPD did. "How about you stop fucking around and go get your boss?"

Silence. Heavy, damning silence.

Morales stiffened and turned slowly in his chair. The room pulsed with tension for what felt like a full minute before Morales stood up. His chair's creak sounded like a scream in the silence. His boot heels made ominous thumps on the stained wooden floor. Finally, he pushed past the chick. She looked up at him with something resembling worship, and I figured he was most likely Gardner's number two.

He looked like the kind of guy whose cologne was made from gasoline and whisky. The dark scruff of beard was probably a look he used for undercover work, but combined with his full lips it was hard not to think about work under the covers. Broad shoulders and large hands that looked as if they weren't strangers to making fists. The kind of cop who'd laugh if a suspect punched him. Then smile as he applied a boot heel to the perp's neck.

Despite the dark and dangerous exterior, his brown eyes sparked with intelligence that told me he wasn't a typical muscle-bound idiot. Looked like Pen had been right about the eye candy. But then, I'd always been attracted to assholes. They were so much less complicated than nice guys.

"Officer what?" His voice was as calloused as his hands.

I raised my chin. "Prospero—Kate."

"Officer Prospero, were you born this way or has working patrol for the BPD forced your head up your ass?"

My jaw fell open. "Excuse me?"

"One, no cop with any real tactical experience would show up to work on a task force wearing a cheap suit and high heels." He ran his fingers over the lapel of my jacket.

The chick laughed. "Aw, snap!"

I swatted his hand away only to receive his nose in my face. His voice lowered to a menacing tone. "Two, no one with half a brain would walk into a room full of veteran MEA agents and insult them unless they're begging for an ass kicking."

The Asian guy frowned. "Drew," he said in a warning tone.

Morales shot a look at him and crossed his arms. When he looked back at me, he leaned in and whispered, "You want to play with the big boys, Cupcake? Stop acting like an idiot."

I stared him in the eye. Looking away would have been like offering up my backside for an alpha dog. He might be hot, but there was no way the cocky bastard was coming anywhere near my ass.

"That's quite enough, Special Agent Morales." Gardner's voice cut through the room like a gunshot.

The corner of Morales's mouth lifted. He hooked a finger in my necklace and flipped it up. "Nice pearls, by the way."

My cheeks flared with a mixture of shame and anger. A thousand words burned like fire at the back of my throat. Before I could spit any of them at him, Gardner's voice rang out like a shot: "Prospero, my office—now!"

# Chapter Nine

Gardner's office was really little more than a storeroom in the rear of the gym with a desk wedged in among metal shelving and file boxes. Dishwater-gray light filtered through smudged glass in the rusted window frame. The only decoration in the room was a plaque on her desk that read NO BULLSHIT BEFORE 5 P.M.

"Sit," she snapped.

It wasn't that I'd expected a warm welcome, but I hadn't anticipated so much outright hostility. "Did I do something?" I lowered myself into the folding chair across from the desk.

She threw a file folder on her desk and blew out a sigh. "Little advice, Prospero. You want to be a member of this team, you need to try to make friends, not enemies."

"You might want to remind your team of that. Where I'm from—"

She held up a hand. "I know exactly where you're from." Her tone was heavy with subtext. "But this is the MEA, not some dirty magic coven where your street cred is your destiny.

Here you earn respect through professionalism and good police work."

I ground my comeback between clenched teeth. Saying it wouldn't get me anything but more headaches, and I already felt a tiny ice pick *tap, tap, tap*ping away behind my left eye. "Understood. I'll try not to hurt their feelings anymore."

Her eyes narrowed, but the corner of her mouth twitched. "All right. We need to discuss some details of your assignment."

I sat up straighter, glad to put the awkward meeting with the team behind me—for now.

"This is a trial run, not a permanent gig. You want that, you'll have to prove you've got the chops to work at the MEA level. You can't keep up—you're out. You can't follow orders—you're out. Got it?"

I nodded.

"That said," she continued, "this case is only the first in what I hope will be a long-term mission to rid Babylon of the dirty magic trade altogether."

"Question," I said. "Why did you agree to give me a try?"

"Honestly? There were a couple of other qualified Adepts on my list, but not one of them is related to Abraxas Prospero. None of them used to cook potions before they were old enough to read. And none of them have that hunger in their eyes."

I tilted my head. "Hunger?"

"Desperation to prove yourself."

My jaw dropped. "Screw you, lady."

"You've got some balls, huh?" She smiled like I amused her. "That's good because this job will test you on every level." She crossed her arms and leaned back. "Judging from the high scores on your tests combined with the lack of promotions, I think it's safe to assume you've had some issues at BPD because of your background."

I nodded stiffly. "So?"

"So I want you to know that the BPD might not see the advantages of having an Adept on their squad, but I do. That's why I convinced the MEA to set up this task force. To leverage the magical knowledge of Adept law enforcement officers to fight the dirty magic problem."

I glanced at the door. "You mean, everyone's—"

She shook her head. "Just Mez. And me," she added almost as an afterthought, "but you already knew that. Shadi's Mundane and Morales is a...special case." I already knew who Morales was. I wanted to ask what was special about him besides his being an asshole, but I resisted. I assumed that Shadi was the chick, since she basically screamed Mundane. That meant I'd been right about the guy with the dreadlocks—Mez?—being a wizard.

"Does this mean you're planning on recruiting more Adepts?"

She grimaced. "The MEA and BPD want to see what we can do with what we have for now."

Translation: No more resources until we get some collars on the books.

"I'm surprised the MEA agreed to this at all. Most federal agencies refuse to even hire Adepts, except as lab geeks."

"Well, it wasn't easy." Her dry tone implied she wasn't just referring to how hard it was to get an Adept cop on her team. The fact she'd been able to work her way up to special agent in charge of an MEA task force spoke volumes about her own skills and tenacity. "Have you heard of Sun Tzu?" At my frown, she continued. "The Chinese military strategist. He wrote a book called *The Art of War*?"

My night-school degree hadn't covered Chinese military strategy. I grimaced and shrugged.

She waved a hand. "Anyway, he said many smart things. One of which was, 'If you know the enemy and know yourself, you need not fear the result of a hundred battles.'"

I squinted at her. She watched me expectantly, so I smiled and nodded. "Right on."

"The point is that Adepts understand how magic works better than any Mundane ever could. And you, Kate, you understand our enemies more than anyone else in this city."

"I'm thrilled you are willing to give me a shot to prove that's the case."

"I hope you do. This task force is a sort of pilot program. If we have success, Eldritch agreed to give us more bodies for the team. Plus there's a possibility the agency will create Adept teams for other hot spots—New York, Boston, LA. We may finally have a real chance to cripple the covens across the country."

My pulse kicked up and pressure pushed down on my lungs. Suddenly this wasn't just about my career ambitions or making enough overtime to buy Danny new sneakers. Gardner was talking flipping the script on the entire war on magic.

She slapped her palms on the desk, as if to dispel the heaviness that had settled over the room. "Now, since you're on the team, you need to know that I only have two rules. First, no excuses. I'm not your mama so I don't want to hear why you're running late or that someone else is to blame for your fuckup." She pointed to the sign on the desk to emphasize her point. "I discourage bullshit after five, too, just so we're clear."

"Understood." I raised my chin.

"Second, we do things by the book here."

I opened my mouth to tell her that wouldn't be a problem, but she held up a hand.

"I've read your file, Kate. The fact you made it through the academy and came recommended by Eldritch goes a long way to make me ignore your past associations. But please understand: We solve crimes using police work. Mez is the official team wiz. You need a defense potion or evidence analyzed—you go through him. No magical shortcuts to get evidence and no cooking potions—dirty, clean, or in-between—period." She looked up from the papers she'd been arranging into a neat stack. "No reading potions, either, Prospero."

I cringed. She really had done her homework on me. Back in the day, I'd had a talent for reading a potion's energy to figure out the ingredients and sometimes even the identity of its maker. But I could tell from the look in her eye it wasn't any use trying to explain that I didn't touch any magic at all anymore. She wouldn't have believed me anyway.

"Do things by the book," she continued, "or you'll find the book thrown with great force at your ass. Am I clear?"

Transparent was more like it. I'd hoped for a fresh start on the task force, but it appeared that the specter of my past haunted this gym just as it had the precinct. Gardner might be an Adept, but she clearly wasn't letting that shared trait soften her attitude. I didn't point out to her that my jaded past was part of the reason she'd hired me in the first place.

I raised my chin because I'd danced this dance before. I knew all the right moves. "That won't be a problem."

A slow smile spread across her lipstick-free lips. "Good." With that, she got out of her chair and flung open the office door. "Morales!"

A few seconds later the dick from earlier appeared in the doorway. He slid me a smirk before raising his brows at his boss. "What's up?"

"Round up the team. We've got crimes to solve."

♦ ♦ ♦

Morales wasted no time getting down to business. Without sparing me a glance, he walked back out the door. "Round up!" he called to the others.

Gardner passed me to follow him out. "Well? Come on."

I blew out a sigh and followed. The sooner we got the formalities out of the way, the sooner we could get moving on the case.

We all gathered by the entrance of the makeshift lab I'd spied earlier. Well, "lab" was a generous term for what was basically a long table and a counter with cabinets overhead. The shelves were filled with various herbs and liquids—all neatly labeled. Bunsen burners flickered under glass beakers with simmering liquids of varying colors and viscosities on the counter. It had been a long time since I'd entered another wizard's lab. Despite the bare-bones setup, I still experienced a little quickening in my veins. My eyes eagerly inspected the liquids, identifying most from scent or color. The rest I couldn't name without further inspection, but I wasn't about to do that until I was invited to do so. First rule of visiting another Adept's lab: Don't touch without permission. Usually this was as much a safety precaution as just good manners, and for me it was also self-preservation. Just being this close to the apparatus was making my palms itch.

I glanced toward the window and saw that the wizard's view was a large billboard rising high above the freeway a couple blocks over. It advertised a new self-tanning elixir from Sortilege, Inc., that no one in the Cauldron could afford. Clearly the picture of a young blond woman playing on the beach was meant for the Mundane commuters who zoomed through the Cauldron on their commute to the suburbs.

Now that the team was gathered again, the jokey, hazing atmosphere had been forgotten entirely.

Gardner jerked her thumb toward me. "You've met Officer Prospero."

I bit my tongue since I wouldn't exactly describe the scene earlier as an introduction.

"The Cauldron's her beat," she continued. "I've invited her on the team because of her extensive knowledge of the covens and their key players. Officially she's a consultant, but as far as we are all concerned she's as much a full member of this squad as any of us. Is that clear?"

I blinked at her public support after the warnings she'd just delivered in her office.

The guy with the dreads shot me an impish smile. Gardner pointed to Morales. "I believe you caught Special Agent Morales's name when you arrived."

I nodded. "Hey."

He crossed his arms over his chest. "What's up?"

"Morales is second in charge around here. If I'm not available you take your cues from him."

"Okay," I said. Inside, however, I was thinking, Oh shit. The shit-eating grin he shot me confirmed my concern that he wasn't done with the hazing.

"That's Shadi Pruitt," Gardner continued. "She was recruited into the MEA from Detroit PD. She's our surveillance expert."

The female jerked her chin up in greeting.

"Agent Pruitt," I said.

"Shadi," she corrected. Her tone wasn't combative, exactly, but she was definitely sending off a vibe that our shared gender didn't make us automatic allies.

"And this," Gardner continued, "is Kichiri Ren."

The other guy came forward and held out his left hand. "They call me Mesmer."

"Mesmer?"

"Mez, for short." He nodded back knowingly. "I'm the team wiz. You need a protection amulet or magical weapon, I'm your man."

"He's a magical bad ass." Shadi winked at him. "Right, Mez?"

He shrugged, but his smirk was self-assured. "I try."

Gardner decided the social hour was over. "Any hits on the blood sample yet?" she asked Mesmer.

"Yeah, about that," Mez hemmed. "There's some bad news and some bad news."

"Start with the bad." Gardner leaned a hip against the counter.

"I've never seen anything like this in a dirty alchemy potion before. It's got some elements I haven't identified yet."

"Because you can't?" Gardner asked.

"Don't insult me." Mez rolled his eyes. "I will be able to identify every component—it just takes some time. It'd be easier if we could get a sample of the potion off the street to break down."

"What's different about it?" I asked.

He looked up as if he'd forgotten I was there. "In addition to the antimony, there's also oil of rose quartz."

My eyebrows slammed down. "You're sure?" Oil of rose quartz was a distillation often used by alchemists to improve physical stamina. It was even thought to make men more virile, which is why the Big Magic companies used it in erectile-dysfunction potions.

"Why?" Shadi asked.

I glanced at her. "Most street wizards use down-and-dirty ingredients to cook. Their potions have more in common with moonshine or a meth lab than a true alchemical potion," I explained. "They prefer quick and cheap so they can turn a faster profit."

"It's kind of like alchemy's redneck cousin," Mez added. "But oil of rose quartz of this quality is not cheap to come by, and even if a wizard saves money by brewing it himself it's pretty time consuming." He turned and looked at me, clearly enjoying talking to someone who spoke his language. "But that's not all—there's also blood."

Shadi raised her hand. "And that's bad why?"

"Most wizards from the alchemical tradition won't touch blood potions," I said. "They think it's the dirtiest kind of magic."

"But alchemy's dirty, too," Morales said, coming closer.

"It's one of those weird hierarchy things," I said. "The street alchemists see themselves at the top of the food chain, magically. Sex and blood magic are bastardized from other magical traditions, so alchemists consider those potions beneath them."

My fingers itched to get a hold of a sample of Gray Wolf. Unfortunately, even if we had a sample and I somehow overcame my aversion to using magic, the fact remained that the courts had deemed evidence gathered through magical means inadmissible. Still, part of me wished that shortcut was available to us because I had a feeling getting the evidence through conventional means was going to be a pain in the ass.

"Keep working on it," Gardner said to Mez. "Let us know what you find out. Soon."

The wizard nodded.

"Shadi?" Gardner prompted. "Any leads on your end?"

"I hit all the apartments that looked down on that alley where Harkins killed the vic. People ain't talkin' as usual."

"Keep trying. I want to know if Harkins knew the vic or if

he just attacked at random. You find out anything about who she was?"

"Her name was Jessica Sprote. She was on her way to work." She glanced down at her notebook. "She's a cleaning lady at Volos Towers."

My head jerked up. "Really?"

"What?" Gardner said.

Part of me wanted to keep the whispers I'd heard about Volos's involvement close to my vest. But in the end, I accepted that if I was going to prove myself good enough to stay on this team, I'd have to start sharing intel. "Not sure it's solid. Lots of people work in Volos Tower." I shifted on my feet and crossed my arms. "But John Volos's name has been cropping up ever since I killed Harkins. He's got the mayor and the chief convinced he's gone straight, but no one at the street level believes it."

"Wait," Morales said, "isn't Volos the hotshot land developer?"

I nodded. "Yeah. He grew up in the Cauldron, though. He was Abe Prospero's right hand." I didn't add that he'd gained that position once I'd walked away. "He'd certainly be capable of cooking a potion like this."

I waited for someone to question me about sharing a last name with the former leader of the covens, but no one did. That meant they'd probably already been briefed on my background, which, frankly, was a relief.

"But you don't think it's him?" Morales asked.

"Not likely," I admitted. "Volos is an alchemist, sure—a talented one. But I can't wrap my mind around a motive for him. He's already got money and power. Why screw up his sweet position as Babylon's golden boy with a dirty potion?"

"Just because we can't think of a motive doesn't mean one doesn't exist," Morales countered.

I nodded. "Sure."

"We shouldn't rule anyone out at this point," Gardner said. "But I'm inclined to agree that it's too soon to focus our lens too tightly on Volos."

Morales nodded, but I could see his detective instincts filing away that conversation for later use. He turned to Shadi. "What about the blueprints of the Arteries?"

I raised my brows to Gardner—a silent request to be brought up to speed.

"Since Harkins was trying so hard to get there, we thought he'd probably already been in the tunnels. Maybe someone saw something."

I snorted. "No offense, sir, but even if someone saw him questioning the tunnel rats it wouldn't help much. Between them all, they don't have ten brain cells left to rub together."

"Still," she said, "it's an angle I intend to pursue."

I nodded and shrugged. "Of course."

Shadi sucked at her teeth. "Gettin' the runaround down at the department of records."

"Who you talking to down there?" I asked.

She pulled out her notepad and flipped through a few pages. "Guy by the name of Stewart."

"Ah," I said. "You need to go through his assistant instead. Her name's Nancy and she's a sweetheart if you use your polite words."

"Thanks," she grunted. She turned to Gardner. "On that note, I'm heading back to the hall of records before I go back for more interviews." She snatched a few ampoules off Mez's workbench. "You mind if I take a few of these protection shots?"

Mez shot her a look. "What happened to the doses I gave you last week?"

"It's a dangerous world out there."

"Hmm."

With that Shadi pocketed the vials. As she walked away, she said, "Thanks for the tip, Prospero."

Once she was gone, Gardner turned toward Morales. "All right, that leaves you two," she said to us. "Any idea where to start tracking down Bane's involvement?"

I did an inner high five with myself for having the forethought to talk to Little Man. "A bar called the Green Faerie on Exposition. I have intel that indicates a dealer might be dispensing Gray Wolf from there."

Morales crossed his arms and shot me a dubious look. "Where'd you get this intel?"

I shrugged. "I got a source." I was willing to share intel, but I was too protective of my CIs to hand LM's name over. If they wanted to use my sources, they needed to keep me around.

"How reliable is this source?" Gardner asked.

"Reliable enough to bring it up to you."

"Morales, you have any leads?" she asked.

His jaw clenched. "No, sir." A chill filled the space between him and me. Guess he didn't like the new girl showing him up.

Gardner's eyes narrowed as she considered her options. "All right. You two check it out. Let me know what you come up with."

"Probably nothing," Morales said under his breath. To me, he turned and snapped, "Well?"

I smiled sweetly. "After you."

# Chapter Ten

On the dark side of Exposition Boulevard, a discreet green door sat in a red brick wall. Over that, a small, faded sign depicted a faerie with green wings. The Green Faerie—a whimsical name for an establishment that catered to some of the most dangerous magical criminals in all of Babylon.

The club used to be an old speakeasy dating back to the dark decade in the twenties when the US government tried to outlaw alcohol during Prohibition. Little had Uncle Sam known that magic would pose a far greater threat to the moral fabric of America than alcohol ever could. Unfortunately it took another four decades for that lesson to hit home and by then it was too late to close Pandora's box.

You didn't need a password or secret handshake to enter the club these days, but it was probably a good idea to have a gun or other weapon easily accessible.

As it stood, Morales and I weren't planning on entering the club, since they'd smell the bacon on us the minute we crossed the threshold. Instead, our goal was to watch the perimeter for any of the usual suspects or signs of deals.

"Gardner seems like a real ballbuster." My tone was conversational instead of accusatory. We'd been sitting in the car for more than an hour without much conversation and I was getting antsy.

Morales lowered his sunglasses, performed a leisurely once-over of my person, and smiled. "Takes one to know one, right, Prospero?"

"Suppose so." I shrugged. "It's a common enough act for most female cops."

He pushed his glasses back up on his nose before answering. "Gardner's not acting. I haven't verified this, mind you, but I'd bet money she's hiding an impressive pair of stones in those panty hose."

I grimaced at the mental image this conjured. "What's her story?"

"All you need to know about Gardner is she's good, real good. Fair unless you cross her and she has a long memory. So don't fuck up." With that he seemed to dismiss me entirely in favor of reading the magazine in his lap.

"What are you reading?"

He sighed and held up the magazine. *Trigger Happy* was a rag that catered to men who enjoyed looking at pictures of well-endowed women holding guns.

"Nice," I said, my tone arid.

He shrugged. "Read it for the articles."

I rolled my eyes, but I wasn't offended. The magazine was a regular fixture in the coed locker room at the station. If you overlooked the centerfolds of silicon-inflated bimbos licking AK-47s, they had some decent features on the latest trends in Mundane weaponry. However, I noticed Morales kept skipping the pages covered in text in favor of the ones filled with boobs and ballistics.

As I watched, I noticed for the first time that his left hand was badly scarred. The scars webbed across his wrist and knuckles like melted wax. I cringed inwardly as I imagined the pain he must have gone through. The urge to ask where they came from was strong, but I figured I'd save myself the time. Guys like Morales weren't big on discussing anything that made them seem vulnerable. Plus, he didn't seem real eager to bond with me anyway.

I dragged my gaze from the hand to look outside. The corner was quiet, but I had a feeling it wouldn't stay that way long. "You done many of these?"

"Hmm?" He didn't look up.

"Stakeouts."

He sighed as if I were a five-year-old who asked too many questions.

"Hey," I said. He ignored me.

I grabbed the magazine. His head jerked up and a fierce scowl was suddenly aimed at me. "What the fuck?" he snapped.

"I was talking to you."

"So?"

I jerked my chin up. "You got a problem with me, Morales?"

He chuckled bitterly. "Yeah, I got a problem, Cupcake."

"Well?"

He sat up straighter. "Look, I can tell you're ambitious, and that's great. But don't be getting your hopes up that we're going to be real partners or anything."

I blinked once, twice. Finally, I said, "Let me get this straight: You're being a dick because you don't want me to get too attached to you?"

The corner of his mouth lifted. "Something like that."

"Get over yourself. This isn't a fucking date. I'm here to do my job. For the record, I've worked for five years without a partner and that suited me just fine. But if Gardner wants us to work together to get the job done, then we'll have to make the best of it. Starting with you never calling me 'Cupcake' again." I tossed the magazine back to him. "Asshole."

He stared at me with a poker face for a good five seconds. Then he lifted the magazine and started "reading" again without another word. But he was smiling like he was amused, so that was something.

I sighed and resumed my surveillance of the corner. Luckily, a bum limped on the far side of the building and distracted me from being irritated with the knucklehead next to me. The bum's skin had the jaundiced cast of a man addicted to a greed potion. Poor bastards took the stuff hoping the potion would help them win the lottery or get a raise at work. First time, the potion usually worked. They'd find a twenty on the sidewalk or win ten bucks on a scratch-off ticket. Barely enough to cover the cost of the potion, but enough to make them go back for more on the chance they'd get even more money next time.

Wasn't long before the potion started working on them from the inside. Large, yellow warts would sprout all over their skin. Even as the outward symbols of their greed appeared, their money—what was left of it—disappeared down the black hole of the Cauldron. Eventually, their addictions would take away everything: their houses, their families, their jobs. Most ended up digging in trash for aluminum cans to sell so they could buy their next hit, hoping this next time they'd finally get lucky.

Unlike Mundanes, Adepts rarely became addicted to potions. Some did, but since we could manage the magical energy better it rarely changed how we looked. Instead, Adepts who cooked dirty became slaves to the two Ps: Power and Profit.

That's why I knew street wizards like John Volos never fully got out of the game. He had plenty of money through different sources, but he'd always be addicted to magic's power.

My inner skeptic spoke up: You're addicted to power, too, you just found a different source for it. A sudden awareness of the weight of the gun and badge at my hip made me shift uneasily.

"According to Harkins, the dealers are being really selective about who they'll sell Gray Wolf to." Morales's casually shared information after he'd been so standoffish caught me off guard. Maybe I'd gained some ground there after all. "That's why we sent him out alone to do a buy to begin with. We were hoping he'd have a better chance of scoring a potion than we'd had on the corners with buy walks."

"Buy walks?"

"That's what we call it when we send an agent in undercover to buy a potion. Corner boy got a little trigger-happy with Shadi, so we put a stop to that."

My pulse sped up a little. Maybe it was lame to be excited about learning MEA lingo, but I was. After spending most of my time performing reactive police work—chasing perps after the crime had happened—I was excited to be involved in building a case proactively. It felt more...I don't know, productive. Which was ridiculous since all we were doing was sitting in a car.

"Has anyone on the team actually seen Gray Wolf?"

"Harkins said he saw it once." He nodded. "It's a gray powder, like ash, he said."

I nodded. Most potions were sold in powder form. Alchemical

potions were usually mixed with alcohol or narcotics and smoked, while blood potions were mixed with blood and injected or snorted.

"He also said it can be smoked or injected," he continued. Which supported Mez's theory that it was a combo of alchemy and blood magic.

"What's the street price?" I asked.

He finally put down the magazine and turned toward me fully. "Two hundred an ounce."

"Fuck off! Who the hell are they selling that shit to at those prices?"

"My guess is they're trying to scare off the curious."

I frowned. "The demographic in the Cauldron that can afford that kind of scratch is so small it's laughable."

He shrugged. "Well someone's buying. Gardner got a call from your boss at BPD this morning. There was a mugging last night. Vic said the perp bit him, but he managed to beat him back with his briefcase, which the perp promptly ran off with."

"Why do they think it's related to Gray Wolf?" I lifted the binoculars to watch the corner again.

"The vic said the guy looked like, and I quote, 'One of them ugly werewolves from the movies.'"

I nudged him with my elbow. "Speaking of ugly—get a hold of that mug."

The guy leaned against the building, smoking a cigarette. He was a six-foot-plus-tall sack of tough meat and gristle. His lanky frame was pretty much the only thing noteworthy about him. Brown hair, ashy skin, brown eyes.

Morales turned and lifted the binoculars to get a gander. "Recognize him?"

I nodded even though he couldn't see me. "He's a regular

corner boy. One of the Votary boys." Which wasn't a surprise since the Green Faerie sat smack-dab in the middle of the territory Uncle Abe used to run. Now, of course, no single wizard was in charge of these corners—just low-level guys duking it out for prime real estate.

"I busted him a couple of times for vandalism. Real name's Marvin Brown, but on the streets he's known as 'Picasso' because he's a coven Herald." Personally, I thought the nickname fit because his face looked like one of those cubist paintings—all angles with no symmetry.

"Herald?" Morales shot me a curious eyebrow raise.

"Covens sometimes use graffiti to spread messages to the troops. The ones who paint the symbols are called Heralds."

Morales nodded. "Some of the covens in Los Angeles do something similar. What kind of code do they use?"

"The Sangs tend to use Egyptian hieroglyphs. The Votaries use the alchemical language of birds."

He shot me a look that I was too smart to mistake for respect. "What about the Os?"

"Aphrodite Johnson doesn't bother with that cryptic bullshit."

"So our friend is a tagger. Any history of dealing?"

"Hasn't been collared for it yet," I said. "But he's looking awfully nervous for a graffiti artist without his paints."

Marvin's posture was casual, but his eyes worked over the street as if he was waiting for someone to attack. Morales and I were parked in a lot down the street, so he hadn't eyeballed us yet.

"Should we have a chat with him?" I asked.

Morales watched for a few moments. Finally, he picked up his magazine again. "We'll wait."

"Why?"

He sighed and dragged his eyes from the magazine.

"Because, Nancy Drew, we're trying to find evidence, not have a heart-to-heart with the guy."

I considered calling him to task on the Nancy Drew thing, but it was better than Cupcake, so I let it slide. Plus, as soon as Morales said it, a limo pulled up to the corner. We both sat up straighter. Marvin sauntered to the car and leaned in through the open window. I tried to adjust my angle, but I just couldn't see inside past Marvin's skinny ass.

"Wait for it," Morales said.

Just then, the Herald pulled something out of his pocket. Couldn't tell what, but I was guessing he wasn't passing notes. "Can you see it?"

"Shit," Morales said. "No."

A split second after Marvin passed the item into the window, it rolled up and the limo took off like a shot. I spun around to grab the license plate. "Got it."

Morales picked up the cell he'd stashed on the dashboard. "Shadi. Yeah. Need you to run a plate for me."

I held up the pad with the numbers while he read them off.

"Call me back when you got it," Morales said and hung up. "All right, let's go have a chat with Marvin."

He put the car in gear and drove toward the front of the club. The closer we got, the more alert Marvin's posture became. His eyes narrowed as Morales slowed near the corner.

I didn't know if he recognized me or if his criminal Spidey-sense just told him who we were, but he started walking at a rapid clip down the side street. When he reached the alley behind the building, he sprinted off like a gazelle.

"We got a runner," Morales said in a bored tone. "Go get him."

I frowned. "Why me?"

"I'm driving." He glanced over. "Go on."

The sly tilt of his lips told me he expected me to balk. Trust me, I considered it. After all, I was still in the stupid suit and heels, a detail my new partner had clearly not forgotten.

"Fine." His eyes widened as I reached for the handle and threw the door wide. I hit the ground running. A jolt of pain raced up my ankles as I sprinted in front of the car, but I dug in and ran faster. The heels were a bitch, but damned if I was going to let Morales think I couldn't hold my own.

I shot off down the alley, my gaze lasered on Marvin's rapidly retreating back. "We just want to talk to you, Marvin."

"Ah, hell no!" he yelled over his shoulder. He hurdled a cardboard box and headed straight toward a chain-link in the distance.

"Goddamn it." My heel skidded on a puddle of grease. I windmilled my arms and caught myself before gravity won the battle. Now that I was good and pissed, I was able to put a little extra gas in my stride.

I managed to grab a handful of Marvin's shirt.

"Bitch, you crazy!" he shouted, struggling for the top.

I managed to get my other hand on his waistband. A good yank later, he came tumbling down like a sack of pointy elbows and ass cheeks. He landed directly on top of me.

"Uh!"

Marvin struggled against my hold, but I gripped hard despite the pain in my ass and my twisted ankle.

"I told you to catch him, Prospero," said an amused voice behind me, "not make out with him."

"Shut the fuck up and help me."

Two scuffed boots entered my field of vision, followed by a face bearing a shit-eating grin. In two seconds, he had Marvin subdued. While they both watched, I dragged myself off the nasty pavement.

My right shoe lay to the right, so I limped over and grabbed it. As I bent down, I noticed a vomit stain on my elbow and a smudge of something disconcertingly brown on my skirt. "You're paying for my dry cleaning," I said.

Morales opened his mouth to respond, but Marvin beat him to it. "I was you, I'd burn that shit."

◆ ◆ ◆

Fifteen minutes later, we were parked in a lot a few blocks from the Green Faerie. Mr. Funny Guy was pouting in the rear seat. I was back there with him because Morales said he didn't want his passenger seat to get dirty.

Ass.

"Y'all gonna get me killed picking me up in broad daylight!" The paint spatters that decorated his hands were brilliant against his white-knuckled grip on the tail of his T-shirt. The black shirt also sported fresh red paint stains over the logo for the popular Alchemist rock group, Spirit of Vitriol.

"And selling potions won't?" Morales said from his spot in the front. "Come on, Marvin."

"Picasso," he corrected. "And I already told you, my home-boy PeeWee got a sweet gig as one of them chauffeurs. He was asking for directions."

"A chauffeur was asking for directions?" Morales asked.

"Didn't say he was a good chauffeur."

"Where was he headed?" I asked. "To the stash?"

Marvin feigned an almost convincing frown. "What's a stash?"

I rolled my eyes. "Who's putting Gray Wolf on the streets?"

"What's Gray Wolf?" This time his pupils dilated, as if his eyes were trying to hide secrets.

Morales raised a brow. "You know, Marvin, the jails are full of assholes who wouldn't talk."

"Stop calling me Marvin," he said, setting his jaw at a stubborn angle.

Morales's cell chimed. He grabbed it and punched a button like he wished it were Marvin's face. "What? Hey, Shadi."

While he talked to her, I stared down Picasso. He met my look with a curious one of his own. Finally, he said, "What's it like?"

"What's what like?" I snapped.

"Being a traitor." He didn't say it in an accusing tone. More curious. Like maybe he was thinking of becoming one himself.

Since that's exactly what I wanted him to do, I thought for a moment about my answer. "Not gonna lie. It's not easy." He nodded as though that's what he expected me to say. I leaned forward. "But I'll tell you this: I don't miss looking over my shoulder and waiting for the fuzz to snatch me up."

"Cut the shit, Prospero." He laughed. "Helping you two might get the fuzz off my back, it might not. But it sure as hell will get me ass-fucked by Volos."

I raised a brow. "So he's back in the game?"

"You already knew that, right?" He shook his head. "Problem is you don't got the evidence. And I ain't got none to give you."

At that moment, Morales ended his call. "Plates checked out. National Limo owns the car and the registered driver is Jerome Simmons, who goes by the alias PeeWee."

"I told you," Marvin said. "PeeWee works for them."

"That doesn't mean you weren't selling him a potion."

Marvin made a disgusted sound and jerked back toward the seat. "If I sold to the man, where's the money at?" He raised his hands. "Ask me, y'all are holding a brother against his will. This is some straight-up kidnapping and shit."

Morales and I exchanged a look. Technically we couldn't hold him without charging him with something, but there were ways around that. We were grasping at straws now. When we'd patted him down, we'd found only a box of breath mints he'd clearly forgotten about, a Velcro wallet, and a pack of generic cigs in his pockets. His wallet turned up a bus pass, a few bucks, and a condom that looked like he'd stolen it from a Gas 'N Gulp in the '90s.

I glanced at the glowering Herald. As much as I didn't want to let this go, we weren't getting anywhere. I shook my head at Morales.

"All right, Marvin," he said. "Looks like we gotta throw you back."

"Wait," he said. "Don't suppose you could spare a little extra scratch."

Morales and I shared a look. "For what, exactly?" I asked.

He sat up straighter. "Seeing how I told you it's Volos."

Morales laughed. "I'm pretty sure the judge won't accept hearsay from a known vandal as proof."

The kid chewed his lip. "Okay, look. All I know is Volos has some plan cooking. A big one."

"What kind of plan?"

"I don't know exactly." His eyes darted around quickly, like he was looking for ideas. "Maybe he's trying to take over where Abraxas left off."

"Good-bye, Marvin." Morales reached for the door.

"Wait! I helped you, right?"

I snorted. "That's about as useful as you telling us Volos prefers boxers over briefs." For the record, he preferred nothing at all. At least he hadn't a decade earlier.

"Hey! What do you want here? You ain't gonna get that kind of evidence interviewing low-level assholes like me."

"So we'll go up the chain," Morales said. "Bye now."

"Shit," Marvin said, not moving. "Good luck with that. Ain't no one want to get in the middle of this turf war."

I tilted my head. "Wait. What turf war?"

The kid froze and swallowed. "Just, you know, everybody trying to stake a claim."

"Out!" Morales threw open the door and pushed the kid out. Marvin stumbled into the alley.

"Hold on," I said, grabbing Morales's arm. "He knows something."

"Should have shared it when he had the chance." He threw a couple of crumpled bills out the door after Marvin. "Here's a little something for your dry-cleaning bill." He hit the gas before I could grab the door and slam it shut.

I leaned over the back of his seat. "I don't think we should leave him here."

"Why not?"

"Because we're in Votary territory. If anyone saw him with us—"

"Sounds to me like Marvin needs to be more careful about the company he keeps." Morales elbowed my hand away and slammed the car into drive.

As he drove away, I cast a final, apologetic glance out the back window. Marvin was pulling himself off the filthy alley floor, clutching the bills in his hand, and watching our exit with eyes that glittered with hate.

# Chapter Eleven

That night, I pulled Sybil into the driveway after picking her up from Joe the Mechanic's shop. In the passenger's seat was a bucket of chicken, a bag of groceries I couldn't afford, and my shoulder holster. Part of me wanted to just hide out in the car and eat the extra-crispy in silence. But I'd already received two impatient texts from my brother demanding to know when I would be getting home with food. So I gathered my stuff and trudged toward the door.

Mez had been nice enough to drop me off at the mechanic's shop after work. He drove one of those fancy, potion-fueled cars and spent the entire drive trying to talk me into buying one, too. I just smiled and nodded because I appreciated the ride, but I resented the hell out of the suggestion. The Jeep had been the first major purchase I'd made in my life that hadn't been funded by dirty magic. It had taken six months of riding the bus, eating ramen, and forgoing any sort of luxuries to buy it from the fry cook at the diner I'd worked in after I left the coven. I mean sure, she was primer gray, needed enough repairs to put my mechanic's kid through college, and the interior smelled like dirty gym socks, but she was mine.

According to Joe, the culprit of that morning's no-go was a corroded battery that had eaten through all the surrounding connectors and terminals. Because I'd let the problem fester so long, the repair cost twice what it would have if I'd just needed a new battery. It would have cost three times that had I not also promised Joe to help Joey Jr. with his latest speeding ticket.

I used my foot to push open the kitchen door. The bucket of chicken was hot against my rib cage, and the groceries and holster were balanced precariously in my left hand.

Danny was doing homework at the table. "Hey," he said without looking up.

"Grab something, will ya?" I asked.

He sighed and took the chicken from me. Instead of setting it down, he ripped off the lid and pulled out a drumstick. I grimaced at him and lugged the groceries to the counter. The sounds of him munching on that chicken leg made me want to claw my skin off.

"Oh yeah, Pen called. Said she wanted to hear about your new assignment or something."

"I'll tell her later at group." I nodded and pulled a box of cereal out of the bag.

"Ah, shit." *Smack, smack.* "Why didn't you get the cinnamon kind?"

I pointed to the large ceramic jar set up by the sink. On it, I'd written CURSES $1. "Pay up, kid."

He sighed and shoved the drumstick between his teeth. Then he dipped into his pocket and dug out a handful of change. With exaggerated movements, he dropped the coins in the jar. "Happy?" he said over his mouthful.

I nodded. "Now, back to your complaint. When you get a job

you can pick the fu—" I caught myself just in time—"freaking cereal." The box slammed onto the counter like a gunshot. "Now put that chicken down and help me put these away."

His expression became the one teenagers had used on their parents for generations. The one that made you long to walk out the door and never look back.

He threw the chicken bone at the sink and wiped his hands on his jeans. "Jesus, what crawled up your butt?" He took a six-pack of soda from me and went to put it in the fridge.

I closed my eyes and counted to ten. Then twenty. Ah, hell—why not thirty just to be safe?

"Katie?"

When I opened my lids, Danny was staring at me with a worried expression. Guilt washed through me like an acid bath. Sure, his selfishness was annoying, but the kid was only sixteen. I'd overreacted and we both knew it. I sighed. "Sorry. I just had a long day."

"Tell me about it," Danny said with a sage nod. "Miss Bell gave us a pop quiz in calculus today."

I snorted as I kicked off my pumps. After I spent my day chasing junkies down alleys and investigating the scum of the earth, coming home to someone so naive about the realities of the streets was nice. Yet another reason why I was determined for him to have a normal life—far away from the corrupting influence of magic.

"Yeah, that sounds pretty brutal." My tone was sarcastic but not mocking. I barely passed statistics in night school and would rather face down a hexhead with a knife than a calculus test.

Now that I'd shaken off the bitch funk I'd walked in with, I refocused my efforts on putting away the groceries. The delicious scent of chicken was making my stomach growl.

We worked in companionable silence for a few moments. "So how do you think you did on the quiz?" I asked.

He opened the cabinet to put away a box of snack cakes—I'd finished the ones we had for breakfast that morning. "Pretty well."

I lifted his backpack off the table. The zipper was open and a book fell out on the floor. "Crap." I bent down to pick it up without looking at the title. "Anything else happen at school?" I started to shove the book back in the bag, but he grabbed it from me before I could manage it.

"I got it." His voice was an octave higher than usual. Cue the police instincts.

"What you got there?" I said casually.

He froze and his gaze flicked to my face, which I purposefully kept clear of emotion. He tensed, as if bracing himself. "Nothing."

I stayed quiet but raised a brow.

Finally, he sighed. "It's a stupid book I found," he grumbled, eyes focused on his sneakers.

The hair on the back of my neck prickled. "Hand it over."

"Kate, it's just a—"

I snapped my fingers, trying to keep a lid on my temper. I had a really bad feeling I knew what kind of book he had, but I wanted to see it before I boiled over. He handed it to me the way one might a piece of dynamite.

When I saw the title, I wanted to throw the book out of the window. No, that was too nice. I wanted to light it on fire and spread the ashes to the four corners of the earth.

In truth, the term "book" applied in only the loosest sense. Really it was a pile of mimeographed paper with a flimsy cover stapled along the spine—more of a pamphlet, really. A pamphlet I unfortunately knew by heart.

*The Alchemist's Handbook* was the bible of the dirty magic

underworld. Potion cookers, street-level spell dealers, and all manner of lowlifes referred to this piece of trash constantly for recipes, arrest-evasion strategies, and general criminal inspiration. Every cop who worked the Arcane beat knew and cursed the existence of the textbook for criminals.

The clock on the wall *tick, tick, tick*ed like the bomb's timer counting down to explosion.

Danny crossed his arms and slouched against the counter. A bullish expression told me he'd convinced himself he had a fighting chance of winning this battle of wills.

Dumb kid. You'd figure he'd have learned never get into a silent standoff with a cop. Especially when the proof of his guilt had just been in his sweaty palms.

He cleared his throat. "I can explain."

Bingo. Cop face one, the kid zero.

"Save it." I held up a hand. Using the same tone I employed when interrogating a hostile suspect, I pointed to the table. "Sit."

He looked taken aback that I hadn't started screaming. He dropped into a chair with a sigh.

I lifted his game player off the table. "Do you know who bought this?"

His head tilted to the side like he suspected it was a trick question. "You?"

"Do you know what I do for a living to earn the money that paid for it?"

He crossed his arms. "I know," he grumbled.

"Do you? I think I need you to say it out loud just to be sure."

His lips puckered and he rolled his eyes. "You're a cop."

"Where am I a cop, Danny?"

A martyred sigh. "The Cauldron."

"Right. I patrol slums filled with Arcane criminals who learned the tricks of their trade from that book."

"I got it, Kate," he snapped.

"No, Danny. You don't fucking got it." My voice rose and I leaned across the table. His eyes shot toward the curse jar, but he thought better of mentioning my slip. I rose abruptly, shoving my chair back, and stuck my hand in my purse. From it, I removed a handful of bills. As he watched with his mouth hanging open, I dropped probably ten crumpled ones in. His eyes widened. Without missing a beat, I continued, "Because if you fucking got it, there'd be no way you'd bring the mother-fucking *Alchemist's Handbook* under my goddamned roof!"

"It's just a book. Jesus, don't be such a fascist."

"This isn't just a book, Danny. There's nothing in here that won't get you into a world of trouble with the law." I paused to get control of my temper. Releasing a great sigh, I dropped into the chair across from him to get on his level. "Where'd you get it?"

His eyes shifted left. "Found it."

I snorted. "Please don't insult me."

He threw up his hands. "I found it in the attic!"

My mouth fell open. With trembling hands, I opened the cover. Sure enough, there was the familiar inscription.

*Welcome to the magic game, Katie-girl.*

My stomach dipped. Shit. He'd found my copy. The one Uncle Abe gave me on my birthday when I turned eight. I had clutched it to my chest like a precious treasure while I blew out the candles on my pink princess cake.

I shook off that nausea-inducing memory and frowned at my brother. "Why were you in the attic?"

His discomfort was palpable and not just because he knew what he'd done was wrong. There was something underneath the defensive posturing. His reddened cheeks hinted that he was embarrassed. "I needed to find a picture of Mom." His gaze was hot, like he hated me for making him say that out loud. "In history class we're doing a genealogy project and I needed a picture."

I chose my tone carefully because this conversation was the verbal equivalent of thin ice. "Why didn't you just ask me?" I sat down heavily because the turn the conversation had just taken made me feel sucker punched.

"Because you never want to talk about her. Or anything having to do with the past or the family. Whenever I try to bring it up, you give me that look."

I pulled back and relaxed my face, knowing I'd just been giving him the look in question. Here I thought I'd been so clever and in control, but my little brother just managed to gain the upper hand. If there was one topic sure to cripple me it was a discussion about "the family."

With a sigh, I placed my elbows on the table and looked at my brother. "Look, Danny, I—"

Before I could continue, he shoved his chair back. The wooden slats banged into the fridge. "Just forget it, okay? I'm sorry I took the stupid book. I was just...curious, I guess, since it's, like, part of my heritage or whatever."

I rose slowly, scrambling to think of the right thing to say. "No, I—"

"I already took the picture of Mom to school, but I'll give it back to you after I get the assignment from my teacher." He grabbed his books off the table and his backpack from the floor.

"No, it's okay. You can keep—"

"I gotta finish my work."

With that my little brother stormed out of the kitchen. I looked up at the ceiling for help. Luckily, I still had some credits left in the curse jar. "Fuck, fuck, shit, shit, damn it, fuck."

# Chapter Twelve

Two hours later, the argument with Danny chased me down the concrete steps into the basement of the Sacred Heart Church. Despite the Catholic setting, recovering dirty magic abusers of any faith could attend the weekly Arcane Anonymous group meetings.

I was late, so I slid in as quietly as I could and took a seat beside Pen. She glanced over with raised brows. I mouthed "Later." A very loud, very pointed throat clearing sounded. I glanced up and shot an apologetic smile to our fearless leader, Rufus Xavier.

He sat in a blue plastic chair—the kind found in every school cafeteria in America. The other chairs were formed into a circle so you couldn't really say he sat at the front, but his sheer size and bearing left no doubt about who led this support group. He wore a black T-shirt and jeans with a crocheted slouch hat done in stripes of red, green, and yellow perched on his braided hair. The meeting had only just begun, but already he was worked up into a feverish sermon as if he were standing in a pulpit on Sunday morning.

"Everyone has a hole in their center," he said, placing a fist over his diaphragm. "A gaping shadow that demands to be filled. Some people fill it with faith and God. Others with money or fame. Then there are those who fill it with food, alcohol, nicotine or, yeah, potions." He looked around the circle to each of our faces. No matter how hard you tried, you couldn't keep much from Rufus. He had an almost preternatural ability to see through people's bullshit.

I'd spent enough time on the streets as both a pseudocriminal and then as a cop to know his words were true. It was the eyes. No matter how tough you acted or how much you tried to disguise it with makeup or a strut or other masks, the eyes always exposed the void. Generally, it was whatever the perp used to disguise or fill the hole that got me called out by Dispatch, but I could always see the shadows in their eyes. The darker secrets behind the violence and addictions.

"But the potions and sex and the religion, they're just symptoms," he continued. "Truth is, the real problem is whatever created that crater in your chest. Most of us got ours 'cause our mamas had their own holes they was trying to fill and didn't have enough time to prevent ours from forming. Or maybe it was our daddies. Maybe he left when we were too young. Or maybe he stayed around too long."

A couple of ironic chuckles filtered through the room. Several studies had been contracted by the government to figure out a link between upbringing and magic addiction. I'm no scientist, but from what I've seen, the most common denominator for addiction was simply being human.

"Maybe you weren't born into poverty and maybe your daddy didn't sneak into your bedroom at night to touch your no-no place," Rufus continued, "but somewhere along the way some other human fucked you over but good. Probably lots more than one. And getting fucked by your fellow man drills a hole in your center. So you either find a coping mechanism or you check out early."

He let that settle over us like a gray cloud. Most of us gathered that night were veterans of the group. Addicts with lots of years between them and the rock-bottom moment that made them finally seek help. But magic sank way down deep inside and it was almost impossible to exorcise its roots completely.

"So what do you fill your hole with now that you're off the junk?" he asked.

I chewed my lip and thought it over. Justice, I thought, feeling smug. Problem was, the longer I was a cop, the harder it was becoming to keep my faith in that particular religion. Not when I saw justice fail so many people so often.

"Maybe you joined a gym," he said. "Maybe you spend most of your Sundays on your knees praying to the good Lord. Don't matter what it is, long as it's legal and healthy and doesn't hurt anyone—specially your damned self. You just got to fill it with something or else that blackness gonna rise up and consume you whole, brother."

My inner skeptic snorted. She reminded me that I was never addicted to potions. I never shot up, lit up, or snorted up. Unlike the rest of my companions, I wasn't a Mundane looking to recover from addiction to dirty magic. Instead, I was an Adept trying to overcome an addiction to the power I felt from cooking. An addiction's an addiction, but I never pretended my struggles compared to theirs. It was easy to find other sources of power. Not so easy to replace the chemical changes forced on one's body from dirty magic.

Now that his introductory speech was over, Rufus raised

his hands and invited us to join him in reciting the credo of Arcane Anonymous. "Everything I need to transform myself already exists within me. I am enough."

When we sat back down, Pen nudged me with her elbow. She looked over and nodded to a new member across the way. The girl couldn't be more than eighteen. Her hair hung in long greasy ropes around her pale face. Her irises were still the cornflower blue of a heavy potion-user and her hands shook as though she'd been stricken with palsy. Scabbed-over track marks peeked over the top of the black turtleneck she kept tugging up.

Poor kid, I thought, she couldn't be more than a week or two sober. She had a tough road ahead.

Closer to us, a few people over, was a guy in his mid-forties. His skin had a definite yellowish tint, except for where the angry flush into his cheeks made them appear orange. His arms were crossed and the foot perched on his knee bobbed up and down. I'd come to enough of these meetings over the years to recognize a court-order case when I saw one. Probably he'd be defiant and sullen during the meeting until it was time to ask Rufus for a signature on his forms.

"Welcome, everyone. Congratulations on taking the first, most important step in recovery: showing up. We gather here every week to share our experiences and help each other through the maze of recovery from dirty magic." He paused and looked around the circle. Naturally, the new people kept their eyes downcast. Typical. They thought not making eye contact would spare them from having to share, but Rufus always called on those types first.

"Mr. Callahan?" Ru said finally. "Do you have anything you'd like to share tonight?"

The jaundiced man shook his head, refusing to meet Rufus's gaze.

"Just so you know," he said, his tone friendly, "I don't sign court documents for people who don't do the work."

Callahan's head snapped up. His lids squinted over ice-blue irises. "What do I have to talk about?"

"Anything that's on your mind." Ru spread his arms wide. "We're here to listen."

"I shouldn't even be here." His lips puckered like a bitter lemon. "That fucking judge had it out for me."

Ru's expression remained calm. He'd heard all of this before. "So you don't think you have a problem with potions?"

Callahan adjusted his ass in the chair, warming up to having a sympathetic ear. "Of course not. I mean, sure, I take a little nip of a virility potion every now and then. Just to give me a little edge with the ladies."

That explained his color. Virility potions attacked the liver first. However, if he kept up with it, he'd turn bright red, like a horny baboon's ass.

Rufus looked down at the clipboard in his lap. "According to the notes I was sent, you were arrested for masturbating in your car at a red light."

Callahan's cheeks pulsed orange. "I was in the privacy of my own vehicle. Wasn't my fault that school bus pulled up next to me. I don't have a problem."

"When the medic wizards checked you out, your penis was covered in friction blisters."

Callahan started rocking back and forth. "I can't help it that I have a healthy libido."

On my left side, Jacob, who used to be addicted to sex magic, too, snorted. "Is that the same excuse you'll use when you rape someone?"

"Hey!" Callahan's eyes flared. "I would never—"

"Before you started that virility potion, I bet you also swore you'd never masturbate in front of school kids, either." Jacob was six feet tall, covered in tattoos, and bald. He's served five years in the pen for stalking a woman after he'd taken a dirty love potion to attract her. After he'd been released, he joined the group and redirected his addiction into a successful career as a sculptor. "Face it, man. You're an addict. Unless you stop taking that shit, you're going to end up seriously hurting someone besides yourself."

"Can he talk to me like that?" Callahan sputtered.

"Yep." Rufus smiled. "This isn't show-'n-tell, brother. Recovery ain't pretty. Jacob there has been potion-free for three years now. You'd do well to listen to him."

Callahan crossed his arms and scooted farther into the seat. The move revealed that he was sporting an erection. He quickly realized his mistake. Scooting his butt back, he lowered his head into his hands and rested his elbows on his knees. "I don't know how to quit," he whispered.

I pressed my lips together. Part of me wanted to shake the guy and tell him to stop feeling sorry for himself. The other part felt some compassion for him. Using potions changes who you are in the most fundamental ways. Probably Callahan was a guy who lacked self-esteem and started taking the virility potion to feel more confident and attractive. He'd had no idea when he started using that he'd turn into the type of guy who'd jack off in front of kids.

"Being here is the first step," Rufus said. "Come talk to me after and I'll hook you up with some other resources, okay?"

Callahan nodded and wrapped his arms around himself protectively.

"Miss Pen?" Rufus prompted.

Next to me, Pen sat up straighter. "I've been feeling really tested lately. Some of these kids I talk to at school?"

Rufus nodded.

"Their parents got them so messed up they don't know their assholes from their elbows."

"That's horrible." This from Darla, the fortysomething mother of four, who'd been sober for six months after kicking her addiction to vanity potions. When she'd first attended group, her size 42 GG breasts had defied several laws of physics, but now the pendulous lobes drooped over the distended shelf of her stomach.

"It's the truth," Pen said. "Some days I don't know why I even try. Money doesn't buy class or morals. Today, this kid was brought into my office because she got caught taking a diet potion. She's eleven."

Darla made a distressed sound and shook her head. I raised a brow, but not much shocked me anymore. Working the Cauldron beat helped me develop a nice, tough callous where my naïveté used to live.

"What did you say to her?" Rufus asked.

"I asked her where she got it. Said her mama gave it to her because she wasn't losing her baby fat fast enough."

"How does dealing with these kinds of cases make you feel?"

"Frustrated. Angry." Pen sighed. "Powerless."

Rufus leaned forward. "Sometimes you got to fight the good fight even if you'll probably lose the war."

Pen nodded. "I have a call in to CPS, but they're so backlogged it'll be a long time until a social worker gets over there."

"Did you talk to the principal?" I asked.

"Yeah." She grimaced. "He said as long as the diet potion is clean magic, we can't get involved. But you ask me, he's just worried about losing that family's fat fund-raising checks."

"Pen, we've talked about this before—" Rufus began.

She waved a hand. "Yeah, yeah, I know—I can't control other people's behavior."

"I was going to say that you can't save everyone."

Pen laughed bitterly. "You just said I had to fight the fight even if I'd lose."

Rufus shook his head. "Sometimes the fight's not even worth starting."

My best friend went silent. Rufus had just poked her most sensitive bruise. She raised her chin. "Maybe not, but at least I have to try to save them."

Rufus winked. "Just be sure you're doing it for them and not because your savior complex has replaced your old addiction to energy potions."

Pen had been addicted to potions that helped her stay awake and energized during her rigorous master's-level work in psychology. She'd purchased the potion patches from some two-bit cook on campus, who put God-knows-what in the formula. After using the potion for six months, she'd had a minor heart attack that almost ended her life and her future career and definitely ended her love affair with dirty magic.

Instead of being angry for being called out on her issues, Pen simply nodded. She'd put enough people through the psychotherapy wringer to know Rufus was not only justified, but also right in his assessment.

"Kate?" Rufus said.

I jerked my head up. Usually I didn't talk much at group. I wasn't mad he'd called on me, just surprised. "Don't have much to report," I lied.

Beside me, Pen leveled me with a look. "Mmm-hmm."

I swiveled to stare at her. She raised her brows. When I looked at Rufus, he had a knowing look on his face. "What?"

Pen nudged me with her elbow. "Your anniversary."

My first reaction was relief. For some reason, I'd been expecting Pen to call me on lying about my problems. But then

I remembered she'd have no idea about my fight with Danny or the fact that my first love was now a suspect in the most important investigation of my career.

My second reaction was frustration. "How many times do I have to tell you guys I don't feel right celebrating anniversaries?"

All these years I'd resisted because I was never actually addicted to using magic. I'd never taken a token or anniversary pin because I felt it was disrespectful to those who'd been through hell to kick their dependencies. I'd just showed up to a meeting one day with Pen and kept coming because it helped me remember why I didn't cook anymore.

"But this is ten years," Rufus said.

"It's still a couple months away," I added loudly over the round of applause from the group. I'd stopped cooking the day my mother died. The anniversary Pen was referring to was of my first time attending a meeting. After I'd started working at the restaurant where she was already a waitress, it had taken a few weeks for us to feel each other out, and even longer for her to convince me to come to a meeting with her.

"Ten years?" the new girl asked. "How did you do that?" Her eyes were wide, as if the answer to this question would dictate her own failure or success on the road to sobriety.

I looked at Ru for help, but he simply raised a brow and smiled. "One day at a time, baby girl. One day at a time." To me he said, "We'll talk about it later, okay?"

With a nod, I crossed my arms and slid down in my seat. Part of me was kicking myself for not using the opportunity to talk about my shit, but the rational part reminded that part that I couldn't discuss a case in front of these people. And I simply wasn't ready to talk about Danny's sudden interest in magic because it brought up too much shit.

"Kate?" Rufus was saying.

I looked up. "Hmm?"

"Will you lead us in the pledge?"

Inside, my sense of irony laughed and laughed. On the outside, though, I rose and said the words I'd memorized and repeated more times than my own name in the last decade. "Magic is a tool. If I am unable to use it responsibly, I will not use magic at all. I am responsible for my own actions, and I pledge to act with compassion for myself and others, always."

♦ ♦ ♦

At the top of the steps leading up from the basement, Rufus stood by the door to say good-bye to everyone. When he saw me coming, he smiled, showing a full mouth of strong, white teeth. "What's shaking, white girl?"

I smiled and went in for a hug. The familiar, pungent-sweet scent of Mary Jane clung to his clothes like cologne. Rufus might be a magic-recovery counselor who met with addicts in a Catholic church, but he worshipped at the altar of Mother Ganja. He'd overcome a pretty devastating addiction to performance-enhancing, dirty magic potions that ruined his career as a pro baller in the early '90s. Now he worked at a gas station by day and led junkies toward salvation at night.

"Can't complain," I said. "How about you?"

"Oh, you know, SSDD." Same shit, different day. He laughed. "So about this anniversary."

I was shaking my head before he finished the last word. "Don't start on me."

"I know, it's just—" He reached into his pocket. "Your success gives the newer ones hope."

He nodded toward the new girl, who scurried out of the basement and sped by without looking up to see Ru's wave.

"Think she'll be back?" I asked, watching her retreat.

"We'll see." He shrugged. "Look, just think about it. If you don't do something here, at least do something privately to mark the occasion. Rituals matter, Kate."

I nodded because I didn't want to lie to him. I'd think about it, all right. About how the anniversary brought up all sorts of complicated shit for me. Like guilt that I hadn't visited my mother's grave since her funeral. About how my little brother was poking his nose into magic because I'd been such a hard-ass about keeping him away from it. About how after ten years I should have been able to relax, but instead John Volos was sniffing around the edges of my life again.

"Hey," Rufus said, "you okay?"

I smiled quickly. "Yeah. I'm good."

"You ready to go grab that drink?" Pen asked, approaching us. "Great talk tonight, Ru."

He smiled and gave her a hug. She'd been coming to group longer than I had. Her ten-year anniversary had been a couple of years earlier.

"You know," I said, "I think I'm gonna pass tonight. I've got some work to do." I still had some files to review for Shadi. "I'll call you tomorrow, though, okay?"

Once we'd said our good-byes, I walked away feeling relieved. I felt guilty for not wanting to hang out with Pen, but part of that decision had been self-preservation. No way could I get through one beer with her without spilling my guts about the case, and I really needed not to be analyzed right then. I knew I was taking risks, but I also knew the possible benefits outweighed any of the risks. If I could make this case, I'd make the team and then Danny and I would be set. And if John Volos had to go down to make that happen, I'd do whatever it took.

# Chapter Thirteen

When I pulled into work the next morning, I was determined to make it go smoother than the day before. Sure, Danny hadn't spoken to me over breakfast, but the sun was shining, I found a new penny in the parking lot, and I'd brought coffee and a box of bagels for the team. No bad days begin with free money, good coffee, and warm carbs.

When I reached the top of the stairs, I found the team huddled around Gardner's open office door. Male shouting came from inside the small room. Tension filled the air like smog.

"What's up?" I whispered to the others. Shadi made a pained grimace and shook her head. Mez, whose dreads had turned an inexplicable blue overnight, looked disgusted by the outburst, and Morales leaned against the ring with a smirk that said he was enjoying the fireworks.

Captain Eldritch's back was to the open door. The way his hands were flapping he was capable of taking flight any second. Standing across from him at her desk, Gardner looked cool and calm, like she was used to having police captains chew her ass out before breakfast.

Closer now, I could make out the captain's words. "—explain to me why I got the mayor's office breathing down my fucking neck?"

I slowly slid down into a seat. "I brought bagels," I whispered.

The other three perked up and dug into the box like a bunch of hyenas. Shadi and Mez retreated to their listening posts to enjoy the refreshments while they watched the show. Morales stayed near me. "He stormed through about five minutes before you got here."

I nodded and took a sip from my coffee, suddenly wishing it were bourbon instead.

"Can't say that I do," Gardner replied in a calm tone. "But I'm guessing you have an idea."

"Seems a good friend of the mayor's is being harassed by this task force."

"Who?"

"John Volos."

I cringed. Had Volos seen me the other day outside his building?

"Shit," Morales said under his breath. "I thought we were more careful."

I relaxed instantly. I'd forgotten that Gardner had him and Shadi tail Volos the day before.

Gardner shot a quick, hard glance in Morales's direction. "Harassed?" she said. "I highly doubt that, Captain. My agents know better."

"According to Mr. Volos, members of this task force followed him for four hours yesterday and then sat outside a fund-raiser at the mayor's own campaign manager's house last night."

"Maybe you should remind the mayor that his biggest

backer was and probably still is a major player in the Cauldron's potion trade."

"I'd be happy to if you can hand me one piece of evidence that backs up that accusation."

"As it happens, Agent Pruitt found some manifests from Volos Transport's freighters yesterday. Mr. Volos has been receiving shipments of alchemical materials from Canada for the last five weeks."

He laughed. "As an Adept, he's allowed to use alchemical materials for his own purposes."

"What do you suppose a solitary practitioner would need barrels full of oil of rose quartz for, Captain?" Mez challenged.

"It's well known Mr. Volos does consulting work for Sortilege, Inc. Maybe it's for a project with them." Eldritch crossed his arms. "So far I have only heard conjecture."

"We're working on it," Gardner snapped.

Eldritch's mustache twitched. "John Volos isn't just bankrolling for the mayor, he's also a goddamned hero in this city. If you're going to go after him, you better be sure you can back up your accusations with evidence that's more watertight than a frog's ass."

"I'm sorry the mayor's on your case," she said. "But Mr. Volos is involved in this investigation whether any of us like it. How are we supposed to do our job properly if all the mayor's cronies are off-limits?"

"Gee, Gardner, I don't know. Maybe with police work? Finding hard evidence, instead of guesswork? Or does the MEA only know how to harass city leaders and get informants killed?"

His comment lay on the ground between them like a tossed gauntlet. Gardner's jaw tightened.

"I can promise you that my team"—she shot a weighted look at Morales and Shadi—"will be more careful moving forward."

Message heard loud and clear if the stiff postures of my teammates were any indication.

"However, I'm not here to play politics," she continued. "I'm here to catch the criminal whose handiwork has already gotten two people killed and potentially more wounded. The evidence you respect so much is telling me Volos is involved somehow, so he will continue to be monitored."

"Good luck with that."

She narrowed her eyes. "What do you mean?"

"I'm meeting with the mayor later to discuss options." He crossed his arms. "He's considering pulling the plug on this case altogether."

"Shit," I breathed and shared a worried look with Morales.

Gardner grew very still. "You're going to tell him not to, right? Because there will be more violence, guaranteed. A spike in violent crimes won't look too good to the voters right before the election."

"Not so sure it's the wrong move. We only have one confirmed crime connected to this potion."

"I found five in the files that could be tied as well," I said quietly.

"Then we'll raid the Arteries and any known potion houses. The BPD can handle that without the MEA's assistance."

"Unacceptable," Gardner said. "We simply need more time. Regardless of who is responsible for this potion, we're looking at federal charges and I won't let cronyism prevent us from doing our job."

"If you can show me one piece of solid evidence tying Volos to Gray Wolf, I'll go to bat for you with Mayor Owens."

Gardner and Morales shared a weighted look. Finally, my partner shook his head a fraction to either side.

"That's what I thought," Eldritch said.

"Imagine what it will do for the mayor's reelection if we can bring down one of the biggest coven leaders in the city. Imagine how grateful he'll be to you for making it possible."

He sucked on his teeth for a moment. Finally, he said, "I'll see what I can do to buy you some time, but you need to watch your ass around Volos."

Morales and I shared relieved glances. Gardner smiled at the captain. "You made the right choice."

"We'll see," he said. He turned to me and raised his brows. "Prospero? A word?"

I glanced at Gardner. She tipped her chin down, but shot Eldritch a warning look. He looked offended that I'd even silently asked my new boss for the go-ahead. Jesus, this was getting more complicated every second.

He stormed back down the stairs without waiting to see if I'd follow. I dragged myself after him. As I descended the stairs, I heard Gardner talking rapidly to the team. No doubt they were hatching some sort of Hail Mary play.

Eldritch was waiting for me on the sidewalk. The instant the door shut behind me, he started in. "I didn't get you a place on this team so you could betray your entire unit, Prospero."

I jerked my chin back as if he'd struck me. "First of all, sir," I said with sarcastic emphasis, "you couldn't get me out of your hair fast enough, so enough with the bullshit about doing me a favor." He shrugged—as close to a "You're right" as I was getting. "Furthermore, I don't control Gardner. Neither does the mayor, for that matter. And as for Volos, you know damned well he's probably playing the mayor to knock us off his scent."

"Do you really think he's behind this?"

I threw up my hands. "I don't know. I hope not, but I do know that not investigating him because he threw some money at the mayor is a huge mistake."

He crossed his arms and pierced me with the old laser eye. "I could revoke the exception I made to allow a suspended officer to consult on a federal investigation."

"No offense, sir, but that's not gonna happen. Gardner needs my insider knowledge of the Cauldron to make this case. Especially since my childhood friend John Volos looks to be the lead suspect." This far I'd managed to avoid letting Eldritch know about the real nature of my relationship with Volos, but I wouldn't be so lucky with Gardner, whom I'd have to tell before the day was out. I was gambling that she'd see the connection as an advantage.

"Don't get cocky, girl. Gardner will only like you as long as you keep producing results. What happens when your luck runs out? Or if the MEA pulls this team out of the Cauldron? Where are you going to go then if you burn all your bridges with the BPD?"

I squinted up at him. "Haven't you ever imagined what it would be like to shut all this down?" I motioned to the trash-strewn street, the broken-down buildings, and the disenfranchised junkies who scrambled through this part of the city like rats in a dead-end maze. "What if we could clean up these streets and run the wizards out of town?"

Eldritch laughed bitterly. "I was arresting potion cookers before you were born, Prospero. Have I imagined a world free of dirty magic? Shit, yeah. But then I grew up and realized that the minute you get rid of one asshole, another one takes its place. Usually worse than the last one. Face it: In order to get rid of dirty magic, you'd have to figure out how to rid all humans of their greed, vanity, and fear of pain." He took a deep breath, as if resigning himself to something. "The best we can do is try to help the victims and minimize the impact of the dirty potion trade on innocent people. That means making it as tough as possible for the corner guys to ply their wares and chasing down the bad guys after they victimize the innocent to feed their habits. It's good, honest work."

"So you think the MEA's wasting their time going after the covens?"

"I'm saying I'm terrified of what would take their place once they're gone. Better the assholes you know, right?"

I shook my head at the jaded bastard. "I'm sorry you think I'm choosing sides, but I'm just trying to do my job."

"Yeah, you keep telling yourself that, Prospero." His eye twinkled like he was in on some joke I didn't catch. Finally, with a sigh, he said, "I'll buy us some time with the mayor. But you tell Gardner that if you guys take Volos down, I want some camera time." His phone started chirping during the middle of his speech. He ignored it until he was done and then pulled it out to check the screen.

I tried not to feel disillusioned. I'd been around the politics of policing long enough to understand how important face time was to the brass. Still, his opportunistic approach left the taste of bile heavy on the back of my tongue. "Understood, sir," I forced out. "If that's all, I need to head back inside."

He nodded absently and read the screen on his phone. "Fuck me," he whispered as I turned to go.

I stopped.

"What's wrong?"

He looked up slowly. "There's been another murder. According to the responding officer, the body appears to have similar wounds to the Sprote woman from the other night."

I stilled. "Another Gray Wolf murder?"

"Maybe," he said. "But that's not the bad news."

I frowned at him. How could a mutilated body not be the bad news?

"She's going to gloat now." He looked like he'd been sucker punched.

"Sir?"

"Gardner," he said. "She's going to love this." I continued to look at him with a confused expression. Finally, he shook himself and looked me in the eye. "You're going to tell her."

I shook my head. "Tell her what?"

"The body was found at Volos Towers."

# Chapter Fourteen

Volos Towers loomed over the Steel River like a shiny hypodermic needle. Far below, the cul-de-sac and parking lot in front of the building were cordoned off with police tape. The rest of the scene was clogged with crime-scene investigators, cops, and the morbidly curious.

As Morales, Mez, and I made our way toward the crime scene, several looks were aimed our way—some merely curious, others downright hostile or smug. I guess word had spread through the station house that I was working with the MEA. I wasn't a mind reader, but at that moment I could have given Carnac a run for his money. They were all thinking: Who'd she fuck to get that gig?

I ignored them and focused on looking as if I belonged with the MEA guys instead of with the uniformed cops who were dealing with less glamorous duties, like crowd control and traffic direction. It didn't help that I was lugging one of Mez's tackle boxes like a wizard's apprentice. Meanwhile, he carried one of those old leather doctor's bags and a special padded backpack containing all sorts of glass tubes and bottles filled with herbs and elixirs. Morales, naturally, didn't offer to help carry any of the magical gear. Made sense considering he was already weighed down with that huge ego.

"Hey, Mez?" I said as we walked to distract myself from the stares.

"What's up?" He raised a single brow, which, now that I was really looking, also sported a new hoop piercing I hadn't seen the day before.

"Did you do something different with your hair today?" I asked with awkward diplomacy.

He chuckled. "I get bored a lot, so I like to change things up."

"This is nothing," Morales said. "Remember that day you tried the potion that turned your skin purple?"

"Hey, I liked that look." To me, he said, "Anyway, if you ever want a makeover, I brew up vanity potions on the side."

I shook my head. "Thanks but no thanks." I was fine with my quarterly twenty-dollar trim from the Snip 'N Curl on Juniper Sreet.

"You sure? It's clean magic, but I sell it to friends at a discount."

Luckily we'd reached the crime scene then, so I didn't have to get into the whole thing about how I avoided all magic, especially when it changed my skin color.

The CSI guys had erected a tent in front of the bank of glass doors. The covering protected the body from the drizzling rain and the helicopters full of cameramen hoping to get the money shot for the five o'clock news. Eldritch stood just outside the tent, speaking to Gardner. Behind them, an Adept CSI supervisor named Valerie Frederickson examined the body.

"Oh good," I said to Mez. "The CSI lead today is a friend of mine. That should help if you need access to any of the samples the BPD gathers."

"Cool." The wiz looked over to where I was pointing. "But I've never had problems charming samples out of cute lab wizes."

"You will if Eldritch cock-blocks us first," Morales said, nodding toward Gardner and Eldritch, who looked as if they were trying very hard not to shout in front of so many subordinates.

The three of us skirted them and headed toward the other side of the tent for a peek at the scene. Val was kneeling in front of the body as she discussed something with one of the other techs. But once they moved and I got a clear view of the body, I wished they'd come back and block it again.

Morales whistled low. "Brother done lost his head."

I cringed. What was left of the cranium was a red and gray pulpy mess mixed with skull shards. Except for the generous coating of blood, the rest seemed intact.

"Jesus," Mez said.

"Amen," I quipped. I suppose I should have felt more horrified by the scene. Normal people don't gaze upon mangled corpses without some sort of visceral reaction. Instead, I felt completely detached. The only emotional thread—and we're talking dental floss–thin here—was feeling relief that I wasn't responsible for identifying the deceased or notifying family.

"Hold on." Morales stiffened beside me. He raised a finger to point toward the body. "Look at the hands."

The body had one arm extended up over the place where his head used to be, but the other lay palm down about a foot away from the hip. I squinted toward it, wishing I could get closer to see better, but also glad I couldn't because being that close to a body wasn't my favorite thing on earth. But sure enough, if you ignored all the blood, it was possible to see darker colors on the skin. "Is that a tattoo?" I glanced up at Morales.

His face was grim and he kept his eyes on the body as he shook his head. "It's paint, Kate."

I looked again. This time, yeah, I could kind of see splotches of green and black across the knuckles. "I don't—" I began and stopped because my eyes had strayed toward the torso. The blood-soaked shirt had initially concealed the logo on the front.

"Fuck." I grabbed Morales's arm. "Fuck!"

He nodded back. "Triple fuck."

"Does someone want to fill me in?" Mez asked in a dry tone.

I swallowed the bile rising in my throat. Luckily, Morales informed the wizard, "That's the guy we interviewed yesterday outside the Green Faerie. Melvin."

"Marvin," I croaked. "His name was Marvin." And he was dead because of us. I knew that as sure as I knew my own name.

Mez didn't look convinced. "You positive?"

I nodded. "He was wearing that shirt yesterday."

The wizard squinted at the logo. "Spirit of Vitriol, huh? Their last album was bullshit. It's a cool shirt, though."

"Or was before someone got blood all over it," Morales quipped. I shot him a glare. How could he be so flippant about this? On my look, he sighed. "Relax, Prospero. This isn't our fault."

I snorted. "How can you believe that?"

He shrugged. "Because I choose to. Fact is, Marvin made his own choices. Members of street covens don't have long life expectancies."

"Right, because covens tend to take things like snitching to the cops pretty fucking seriously. I told you we should have taken him somewhere less conspicuous."

"Hey," Mez said, "how about we get busy doing our jobs so we can find out what really happened instead of bickering in front of everyone?"

I snapped my mouth shut and walked away. Someone needed to tell Val about Marvin's identity and doing so was the perfect excuse for getting away from Morales for a few minutes.

"Kate!" she exclaimed when she saw me. Val was a petite brunette who looked as if she belonged on the sidelines of a peewee soccer game cheering on a kid named Conner or Scotty. Instead, she spent most of her time up to her elbows in dead people's DNA, and to hear her tell it, she couldn't be happier about hanging out with stiffs instead of rug rats. She snapped off a bloodstained glove and shook my left hand. "Heard you got a big promotion."

"It's only temporary." Considering the politics and personnel issues, I didn't think getting too hopeful was healthy at that point. Better to expect the worst and then be pleasantly surprised if things did actually work out. "Anyway, I think I know this guy."

Her brows rose. "Do tell."

I spent the next five minutes telling her everything I knew about Marvin, which, admittedly, wasn't that much. "I know his prints are in the system because he's been collared for tagging a few times," I finished.

"He won't be doing much of that anymore," Val said in a dry tone. "Thanks, Kate. I'll get the print techs on this immediately."

"No problem." I paused. "Listen, do you mind if our lab wiz takes some samples?" I pointed toward Mez on the other side of the tent. He winked at Val as though I were setting up a blind date instead of securing permission for him to take body fluids from a crime scene.

Luckily, Val didn't see the wink since she was too busy looking in her gear bag. "As long as he doesn't contaminate my scene, he's welcome to."

"Awesome." I waved Mez over and made a quick introduction. With a final warning glare at him not to sexually harass my friend, I went to join the others.

By the time I headed back, Gardner and Shadi were with Morales.

This time, I kept my eyes averted from the body. Just yesterday, it was a walking, shit-talking, breathing human. Now he was just another casualty in a war that no one was winning. Morales was right: Marvin had made his own choices. But whether we liked it or not, some of the blood coating the pavement outside Volos Towers belonged on our hands. The only way to remove the stain was to arrest the responsible party, which, like it or not, was looking more and more like John Volos.

I joined the rest of the team in time to hear Gardner say, "Eldritch is allowing us to conduct interviews, but that's it. I didn't mention that we'd want to speak to Volos directly, but he's not here yet anyway."

"He's on his way?" I said, trying not to sound as worried as I felt.

Gardner nodded. "We're going to have to be smart and move fast to secure an interview. Eldritch has already warned me that the mayor's expecting hourly reports on this situation. If we step out of line, we'll risk this entire case. Got it?"

"Sir, I need to speak to you," I said. If John was on his way, now was definitely time to come clean with Gardner about my connection to him.

She raised a brow. "What is it?"

"Alone?"

Everyone froze. Gardner looked curious, but Morales and Shadi looked like bloodhounds who smelled fresh drama in the air.

Finally, Gardner jerked her head toward a spot a few feet away. "Make it quick, Prospero."

I turned my back toward the others, so I could ignore the

fact they were not even trying to hide their eavesdropping. "Listen, there's something you need to know—about me and Volos."

She raised a brow. "You mean the fact you two used to be an item?"

The unexpected question struck me dumb for a minute. At my shocked expression, she sighed. "Prospero, do you really think I would have brought you on the team without doing some digging?"

"But—but—" I shook myself. "But Eldritch doesn't know about that. He couldn't have told you."

She smiled like a sphinx. "I have other resources."

I wanted to ask her what other skeletons she'd unearthed from my closet, but I didn't have time for that. "Does this mean you're not worried about my objectivity?"

"Why? Are you planning on freaking out?"

I reared back. "Of course not. A lot has changed since those days. I'm perfectly capable of doing my job."

"I never doubted it," she said in a tone that hinted she was well aware of my own doubts. "But just in case, Morales and I will be handling the interview."

Relief flooded through me. It's not that I didn't trust myself. I just had no idea how John would react to my interrogating him. That wild card could fuck up our case about ten different ways. No, it was better I sat this one out. "Okay. You want me to help Shadi with witness interviews?"

"Yes, and then I want you to make a list of Marvin's known associates. See if maybe one of them can tell us what happened after you two left him yesterday."

"Got it."

She was about to say something else, but her gaze jerked to a point somewhere behind me. I turned to see what was up and froze. A long, black car had just turned into the lot. The license plate on the front read VOLO$.

A buzz of excitement rose over the area as everyone else noticed the arrival of Babylon's golden boy. My stomach suddenly felt as if it took a nosedive off Bessemer Bridge.

"Showtime," Gardner said. She flicked a glance at me. No doubt she saw something on my face that betrayed my nerves at seeing John again. "Never let them see you sweat, Prospero." With that, she walked away to join Eldritch at the curb. When the captain saw her approaching, his smile morphed into an acidic glare. If I hadn't been so distracted by the imminent arrival, I would have enjoyed watching those two jockey for position.

I went to Shadi. "Let's go," I said, failing to keep the urgency out of my voice. She shot me a sharp look and hung back even as I started moving toward the door.

"Hold up," she said. I turned to see her jogging toward me. "What's your problem?" She didn't sound confrontational as much as curious.

"Nothing. Just want to get these interviews done."

While I spoke, the commotion at the curb caught her eye. By that time, the limo had pulled up directly in front of the building. Eldritch stood next to the door like a nervous teen about to help his prom date out of the car. Gardner stood next to him, looking cool but also determined. Two large bodyguards exited the front of the car and kept back the reporters who swarmed the area like locusts.

The redhead I'd seen with Volos a couple of days earlier stepped out first. She said something to Eldritch and pulled him a few steps away for a confab. He cast a worried glance back at Gardner, who was suddenly smiling like the cat about to eat the canary.

Volos unfolded from the backseat with the grace of a jungle cat: long, muscular lines and the barely leashed energy of a corporate predator. Gardner flashed her credentials immediately. If he was surprised to be approached by an MEA agent he didn't show it. His smile was polite. Not the expression of a man who worried he might be the center of a federal Arcane investigation.

Everything about him was sharp: his suit, his posture, his gaze. He'd aged over the last decade—we both had—but damned if he didn't look more handsome at thirty than he had at twenty. More dangerous, too.

Eldritch sidestepped the redhead and moved toward Volos and Gardner as the pair walked toward the building. In his eagerness to join the conversation, he looked like a puppy nipping at their heels. The captain's admiration wasn't a surprise. With him angling for chief, it could only help to have a man like Volos on his side.

Also, I couldn't exactly blame Eldritch for acting like an idiot, since I wasn't exactly immune to the Volos thrall, either. I could only stand frozen, waiting for the moment when he spotted me.

Time slowed. He frowned at Eldritch the way one might at an annoying housefly. The redhead kept pace behind the trio while she talked on a cell phone. Volos turned toward her to say something, but on the way his gaze intersected with mine briefly before continuing. Slammed to a halt. Reversed.

*Boom.*

I must have gasped because suddenly my lungs felt too full. Sweat broke out over my chest, where my heart thumped like jungle drums.

One second, he was as frozen as I had been, but then, inevitably, he left the others behind and came at me with the determination of a heat-seeking missile. His expression belonged in a high-stakes room in Vegas. I'd seen that poker face more times than I could count. I'd also seen the slight tightening of his jaw that indicated he wasn't pleased by my presence.

"Kate."

Jesus, his voice cut to the bone. Energy sizzled along my spine and put every protective instinct in my body on code red.

"Mr. Volos." My voice was steady, professional despite the sweat on my palms and the slight tremor in my midsection.

It felt as if everyone in the vicinity stopped to watch this momentous meeting, but no one had. Not really. Just Eldritch, who didn't make an effort to hide his naked curiosity, and Gardner, who had on her cop face. Morales came to join Shadi off to my left and the pair openly stared at us.

"Mr. Volos, about that interview," Gardner said into the tense silence.

Those hard eyes left me alone to stare down my new boss. "I thought BPD was investigating."

"We are, sir." Eldritch stepped in. "The MEA is assisting because they believe the murder might be linked to an Arcane investigation they're working."

Volos looked back at me. "You've been spending a lot of time on this side of town lately. Thought you patrolled the east side."

I stilled as his meaning sunk in. He'd seen me here the other day and he wanted me to know it. He also apparently had kept tabs on my position in the department. Dread settled over me like a cold mist. When a man like Volos kept tabs on you, it usually meant he wanted to use you—or he wanted you dead. I forced a casual shrug. "Things change."

"Some things change." His eyes performed a leisurely stroll

over my body. I suddenly felt dowdy in the jeans and button-down I'd chosen that day. Especially since his suit probably cost more than my rent. "But most things stay the same."

"Does that include you?" I shot back. "Are you the same, Mr. Volos?"

"Touché." His expression lost its humor. "Who punched you?" He started to reach up, as if to touch my black eye, but then caught himself before he could invade my space. But my eye caught the Ouroboros tattoo he bore on his left wrist—the one that matched my own and that of every other Adept in the Votary Coven, for that matter—peeking out from under the French cuff of his dress shirt.

I didn't flinch. Just smiled politely as if the shiner was nothing of consequence. "All in a day's work, Mr. Volos."

His lips twitched like he knew I was doing it on purpose to keep distance. He didn't say anything else. Just watched me, perhaps thinking if he stared long enough he could see through my skin and into the shadowy parts where all my secrets were hidden.

"If you can spare the time," Gardner cut in, "Agent Morales and I would like to speak to you about our case."

Volos's smile didn't reach his eyes. "I thought we were talking, Special Agent."

Gardner, God love her, simply stared Volos down. He flicked a glance at the redhead. She stepped forward. "I'm afraid Mr. Volos has a tight schedule this afternoon."

Gardner tilted her head and smiled tightly. "Perhaps he'll be able to squeeze us in once we secure a search warrant."

The assistant, or whatever she was, leaned in and whispered something to Volos. His jaw hardened but he let out a resigned sigh. "As it happens, I have a few minutes now."

The one-eighty happened so fast I had to blink.

"Excellent—" Gardner began.

"On one condition," he cut in.

"You can name it," Gardner shot back.

"I'd like Detective Prospero present."

Almost automatically I corrected him. "Officer Prospero." And then the rest of his request sank in. "Wait, what?"

Gardner ignored my shocked reaction. "That wouldn't be appropriate, all things considered."

"She has insight into my background and personality that could only benefit you, correct?"

Gardner hesitated and shot Eldritch a look. The captain, clearly enjoying himself, merely smiled back serenely instead of supporting her. "That explains why we'd want her in there," she continued, "but not why you do, Mr. Volos."

Everyone's eyes ping-ponged as the pair played verbal chess. For the rest of them it was merely a spectator sport, but I felt like a rope tugged between two bulldogs. Part of me wanted to attend the meeting, but now that John had specifically requested my presence I was wary as hell.

"My motivations are my own business, Special Agent." He said it too casually to be casual. "Suffice it to say, as requests go it's a minor thing, is it not? Considering none of us here believes that I am not a suspect in this case you're investigating and I am well within my rights to refuse an interview until such time as you are ready to charge me with an actual crime."

Gardner's jaw clenched. "Your office then?"

Volos's clipped nod was the only response.

"Mr. Volos—" Eldritch stammered.

"You're here to solve a murder, Captain. I suggest you get back to work." With that Volos turned his back on the veteran cop and walked away. Eldritch looked at a loss for a moment and then shot me a look that promised retribution, like he held me personally responsible for the rebuff.

Gardner marched off with Volos, as if she expected him to renege if she didn't stay next to him every step to his office.

"Well?" Morales said. I spun to look at him, but I felt totally disconnected from myself. As if I'd just watched some other woman get shanghaied into a situation she wanted no part of. I opened my mouth but no words came out.

"When this is all done, we're going to go grab a beer so you can explain to me why our Big Bad Wolf just looked at you like you were Little Red Riding Hood."

I grimaced. "Make it a couple of shots of tequila and you've got yourself a deal."

He didn't crack a smile. "You're turning out to be a real pain in the ass, Cupcake."

# Chapter Fifteen

As it turned out, Volos, Gardner, and the redhead hadn't bothered to wait for us. We grabbed the next elevator and popped out on the top floor of the tower. The outer offices of Volos Real Estate Development were designed with lots of bamboo and black-lacquered wood with touches of bloodred. A large wooden panel behind the front desk depicted a scene of two samurai warriors hacking away at each other with swords. The Asian-inspired motif wasn't surprising since John had always had a fondness for the Eastern alchemical traditions.

The redhead stood in the center of the room to greet us. Her hair was again pulled back into a professional chignon. That day she wore a black skirt and an expensive-looking pink silk blouse, which managed to look both feminine and dominatrix-y at the same time. Especially when paired with the skyscraper black stilettos.

"I'm sorry I didn't have the opportunity to introduce myself earlier." She came forward with her perfectly manicured hand extended. "I'm Jade Turner."

Morales shook her hand first. "Special Agent Drew Morales," he said with enough baritone to make my eyes want to roll. "And this is my colleague, Officer Kate Prospero."

She flicked her cat eyes toward me with a fake smile. "A pleasure."

I tipped my chin in greeting. "You're Mr. Volos's secretary?"

Her smile froze. "Attorney."

Morales cleared his throat to remind me to shut up.

"Sorry," I mumbled, not really meaning it.

"If you'll follow me, Mr. Volos and Special Agent Gardner are waiting," she said in a permafrost tone. She sashayed away. My eyes went immediately to her legs, which were a mile long and featured those back seams that made pulp novel detectives wax poetic. I sneered inwardly and glanced at Morales. His eyes were on her legs, too, but his expression wasn't judgmental so much as downright predatory.

I shot him a disgusted look.

He just waggled his brows and smirked. Then he nudged me to follow the Frost Queen into the office.

Volos was ensconced behind a large bamboo desk. Behind him a massive window offered a panoramic view of the river and the skyline of downtown Babylon in the distance. I couldn't help but feel I'd just walked into the nest of a bird of prey.

"We don't have much time." He waved us into the chairs across the desk from him. "I have a meeting in thirty minutes."

Gardner and Morales took the chairs since they were leading the interview. I settled for leaning against a black-lacquered credenza set on the wall behind them. Volos noticed the seating arrangements with a clenched jaw. What the hell was he playing at?

After she sat, Gardner looked at the attorney. "May I have some water?"

Jade froze. Clearly being thought of as Volos's assistant was a sore spot.

"Please," Gardner added with a fuck-you smile.

The attorney glanced at Volos, clearly expecting him to countermand the request. Instead, he nodded. "I'll take one, too."

As she walked out, Jade's movements were stiff and her hands clasped at her side. Someone was silently cursing everyone in the room.

When I turned from watching her go, I caught Gardner and Morales exchanging a quick victorious glance. Their gamble to get rid of the attorney paid off, but I had to wonder about Volos's easy compliance. Either he wasn't concerned about being questioned without an attorney present or he merely wanted us to think he was.

"So?" Volos prompted.

Gardner cleared her throat and sat forward. "Three nights ago, a suspect murdered a woman in an alley off Canal. He was drinking her blood when Officer Prospero arrived on the scene."

Volos shot me a speculative glance. "And you think he's the one who killed the gentleman downstairs?"

Gardner shook her head. "No."

When he dragged his gaze from me back to Gardner, I felt visceral relief. "How can you be certain it isn't the same perpetrator?" he asked her.

Morales glanced back at me. "Prospero was forced to shoot the suspect when he attacked her."

Volos stared at me. I met his searching gaze without flinching. He opened his mouth to say something but thought better of it. He cleared his throat and looked back at Morales. "So what's the connection to this murder?"

"The man Prospero killed was freaking on a new potion,"

Morales said. "Yesterday, we questioned the dead man downstairs about it."

"And what did he say?"

I stiffened. Were they going to show all our cards?

Morales rested back in his chair like a man without a care in the world, but then he wasn't the one about to be accused of federal Arcane and homicide charges. "He said it was your potion."

Volos didn't flinch. "So you figure I had him killed."

"That's for the BPD's homicide detectives to determine," Gardner said. "It's quite a coincidence, though, don't you think?"

"Perhaps. Luckily for me the courts haven't suddenly started accepting coincidences as proof of guilt," he said. "But as it happens, my attorney, pilot, and business associates can attest I was at a meeting in Toronto last night. I only found out about the murder when I got off the plane this morning and I headed right over."

Gardner didn't argue that it would have been easy enough for him to communicate with his people here to make the kill order. "Did you know the deceased?" she asked instead.

"I was told he hadn't been identified yet."

"His name was Marvin Brown," Morales offered. "On the streets he was known as Picasso."

Volos frowned. "I knew him back when Abe was still in power. He was young then. As I recall he was always doodling on stuff."

"He was arrested a couple of times for vandalism. Graffiti," Morales supplied. "It's believed that the Votary Coven used him as a Herald."

Volos raised his hands. "I wouldn't know anything about that. It's a shame, though. He was pretty young, yes?"

"Twenty," I said, looking at him. "Older than a lot of coven kids get to be these days."

"Sadly true," he said, shaking his head. "What's the potion you're investigating?"

"It's a strange formula," Morales began. "Blood magic—"

"You're on the wrong side of town, then," Volos interrupted. "You need to be having this conversation with the albino."

Technically Ramses Bane was not an albino, but since he spent all of his time underground, he was somewhat melanin-challenged. "You didn't let me finish," Morales said. "There are some minor characteristics of blood magic, but the main components are definitely alchemical. That's your specialty, yes?"

"One of them," Volos said, smooth as an elegantly extended middle finger.

Morales sighed heavily at the other man's obvious obtuseness. "Are you familiar with the Gray Wolf?"

He leaned back in his chair and steepled his fingers. "It's another name for the purifier, the king."

"Huh?" Morales said.

"Antimony," I explained. "The king is an alchemical symbol for gold. Antimony dissolves all metals except gold so it is often added to molten gold to destroy any impurities."

Volos nodded to confirm what I said. "It's used in the *calcinatio* phase of classical alchemy—baptism by fire."

"Yes, that's fine," Gardner said, losing her patience. "What do you know about a potion by the name of Gray Wolf?"

Volos smiled. He was enjoying this. "More than I want to know, but less than you want to hear."

"Humor us."

"It's exceedingly dangerous. Both to the user and anyone who crosses their path." He held up his hands. "But you already know that. My guess is whoever is behind it has a motive beyond profit. Otherwise, why put so much of their customer base in danger?" He leaned forward. "Obviously, Kate has told you that my specialty is alchemy and that's true. But before you decide to pursue me as a suspect I'd ask you to consider what possible motive I'd have. For the last several years I've worked to improve the Cauldron and haven't had so much as a speeding ticket. You ask me, the wizard behind this potion left that body here as a message."

The door opened and Jade returned with a tray bearing a few glasses and a bottle of some fancy sparkling water. "What did I miss?" Her tone was cheerful, but her posture was stiff. She set the tray down and handed glasses to Morales and Gardner. I shook my head when she offered me one and mulled over Volos's words. He sounded genuinely pissed off. I couldn't tell if it was because he was guilty and didn't want to get caught, or if it was because he was innocent and angry about being dragged into the case.

Plus, I'd been wondering myself about the motives someone might have for putting Gray Wolf on the streets. No wizard looking for a quick buck would mess with such a dangerous potion. Not only was the market extremely small given the cost, but they also risked killing off potential customers. We had to be missing something. Question was, did Volos know what that something was?

"Mr. Volos was just about to tell us what kind of message the body downstairs is intended to convey," Gardner said.

The executive across the desk took a sip of his water before answering. "I'm afraid I don't have solid proof."

"Did you tell them about the letters?" Jade asked.

"What letters?" Gardner asked.

"After plans to build a community center near the Arteries were announced, my client began receiving threats in the mail," Jade said.

"Why didn't you take them to the police?" Morales asked Volos.

"I knew the plan wouldn't be popular among all the residents of the Cauldron," Volos admitted, "so I wrote them off. Initially."

Jade stepped in. "In the last couple of weeks, they've become more frequent and the tone has shifted from vague threats to specific warnings."

Gardner leaned forward. "May we?"

Volos nodded at Jade, who handed a stack of photocopies to Gardner. She scanned them for a moment. After a couple of pages her posture went stiff and she muttered a curse. Without looking up, she passed the ones she read to Morales. I came forward and took the first one, which he waved at me over his shoulder.

I scanned them quickly. The first was a formal, typed letter stating the author was unhappy about the land development plan, but not overtly threatening. However, on the second page—dated the day before my run-in with Harkins—only one sentence had been written: "The Cauldron will run red with blood."

"Jesus," I whispered. When I looked up, Volos was watching me.

"Even after this one, you still didn't feel it was worth going to the cops?" Morales demanded.

Volos leaned forward with his elbows on the desk. "I didn't take them seriously until a body showed up on my property."

"May we have photocopies of these?" Gardner asked Jade.

"We already gave a copy to Captain Eldritch." Her tone bordered on insult. "Perhaps he'll share."

Bitch.

"What about surveillance from last night?" Morales asked.

"Also with Eldritch," Jade said before Volos could talk. "Perhaps instead of taking up my client's time issuing vague accusations, you should have a conversation with your colleagues."

Morales nodded, sucking air in through his nostrils. "Who do you think sent these?"

"You asked for theories, Special Agent," Volos said. "All you have to ask yourself is this: Who in the Cauldron would feel most threatened by the location of the community center?"

Gardner and Morales weren't from the Cauldron, but I knew whom he meant immediately. "Ramses Bane." The minute I said his name, my brain spun off in about ten directions. The most compelling of which was Bane's little stunt at the precinct the other day.

Gardner, however, was playing catch-up. "Isn't he the head of the Sanguinarian Coven?"

Volos nodded. "Bane considers the Arteries his kingdom. Not hard to imagine he would see my plans as a direct threat to his turf."

"But you knew he'd see it that way when you proposed the project," I countered. "Why risk it?"

Volos smiled. "The lot in question has been empty for years and I managed to buy it at a steal because the owner was tired of the covens' using it to peddle their wares. Now it will be a safe place for kids to go after school so they'll stay off the streets. The benefits outweighed the risks, in my opinion."

"I doubt Marvin Brown would agree with you," I shot back.

His jaw tightened. "I will not be bullied into backing down by that anemic tunnel rat."

"You're conveniently forgetting that Gray Wolf is an alchemical potion. Bane's into blood magic. He doesn't have the chops to pull off that kind of alchemy."

"I'm not forgetting anything, Kate." The words conveyed a

world of subtext I couldn't begin to unravel. "It's not my job to prove Bane is responsible. It's yours."

"No, Mr. Volos," Gardner said. "Our job is to find the truth." She rose. "Thank you for your time. We'll be in touch if we have more questions."

For the first time Volos looked taken off guard, as if he couldn't fathom why Gardner wasn't taking his word for it. "The ground-breaking is in four days. I suggest you move fast before Bane does something more drastic, like unleash an entire pack of bloodthirsty beasts on the innocent citizens of this city."

Morales held up his hands. "If you believe that's possible, why not postpone the ceremony?"

Volos shot my partner a pitying look. "I assure you that's not a possibility."

"Why not?"

"Too much time and money have been invested to delay. If we haven't broken ground by winter, we'll have to wait until next year and that is not an option. The mayor wants the project well under way before the election." He smiled coldly. "Besides, postponing would be surrender and I assure you that is not my style."

"And if we don't catch him before you break ground?" Gardner asked.

"I'll convince the mayor to send the BPD in to clean out the tunnels and charge everyone they find with trespassing. That will give us the window we need to move forward."

"But if you do that," I said, unable to help myself, "and Bane is guilty, we will lose any shot of nailing him on federal charges. Or he'll retaliate by flooding the streets with the potion and even more lives will be lost."

He leaned back and crossed his arms, smiling like the cat that devoured the canary. "Then I suppose you better get to work."

# Chapter Sixteen

An hour later, Morales and I were back in his wheels headed to the morgue. Mez was still tied up going over the physical samples from the scene with Val, so we got the job of hitting up the ME for access to samples from the body.

I wouldn't say the ride over was awkward so much as tense and downright glacial. Morales made no effort at small talk, and I obliged his obvious desire for silence by ignoring him.

When we'd pulled up to the morgue, he finally turned to me. "I'll do the talking in here."

I considered arguing, but my instincts told me to keep quiet. I was pretty sure he was pissed about my not telling him about my past with Volos. After the meeting, he'd pulled Gardner aside for a heated discussion. I couldn't make out their words, but the way he kept shooting me looks while he ranted, it didn't take a cop to figure out the evidence pointed to his wanting me off the case. I supposed I couldn't blame him for worrying. The meeting had left me feeling worried, too. Obviously Volos had some sort of reason for wanting me in that room, and I was pretty sure it wasn't anything that would turn out well for me—or the case.

But apparently Gardner disagreed because she shut him down and then told him to take me with him to the morgue.

"Fine," I said, finally, forcing an amiable smile. It wouldn't hurt to try to get on his—well, not his good side, exactly. His less shitty side, maybe.

The first sign of trouble was when Morales strutted into the morgue as if it were an Old West saloon. "I'm looking for Thomas Franklin."

If he'd had asked me, I might have warned him to take a cautious approach with the ME. But he didn't ask, so I just hung back while he swung his dick around the man's icebox.

The tall, African American man in question had been leaning over a body when Morales entered. Franklin slowly levered his tall body upright, pulled down his mask, and said, "Who the fuck are you?"

Morales stilled like the guy had spit at his feet. I covered my mouth with my hand. This was going to be fun.

"I'm Special Agent Drew Morales, MEA—"

"In case you're blind as well as rude, I'm in the middle of an autopsy. Get out!"

"We called ahead." Morales's tone was cool, unruffled. "We're here to see the body of—"

Franklin made a rude noise with his lips. "This ain't the motherfuckin' Red Lobster, son. You can't make a reservation. First come"—he pointed a goo-covered, gloved hand down at the body—"first served. Bye now."

I watched Morales closely, just waiting for him to lose it and threaten to shove that scalpel down Franklin's piehole. Instead, the big guy relaxed his shoulders and lowered his tone. "The last thing we want is to inconvenience you. If you could simply point us to the proper drawer."

My eyes pinged back and forth between the two men.

"You can't view a body unattended." Franklin sighed the sigh of the martyred. "You Feds are all alike. We got a backlog of bodies and you need me to take my assistant away from her work to babysit your bossy ass?"

Morales stared down the taller man. "You got a problem, you can take it up with my field supervisor, but we're going in there." He moved toward the doors.

Franklin started after him, "Hey!" But then he stopped because he finally noticed me lingering by the entrance. I waggled my fingers at him.

"Kate Prospero! I almost didn't recognize you with that black eye."

Morales stopped and turned slowly. His accusing glare burned my skin but I didn't look at him. Instead, I smiled real wide at Franklin, ignoring the comment about my eye. "How's it going, Franky baby?"

"Ah, you know." He shrugged. "Motherfuckers keep dying so at least I got some job security."

I laughed. "I hear ya."

"Wait, what you doing with this one, Kate? You working a case? And what's with the shiner? Do I need to kick someone's ass?"

"We're tracking the source of that new blood potion." I placed a hand to the eye I'd forgotten was still bruised. "This was courtesy of one of the stiffs you've got in there." I jerked a thumb toward the door. "Speaking of," I said, "could you do us a solid and let us take a gander at Marvin Brown's body? He just came in but we won't disturb him too much."

Franklin pursed his lips and glanced at Morales, like he

was weighing the other man's character. Morales shifted on his feet.

Just when I was convinced Franklin was going to start yelling again, he laughed instead. "Well, shiiit." He dragged out the vowel like a match against a striker. "Why didn't you just say so?" He pointed a dripping hand toward a set of swinging doors. "Body's through there. Knock on Janet's door on your way. She'll help you."

The tension escaped the room. "That would be great, thanks." Morales flashed a tight smile, like he didn't really trust Franklin's expected one-eighty to last long enough to get results.

He turned and loomed toward the doors like a thunderhead. Franklin turned to me and winked. "Have fun with that."

"You're a bad man, Franky."

He shrugged. "I spend my days collecting the human waste of this fucking city, Prospero. I gotta get my laughs where I can." We both paused as the truth of those words sank in. Then, as if breaking a spell, he clapped his gloved hands together. "All right, get on with ya. I gotta remove a bullet from this poor asshole's trachea."

I glanced at the body. The vic was a white male, probably early forties. His skin was blue and he'd been cut from sternum to pelvis. Franklin had closed the guy's eyes, but the gaping mouth caught my attention. Fuck me if it didn't look like he was silently screaming.

◆ ◆ ◆

As if she'd been invoked magically, Janet was already waiting for us in the room. She had her trusty clipboard at the ready and quickly found the locker containing the mortal remains of one Marvin Brown. She opened the door, pulled out the drawer, and turned on her heel.

"Humph." She pushed her spectacles back up her overly large nose. No "Let me know if you need anything else" or even a good-bye. She just walked back into her office. A large window over her desk ensured she could see everything we did. However, the instant she sat down she began tackling the mountain of file folders covering the desk's surface.

"Charming," Morales said. He paused a beat and then turned toward me. "Thanks for making me look like an asshole out there."

I bit my lip. "You didn't need my help for that." Okay, so maybe I wasn't so hot at getting on people's not-shitty sides.

His eyes narrowed for a moment, but then he sighed. "Just grab a slide, will ya?" He pointed to the black duffel he'd carried in from the car.

"What's the hurry, Morales?" I said. "Feeling woozy?" I said this despite the fact that I always had nightmares about rotting slabs of pork for days after I visited the morgue.

"Not at all," he said. "I just have real police work to do. We're not going to find jack shit on this body linking this murder to Volos."

The problem was, I totally agreed with him. Even if he'd killed the guy himself, Volos was too smart to leave evidence. "Then why are we here?"

"Gardner." He might as well have said God's name.

While I rummaged for the slides in the black bag, he started examining Brown. "What's your story with Volos?"

I paused and looked up. "The kind that's none of your business."

He glanced at me. "Look, Cupcake, I get that a lady likes to have her secrets, but as long as we're working together on a case involving your ex, that history has a direct impact on my well-being. So spill it."

"There's not much to tell." I handed him the package of lab slides I found in the bag. As I did, I noticed those scars again. Curiosity itched the back of my brain, but he would never share his secrets until I spilled mine.

He accepted the slides with his right hand. "We both know that's bullshit. I saw you two today. There's some shit between you that time hasn't erased."

I sighed. "We didn't end...easy."

He snorted. "What relationship does? Otherwise why end it?"

"True enough." I was stalling. "The short of it is, I wanted out of the coven. I finally convinced Uncle Abe to let me go—"

"Why did you want out?"

Now that topic was definitely off-limits. "Let's just say I lost my taste for magic and leave it at that." I could tell he wanted to press me, but he nodded. "Anyway, Abe was ready to let me go, but John—not so much."

"You dumped him?"

I nodded. "And I said some things to make sure it stuck."

He whistled low. "Guy like that doesn't seem like he'd take rejection well."

My stomach clenched at the memory of that night. I pushed it ruthlessly aside. "Anyway," I said, "today was the first time we'd been in a room together in a decade."

Morales nodded but I could tell by his expression he was mulling it over. "Do you think he's guilty?" He nodded toward the body bag to indicate Marvin's murder.

I blew a long breath out through my nose. "Do I think he's capable of murder? Yeah. Do I think he's responsible for this particular one?" I paused. "Not really. I mean, someone on Gray Wolf probably killed Marvin. And maybe Volos put that potion on the street. But did he send a hexhead hopped-up on his new junk after Marvin as retaliation for talking to us?" I shook my head. "Seems like a stretch." Low-level guys like Marvin never knew enough about what happened at the top to be a threat.

"Hmm," Morales said.

Clearly he wasn't ready to tell me his own theories, which was fine. I was tired of speculation. We needed to find some hard evidence soon or our case was going to get torpedoed by the mayor and Volos's lawyer before we could say "warrant."

"What about this Bane angle he threw out today?"

I shook my head. "Also a stretch. Bane's a lunatic, no doubt, but he's a blood magic wizard. To pull off this kind of alchemy?" I sighed. "It's not impossible, I guess, but he'd have to have help. And the only wizard I can think of who can pull off a spell like this is—"

"Volos."

I nodded. "Round and round it goes. There's got to be something we're missing. Hopefully Marvin will help us." I looked down at the body. On the way over, Val had sent a text confirming his identity from the print database. "Did he have any next of kin?" Morales had pulled Marvin's file from ACD at the crime scene.

He shook his head. "Never married, no kids. Mother died ten years ago."

A loud snap sounded. I looked up to see him pulling on a pair of rubber gloves. He leaned over the body and began to inspect it for Lord-knew-what. With nothing to do, I scanned the rows of drawers, wondering which one held Ferris Harkins's body.

"How'd you hook up with Harkins as a snitch?" I asked to distract myself.

"He'd served a couple years in Crowley," he said referring to the penitentiary for magic criminals on Philosopher's Island. "His roommate was a CI of mine from a case I ran a few years back. I remembered him talking about his buddy who lived in the infamous Cauldron. Tracked him down through the shelters."

I raised my brows. "What was he hooked on—before the Gray Wolf, I mean?"

Morales shrugged. "He worshipped at the altar of the Os for a time, but he claimed he'd been clean for a while."

As if Harkins hadn't been unsavory enough, I thought with a memory of him grabbing his crotch and shuddered inwardly. It was hard not to picture the werewolf he'd become humping away at someone like there was no tomorrow.

"And you believed him—about being clean, I mean?"

"He didn't show any signs of heavy use," Morales said. "When I found him he was washing dishes in the kitchen at the Catholic mission on Salado Street."

I didn't ask why Harkins had become a CI. If he'd been living at the mission, the income alone would have been enough of a motivator. Experienced CIs with excellent intel raked in decent paydays, but even a low-level guy could make a nice little nest egg—or potion bankroll. But now Harkins's body would be donated to the state's alchemy labs for experiments, and Marvin would probably end up in some remote potter's field. Crime and snitching might pay, but, as they also say, you can't take it with you.

"So what exactly are we looking for here?" I asked.

He looked up from scraping under the nails and carefully placing the results on the glass slides. I glanced to make sure Janet wasn't looking. If Frank saw Morales taking evidence off a body, we'd be toast. "I'm hoping Marvin struggled with our perp. Maybe some DNA under the fingernails."

"Good luck with that. The state lab will take months to run that sample."

Morales snapped the lid on the test tube. "Don't need the state's lab—we've got ourselves a Mesmer."

# Chapter Seventeen

That night, I went to Pen's to pick up Danny because he'd gone home with her after school, since Baba had her weekly smutty-book-club meeting that night. I had to make three passes before I found a spot halfway down the block from her building. I killed the engine and soaked in the silence, trying to collect myself before I headed in.

But soon the silence was pushed aside by a jumble of worries that stumbled noisily into my head. To escape them, I grabbed my purse and hauled my tired ass out of the car. Pen's apartment was on the first floor of a building that used to be a whorehouse. Back when the Mundane mob ruled Babylon—back before the magical criminals took over—they'd used this place to stash their ladybirds.

Pen said she liked living there because of its scandalous history, but I couldn't figure out how that was enough to make her overlook the tricky outlets, shitty plumbing, and lack of decent parking.

When I entered the building, the air was saturated with the

scent of hot grease and five-spice powder. My stomach grumbled and I realized I hadn't eaten since that morning's bagel.

When Pen opened the door, her smile wasn't as bright as usual. "Hey."

I glanced over her shoulder but couldn't see more than the TV flickering in the corner of her shoe-box living room. "What's up?" I asked with a frown.

She shook her head. "Tough day."

Even though I'd had one of those myself, I pushed aside my own worries. I leaned on Pen way too much to put my problems ahead of hers. "What happened?"

She waved me in. "That girl I told you about? With the diet potion?"

I nodded and set my purse down. Danny was slouched at her dining-room table doing homework with his headphones on. "Hey, Danny." When he didn't respond, I bent over and waved a hand to get his attention.

He glanced up from under his bangs and lifted his pencil in something approximating a wave but didn't speak.

Turning my attention back to Pen, I said, "What about her?"

She pulled me into the galley kitchen. "She OD'd," she whispered. She shot a worried glance to see if Danny heard, but the headphones prevented it.

"God, is she okay?"

Pen slowly shook her head. Her eyes were bright with unshed tears. I pulled her in for a hug because what else could I do?

Her shoulders shook and she held on as if I was the only thing keeping her upright. "I'd reported the case to child welfare," she sobbed, "but they're so backlogged they couldn't make it in time."

"Shh," I said and rocked her. "You did what you could."

Her head shook wetly against my collarbone. "No, I didn't.

I should have called her mother myself. I should have gone over there—"

I grabbed her by the shoulders and forced her to look at me. "Stop. Don't do that to yourself. You can't save everybody."

Her tear-stained face morphed into a fierce scowl. "I have to try, Kate. I have to."

I swallowed the emotion that gathered in my own throat because I understood. I understood all too well why she needed to help those kids. I wasn't the only one with a past that still haunted her.

"I know," I whispered. "And you did try."

She wiped her nose and eyes with a paper towel. "I filed a report at the BPD," she said, standing straighter. "They've already picked up the mother."

"Who did you talk to?"

"Detective named Duffy."

My eyebrows rose. I knew Pat Duffy's name only by reputation. "I don't know him personally," I said, "but he's an Adept. He managed to claw his way up to detective from patrol, which means he must be the real deal."

She licked her lips and nodded. "Good," she whispered. "That's good."

I hugged her one more time to reassure us both. "Anyway." She sniffed and tried to swipe the mascara from under her eyes. "How was your day?"

I bit my lip. After hearing the shit she was dealing with, I decided not to unload about my own problems. "Just another day at the office."

She leaned forward. "You do remember tomorrow's his birthday, right?"

I blew out a breath. Shit. I'd been so caught up in the case

I'd lost track of the date. "Of course," I lied. "I'm taking him to the Blue Plate tomorrow for lunch."

The Blue Plate was a diner that sat in the shadows of the Bessemer Bridge, on the Mundane side. Going there was a yearly tradition for Danny's birthday. Just as it had been for my mother and me, before Danny was born.

"You're taking him out of school?" she said, sounding dubious.

Crap, I hadn't thought of that. "Yeah, just for lunch, though."

She nodded absently. "How's the case?" The fact that she wasn't nailing me to the wall with questions about my lame story told me how upset she was about the kid who'd died.

"It's coming together."

Her brows lowered and her mouth formed into a thin line. It was a look I called "the Analyzer." "What aren't you telling me?" I guess that lie had been such a stinker it shook her out of her funk.

I sighed and decided to tell her the least dangerous development to get her off my trail. "I saw Volos today. Someone dumped a body at his building. I had to sit through the questioning."

"Oh shit." She blew out a breath. "How was that?"

"Awkward, frustrating, you know." I tried to shrug it off.

"Is he still a malignant narcissist with megalomaniacal tendencies?"

My lips quirked. "I love it when you speak shrink."

For a few years I'd nurtured a lot of guilt and pain over leaving John. However, one of the benefits of having Penelope Griffin as a best friend was the free therapy. With her help— as well as working the steps through Arcane Anonymous— I'd realized that my relationship with John had been far from healthy. Things were fine between us only as long as I let him call the shots. I liked the music he'd liked, preferred the same types of food. Hell, it had taken me years after I'd left him to realize I hated my coffee with cream, but I'd drunk it that way forever because it was how John liked his. Pen's theory was that I'd been attracted to him initially because he'd reminded me so much of the other overbearing male role model in my life: Uncle Abe. Not exactly the foundation for a faerie-tale romance.

She shrugged. "Seriously, though. Are you okay?"

"Yeah," I said honestly. "It wasn't easy, but I think I can keep things on a professional level."

"Of course you can, Kate. You're not the same kid who used to let him manipulate you. You're all grown up now, girl."

I forced a laugh. That was the problem. He was all grown up now, too. Seeing him again had affected me on a physical level—more than I'd ever admit out loud to Pen—or myself. Old self-sabotage habits die hard, I guessed. Luckily, Pen was right about one thing. I wasn't the same kid who let her emotions—or her libido—guide her actions anymore.

"Anyway, hopefully I won't have to see him again for a long time."

Pen yawned as she nodded. "That's good."

"All right," I said. "We'll get out of your hair."

I paused because I didn't want another lecture, but I needed to know. "Did he say anything to you?" I said, finally. "About the argument?"

"I can't talk about it if he did."

I frowned at her. "Don't pull that patient privilege crap with me, Pen."

"And don't take that cop voice with me." She crossed her arms. "If I came running to you every time he vented about some fool thing you did, he'd never trust me again."

I narrowed my eyes. "What do you mean, 'every time'?"

She rolled her eyes but softened it by putting a hand on my arm. "Look, he'll talk to you when he's ready. In the meantime, just play it cool."

I looked over at the back of my brother's head, which bobbed to some beat I couldn't hear. Meanwhile, seeing Volos had opened old scabs and a nagging voice in my head whispered dire predictions about having him slink back into my life. And now, my little brother, whom I'd struggled to save from the Cauldron, was trying his hardest to run right back to magic's strangling embrace.

"Right," I said, "I'll just play it cool."

# Chapter Eighteen

The Blue Plate Diner had been around for as long as I could
remember. Mom used to take me every year on my birthday. We'd sit at the counter and order shakes and burgers and
giggle as if we were a normal mother and daughter, instead of
a sex magic practitioner and her budding magical criminal of
a kid.

The diner sat on the corner of a street just across the Steel
River from the Cauldron. It was an institution at the crossroads
between the Mundane and Arcane worlds.

The place looked exactly the way I remembered it from my
childhood. It had been the one comfortingly Mundane thing
in my life as a kid, so it made an impression. The red vinyl
booths were cracked and slick from decades of greasy mist. The
gold-flecked composite countertops had yellowed and warped
from years of coffee spills. The old Wurlitzer jukebox boasted
all the greatest hits of the '40s and '50s, which added to the
time-warp vibe.

Once Mom was gone, I kept up the annual tradition for

Danny's birthdays. I told Danny I did it so he'd maintain a connection to Mom, but I suspected I got more out of it than he ever did. Like always, Danny got a vanilla shake while I ordered chocolate. We ordered that way so we could share and not have to choose between flavors. But he always ended up drinking both. He always got Tater Tots. I always got the famous crinkle fries. And when they arrived we dutifully divided them between the two plates. Like clockwork, we had been repeating this ritual for the last decade.

Danny dabbed a Tater Tot in the lake of ketchup on his plate. His eyes were downcast and he'd been unusually quiet. So it surprised me when he said, without looking up, "Did Mom do magic?"

Shock at the question forced a sharp intake of breath. The fries I'd shoved into my mouth a few seconds earlier slammed into my throat. The waitress was still making our shakes behind the counter, so I groped for the glass of water she'd brought in the meantime. I coughed until my throat was sore and the other patrons turned on their stools to gape. I held up a hand as the man in the next booth over started to rise, his face set in a determined line that hinted at a painful Heimlich in my future.

I waved my hands to show I was okay and gulped some more water.

Normally, we spent our meal people watching and laughing over stories I made up about Mom. As far as Danny knew, Mom had been a hardworking laundress who'd been hit by a stray bullet in a drive-by shooting. Maybe over the years he'd realized there was more to that story, but he'd never pressed me about it until now.

By the time I recovered and saw Danny's worried but determined expression through my teary eyes, I almost wished that guy had done the maneuver and broken a couple of ribs so I wouldn't have to have this conversation. Not right then. Not ever, if I had my way.

But Danny, even though he hadn't grown up in the family, was a Prospero through and through. I wouldn't walk away from that table until I delivered the answers he wanted. I just prayed he was prepared for the truth because it wasn't pretty.

"You know she was an Adept." I sighed and took one last sip of water before I proceeded. "Why are you asking?"

He rolled his eyes. "Not all Adepts learn how to cook magic, Kate."

He leaned forward and removed his wallet from his back pocket. From it he withdrew a small photograph and tossed it across the table. I cursed under my breath. The image was old, twenty years at least. In it, my mother wore the *memento mori* makeup of a member of the O Coven. White greasepaint, colorful shadows creating a sugar skull motif on the delicate planes of her face. Her hair was piled on top of her head and a tight red corset contained her...assets. I considered playing it off as if the picture was of someone else or maybe write it off as a Halloween costume. But when I flipped it over, the faded ink read, "Maggie Prospero, April 1985" in my mother's own hand.

Shit.

"Where'd you get this?" I hedged.

His eyes shifted left. "In the attic with the other stuff." The admission confirmed that he'd had this picture the other night when we fought but had hidden it from me. "Why is she wearing that weird makeup?"

I scratched my forehead, as if doing so would make my brain come up with the perfect response. When that didn't work, I just decided to wing it. "Look, I'm sorry I yelled at you about all that. It just caught me off guard." I blew out a breath. "You didn't, um, take this picture in to school, did you?"

The look I received in response made me feel like an idiot. Teenagers have a way of reducing you like that. "Of course not. I found a normal one, too."

Well, that was something, I thought. I couldn't imagine the crucifixion my brother would receive if he brought a picture of his mom in full-on sex ritual regalia into that snobby school. "That's good," I said, slowly. "So you've never seen this makeup anywhere before?"

"No." He drew the word out as if I'd asked the most obvious question ever. "But it's not exactly normal, so I figured..." he trailed off.

Moment-of-truth time: I could either come clean and shatter my brother's limited but positive impression of the woman he'd barely known or I could lie and risk his finding out later and never trusting me again.

Shit.

"The makeup is kind of a costume she wore for work," I hedged.

"I thought she worked at a laundry."

I chewed on my lip and cast a hopeful glance toward the waitress, praying she'd interrupt. But her back was to us. "She did sometimes—for extra cash," I said honestly. "But she was also kind of a... performer of sorts."

His eyes narrowed, but he didn't say anything. Guess the kid had picked up a few of my techniques. Damn it.

"Like a burlesque dancer, kind of." I couldn't look at him.

"Wait a minute—Mom was a stripper?" he shouted.

The volume in the restaurant dipped as patrons tasted drama on the air.

"No, Daniel, she wasn't a stripper." Not really. "There was more art to it—and magic."

My kid brother gave me a look with eyes that appeared way

too wise for his young face. "Hold up, are you talking about one of those sex magic shows?"

My brows slammed down. "How do you know about those?"

"Kate, I'm sixteen. What the heck do you think my friends and I talk about all the time?"

Jesus, I really wished I could change the milkshake order to a whiskey. I slammed another gulp of water. "I was hoping you discussed sports and homework."

He snorted. "Andy Lipshitz's older brother went to one of the shows. Said it was like some kind of boring religious ceremony but that the hand job at the end made it worth it."

Hearing the phrase "hand job" mentioned so casually by the kid made me want to gouge my ears out with my spoon.

But before I could deafen myself, he leaned in with an expression that was part shocked and part intrigued. "So Mom was a whore?"

"Shut your mouth." I jerked forward and lowered my voice into a harsh whisper. "Whatever else she was, that woman gave you life. She deserves more respect than that from you."

He looked away, his cheeks reddening with shame. "What do I care? I didn't know her." His eyes flicked to mine. "Not really."

My heart contracted in my chest. "How can you say that?" He was almost six when she died. Old enough to have some memories.

He was saved from having to answer when the waitress arrived to deliver our shakes. She set the vanilla in front of Danny and the chocolate next to me. I thanked her while Danny dug into his with gusto.

I watched him for a moment, wondering how we'd come to this juncture. Seemed like just yesterday he was that cute kid who wanted me to read him a story before bed. Now he was hiding things from me and rolling his eyes as if I were the most ridiculous person ever. Pen was right, I guessed. Danny was old enough to make his own decisions. But what kept me up at night was that he was still too young to understand the long-term consequences of those choices.

But one thing was becoming clear: Hiding secrets wasn't protecting Danny from the past.

"What do you want to know?" I said.

His head jerked up. He had a smear of shake on his chin. He wiped it with his hand instead of the napkin on the table in front of him. "Really?"

I blew out a long breath. "Yeah."

"How did Mom really die?"

My stomach contracted. Jesus, the kid really came out swinging, didn't he? "Why do you ask?"

"The death certificate," he admitted.

I opened my mouth in a silent "ah." Inside, I cursed myself seven ways to Sunday that I'd kept all that old stuff in the attic.

"The cause of death was listed as coronary failure caused by complications from Arcane substances." The accusation in his tone cut to the bone. "Why did you tell me she was shot?"

I hardened the part of me that was still tender after all these years. The wound in my chest that was put there by guilt. "Because it was easier for you to understand when you were younger."

He nodded, seeming to accept that. He'd been ten the first time he asked what happened to his mama. "So why didn't you tell me the truth once I was older?"

I fidgeted with a straw wrapper on the table. My eyes stayed on my shake, which was melting into soup. "Because it was easier for me."

He stayed quiet, like he expected one wrong word would

spook me. Eventually, I looked up, my chest so damned tight, and confessed my sins.

"It was a new potion. Uncle Abe was sure it would be the hot new commodity. It hadn't really been tested, but the plan went ahead to get it in rotation quickly." I lifted my water with a shaking hand and took a sip to wet my dry throat. "Back then, Abe had a deal with Aphrodite Johnson. Her girls were to act as couriers because the cops knew all his guys too well."

"Why wouldn't they recognize the girls?" Danny asked quietly.

"Because of the makeup. When they weren't working, they were clean-faced and less suspicious, I guess."

He nodded for me to continue. His hands slowly twisted a napkin into knots.

"Mom volunteered to do the drop," I said. "I didn't know until later that she'd been saving up for a bike for your birthday so she needed the money." My voice cracked. I cleared my throat, knowing there was no turning back now. "Best we could figure afterward was she decided to help herself to a sample."

I closed my eyes against the sting of hot tears. In my head, I was back in that cramped room ten years earlier. The one Uncle Abe brought me into to tell me the news. Funny, I don't remember exactly what he said, but I remembered he had a small cut on his neck, from shaving. A dot of blood had held a small scrap of paper to the wound. And when he smiled, his teeth bore the sepia stains of a man addicted to caffeine and cigarettes—"coffin nails," he'd called them.

I felt a touch on my hand, warm against my clammy skin. When I opened my eyes, Danny's face was all lit up with gratitude I didn't deserve. "Thanks for telling me the truth."

I laughed bitterly. "That's not all of it."

He frowned. "What do you mean?"

I licked my lips. "The potion."

"Yeah, I get it. It was bad. Uncle Abe shouldn't have put it out there."

"It wasn't Abe's fault." I shook my head. "He was told it was safe."

"By who?"

I looked my baby brother in the eye and pulled the trigger. "Me."

He blinked hard.

I forged ahead. "It was my potion."

All the blood leaked from Danny's face. "What do you mean?"

I reached for his hand, but he jerked away. "It was supposed to be my big break. It's a big deal for a potion-cooker to get their own recipe chosen for the streets. I-I wanted to prove myself to Uncle Abe, and I got cocky. Told him it was solid even though I hadn't tested it."

Danny stared at me as if I were a stranger.

"Anyway." I swallowed the hard lump of shame in my throat. "Abe tried to tell me it was just part of the game. Happened to everyone at some point." I shook my head, remembering the smile on his face as he told me how many of his potions had killed people when he was starting out. That conversation had been the first time Abe ever really scared me. He'd acted as though killing my own mother was just a cost of doing business. It wasn't too much of a stretch to imagine his writing my life off just as easily. "I knew then that I had to get us away from that life. So the day of Mom's funeral, I told Abe I was out."

"What did he do?"

"He tried to get me to stay, of course. We fought for hours, but eventually he gave me his blessing. I told him even if he made me stay I'd never cook again."

"I don't get it."

I smiled sadly. "In the end, after all those years of telling me I was his heir and building me up, it turns out all he wanted from me was my magic. Without that, I was useless to him."

Luckily Danny had been too young at the time to show any signs of potential with magic, otherwise Abe would have fought tooth and nail to make me leave the kid behind. But the fear that Abe would change his mind one day and try to woo Danny into being his new protégé kept me up at night. I would stop at nothing to ensure he never got his dirty magic or his malignant influence anywhere near my baby brother.

Danny said nothing, just watched me with those wary eyes.

"So that's it. The big dirty secret." I blew out a shaky breath. "Well? Aren't you going to say anything?"

Silence hung over us like a funeral shroud. I'd been afraid a lot of times in my life, but waiting for my little brother to hand down his verdict was definitely in the top three.

He took a sip of his shake, watching me over the straw. Finally, he licked the residue from his lips and leaned forward. "So let me get this straight. Our mom was a junkie who killed herself using illegal magic."

My mouth fell open. "No, Danny, it wasn't like that. She used that potion because she knew I'd made it."

"How do you know that? Were you there?"

I shook my head and admitted that no, I wasn't. "But Mom wasn't an addict, Danny."

"Whatever." He crossed his arms and slouched down. "I say it's pretty unfair that because of your mistakes I can't learn about any magic at all."

I paused and spoke slowly because he wasn't getting it. "It's illegal and dangerous. Of course I don't want you to mess with it."

He leaned back with arms crossed. "Not all magic is illegal."

"No, but it's all dangerous."

"The government doesn't think so."

I snorted. "Yeah, at one point they also said slavery was moral and smoking was safe."

He shrugged to dismiss my argument. "Look, I know you feel guilty. But you shouldn't. You didn't force Mom to try that potion."

I leaned back and shook my head at him. I'd been expecting recriminations for my sins, not exoneration I didn't deserve. "Must be nice."

"What?"

"For everything to be so simple. To have an answer for everything. I used to be that way, too. Right before Mom died."

"Look, you want to beat yourself up for that, it's your business. But it's not fair for me to suffer for your mistakes."

I got it then. He didn't give a shit about Mom's death. Asking about it had been a lead-up to lobbying for magic training. My stinging guilt morphed into something sharper. I threw my hands up. "What do you want from me?"

Several patrons turned to gape.

He leaned forward, his jaw set in that stubborn Prospero line. "I want you to teach me magic."

"Absolutely not."

His eyes sparked with challenge, the kind spurred by the thrill of rebellion. "Fine. I'll just find someone who will then."

I slapped my hands on the table. "I forbid you!"

"You can't do that! You're not my mom!" He jumped out of his seat, knocking over the shake as he went. My shock nailed me to my seat just long enough for him to bolt for the door. In the next instant, I sprang from the booth to follow.

"Miss! Your bill!" The waitress grabbed my sleeve just as I reached the door.

Cursing, I pulled my wallet out of my pocket and shoved a couple of twenties in her hand. I swiveled and ran out the door just in time to see my brother standing on the corner, looking around as if he were lost.

"Danny!"

He flipped me the bird.

Gritting my teeth, I stiff-legged it over. As I moved, I was very aware of the eyes tracking us. Of the judgmental gazes of the women who already condemned me as a bad mother. Of the men who thought I should take Danny in hand. What the hell did they know about our problems?

When I finally reached Danny, I grabbed his arm. "What the hell, Danny?"

Every cell in my body yearned to read him the riot act right there on the corner. Maybe drag him down to the precinct so he could see what magic did to people. Perhaps ground him for the rest of his life so he'd never have a chance to make good on his threat to seek magic training from someone else. Luckily, my conscience kicked in. It was the kid's birthday, for Christ sakes. I blew out a long breath. "Look, I'm sorry you don't like my rules, but I know more about the dangers than you do. I'll answer questions and I'll talk to you more about Mom if you want, but I cannot condone you learning how to cook."

He set his jaw in a mulish line. "I have to get back to school."

I deflated. What? Had I hoped he'd see reason and tell me it was okay? I gritted my teeth because I knew this battle would have to be fought another day. "Let's go."

# Chapter Nineteen

A few hours later, the sun was a glare in the rearview and Morales and I were looking for a man named PeeWee. According to the dispatch for the limo company he worked for, Marvin's friend had failed to show up for work the last two days. We wanted to find him and ask him if he'd seen or spoken to Marvin after we'd left him in that alley so we could begin piecing together a time line for the murder. But it was looking more and more as if PeeWee didn't want to be found.

Morales drove us. By that point, he'd stopped trying to make small talk and had settled for casting me worried glances. I sat with my face turned toward the window, chewing my bottom lip raw while I endlessly replayed the lunch with Danny in my mind.

"Is this about Volos?" Morales asked quietly.

I kept my eyes on the road but shook my head. "Don't be an idiot."

"So what's up?"

I had a brief moment of thinking I'd prefer to roll out the car door than to ask Drew Morales for advice. But then I thought,

What the hell? It was not as if he was going to take Danny's side anyway. "My brother wants to begin magic training."

His eyes slammed down. "Back up. How old is this kid?"

I told him. "And, yeah, he's an Adept."

"So what's the problem?" Morales shrugged.

I paused. "What do you mean? My little brother wants to learn magic, that's what's wrong."

"Am I missing something?"

It hit me then that Morales didn't know about my personal ban on magic. He knew I'd left the coven behind, sure, but not that I didn't cook or use any magic. Something told me that, even though he was, according to Gardner, a Mundane, no one shunned all forms of magic in our world. Hell, Rufus was the most hard-line, antidirty-magic guy I knew, but even he thought I was crazy for spending more to buy produce from farms that didn't use potions to fertilize their vegetables and fruits. I was saved from having to wade into that mess when my cell started dancing on the dashboard. I punched the button. "Prospero."

"We need to talk."

Electricity skittered up my spine. "John?"

Beside me Morales went tense and frowned. "Volos?" he mouthed.

I nodded distractedly. Into the phone, I said, "It's not a good time right now—"

"Your brother's here, Kate."

Shock and worry made every muscle in my body go stiff. "Where?"

"My loft."

"I swear to God if you hurt him—"

"Shut up and listen," he snapped. "He came to me. Showed up ten minutes ago. Said he walked all the way here to ask me a favor. I gave him a soda and ducked away to call you."

The idea of my brother's spending time with John Volos made my fingers cramp on the cell. "I'll be there in five. Do not let him leave before I arrive."

I hit the End button and turned to Morales. "My brother is at Volos's loft."

His eyes narrowed. "Why?" Given his qualms the day before after the meeting with Volos, I cursed the dumb luck of being with him when that call came in. I wanted to suggest he just drop me off, but I was pretty sure he'd refuse because he'd want to know the reason my kid brother was hanging with our lead suspect.

"That's the million-dollar question." I looked over, trying to quell the rising panic in my throat. "Step on it."

He smirked at my bossy tone. "Yes, ma'am."

♦ ♦ ♦

Volos opened the door immediately, like he'd been staring through the peephole waiting for our arrival. I was shocked to find him at his house in the middle of the day. Even more surprised to find him wearing a simple black T-shirt and well-worn jeans. It was easier to stay at arm's length when he was all buttoned up in a suit.

He didn't say anything when he opened the door. Just stepped back and waved a hand down the hall, where it opened up into a large living area. I nodded and brushed past him, trying to ignore the dark, earthy, chypre scent of his cologne.

As I walked down the hall, I reminded myself that I had witnesses so I couldn't lose my cool. Behind me, I heard Morales thank Volos for calling. The wizard murmured something I couldn't hear, but the tension in the hallway was palpable.

I found Danny sitting on Volos's couch with a can of soda in one hand and the remote control in the other. The TV on the facing wall was as large as a billboard on Interstate 71. The room was bigger than my entire house, with a sunken seating area filled with an expensive leather sectional and lots of tasteful artwork. To the right, a large counter separated the living area from a gourmet kitchen, gleaming with lots of granite and stainless steel. The entire front wall of the space was made of windows that looked out over the wide terrace. Beyond that, Lake Erie was a sheet of diamonds in the distance.

When Danny saw me appear, he froze with the drink halfway to his slack mouth.

"Do you have any idea—" I began and had to stop myself because I felt the words growing into a shout. I cleared my throat. "What are you doing here, Danny?"

Behind me, I felt Volos and Morales enter the room. They hung back, as if they were concerned I'd turn on them next. I wasn't about to yell at Morales, but Volos was right to worry.

"How'd you find me?" Danny said. He didn't sound afraid so much as disappointed.

"I called her." This from Volos.

"You said you were ordering pizza," the kid whined, sounding wounded.

Volos crossed his arms and shrugged. "I lied."

Danny threw his hands up in disgust. "Well, that's just great!"

"That's all you have to say?" If he'd been smart he would have recognized the quiet chill in my tone. "The school called me right after John did. Danny, they're frantic with worry. You never should have come here."

"He said he wouldn't call you until I told him why I was here."

"Tell you what." I crossed my arms. "Since I already came all this way, you can tell us both."

Morales cleared his throat. "I, uh—think I'll go call Gardner. Check in."

"Thanks." I nodded, grateful for his tact. Once he'd disappeared into the hall and out the door, I looked back at Danny. "Well?"

He slumped back into the plush couch. "I was going to ask him if I could be his apprentice."

Even though I'd suspected his motivation, hearing the words come out of that young face made me want to punch something. "We discussed this earlier."

Danny hopped up. "No, you didn't listen to my side at all."

"Why come to me?" Volos's voice was calm despite the charged atmosphere.

"Because of what you said."

My brows slammed down. "You've been talking to him?"

Volos shot me a bemused look and shook his head.

"No," Danny said, exasperated. "Back when I was little. Remember? The night before Kate and I moved away?"

I stilled and turned to look at Volos in time to see some emotion pass across his face before he slammed down the walls. "I don't know what you're talking about, kid."

"You do, I can tell," Danny said. "I'll never forget it. I was six and something woke me up. There was a lot of shouting coming from Kate's room. I walked in the hall. It was really dark, but I remember telling myself to be brave."

Memories of that night came rushing up, like ghosts rising from deep graves. Suddenly, my ribs felt too small to contain my lungs and heart.

Danny, oblivious to my emotions, soldiered on. "You were yelling at Kate, asking why she was leaving you," he said to Volos. "She said something real quiet, so I couldn't make it out."

John glanced at me, as we both remembered the words I'd said to stop the argument: "Because I don't love you."

177

It had been the only lie I ever told him. But I knew if I didn't break both our hearts, he'd never let me leave.

"Anyway," Danny said, "a couple minutes later, you burst into the hall. You looked real mad. But then you saw me standing there and knelt down. Do you remember now? What you said?"

Volos's jaw clenched. With a sigh, he nodded. "I told you if you ever needed anything to come find me."

Danny nodded eagerly. "You made me repeat it back to you, too, so I wouldn't forget."

I closed my eyes and damned myself for being the reason Danny felt the need to go to Volos in the first place.

"That was a long time ago, kid," Volos said. "Things have changed."

"So you were lying?" The betrayal in my brother's voice had me snapping my eyes open again.

"I wasn't lying," John said. "I meant it—at the time."

"You still do magic, don't you?"

Volos shot me a look. "Occasionally."

I gritted my teeth. "Look, even if nothing had changed, I'd never allow you to become an apprentice." Especially not *his* apprentice, I amended silently.

Danny's expression became mulish. "That's why this was supposed to be *secret*."

"Please apologize to Mr. Volos for interrupting his day."

He looked as if he was about to fight me on it, but I put on my best cross-me-and-regret-it look. With a sigh, he finally muttered, "Sorry."

"Don't worry about it, kid. But maybe instead of running away you could have just called me."

"Whatever." Clearly the conversation had put a serious dent in Danny's hero worship of Volos. Good.

"Why don't you wait on the terrace while your sister and I have a little chat?"

Without a word, Danny stomped toward the sliding door set into the windows. He slammed it so hard, the entire panel of glass shook.

"Well, I see he got the Prospero temper," Volos said.

"What the hell are you doing home today anyway?" I shot back because I needed to vent my anger somewhere.

He crossed his arms. "Gee, Kate, I don't know. Maybe because your investigation has required me to shut down my offices for a few days?"

I opened my mouth but found my brain totally incapable of a battle of sarcastic wits. The awkwardness of the situation swooped in to replace my anger and fear. "Look, I'm sorry he came here. It's been—" I shrugged instead of trying to find the right word.

"Why won't you let him learn the art, Kate?"

"It's none of your business."

"Considering he just asked me to mentor him, it is."

"I appreciate you calling me, and that you let him down as gently as possible. But that's as far as this goes."

Just then the door opened again and Morales came back in, looking wary. When he saw Danny outside and Volos and me squaring off, he relaxed. "What'd I miss?"

"Nothing," I said. "We're leaving."

Volos held up a hand. "Not so fast. We need to talk about this misguided investigation—"

"Oh good, so you're ready to confess?" Morales cocked his head to the side.

Volos shot him an eat-shit-and-die look. "Confess what, exactly?"

"Cut the crap," I said. "You know how all this looks."

"You should understand more than most how dangerous assumptions can be." He moved in closer, trying to establish intimacy. I stepped back to let him know it wasn't welcome. He absorbed the rebuff smoothly and continued, "Use your logic. What would I possibly gain by cooking a potion that turns men into monsters?"

"What's your game here, Volos?" Morales demanded.

"No games," he said. "I'm just protecting my interests."

"You mean like having snitches killed?" I asked.

His expression hardened. "You're grasping and you know it. Do yourself a favor and start looking into Bane."

"Or we could call the state attorney and get a warrant for your warehouses."

"An empty threat," Volos said dismissively.

Morales held up a hand. "Actually, it's not. We have manifests from the port authority that prove your import company received a shipment of oil of rose quartz just last week."

Volos smiled. "Let me ask you a question, Agent—"

Drew clenched his jaw. "Special Agent Morales."

Volos nodded. "If I were importing materials to create an illicit potion, don't you think I'd have those ingredients smuggled in and kept off the radar?"

"The more important question is, What possible use would you have for twenty barrels of oil of rose quartz?" I shot back.

"If you want the answer to that you will definitely need to charge me with something or get a warrant. If not, I'll kindly ask you to leave because I have a meeting with the city council about the community center."

Morales snorted. "Yeah, you're a real humanitarian, right?"

"Some say so. I just try to do what's best for the city."

"Only if it's in your best interests, though," Morales challenged.

"That doesn't negate the benefits to the people of Babylon."
He shrugged.

I'd heard enough. I marched over to the windows and
rapped against the glass. Danny turned away from the railing
he'd been sulking at and glared. I held up my watch. "Time to
go," I mouthed. His shoulders drooped, but he started for the
doors anyway.

I marched back over to where Volos and Morales were standing. "You know what?" I said to Volos. "If you're telling the
truth about Bane and you really cared about this community
as much as you claim, you would postpone plans for that community center."

Volos raised a brow. "Are you claiming you're not using this
situation to advance your own ambitions, Officer Prospero?"

"Fuck you," I said, stepping up to him.

"Kate," Morales said in a warning tone.

Volos flicked an amused glance at Morales before aiming
that knowing gaze back at me. "Truth hurts, doesn't it, Kate?"

"It might," I said, "if I believed for a second you knew how
to tell it."

"Kate?" Danny said in a small voice from the door.

I forced myself to relax and turn toward him, forcing a reas-
suring smile. "It's all right, Danny." I motioned to Morales.
"Let's go."

Morales led the way with me behind.

"Bye, John," Danny called as I dragged him in my wake.

"See ya, kid," he said with a warm smile that made my skin
turn cold. "If you can't convince her to teach you, give me a
call. Maybe we can work something out after all."

I froze and turned, pushing Danny behind me. The speculative gleam I saw in Volos's eyes scared me. "Over my dead body."

He smiled sadly. "I sincerely hope it doesn't come to that."

# Chapter Twenty

anny wasn't speaking to me. Again. This time it was fine because I didn't trust myself to speak to him, either.

Morales kept stealing glances at the two of us like we were bombs about to go off. Finally, he cleared his throat. "So I talked to Gardner."

I jerked my gaze from the window I'd been glaring at. "And?"

"She wants us to meet her at the gym."

I frowned. "Why?"

"Mez found something from those samples we got at the morgue."

My eyebrows popped up. "Good news?"

"She wouldn't say." He glanced over his shoulder at my pouting brother. "What do you want to do?"

I shot a look at Danny, too. The last thing I wanted to do was let him out of my sight. But the alternative was to take him to work, which didn't sit well with me, either. Still, I was pretty sure Gardner would be more annoyed by a delay than showing up with the kid.

I sighed. "Go to the gym."

"You're sure?"

I looked at Danny as I spoke. "He'll be on his best behavior," I said in an *or-else* tone.

Danny rolled his eyes but didn't comment.

"Yes, ma'am," Morales said.

About five minutes later, I realized he was headed in the wrong direction. "You should have turned right back there."

He glanced at me with mischief in his gaze. "Figured a little detour wouldn't hurt." He pulled to a halt at a stoplight. On one corner of the intersection, a man huddled against a trash can. His skin was blue. Not a subtle tint, like Mr. Callahan's jaundiced skin at group. No, this was deep indigo.

"What's that guy's deal?" Danny asked suddenly.

Morales winked at me. I nodded, catching on. He'd taken us to one of the worst parts of the Cauldron to help drive home my point about magic for Danny. Guess my partner finally realized Danny's interest in magic was a big deal after all. "He's hooked on an antidepression potion." I kept my tone casual. "From the looks of it, he's been using for a while. Before long, the addiction will drive him to commit suicide."

"Wh-why would he do that?"

"That's how addiction works," Morales said. "After a while the potion stops being effective, so the user has to go to more and more extreme measures for relief. In the case of the antidepression potion, it makes him more deeply depressed until he can't stand to live anymore."

"Why is he so blue?"

"Because when you use them a long time they change you at a cellular level."

"But that's just dirty magic, right? Clean magic is safe."

I turned fully and shook my head. "Danny, no. Magic is

magic, and it all changes you. It's just that clean magic companies use safer ingredients and are more controlled. There are still side effects."

Danny crossed his arms. "Hmm."

"And usually, you gotta take more potions to mask the side effects." I added, "It becomes a vicious cycle, and before you know it, you're on ten potions for that one defect you were trying to treat."

"From the looks of that guy," Morales added, "he's been hooked for several years."

I turned to see that Danny's complexion had gone paperwhite. "Can't someone help him?"

"There are antipotions, but they're too expensive for most potion freaks to afford since their addictions probably got them fired from their jobs. Some have success with recovery programs."

"You mean like the group you and Pen go to?" Danny asked.

From the corner of my eye, I saw Morales's head swivel toward me with a speculative gaze. I ignored him and spoke to Danny. "Something like that, but usually they have to go through a really painful detox period. Some people don't survive that part. But before any of that, the addict has to want to stop."

"If it makes him that sad, wouldn't he want to quit?"

"Potions change a person's brain chemistry, Danny," I said. "He's not thinking rationally. The addiction is controlling his decisions."

The light turned green and Morales slowly pulled forward. As he drove, we passed more addicts. I pointed them out as we went. "That girl over there? With the lips that look like two sausages on her face? She's addicted to a vanity potion." I pointed to the other side of the street. "He's probably hooked on a strength potion."

"How can you tell?" Danny asked, almost grudgingly.

"No human can gain that kind of muscle mass without chemicals," Morales said. "Soon his body won't be able to carry all that extra weight and he'll either have a heart attack or an aneurysm."

"Oh, look at that one," I began, "she's definitely on a—"

"Stop," Danny whispered. "I get it, okay? Becoming addicted to magic is dangerous. Just say no, blah, blah, blah."

I turned fully in my seat. "No, you don't get it. I'm not worried you'll become an addict."

"What then?" He set his jaw in a stubborn line.

"You need to see that there's a very real human cost to the potion game. The Adepts who cook and sell potions are profiting off people's misery and desperation. And in the process, they're ruining lives."

"Kate, I don't want to sell potions. I just want to learn how magic works."

"To what end, Danny?"

He sighed and leaned back with his arms crossed. The pleading vanished and a ruthless glare replaced it. It was an expression I'd seen on Uncle Abe's face more times than I could count, and seeing it on Danny made me go cold. "Maybe you're just afraid I'll be better at it than you."

"You know what? I bet you would be." I shook my head sadly. "In fact, I'm sure of it." Danny was a lot smarter than I was as a kid.

He paused, as if sensing a trap. "Really?"

I nodded. "Which is why I'm terrified to let you try. If you show talent, it will only be a matter of time before the covens come calling."

For a moment the only sound in the car was the echo of the wheels slapping pavement. Morales kept his eyes on the road, but I could feel the tension coming off him as if he was holding himself back from jumping into the argument. Part of me was embarrassed for him to see this personal drama at all, but making Danny see was more important than my pride.

"You know what your problem is, Kate?" Danny said quietly.

"No, but I'm sure you'll tell me."

"You assume everyone's like you." He speared me with a look. "Just because you couldn't handle your power doesn't mean I can't."

"That's not fair."

"You know what's not fair?" he shot back. "The fact that I've done nothing but follow your rules, but you still treat me like I'm a criminal."

I felt like he'd punched me. I opened my mouth to say—I don't know what, but he turned away, as though he couldn't stand to look at me.

Morales, whose presence I'd forgotten, cleared his throat. "We're here."

◆ ◆ ◆

When we got back to the office, the entire team was waiting for us with grim expressions. Needless to say, when Gardner saw me leading my sulky teenaged brother behind me on the stairs, her expression did not improve.

"Who's the kid?" she snapped.

After shooting Danny a warning look, I walked over and pulled her aside. "That's Danny, my little brother."

Her eyes narrowed. "Why isn't he in school?"

"Look, I could bullshit you, but the truth is he ran away from school to go see John Volos."

Gardner's eyes widened.

"He's been wanting to learn magic—Danny, that is,"

I rushed ahead. "When I told him I wouldn't teach him he decided to go see John." She blinked. "Sir, I know how this looks, but Danny had no idea we were investigating Volos. He thought he was just going to see an old friend to ask for a favor. Obviously I shut that option down," I said quickly. "Anyway, I brought him here because it's too late in the day to go back to school and I don't trust him home alone given the circumstances." I would have called Baba to help, but it was Bingo Day at the senior center and she wouldn't be home for at least another hour.

Gardner looked as if she could chew through nails. "When I brought you on this team I thought your connections would help our case, but all they've done is complicate the shit out of it."

"The case was already complicated without my help, sir."

Her lip quirked. "Ain't that the damned truth?" She sighed. "All right, he can stay but keep him out of the way."

I nodded eagerly. "No problem."

By the time we'd rejoined the others, Morales had already introduced Danny around. When I returned, Mez—today in red dreads pulled back into a thick ponytail—was giving my brother a tour of the lab. Danny's eyes were huge as he took in all the beakers and burners and gadgets. When Mez spoke, the kid looked at him as if he were his own personal Jesus. Crap. I rushed forward to intervene. "All right, kid," I said in a forced cheery voice, "we need to get to work. Why don't you go play one of your games at my desk?"

Danny looked at me like I'd just walked in with shit on my shoe. "I want to hear the meeting."

I narrowed my eyes. "Since when did you get interested in my work?"

"Since Mez here told me how much he loves being a wizard for the MEA."

The look I shot the wiz made him freeze. "I just, uh, meant—why are you looking at me like that?"

Danny rolled his eyes. "She's got a bug up her butt because she doesn't want me to learn to cook."

"What? That's"—Mez glanced at me and cringed—"probably for the best. This job is, uh, superboring."

"But you just said—" Danny started to protest.

"Everyone circle up!" Gardner yelled.

"My desk, now," I said. "And wear your headphones."

Danny's face morphed from confusion to resentment. He muttered "Bye" to Mez and stalked over to my desk. I watched to make sure he put the headphones on before I turned to the wiz. "Thanks."

He shrugged. "No sweat. Maybe later you can tell me what that was about?"

"Now, people!" Gardner sounded ready to nail some asses to walls. Instead of replying to Mez, I rushed out of the lab. Gardner stood in the ring with Morales and Shadi. Judging from her look, this wasn't going to be a fun talk. Maybe that's why she'd decided to deliver her news in the fighting ring.

"Okay, now that we're all here," she began, "we have a lot to cover. Mez, why don't you start?"

Gone was the jokey wizard I'd been talking to a few minutes earlier. Now he looked like a doctor about to tell someone they had six months to live. "I analyzed the samples Prospero and Morales gathered yesterday. The good news, if you can call it that, is that Marvin definitely had fur under his nails, which supports the theory this was another Gray Wolf murder."

"You're sure it was fur and not just hair?" Shadi asked.

Mez shot her a quelling look. She flushed and muttered an apology. "Anyway," he continued, "the bad news is that the DNA I got from the fur didn't match anyone's in the ACD."

A few years earlier, the Arcane Crimes Database added DNA sampling to the fingerprint and criminal histories they kept on file. Problem was, it took time to collect and process DNA samples from all the Arcane criminals in the country. Mostly it had samples from crooks who were already in jail, which wasn't so helpful because if they were behind bars, chances were good they weren't guilty of current crimes.

"Shit," Morales said.

Mez held up a hand. "Not so fast. As it happens, Prospero's friend in CSI at BPD is a real peach. This morning, she faxed over her preliminary report from the crime scene."

My eyebrows popped up. "Does Eldritch know about that?" I asked Gardner.

She shrugged. "Not our business." Which meant, no.

"Anyway," Mez continued, "according to her, there wasn't enough physical evidence to support the theory that Marvin Brown was killed at Volos Towers."

"His body was moved?" Morales asked, glancing at me.

"Wait," I said, recalling the gruesome scene, "no way his head was bashed in elsewhere and moved."

"According to Val, it happened postmortem."

"Someone didn't want the cops to have an easy time of identifying Mr. Brown," Gardner concluded.

Mez nodded. "Unfortunately, the surveillance cameras weren't much help. They show a black van arriving at 2:08 in front of the building. But soon after there's a blackout in the footage."

I sighed. "So whoever did this is organized and resourceful."

"Not so fast," Mez said with a smile. "Val sent over a few stills taken from the footage just before the cameras went dark." He pulled them out of the file to pass around.

I looked at the first one he handed me. The van he mentioned was maybe twenty feet from the camera. There were no identifying marks on the vehicle and no license plate was visible. Likewise, the windows were too tinted to see inside. Next couple of images were the same. By the fourth, I was getting antsy that Mez was just fucking with us. But this one showed a person dressed in black from head to toe exit the driver's side, which was closest to the camera. The suspect was slim in build, but tall—lanky. The only part of his skin that showed was the mouth and chin as he finished a cigarette. The next still showed him pulling down the mask and tossing the cigarette on the ground. Another figure was coming around the van, but he was wearing a mask, too.

I passed the last image to Morales, wondering what I was missing. Then it hit me. I snatched the picture back from Morales and spun around to Mez. "Tell me you got it."

"What?" Morales asked, frowning.

Mez smiled at me. "Val had her team get it. She sent it to me because she knew I could rush the DNA."

"Hello?" Shadi snapped. "Anyone want to fill the rest of us in?"

I turned and held up the picture. "This asshole was smoking a cigarette when he got out of the car."

Morales's eyebrows snapped up. "Guess they were right—smoking is bad for your health."

I rolled my eyes. "Tell me you got a hit," I said to Mez.

His face fell. "Not exactly. The DNA isn't in the ACD."

The mood in the room plummeted. "Oh ye of little faith," Mez said. "I may not have the asshole's DNA, but I have his number." He held up an evidence bag containing the cigarette butt. The filter was gold and the body of the cigarette appeared to be covered in purple paper.

My stomach started doing jumping jacks. "Fuck. Me."

"This, my friends," Mez said, "is a Vice Royal cigarette."

"Never heard of them," Shadi said.

"They're a specialty brand. Costly," Gardner said. "Rare."

"So we just need to track down people who smoke that brand," Shadi said.

I knew only two people who smoked Vice Royals. One was locked away in Crowley Penitentiary. The other was—

"Don't bother," I said. "I already know who it is."

"Well?" Gardner said. The other three turned to me with expectant expressions.

"Looks like Volos wasn't lying." For some reason that realization made me feel more relieved than it should have. "The only asshole on the streets I know who smokes that brand is Hieronymus Bane."

Morales frowned at me. "The son of Ramses Bane?" At my nod, he whistled low. "Fuck me."

"You're sure?" Gardner asked.

"Sure enough to investigate, anyway."

"There's no way State Attorney Stone will give us a warrant based on a cigarette butt," she said.

"We don't need one for a routine traffic stop," Morales said. "Maybe if we put a little pressure on the prick he'll spill something his daddy doesn't want us to know."

"Guy like that has to have something in his car that would allow us to detain him long enough." I nodded. "It could work. Thing is, Harry's loyal to Bane, but there's also bitterness there. He's been angling to start his own crew for years, but Bane won't allow it. We could maybe play on that."

"Right," Gardner said. "Play that up with him. Tell him we've got enough evidence to put him away unless he gives us something solid on Daddy Dearest."

"We'll have to be careful, though. If he asks to lawyer up, we're toast."

"Do it," Gardner said. "Shadi, I want you to pull everything

191

you can find on Hieronymus and Ramses Bane. Maybe once word gets to Bane that we're targeting his kid, it'll rattle his cage enough to make a mistake."

"What about me?" Mez asked.

"You call the CSI lady and tell her you couldn't find DNA on the cigarette. Don't tell her we're targeting Bane's kid. We don't need Eldritch interfering until we have what we need."

"Sir," I said, "are you sure? If we're right here, this information could make their murder investigation."

"Fuck 'em," Morales said. "If the tables were turned Eldritch wouldn't give us the lead. In fact, he's probably off giving the mayor a hummer as we speak."

Gardner sighed but nodded. "He's right. Keep it tight until we have what we need."

I clenched my jaw. Part of me wanted to call them out for perpetuating the bullshit politics. On the other hand, the prospect of blowing this case wide open without Eldritch's interference appealed to my competitive nature. So I kept my mouth shut. I just hoped that when the dust of this case cleared and Eldritch found out what we'd done, I'd have already secured my spot on the task force for good.

"You guys need me to call DMV to find out Harry's license plate and car model?" Shadi asked.

I shook my head and smiled. "I don't think that will be a problem."

# Chapter Twenty-One

An hour later, we were in Morales's SUV, following a neon-green Trans Am through the Cauldron. The license on the pimpmobile read WIZ-LIFE. Deep bass thumped from its open windows and T-tops. Occasionally, puffs of smoke would escape, too.

I'd called Baba before we left the gym. She had been home celebrating her twenty-buck victory at bingo and said she was happy to keep an eye on Danny until I could get home. When we'd dropped him off, Baba was very interested to meet Morales. She'd pulled me aside and said, "I see the Sexy Juice is already working." I didn't bother correcting her. Mostly because it was funny to see Morales get all uncomfortable when Baba waggled her eyebrows at him and checked out his butt.

As for Danny, he hadn't said much before we left. Eventually I'd have to figure out how to get him to drop this magic business, but for the time being I was off to arrest the kind of asshole I was terrified Danny would become if he started cooking.

Unlike his dad, Harry didn't spend all his time down in

the Arteries; Bane needed a man aboveground he could trust. For Morales's and my sake, I just hoped some of that trust was misplaced.

"What an idiot," Morales complained. "We've been following this douchebag for fifteen minutes and he hasn't gone above twenty."

"He's cruising," I said. "Wants to show off those sweet rims."

We were five cars back, keeping our distance for the time being. Eventually, he'd take a wide right turn or forget to use his blinker, but with the time crunch over our heads it was hard not to be impatient. Any minute now Val and the detective on the case would make the connection to the cigarette brand. We wanted to be sure we had our shot at Harry before they figured it out.

"Tell me something," Morales said, scooting his ass around on the seat like it was growing numb.

"Yeah?" I had my eyes on Harry's taillights, willing one to go out.

"What's the real reason you don't use magic?"

My head jerked around at the suspicion in his tone. "Isn't doing this job for the last five years reason enough?"

"Nope. Every cop I know uses magic in some form."

I sighed. "Most cops didn't grow up in a coven. I've seen firsthand the damage cooking can do to people and those they love."

He shot me a look that made me shift in my seat. I felt as though he saw the truth through my skin. "Who died?"

That one simple question had the effect of a small explosion going off in my midsection. Was I that transparent? "I don't—"

"Cut the shit, Kate. It's obvious. You wouldn't be fighting so hard to keep Danny off the burners and avoiding magic if there wasn't some deep pain associated with it. Who was it?"

I clenched my teeth. "My mother."

His eyes widened. "I'm sorry." The shit of it was he sounded sincere so I couldn't be too mad at him for making me admit it.

I forced a shrug. "It was a long time ago."

"Some pain only sharpens with time."

I jerked my head toward him. He was speaking from experience. I raised my brows in challenge. It was his turn.

He sighed. "Don't pretend you haven't wondered about my hand."

I nodded. "What happened?"

"My dad was an Adept. That's where my sister and I got the gene." My eyebrows rose in shock. Morales always used his right hand. He lifted his left and clenched it. As he did he grimaced. "Doesn't work so well anymore. After the accident." It never occurred to me he didn't use his left because he simply couldn't.

"What accident?"

"My dad wasn't formally trained. He grew up poor and his parents were Catholic. They saw his gifts as a curse from the devil and tried to beat it out of him."

I cringed in sympathy. Over the years, I'd heard too many tales of Mundane parents who couldn't handle having Adept kids. They'd tie the kid's left hand behind his back so he had to use his right—or worse.

"Anyway, I was pretty young when it happened. Eight. My little sister, Blanca, was only three. Dad was in the basement cooking some potion he said was going to make us rich. He was always trying to invent a formula he could sell to one of the Big Magic companies."

I nodded and swallowed, bracing myself for the punch line.

"When the explosion happened..." He swallowed hard, his throat clicking drily. "My mom was helping me with homework in the back of the house. Blanca was down for a nap.

Mom tried to get me out the back door before the fire could reach us, but I ran back in to save Blanca. By that point, the fire was so intense, the front of the house was basically an inferno. Unfortunately, she didn't get to me before I thrust my hand into the flames."

I slammed my eyes shut and cursed silently. "Jesus, Drew."

My eyes opened in time to see him smile tightly. "After we buried Dad and Blanca"—he cleared the catch in his throat—"we moved in with Mom's Mundane family. I learned how to use my right hand, moved to a new school, and started living as a Mundane kid."

"So why did you encourage me to let Danny study magic?"

"I made my own choice." He shrugged. "My mom, as much pain as losing them caused, never said I couldn't study magic. She said if I wanted to she'd figure out a way to send me to a real school so I could learn to use it safely, but she let me decide. I chose to live as a Mundane. But Danny should be able to choose his own path, too."

I blinked at him.

"What?"

"Nothing, I'm just...shocked, I guess. Didn't mark you for the philosophical type."

He smirked at me. "Oh, I got lots of layers, Cupcake."

I shook my head at him but couldn't help smiling. Part of me was relieved to have him back to his cocky self again. The brief glimpse of the sort-of-nice guy hinted at a complexity I wasn't comfortable handling.

"Anyway," he said when I didn't immediately offer a response, "you're gonna have to do something about the kid. If he keeps knocking on our suspect's doors, Gardner's gonna lose it." He looked over at me. "You're a pain in the ass, but it'd be a shame for the team to lose you."

"Thanks, I think."

Morales put his blinker on to follow Harry right down Stark Street. He slowed and pulled over as Harry came to a stop in front of the Green Faerie. "Well, would you look at that?" He pulled his siren from under his seat. "Our friend just parked facing the wrong way."

He lowered his window, popped the light on the roof, and hit the gas. Two seconds later, we pulled in hot behind Harry's car. The kid had been leaning against the driver's door of the car, his arms crossed as he talked to a girl. She wore torn fishnets, a plaid miniskirt, and a halter top that said she either went to the sluttiest private school in history—or she was one of Aphrodite's girls.

When we pulled up, Harry stood and turned to face us. His mouth curled into a sneer. He took one last drag off a cigarette and tossed it into the gutter. It was hard to tell from my vantage point, but I'd bet big bucks it was a Vice Royal.

When we got out of the car, the girl's eyes widened and she took off at a speed I would have thought impossible in her stiletto Mary Janes. We let her go since we had bigger fish to fry.

"Afternoon, officers," Harry said. "You lost?"

Morales lowered his aviators and smirked at the guy. "Are you aware that you're parked illegally, son?"

Harry frowned and glanced back at his car. "No, I'm not. The car's still on. I'm *idling*."

"You can take that up with traffic court." Morales made a show of pulling out a ticket notebook. Where he'd gotten his hands on that, I didn't want to know. "License and registration?"

Harry's look was full of piss and vinegar. "Why are you harassing me?"

Morales looked at me. "Are you harassing anyone?"

197

I shrugged. "I thought we were doing our part to prevent a traffic accident."

Harry swiped his license from his wallet and threw it on the ground.

Morales's posture went from loose and jokey to alpha cop. "Pick it up," he projected. "Slowly. Keep your hands where we can see them."

Harry sighed and did as instructed. He handed the card to me, his eyes scanning me up and down in what I guess he thought was an intimidating manner. "The registration?" I asked. "Insurance?"

"Left 'em in my other pants."

"Uh-oh," Morales said. "We're going to have to write you up for that, too."

"Unless they're in your glove box," I said. "Maybe we should check just to be sure."

"They aren't in there," he said, his voice dripping venom.

"I'd feel better if we checked." I nodded at Morales. "Anything in there you want to tell us about before he goes digging?"

Harry's chin came up. "I got nothing to hide." But his milk-white cheeks reddened.

While Morales began his search, I smiled at Harry. "He'll just be a minute."

He looked down at the ground and kicked a rock with his boot.

I glanced through the windows of the car and saw Morales duck his head under the seats. To distract our uncooperative friend, I started chatting. "So how's your dad?"

His head came up, forcing his white hair to sway. "Do you have any idea what he's going to do once he finds out about this?"

I cocked my head. "I'm dying to know."

He muttered something under his breath. I made out the words "die" and "bitch."

I put a hand to my ear. "What was that? I didn't quite catch it."

He looked at me with hot eyes. "Enjoy yourself now, Kate."

I narrowed my gaze. "Are you threatening me, Harry?" If I could piss him off enough to lose it and threaten me directly, we'd have him.

He looked away, obviously realizing how close he'd been to slipping up.

"Well, well, well," Morales said, standing up with something in his hand. "Let me guess: You left your permit for this in your other pants, too." He raised the pistol high, balancing it on the end of a pen so he wouldn't get his prints on it. It was one of those flashy numbers. The overly large, shiny chrome barrel and inlaid mother-of-pearl handle were probably compensating for Harry's low-caliber pocket pistol.

"That ain't mine," Harry said in a bored tone. "I think you planted it."

Morales laughed. "Then why are your initials engraved in the barrel?" He nodded at me. "Also found these." He held up a purple and gold cigarette box.

"So what? Smoking isn't illegal."

"Neither is being an asshole, but we're taking you in anyway," Morales snapped. "Cuff him."

◆ ◆ ◆

Twenty minutes later, I looked in the rearview mirror, expecting to see red and blue at any second. Morales was in the back with Harry and I was driving. We were miles from the precinct and getting farther away by the second.

"You're going the wrong direction." Judging from his bored

tone, he knew exactly what we were doing, but he wasn't about to let us see him worry about it.

"Oops," I said, "sorry. I get so turned around down here." Which was bullshit, of course. I'd learned to drive on these streets just as Harry had.

"Turn right here," he said.

I turned left.

"What the fuck?" Harry said, finally losing his cool. "Where are you taking me?"

"We told you," Morales said, "the precinct."

Harry looked as if he were ready to spit acid. "When my lawyer finds out about this he'll have your badges."

"Since when is it illegal to have a poor sense of direction?" Morales said. His cell in the console started buzzing. "Hold on, Harry."

Our guest gritted his teeth and muttered, "Hieronymus, asshole."

Morales ignored that and spoke into the phone. "Yeah, we got him. Yep, almost. See you in a minute." He looked up and nodded to me. As agreed beforehand, I turned toward Lake Erie. "Hold tight, Harry, we gotta see a friend about a thing."

Two minutes later, I turned the SUV into a weedy parking lot near the water. This section of town hadn't felt the healing touch of Volos's money. Instead of high-rise apartments and expensive boutiques, the shore was lined with cardboard condos and littered with dirty needles. A beige Camry was already parked in the lot. I pulled up alongside the driver's door. Gardner rolled down her window. "Any problems?"

I shook my head. She nodded resolutely and exited the car. The wind lashed at her hair and clothes as she walked toward the SUV. Things weren't much calmer in the vehicle's interior. Harry saw Gardner and went stiff. "Who the fuck is that?"

Morales smiled. "That's Special Agent Miranda Gardner. Over in Detroit they call her the Velvet Hammer."

Harry frowned. "Why?"

"Because she's got a way of making people talk who don't want to."

Harry swallowed hard. "I want to speak to my lawyer."

"Relax," Morales said, patting him on the shoulder. "We're just giving her a ride to the precinct."

Gardner pulled open the SUV's side door. The cold wind whipped through the small space like a nor'easter. "Gentlemen," she said, nodding to the two in the back. "Prospero, take us to the precinct."

Harry blew out a long breath. "Thank Christ."

Gardner smiled. "Drive slowly."

I nodded and put the SUV in Drive. As I drove, I chewed on my bottom lip and kept checking behind me. What we were doing was highly unethical. Even Gardner, who had come up with the plan, looked tense. Only Morales appeared to see the whole thing as some sort of joyride.

"Mr. Bane, I need you to understand that once we reach the precinct, you will be arrested."

Harry jerked in his seat as if she'd stuck him with a hot poker. "What? I already told them that gun wasn't mine."

She shook her head. "It's not about the gun. In the last couple of hours, my team stumbled on some evidence linking you to the murder of Marvin Brown."

Harry's face morphed into a practiced mask, but his complexion had paled about five shades. "Who the fuck is that?"

Gardner tilted her head. "He was a Herald for the Votary Coven before he was brutally attacked and his body left on the premises of Volos Towers."

"So?"

"So, we know you were there, Mr. Bane. At the very least, you conspired to move the body onto Mr. Volos's property in an effort to frame him for the murder."

"You can't prove that." Harry looked too sure of himself. No doubt he was thinking back to how he and his partner had disabled the video cameras. Also, he happened to be correct. We couldn't prove shit yet, which was precisely why we were applying the heat in the hopes he'd crack.

Gardner looked at Morales, who handed an evidence bag to her. She held it up high so Harry could see it. "Vice Royals. It's your brand, right?"

He frowned. "Yeah, so?"

She reached into the briefcase she'd brought with her. "This bag contains a cigarette butt found at the crime scene." She paused and let that hang there for a good thirty seconds. Even from my vantage point, watching everything unfold through the rearview, I could see the large beads of sweat that appeared on Harry's upper lip. "Did you know that the MEA's lab techs can now process DNA from crime scenes in less than twenty-four hours, Mr. Bane?"

His mouth worked like a fish trying to dislodge the hook Gardner had just wedged in there nice and tight. "Me being there isn't proof I killed that asshole."

*Boom.* Morales and Gardner exchanged a quick victorious look. Now we had the proof we needed that Harry had been the one dumping the body.

"Regardless, we'll be able to pin an aiding-and-abetting charge on you. Combined with the gun charge, you're looking at a nice, long vacation."

"So?" Harry laughed. "I'm Ramses Bane's son. I'll be treated like a fucking prince in Crowley."

"You won't be in Crowley," Gardner said. "I already checked

with State Attorney Stone. The murder rap doesn't fall under federal Arcane statutes. You'll probably go to a Mundane state prison."

Morales whistled low. "Ouch. Better start limbering up your jaw now, son. You're gonna make sweet cell candy for some Bubba."

Harry swallowed audibly. "This is bullshit. I want to see my lawyer."

Look, I didn't like this guy at all. Harry had been a pain in my ass since we were kids. He used to throw tantrums whenever all the kids got together to play Wiz versus the Fuzz. If he didn't win, he'd throw these ridiculous fits. He was so easy to rile up, Volos started calling him "Harry" just to watch how his face turned purple with rage. Plus, given what we knew now, I was reasonably sure he was knee-deep in the Gray Wolf bullshit, along with his father. Still, watching him get shaken down by Morales and Gardner left an acrid taste in my mouth. The one thing that separated the cops from the criminals was that cops followed the rule of law. Those principles were the razor-thin line between them and us. But watching Morales and Gardner work, I felt as if they hadn't just crossed the line but leaped over it with abandon.

On the other hand, I knew that if we granted his request and delivered him to the precinct without getting what we needed, we'd be sunk. His daddy's high-priced lawyers would have him out on bail by nightfall and then he could disappear. Or worse, he and his father could take the next step in whatever their fucked-up plan was to create havoc in the Cauldron.

As I navigated the tricky morality of the situation, I aimed the SUV in tighter and tighter circles nearing the station. Every now and then, we'd pass a BPD cruiser and my fingers would tighten on the steering wheel. "Guys, we need to wrap this up."

Gardner looked up and nodded. "The problem is the murder is the BPD's case, but they don't have the same evidence I'm sitting on. See, my goal is to find the person behind Gray Wolf. If I hand the evidence to the BPD, you're going down, but I'm left empty-handed. Unless..." she trailed off. "Never mind."

Harry sat up straighter after a brief struggle with his cuffed hands. "What?"

She sighed. "Well, it's like this: The US attorney assigned to this case has a real hard-on for getting the guy behind Gray Wolf. So if someone had good information about the wizard behind it, the attorney would be very grateful."

"Don't insult me." Harry pressed his lips together. "You just saw what happens to snitches in the Cauldron."

"You ever heard of the game they play in Mundane prisons? 'Scalping,' they call it." Morales waited for Harry to narrow his eyes before he explained. "It's where they see who can cut off more fingers from the left hands of Adepts. They call it 'scalping' on account of it's like how the Indians used to collect scalps from the gringos who tried to take over their land."

Harry actually laughed in Morales's face. "Go tell your scary stories to one of the peewees on Exposition, asshole. If a fucking Righty comes at me, he'll limp away."

We were burning gas and daylight, so I pulled the van to the side of the road. We were in Sanguinarian territory, not far from the alley where Harkins killed the woman the night this shit began for me. I couldn't help but wonder how things would have been different if I'd just let him escape into the Arteries instead of chasing him toward that inevitable conclusion.

"There's something else you haven't considered," Gardner said. At Harry's raised brows, she continued, "When we get you to the precinct, the first thing that'll happen is a search warrant will be issued for your residence. When they find ampoules of

Gray Wolf in your house, you'll go down for that, too. Maybe it'll get you into Crowley, but you won't be there long enough to enjoy your status. The federal potion charges plus the murder will get you a one-way ticket to the gas chamber."

Harry opened his mouth, but Morales spoke first. "Ah, ah, ah, think for a minute. We're talking about you being put to death for crimes your father masterminded. Are you ready to die for him, Harry?"

"Or you can give us the information we want," Gardner said, "and you'll be free to pursue your own ambitions without your father interfering."

Harry sucked at the front of his teeth for a minute. By this point, we'd been driving around for almost an hour—well past the time when we could claim we'd simply taken a couple of wrong turns. I squeezed the steering wheel so tight my knuckles were white as we waited for Harry's answer.

"So what? I give you some sort of tip and you talk to that attorney?"

"You give us a *good* tip and yeah, we'll have the attorney here with papers reducing charges before you finish talking," Gardner said.

"And if I don't, you'll take me to the precinct to be booked?"

"We'll find the evidence eventually to put you away permanently."

The white-haired wizard looked down at his hands, thinking it over. The tension in the car was thick as Harry's musky cologne. When he finally looked up, his expression was unreadable. I turned full in my seat to get a better look. His eyes met mine for a brief, hard moment. His head tilted as he watched me and then the corner of his mouth lifted, as if he'd remembered something suddenly. "You know what?" He finally looked at Gardner. "Fuck you. I'm no snitch." As the aftershocks of that announcement rippled through the vehicle, Harry started laughing. "Now take me to the precinct or I'll sue all your asses for kidnapping."

I froze and glanced at Gardner. Her expression didn't betray any of the disappointment she had to be feeling, but her stiff shoulders hinted at her anger. She met my gaze and jerked a small nod. I sighed and turned around. As I put the car in Drive, I met Morales's eyes in the rearview. He winked at me. We'd planned for this, but Morales looked as if he had been hoping this would happen instead of feeling like a man pushed to use a last resort.

Our destination was only a few blocks away. On the way, Harry was quiet but the smug look on his face spoke volumes. He thought he'd fucked us but good. Little did he know.

I pulled the van onto Mercury Street. It took Harry a few moments to realize I was slowing down. When he did, he tensed. "Why is she stopping?"

The SUV glided easy as you please next to the curb. We parked about half a block away from a group of Sanguinarian dealers huddled around a trash-can fire. They looked up immediately, mistaking the van as the vehicle of a buyer. A short, skinny kid broke off from the group and started in our direction.

"What the fuck are you doing?" Harry asked. The first notes of panic entered his tone.

"Now that I've thought about it, maybe we were too hasty in nabbing you for that gun," Morales said. "Probably you were telling the truth about having your permit at home." He clapped Harry on the back. "It's getting cold, so we figured we'd take you right to your dad's front door."

As they talked, I kept an eye on the side mirror to track the kid's progress. He couldn't have been more than thirteen, but his eyes already had a street-honed hardness. Luckily the car's windows were tinted so he couldn't see who was inside. Yet. If Harry didn't act soon, everyone in a three-block radius would know exactly whom we had in there.

"Take me somewhere else," Harry said quickly. "If they see me with you—"

"What?" Morales raised a brow. "You'll end up like Marvin Brown?"

Harry's mouth snapped shut.

"You either get out here and receive a police escort to the tunnel entrance or you come with us to the precinct and have a conversation with the US attorney."

"I'll even escort you all the way to the tunnels myself," I said with a smile. "Wanna bet those assholes will recognize me and wonder if you're considering defecting from the covens, just like I did?"

Harry crossed his arms. "You're bluffing."

"Oh yeah?" I unclicked my seat belt. "Remember what happened last time we played chicken, Harry?"

His eyes widened. Back when we were around ten or eleven, Harry got a brand-new bike from his dad for his birthday. It was a cherry-red ten-speed that was the envy of all the Cauldron kids. My mom couldn't afford a bike for me, and I was so envious of that fucking thing it burned me. So one day I decided to challenge Harry to a game of chicken. He was to ride at me full speed on the bike. If I flinched, he'd get to punch me in the face. If I won, he had to give me the bike. After my mom came home to find a red bike in our living room, she made me give it back to him. But the few hours that bike was in my possession were some of the happiest of my childhood.

The look on Harry's face now was a lot like the one that marred his face when he pulled himself off the pavement that afternoon long ago. Back then, his elbows and knees had been bloody, and tears streaked down his pale skin. Now he was an adult and there were no tears, but the hatred remained.

Harry's eyes burned at me. "You will regret this, bitch."

"Maybe." I smiled and reached for the handle. "But it will be fun while it lasts. Shall we?"

The kid outside was even with the rear bumper of the SUV now. His head was tilted up as if he smelled danger, but the promise of a sale kept him moving forward. Harry glanced back. He popped his knuckles and his knee jostled up and down, betraying his nerves. "Fuck!"

"Decision time, asshole," Morales said.

I reached for the door handle. The sound of the mechanism clicking open lit a match under Harry's ass. "Close the fucking door and drive!" he shouted.

I froze and looked over my shoulder. "You sure?"

"I'll talk to the lawyer. Just fucking go!"

I glanced at Gardner. She nodded almost imperceptibly. I pulled the door closed, shocking the shit out of the kid who had almost reached my window. In no time, I had the car in gear and we squealed away from the curb, leaving a confused potion dealer empty-handed at the curb.

"You made the right choice, Mr. Bane," Gardner said to the now-dejected Harry.

"You are all going to fucking die."

I met Morales's gaze in the mirror again. He smiled, but it didn't reassure me. Because Harry hadn't just issued an idle threat. His words had sounded like a vow—or a curse.

# Chapter Twenty-Two

Later at the station, the door to the viewing room opened and Mez walked in. "What'd I miss?"

"Nothing," I said.

"Patience, Cupcake," Morales said. Mez shot us a speculative glance at the nickname. "Gardner's just warming up."

"Did Eldritch buy the story?" the wizard asked.

I glanced around to be sure no one was around but immediately felt ridiculous since we were in a closed room. "Kind of. He looked suspicious, but once Gardner handed over your DNA evidence he stopped asking too many questions." As part of the booking process, we'd gotten a swab of Harry's cheek for Mez to match against the sample he'd gotten off the cigarette. Some quick work on his part in the precinct lab proved without a doubt that Harry had been at the scene where Marvin's body was found.

In the interrogation room, Harry and his court-appointed lawyer—he'd refused to call his dad's lawyer, all things considered—sat at a table across from Gardner, Eldritch, and US

Attorney Aidan Stone. The latter looked to be in his mid-to-late thirties, but it was always hard to tell with lawyers, especially those who worked in the public sector. Most of the local DAs I met aged like dogs—for every year they'd served prosecuting the scum of the earth their faces aged seven. I suppose some women might call Stone handsome, with his salt-and-pepper hair and his piercing blue eyes, but I was too distracted worrying that Harry was going to change his mind to pay much attention.

"We're willing to offer you a reduced charge in exchange for information directly linking your father, Ramses Bane, to the cooking and distribution of Gray Wolf."

Harry's lawyer, a balding public defender by the name of Steve Spalding, dabbed at the sweat on his forehead. It wasn't every day that a low-level defender got the son of a coven leader as a client. Despite his obvious nerves, he didn't seem to have too much trouble keeping up. "What is the reduced charge?"

"We'll reduce the aiding-and-abetting charge to accessory-after-the-fact. Maximum sentence would be three years. Since Harry never has been convicted of a crime before, it'll likely be less. But he's looking at jail time either way—"

Harry blinked. "That's some bullshit."

Stone continued as if he hadn't spoken. "Unless he also agrees to testify against his father in court."

"Hell no! I'm already asking for a bullet just for talking to you people. I stand up in court and I'll be dead before I walk back out of the courtroom."

Stone had already anticipated Harry's being a dry snitch, so he didn't look too shocked by the refusal. "All we're asking today is that you provide information leading to your father's arrest in exchange for a reduced sentence."

"I don't want to spend three years in the can."

"Then I suppose you better be sure the information you give

us today is watertight," Eldritch said. At first he'd been pissed that Gardner got a drop on Harry, but once Gardner promised to give him the camera time when Bane was brought in, his disposition became downright generous.

"I don't know," Harry hemmed.

"Did we mention that while we were waiting for your attorney," Gardner said, "my agents took a closer look at your car? Imagine their lack of surprise when they found a hydraulic trap behind your expensive stereo system."

Harry jerked upright. "Yo, if they fucked up my ride, I'm gonna sue."

She reached in her pocket. "You might have trouble with that"—she laid the ampoule on the table that Morales and I had found in the hidden compartment—"seeing as how they found this."

Spalding snorted. "Please, do you know how easy it will be to prove my client uses that for medicinal purposes?"

"Why don't you tell your counselor what potion this is?" Gardner said to Harry.

He shrugged. "Just a blood potion."

"Tell him the street name."

"Ain't got a name."

Gardner made a show of flipping through a file folder. "That's interesting. According to the lab wizards, the potion found in Mr. Bane's car has chemical components consistent with a popular blood potion sold in the Arteries called Type X."

The attorney's expression remained impassive. "Never heard of it."

"It's for my anemia," Harry said quickly.

Gardner chuckled. "Sure."

"Agent, I suggest you get to the point." Spalding's tone was insulting.

Gardner smiled and leaned back. Harry kept his eyes glued on the ampoule. "My point, counselor"—her eyes were glued to Harry—"is in addition to the gun charge and evidence linking him to a murder, we have enough evidence here to link Mr. Bane to potion distribution."

The attorney laughed. "Based on an ounce? Please don't insult us. And as for the firearm, he has a permit. It also was stored safely in his glove box. That's not illegal."

"It is if the gun is loaded, counselor." She glanced down at the folder. "The firearm in question held four bullets."

Harry shot a glance at Spalding, who refused to look at him.

"In addition," she said, "we are working on a search warrant for Mr. Bane's residence."

After we'd found the ampoule, Gardner called Stone to set the warrant in motion. We were hoping we didn't need it if Harry started singing, but it was always good to have a backup plan.

"Go ahead," Harry said, bravado stamped on his face. "They won't find shit."

"My agents found the trap in your car, Harry," she shot back. "Do you really think they won't find the hidey-holes in the house, too?"

Harry paled. Spalding cleared his throat, a not-so-subtle reminder for Harry to shut the fuck up. "What information do you need on Bane to make this deal happen?"

"Hey!" Harry protested.

Spalding slanted him a look but nodded for Stone to go ahead. Morales shot me a grin. I couldn't see Gardner's face from my vantage point, but I imagined inside she was high-fiving herself.

"We need to know where Ramses is cooking the potion and the location of the stash."

"I don't know that shit," Harry said in a disgusted tone, but his words lacked conviction.

Spalding elbowed Harry. "If you could just give me a minute to discuss your offer with my client?"

Gardner, Eldritch, and Stone rose. "You have five minutes before this offer is off the table," the attorney said. "I'd advise you to take this deal, son. If you say no, you're going away for a very, very long, hard time."

♦ ♦ ♦

They joined us in the viewing room thirty seconds later.

"Think they'll go for it?" Eldritch asked before Stone could even take a breath.

"I sure as hell hope so." He raised his brows and sighed. "We're running out of time. The longer this takes the more likely it'll be for Bane to find out we're on his trail and close up shop."

"You didn't ask him who is helping Bane," I said.

Several pairs of eyes swiveled in my direction. "Why would we do that?" Eldritch snapped. "Bane is the big fish."

"But we know he couldn't have come up with Gray Wolf on his own. What if Volos—"

Eldritch waved a hand. "That again? Look, we know Bane is involved, we just need evidence linking him directly to the crime. Once we nab him, we can try to get him to confess who helped him come up with the formula, but most likely it was some desperate Votary wiz looking to make some quick cash."

I opened my mouth to keep arguing, but Gardner cleared her throat and shot me a look. Pushing Eldritch on this might hurt our chances of continued cooperation. But damned if I didn't feel like brushing Bane's alchemical accomplice to the back burner didn't worry the hell out of me.

Once I backed down, Gardner turned to Eldritch. "We need to have a team ready to go in."

Eldritch nodded. "It'll have to be in the morning."

"Why not tonight?" Morales asked.

"The Arteries are too dangerous at night," I explained. "Even for an army."

"Which is what we'll need," Eldritch said. "Those tunnels are ambushes waiting to happen. I'll call in a favor to the sheriff's office to lend us some of their tactical wizards."

"Once he gives us the location, I'll get the paperwork started for the no-knock warrant."

"How long will that take?" Mez asked.

"Usually not too long, but Judge Akins is on duty today."

"Who is that?" Morales asked.

Stone frowned. "They call him Judge Dread. Likes to watch harried attorneys jump through hoops."

"Just do what you can," Gardner said. "Morales, you and Prospero will need to take lead on our strategy for the raid."

"Now hold on," Eldritch cut in. "This will be a BPD operation."

Gardner raised a brow. "Bullshit. We brought you the evidence, the perp, and the deal that will secure the evidence we need to prove it's Bane."

Eldritch crossed his arms. "And you'll need BPD and county personnel to pull it off."

Gardner gritted her teeth. "I'll let you make the statement at the press conference once Bane's in custody."

Eldritch's mustache twitched as he considered the deal. Seeing the back-room negotiation for camera time left a bad taste in my mouth. "Fine," the captain said finally. "I also get to do the perp walk."

Gardner's eye twitched. "No dice. My bosses will want the MEA to get some camera time."

Eldritch shrugged. "Let's just say whichever agency nabs him gets to do the walk."

She nodded curtly. "Acceptable."

Stone made a world-weary face. "Now that that's settled, we just need to hope this little shit comes through."

As if Stone's words summoned him, Spalding rapped three times on the two-way mirror to indicate they were ready for us. Behind him, Harry slumped defeated at the table. Gardner smiled. "Shall we, gentlemen?"

◆ ◆ ◆

Ten minutes later, Harry was in cuffs and being led out of the room. Eldritch, Gardner, and Stone all shook hands with Spalding and then with each other.

Stone nodded. "I need to get back to my office to get the paperwork rolling. In the meantime, you can put him in lockup."

Morales, Mez, and I went into the hall to watch Harry be taken back to booking. "See ya around," I said as soon as Hanson led him past.

"The game's not over yet, bitch," Harry spat back.

I laughed. "Maybe, but you lost this round."

"True enough." Harry tilted his head and looked me straight in the eye. "But when the final buzzer rings, you'll be the one crying, bitch."

Hanson jerked his arms and pulled him away. "Let's go." Even though Hanson and I didn't get along as a rule, no cop liked to hear another one getting threatened.

As they walked away, Mez whistled under his breath. "Looks like you've got yourself a fan there."

I shrugged. "Harry's had it in for me since we were kids."

"Why?" Morales asked.

"Who knows?" I said with a casual indifference. But I was lying. I knew from an early age that Harry resented the fact that Abe was grooming me to take over the Votaries eventually, while Bane treated Harry like a nuisance or an errand boy. His jealousy had oxidized over time and added to the insult of being forced to betray his coven.

"Anyway," Morales said, not sounding very concerned or interested, "we need to get busy on a plan for tomorrow morning."

I sighed and nodded with a glance at my watch. It had already been five hours since I dropped Danny off to hang with Baba. "Would you guys mind meeting at my place?"

Morales frowned. "You worried about the kid?"

I nodded. "Baba's been known to doze off and I don't want to risk his sneaking out because I'm out late."

"Hey, that's cool," Mez said. "I'll call Shadi to come meet us." She was keeping an eye on the Arteries to make sure there weren't any signs of circling the wagons.

I gave Mez the address. He ran off so he could stop by the gym on the way over to get some files and supplies. After he was gone, Gardner came out of her meeting with the attorney and the captain. We told her the plan. Her eyes flared when she heard we were meeting at my house but she didn't comment. Instead, she said, "Don't fuck this up."

"Thanks for the encouragement," Morales responded drily.

Our boss crossed her arms and looked at both of us with an expression not unlike that of a general before a battle. "Encouragement implies failure's an option."

# Chapter Twenty-Three

When Morales and I got to the house, Danny came upstairs from his basement room looking like someone cancelled Christmas. "I thought you'd be working late."

"We are. We'll just be doing it from here." I held up the box of pizza we'd picked up. "Hungry?"

"No."

Shit, I thought. Teenagers never turn down pizza.

I turned to Morales. "Give me a minute, okay?"

He nodded and turned to chat up Baba. As I led Danny back down to his room, I heard the old lady say, "Uh-oh!" A thud followed—like the sound of a remote hitting the floor. "Would you be a dear and bend over to pick that up for me?" I shook my head and kept going. Morales didn't seem the type to need saving from geriatric sexual harassment.

"I thought you were gonna work," Danny complained as I pushed him toward his room.

I closed the door behind me before I spoke. "In a minute," I said, gathering my thoughts. "All right, so you want to learn magic. I get it, okay? But what you did today was not only incredibly stupid and the exact wrong way to get me to change my mind, it was also dangerous."

The way he jutted that stubborn chin out it might as well have been a middle finger.

"John Volos used to be your friend—"

"He was your friend, too, Kate."

I gritted my teeth and sighed. "Was, past tense. Now, he's a suspect in an investigation I'm working on."

Danny's eyes flared. "Really?"

I nodded. "And when you showed up at his apartment, you put both the case and my job at risk." I wasn't lying. At the time, that had been true. I didn't feel the need to tell Danny that Volos appeared to be innocent now. It worked in my favor for the kid to believe the worst about his former hero.

"I-I didn't know," he said.

"It never occurred to me that I'd need to warn you. But even if I wasn't investigating him, you should know better than to leave school grounds without permission so you can show up unannounced at a stranger's house."

"He's not a stranger!"

"Fine, but, Danny, you know John used to be wrapped up in dirty magic." Still was, probably, I amended silently. He might not be behind Gray Wolf, but I hadn't forgotten that he had imported a large amount of oil of rose quartz. Just because he hadn't committed the crime we suspected didn't mean he was innocent of all crime.

Danny crossed his arms. "You used to cook dirty, too, and you're a good person."

His logic made me press my lips together into a grimace. Damn kids and their ability to make things so simple. So black-and-white. "When you're older you'll thank me for looking out for you."

He snorted.

"Anyway," I said, "magic discussion aside, you'll be in detention after school for the next week for skipping school."

"Come on!" He threw up his hands.

I shrugged. "You should get on your knees and thank Pen for convincing them not to suspend you."

He sighed from deep in his lungs. "This really sucks."

"Could have been worse, kid," I said. I shuddered inwardly to think about how bad it could have been. He could have remembered that Ramses Bane was his godfather and gone to him instead.

"Whatever."

I clenched my fists and pasted a fake smile on my face. "All righty, then. I have to go plan a raid on the Arteries."

His face perked up. "No shit?"

I didn't even bother to correct his language. The curse jar was all the way upstairs, and, frankly, I was starting to wonder if the ban on cursing was more for his benefit or mine. "No shit."

"Will it be dangerous?"

I considered lying, but clearly my attempt to whitewash the darker aspects of my job had backfired big-time recently. "Yeah, but I'll be careful."

"Are you going to use any protective potions?"

I chewed on my lip and changed my mind about honesty. What Danny didn't know might save him lots of worry. "Sure," I said, "the MEA requires them."

He visibly relaxed. "All right. Good."

I nodded. "Good talk," I said awkwardly. "I'll, uh, leave you to your homework then."

"Hey, Kate?"

I paused. "Yeah?"

"You used to like magic, right?"

I paused. Not sure why the question caught me off guard. Maybe I'd spent so much time avoiding magic because it had caused so much pain. But he looked so open and honest, I couldn't wave off the question with a flippant response. "Yeah, I did like. A lot. Too much."

"Hmm," he said. "It's a shame then."

"What?"

"That you had to give up something you loved."

"Sometimes we love things that aren't good for us, Danny."

"I just—I wonder if things were different and you tried using magic to help people maybe you'd be happier."

Something bright and hot exploded behind my eyes. I don't want to call it an epiphany, but it was definitely one of those sharp moments that mark some significant shift in one's perception of the world. Problem was, I was wholly unprepared for it, and, besides, I had a kitchen full of cops who were waiting for me to help them plan a raid on people who used magic to hurt people.

"I, uh," I stammered, "yeah, I guess." I swallowed hard. An emotion I couldn't name was swelling in my chest and I suddenly felt ridiculously close to tears. "I need to get upstairs. Don't forget to do your—yeah, your homework and stuff." With that I exited as fast as possible, closing the door behind me. I leaned back against the painted surface and tried to catch my breath.

All this time, I thought I'd been a good role model. I'd tried my damnedest to give Danny a happy life. But to hear he saw me as an unhappy person felt as if someone had let all the helium out of my balloon. Not to mention, it never occurred to me to think of magic as something I had a choice in using for good or bad. I'd struggled so much with leaving the coven behind that I'd had to convince myself that being near any magic at all was like exposing myself to poison. Back then it was a matter of self-preservation. Still was. And when I'd decided to become a cop I figured it was a way to balance the scales. Erase all the bad stuff I'd done back in the day. Never once had I considered using magic to make amends.

I shook myself. It was ridiculous. Yeah, some people used magic to help others, but my addiction to cooking had come from a selfish place, not an altruistic one. Besides, I did plenty of good as a cop.

"Yo, Prospero?" Morales's voice called down the stairs.

"Yeah?"

"You got any beer in this joint?"

And with that, my brief existential crisis skidded to a halt. I didn't have time for what-ifs or some noble, happy life filled with aiding the downtrodden. I had a raid to plan and a dick partner who sounded like he was going to riot if I didn't make it Miller Time STAT.

♦ ♦ ♦

My kitchen was cramped for a preraid strategy session, but we made do. The blueprints of the Arteries that Shadi scored were spread across the table and held in place by a beer can on each corner.

"Harry said that Bane keeps the stash near his throne room—here," Morales was saying, pointing to the spot on the map. "Makes sense he'd want it close enough to monitor."

"Looks simple enough," Shadi said. "We'll only have to go down a couple of branches of the tunnels to reach it."

"Navigating won't be the problem," I said.

"What will be?" Mez asked.

"Getting to it before Bane's Sentinels can destroy the evidence."

"What's a Sentinel?" Shadi asked.

"Bane's blood fiends," I said. "He pays for their loyalty with blood potions. One or two won't be a big deal. But he'll have several guarding the stash and more on the lookout for intruders."

"Not to mention," Morales added, "he might have some ass-holes hopped-up on Gray Wolf waiting for us."

"Which means we'll need major firepower," I said.

"Not a problem." Shadi smiled. "I'll take lead on ammo and hardware."

Morales turned to Mez. "And we'll need you to bring some magical weapons, too."

The wizard rubbed his hands together. "Excellent. I've been wanting to try this new potion bomb I developed. Causes paralysis and temporary blindness."

"Remind me never to piss you off, Mez," I said. He winked at me.

"All right, so the plan is to go in with the tactical wizards, make sure they have the main tunnel under control, and then split off to find Bane and his cache."

"He'll know we're there the instant we breach the tunnel," I warned. "Probably has an emergency escape route, too."

"Eldritch will post cops at every exit. Gardner will make sure of it if Eldritch doesn't."

"And if he has a secret tunnel or something?" Shadi asked. "Do we chase?"

"Gardner said our goal is to find the stash. That way even if Bane slips away we'll at least have the evidence we need to charge him."

"Okay," Morales said. "Shadi, let's go over weapons."

"Prospero?" she said. "You got any experience with assault rifles?"

I grimaced. "Yes." My mind went back to that day at the academy where I managed to take out the lighting system on the target rig when recoil knocked me on my ass. "None of it good."

"Really? Hmm. There's really nothing like the kick of a Colt in your hands."

"I'm more comfortable with a Glock and a salt flare."

"We'll have to work on that. Maybe hit the range together so I can give you some pointers." She pursed her lips. "In the meantime, Morales and I will lead the charge. You two will have our backs. You with your Glock and Mez with his potions."

I smiled. Not because I was looking forward to shooting anyone, but because her offer to take me to the range meant she considered me part of the team—one who might be sticking around for a while.

"Okay," Morales said. "We're supposed to meet up with Eldritch and the raid team at oh-nine-hundred. Shadi and Mez, go to the gym and make sure we have everything we need. Then try to get some sleep."

They stood and gathered their things, chattering excitedly about how tomorrow we'd finally blow this case wide open. Morales, though, didn't look excited as much as resigned. After Shadi and Mez left, he hung back a second. "I need to talk to you about something."

I stuck my hands in my pockets. "What's up?"

"I didn't want to talk about this in front of everyone else because I know it's a sensitive topic for you."

I frowned. "Okay."

"Defensive potions are required of all officers taking part in the raid."

I opened my mouth to argue, but he held up a hand.

"That's handed down from both Gardner and Eldritch. No patch, no play."

My shoulders drooped.

"I know how you feel about using magic, so I figured I'd talk to you about it now. If you throw a shit fit in front of Eldritch about it, Gardner will cut you from the case. Period. So make your decision now."

"I'll have my wand and salt flare, and I'll be wearing a ballistics vest with salt slabs. Isn't that enough?"

He shook his head. "This isn't a traffic stop, Prospero. Raids are no joke. It's going to be chaos down there and we can't chance you getting hit with a potion from one of Bane's people. If you go down, it'll put all of us in danger."

I knew he was right. If I got hit, he and the rest of the team would be too distracted trying to render aid to complete the mission. Also if I got separated from the team, they'd risk valuable minutes trying to locate me. So I couldn't blame Gardner or Eldritch for requiring the potion for all the cops involved. But that left me with either sitting out and depriving my team of the extra manpower or compromising my principles for the job.

"If it's any consolation, Gardner said that she's really pleased with your contributions to the team. If we're successful tomorrow, it will ensure the MEA giving the green light on us having a more permanent presence in the Cauldron. And that would mean a spot for you, too. Isn't that what you want?"

"Of course that's what I want," I said, raising my hands. "But how would you feel if the MEA required you to do something you didn't feel comfortable with to get the job done?"

He laughed as if I'd made a joke. "Sooner or later, we're all asked to do something we don't want to do, Cupcake." His ironic tone hinted it was a more common than an every-now-and-then thing. "Why did you become a cop?"

I tilted my head. "What do you mean?"

"I mean, just walking away from your coven would have been enough. But you walked away and became a cop. Why?"

I wasn't about to get into my mother's death or how being a cop was a form of penance, so I just shrugged. "I guess I thought I'd see how the other half lived."

He shot me a look that told me bullshit wasn't going to cut it.

I sighed. "Fine. I decided to go to the academy because after so many years of being part of the problem I guess I wanted to make a difference."

"Did you feel like you were making a difference on patrol?"

"Not enough of one," I said honestly. He'd smell the lie anyway. "That's why I talked my way onto the task force."

"Because you wanted to go after the source of the magic?"

I nodded.

"Well, this is your chance. Do you really want to blow it because you're afraid to wear a stupid protection patch?"

I raised my chin. "I'm not afraid."

"Really?"

"Yeah." I almost believed it, too. "I'm just worried it's a slippery slope. Today it's a simple protection spell. What about next month when Gardner wants me to go undercover and I have to use a glamour potion? Or next year when she asks me to cook because Mez needs help?"

"You'll have to take it as it comes, I guess," he said. "For the record, I think you're making a mistake if you walk away from this. You're a good cop, and anyone can tell how much you care about this city. Don't let your pride stop you."

I crossed my arms and chewed on my bottom lip, thinking it over. If I said no, I'd be put back on patrol once the paperwork clearing me of the Harkins shooting came through. That would mean endless nights trolling the streets for low-level pushers while wizards like Bane and Volos got away with murder—both figuratively and literally. Was I really willing to walk away from the real game? Go back to arresting the same junkies over and over while the real criminals lived it up?

I stood straighter. "No," I said. Morales's eyebrows slammed down and disappointment washed over his face. I held up a hand. "No, I'm not going to walk away. I'll wear the patch. Just this once."

A brilliant smile lit up his handsome face. " 'Atta girl."

# Chapter Twenty-Four

I woke up the next morning on a gasp. The dream I'd been having clung to my subconscious with razor claws, but I couldn't remember the details. All I knew was my skin was coated in sweat and my limbs were sore as if I'd been fighting.

The blue lines on the clock slowly focused to form a seven and two zeroes. I briefly considered trying to go back to sleep, but Danny would be up for school soon and I didn't want to miss the chance to see him off. With a sigh, I scrubbed my hand over my face and rose to confront the day. I threw on my ratty robe and walked into the kitchen.

Danny wasn't up yet, so I started pulling out the eggs. As I did, I noticed the pile of mail that I'd tossed on the counter yesterday when I'd arrived with Morales. I flipped through quickly, ignoring the junk mail and bills in favor of a single red envelope, which stuck out from the bottom of the stack like a wound.

It was addressed to Danny in a neat hand. Probably a birthday card. But something about the carefully lettered words made my sensors flare up. I flipped over the card to see the return address and froze. Crowley Penitentiary.

I didn't hesitate to tear it open. It was a greeting card with a birthday cake on the front. Inside, the preprinted message said simply, "Happy Birthday!" But the handwritten note made my blood go cold.

> *Danny Boy—*
>
> *Happy sixteenth birthday! My greatest regret is that I was unable to watch you grow into a man. Maybe one day you can come visit me and we can talk about magic. Has your sister started your lessons? Perhaps not. Regardless, I hope your next year is a good one.*
>
> *—Uncle Abe*

I tore the card up with slow, methodical movements. Tore the pieces so small that even I didn't recognize the fragments of ink-marked shards as parts of words. Once that was done, I placed the pile at the bottom of the kitchen trash can. Then I gathered the bag, tied it closed, and set it outside the back door.

After washing my hands, I continued to gather the ingredients I needed to make breakfast. The Mundane task felt normal and right. It helped me ignore the nausea in my gut, the residue of fear that Danny might have found that card before I had a chance to dispose of it. But I tried to remind myself that this time, like all the others, I'd managed to keep Danny from knowing that his Uncle Abe had been reaching out to him on his birthday every year for the last ten. And if I had my way, he never would.

Over the years I'd tried to convince myself that I hid the cards to protect Danny. But the truth was, I was also protecting myself. Hatred was an easier emotion to live with than fear. As long as I could keep Abe far from us both physically and emotionally, I could go on loathing him. But if Uncle Abe somehow managed to get a fingerhold in our lives, I would suddenly be thrust from anger's warm embrace into the frigid waters of fear. Fear that he'd woo Danny into cooking dirty. Fear that he'd take Danny away from me. But most of all, I was afraid that if he came back into my life, he'd be able to pull me back into the place I'd run from all those years ago. Maybe it was silly to credit him with so much power and myself with so little, but it seemed downright stupid to chance it and give him the opportunity to try. So I'd go on intercepting those cards and doing everything in my power to keep him well away from both of us.

By the time Danny joined me, the room was filled with sizzling sounds and the smoky aroma of cooked bacon. His sneakers squeaked against the faded linoleum floor.

I turned to see him frozen in the doorway. "Oh God," he said. "Who died?"

My eyebrows slammed down. "What?"

He nodded to the stove. "The only time you cook breakfast for me is when there's bad news."

I dismissed his concern with a wave of the spatula. "Not this time." I jerked a thumb toward the fridge. "Get the OJ, will ya?"

He shot me a dubious look before he shuffled to grab the juice. Once he'd set it on the table, he said, "So...you going to tell me why you're suddenly pretending to be June Cleaver?"

I sighed and turned to face him. "All right. I guess I felt bad that we fought on your birthday yesterday." I picked up a strip of bacon I'd already cooked and offered it to him.

"So...what?" He took the bacon. "You're bribing me with pork?"

I nodded. "Pretty much."

He raised it to his mouth and chomped a large bite. "Works for me."

I smiled at him, realizing suddenly that I was looking up at him. When had that happened? He used to be the kid who clung to my knee and now he was almost a full head taller.

I turned away quickly so he wouldn't see the tears that suddenly threatened to give me away. I hadn't been lying when I told him breakfast was a makeup birthday peace offering. But it hadn't been the whole truth, either.

"So what do you have going on at school today?" I asked.

The sounds of the silverware drawer opening and shutting told me he was setting the table without being asked for once. I'd bribed him with bacon, and he was responding by being helpful. I could get used to this quid pro quo.

"Not much," he said. "There's some assembly this morning."

"About what?"

"Oh, you know, one of those Just Say No to Magic programs."

I stopped and looked at him. "Really?"

He nodded. "Guess after what happened to that one kid in the lower school, they're cramming the antipotion campaign down our throats." From the look in his eye, he expected me to launch into another lecture about the dangers of magic. My conscience prickled because it had been a couple of days since I'd talked to Pen about anything other than my own problems. No doubt she was hurting over that kid's death, but here I was calling her for favors to save my brother from suspension. Yet another personal thread that ended up neglected because of the job.

"All right," I said instead. "Sit down and eat before this gets cold."

He did as instructed, but before he dug in he stopped and

looked at me. Really looked, as if he was seeing me as a real human instead of the harpy who made him do his homework every night. "Look, I—I know I give you a tough time a lot."

I opened my mouth to dismiss it, but he held up a hand.

"Let me finish."

I sat back and nodded.

"But I just want you to know that I get how hard you try. You know, to raise me and stuff. I'm sorry I've been a jerk lately, it's just"—he sighed and shrugged—"I don't know. It's just becoming more and more clear that I'm different from the other kids."

I tilted my head. "How?"

He raised his left hand, which held his fork. "This for one thing. I'm one of the few Lefties at school. I might as well be wearing a sign that says 'Freak' on my back, you know? But I'm a freak to the Adepts, too, because I'm not allowed to touch magic."

"Look, I know it's not easy, but kids your age? They jump on anything that's different. In my school, where most everyone was Adept, they picked on the only kid with red hair. It has nothing to do with magic and everything to do with kids needing to persecute others to make their own insecurities less painful."

His lips quirked. "You've been hanging out with Pen too long."

"It's true." I laughed. "But she's pretty smart."

He nodded. "Yeah, she basically said the same thing when I told her."

My chest tightened. How many other issues had Danny gone to her with first because I was working? Or because he thought I wouldn't listen? I reached across the table and grabbed his left with my left. "We're Adepts, sure, but that's just genetics. Same as your blue eyes or the color of your hair. Your choices make you who you really are." I paused to let that sink in. "When I was young, I didn't have a choice. Cooking potions was expected of me and I went along because I didn't know any better."

"But don't you see? You've dictated a magic-free path for me, so I don't have a choice, either."

His words were like a bucket of ice water waking me from a deep sleep. I'd been telling myself I was doing right by him to forbid magic. Instead, I'd managed only to drive a wedge between us. Danny and I were on the other side of the same fucked-up coin Uncle Abe had used to control me. And for the first time, I felt deep in my gut that if I continued to forbid Danny I would lose him—just as Abe had lost me.

"Okay. I get it." I swallowed the lump of fear in my throat. "Maybe later we can go through the boxes in the attic together. You at least deserve to know more about where you come from. If you still want to learn about magic once you learn what it did to our family"—I took a deep breath, as if I were about to jump off a cliff into deep, dangerous waters—"I won't stop you."

His eyes widened. "Really?"

I nodded because I couldn't trust myself to speak.

He jumped out of his chair and came to hug me. In his excitement he didn't notice the stiffness of my limbs. Worry made my chest ache. I closed my eyes and tried to absorb some of his happiness into my skin.

He pulled away too quickly. Before I felt any better. Before I was ready to let go and head out to face Bane. Before I could pretend I wasn't making a huge mistake.

"There's something else," I said, removing the small box from the pocket of my robe. I set it on the table. The simple brown paper wrapping looked so unexciting on the white tablecloth. I suddenly was afraid he'd find the contents unexciting, too, but it was too late to take it back and give him some electronic gizmo instead.

He paused and stared at it. "What's that?"

"Happy birthday, Danny." I nodded at the box. "Open it."

He smiled self-consciously, an expression that took years off his face. His fingers fumbled with the paper, but soon enough he pulled the lid off the box and tossed the cotton square aside. Then he stared into the box with a face I couldn't read for a good, long time. "Was it hers?" he whispered finally.

I licked my lips. "Passed down from her father. She told me once she always intended to give it to you once you were old enough."

When he finally looked up, his eyes were shiny and red-rimmed. "Does it work?" He lifted the pocket watch from its cotton cocoon and raised it to his ear. Hearing nothing, he pulled it away and gazed at the surface of the clock with the blue-enameled night sky and smirking moon.

"We could take it to a shop to have it repaired if you want."

He shook his head. "I can use my phone to tell time," he said. "But I'll keep it with me—for good luck." He smiled at me. "Thanks, Kate. This means a lot to me."

I swallowed hard against the emotion stinging in my throat. "No sweat, kid. I lo—"

A horn sounded from outside. Danny had told me his friend Aaron was driving him that morning because Pen had to be at the school early for a meeting with the principal. The sound shattered the insulating silence that had protected us for a few moments from the outside world. Danny jerked his head to look out the window. "Gotta go!" He grabbed his backpack and leaped out of his seat, shoving the watch into his jeans pocket.

"Wait!" I got out of my seat. With my napkin, I wiped a smear of bacon grease from his chin.

His smile transformed his face from boyish to almost-mannish. On impulse, I grabbed him and pulled him in hard for another hug. This time, I didn't let go until I was good and ready.

"Um, Katie?"

The horn honked again.

"Just one more second," I said, closing my eyes. He smelled like cologne and bacon. I suddenly wanted to tell him to skip school. That I'd unplug the phone, lock the doors, and pretend I didn't have to be anywhere. We could spend the day watching old movies and eating popcorn. And then, after Gardner called to tell me I was fired, I'd pack our things and we'd move far away. Somewhere that didn't have a dirty magic problem. A deserted island or the frozen tundra—anywhere I could protect Danny from the world twenty-four/seven.

The horn honked again. This time the sound was more insistent, angry.

"Kate," he said, "I really gotta go." Danny pulled back, extricating himself from my clinging arms. He looked down at me. "You okay?"

I nodded and widened my too-dry eyes to add credence to the lie. "Just feeling sentimental."

He laughed. "Since when?"

I forced a smile. "Since now." I swatted his arm. "Better go before Aaron storms the house."

"Thanks again for the watch!" He waved and headed toward the door. "Have a good one!"

"You, too," I said weakly. "Be careful."

"I'm just going to school, Katie." He stopped and looked back at me. "You're the one who needs to be careful."

That comment combined with the worry in his eyes told me he knew the score. There was no point trying to reassure him. He knew my job was dangerous. "True enough, kid." I forced a smile. "Now get out of here."

With that he waved and disappeared out the front door. I looked around the kitchen, which seemed so barren without his youthful energy filling it up. Then I shook myself and went to prepare for the raid.

# Chapter Twenty-Five

The sun stabbed the eastern horizon, painting it caution-yellow and bloodred. The assault teams moved in two groups like flocks of heavily armed crows. Our team joined four tactical wizards called in from the county sheriff's office and two BPD guys to attack the main gate of the tunnels. Another team of ten would attack from another entrance and meet us somewhere in the middle of the labyrinth.

As our feet moved silently across the barren lot, Eldritch issued last-minute warnings through our earpieces. My heart thumped like a wild thing under my ballistics vest. The patch Mez had given me when we suited up burned on my arm like hellfire. He'd said the potion was one that would increase my stamina and speed, as well as allow my team to track me if we got separated. All good things, but I still felt off balance and nauseous with it against my skin.

Closer now, almost there.

To the right of the gate, the bright-white sign announcing Volos's ground-breaking ceremony in four days mocked me. I dragged my gaze from it and counted each step to maintain my calm.

Morales and Shadi were in front of me carrying large assault rifles. Mez was to my right. He wore the same black uniform as the rest of us, with his dreads tucked under the helmet. But unlike the rest of us, he also had a bandolier loaded down with potions strapped to his chest. I had a Glock .22, two salt flare guns, two canisters of S&P spray, and a ton of adrenaline ready to go.

Morales would act as the ram man for the raid. In his right hand he carried a large metal cylinder by the handle. When we finally reached the gate, Shadi stepped to one side and one of the other tactical wizards, a large guy they called Diesel, took the other with their guns at the ready.

Morales stepped forward with the ram. He did a quick scan of the team. "On three," he whispered.

I pulled my Glock from the holster and blew out a deep breath. Morales counted.

"One." He stepped forward.

"Two." Pulled the ram backward. Muscles strained for action.

"Three." The ram crashed into the gate. Metal shrieked and surrendered.

Shadi and Diesel rushed forward into the tunnels. Morales stood to the side while the rest of us hurried in. I moved with the tide, yelling along with the rest of them. Morales fell in behind me, his shouts joining mine.

There were two rules about entering the tunnels. First, never, ever go without backup. Second, only the suicidal enter the tunnels after sundown. Night belonged to the blood fiends.

The instant we spilled through the entrance, the stench of shit and stale urine, the tinny bite of blood, and the noxious odor of decomposition bodychecked us. Somewhere inside the fetid slurry was the less disgusting, but no less menacing, scent of ozone that indicated heavy magic use.

"Jesus," said Morales.

I handed him a tube of menthol spray. "This won't help much."

He shot me a look. "Then why bother?"

I shrugged. "Better than nothing." I rubbed absently at the patch on my arm, which bothered me more than the disgusting scene we'd entered.

I figured Morales would take three steps down and lose his lunch all over the place. But when he didn't pause or gasp or bitch, just simply forged ahead like a man pushing his way through a particularly foul windstorm, I grudgingly admitted to myself that maybe some of his swagger was warranted.

The other cops, however, hadn't fared so well. No one vomited, but their movements weren't as assured as they'd been in the fresh air. I caught up with Mez and tried to hand him the menthol. He smiled and shook his head. "Already ahead of you." He pulled nose plugs from his nostrils. "They're filled with menthol and I took a tincture of ginger before I came."

I shook my head at him. He really was good.

"Hand that shit over," Shadi said, grabbing the tube from me. "Damn!" She didn't look upset as much as angry that her concentration was being compromised. But once she squirted the spray, she threw it back at me and didn't mention the stench again.

Only seasoned officers could handle this kind of vulgar scene. When I'd run into my first putrefied body years earlier, I'd puked until I felt as if I'd left my stomach lining on the pavement. Took me a couple of years before I could be around the sickly sweet scent of death without my stomach's revolting.

It's not that I didn't still smell it, just that my body had lost that self-protective instinct to avoid rot and decay. So, like my grim-faced team, I put my disgust on the back burner and moved forward into the dark, yawning mouth of the Arteries.

I pulled a glow rod from my belt. Unlike a flashlight that would take up a valuable hand, this could be attached by a car-abiner to my belt loop and provide a large halo of light around the immediate area. Unfortunately it would also make a very large target for the fiends, but since they tended to avoid bright lights, they'd give us a wide berth.

Once we reached the bottom of the staircase to the main tunnel, the light revealed the dump that the tunnels had become. A repository for used condoms, empty potion vials, dead rodents, and discarded self-respect. A fucking still life depicting the most savage sides of humanity.

"Charming." Morales kicked aside a discarded baby carriage filled with doll parts and hypodermic needles.

"Which way?" Diesel asked.

"Through this area, there's a clearing with a four-way fork." Even though I was speaking in a low voice, my words echoed off the damp walls. "We'll probably run into some hexheads, so be ready."

I used my free hand to scratch the patch again. Fucking Mez with his "slight burning sensation." It felt as if the damned thing was eating through my skin. I glanced up at the rest of the team, but everyone's eyes were too busy scanning the imme-diate area for threats to pay attention to my moral dilemma. I took two seconds to make the decision.

The industrial adhesive ripped the first couple of layers of skin off, but at least the burning stopped. I dropped the patch without a second thought and moved on. I didn't need magic patches to deal with Bane—just my wits.

When I looked up, Morales was watching me. I froze. If he called me on taking off the patch, Gardner and everyone else listening in would hear. But he surprised me by tilting his chin down to acknowledge he wouldn't rat on me. It made me uncomfortable, though, for him to have something to hold over my head.

Once we passed through into the platform with four forks, our lights flashed off flailing limbs as junkies scattered like cockroaches. I hurdled over an overturned grocery cart and tackled a male who was running deeper into the tunnels. My body slammed into his and he came down hard on the concrete, breaking my fall. "MEA! Hands where I can see them."

He went limp. Scabs covered his arms and he stunk of shit. Suddenly glad I'd worn gloves, I made quick work of cuffing him with a zip tie. Once he was secure, I dragged him over to a wall where the others were lining up those they'd collared. "Stay," I ordered.

He lowered his head and huddled into himself. It had been so easy, I found myself disappointed. All the adrenaline pulsing through me demanded action. I turned to find some.

It didn't take long.

Not ten feet away, Morales and Shadi were grappling with a pack of junkies whose addled brains told them it was a great idea to fight back. I rushed forward, pulling my hawthornwood nightstick from my belt.

I arrived just as one of the junkies raised a bat toward Shadi's exposed back. I stashed the gun and took him out at the knees with the wand. He screamed and crumpled, his hands grasping at his right knee. Before I could follow up, a chick with rotten teeth and wild hair ran at me screaming like a banshee. I smiled and wound up. The stick hit her square in the diaphragm. The air escaped her lungs in a whoosh and her eyes bugged out.

I wasn't sure what potion she was on, but it totally overrode her pain receptors. She recovered quickly from the lack of oxygen and came up scratching. I grabbed the S&P spray and pressed the button about two inches from her face. She collapsed in a pile of snot, tears, and pitiful mewling.

While I'd been working, Morales managed to take down three junkies of his own. He had them lined up in a neat row of angst. Shadi had bagged one herself—a hulk of a man who looked like a kicked puppy in his cuffs.

A quick scan of that part of the tunnel told me we'd managed to secure the spot. Morales punched the button on his vest. "This is Morales. We got ten tied up near the entrance for processing."

While he spoke, I got my two cuffed where they lay.

"Good work, Agent Morales," Gardner responded. "Proceed as we discussed."

"Roger that."

Morales turned to the team. "All right, you stay here until backup arrives to collect these guys," he said to the two patrolmen. "You four take the tunnel to the right," he said to Diesel and the other three tac wizards. They nodded and started out. "The rest come with me on the left," he said to Shadi, Mez, and me.

Shadi shot me a smile as we fell in behind Morales. "Fun, right?" she said, sounding as if we were playing paintball instead of raiding the lair of a violent coven.

I realized with a start I was kind of enjoying myself, too. Whatever Mez put in those patches was still working with my adrenaline to improve my stamina. I'd just taken down three perps but I was barely winded. Part of me felt guilty because I shouldn't have been using a potion to begin with, but another part of me—one long forgotten—was getting off on the feeling of power. It was hard to feel bad with the adrenaline and magic giving me such a buzz. Besides, it wouldn't last long since I'd removed the damned thing.

"Prospero?" Morales called. "Let's go!"

Once we entered the mouth of the tunnel, we paused to regroup. "All right," Morales said to our huddle, "be ready. The Sentinels probably heard us coming and may be waiting to ambush. Mez, get those potion bombs ready."

"Already ahead of you." He held something in his hand. He shoved a second one in my left. "If you see any movement, pull the pin and lob this at them."

The metal orb felt heavy in my hand. I raised it to my helmet light for a better look. It had a tab at the top. Like a grenade.

"Just be sure you're at least twenty feet back," he added, "or you might get some of the blowback. Wait thirty seconds. When the screams stop, it's safe."

I swallowed and shoved it in the breast pocket of my vest, hoping I wouldn't have to use it.

"Shadi and I will take point. Prospero, be ready to provide cover."

I nodded and removed my Glock from my belt. "Ready."

"Move out." Morales and Shadi took off at a jog. Mez shot me a here-goes-nothing-look and together we took off after them.

This section of tunnel was enclosed, like a large concrete pipe. Our boots splashed through puddles of liquids best left unexamined. Every now and then, an echo would carry down to us from clashes the other cops were having in other parts of the tunnels. But our path remained unobstructed except for piles of trash.

Eventually, we came to a spot where the pipe opened up to the platform. A throne made from an old armchair, tires, and two rusty bumpers sat empty in the dark. Morales put a fist up to indicate we should halt. Then he slowly worked his way to the lip of the tunnel. We'd all turned off our lights, so we couldn't see much besides vague shadows. The only sound was my heartbeat thumping in my ears and the sound of air scraping in and out of my lungs.

My instincts prickled with something that felt a lot like alarm. It took me a minute to pinpoint the source of my unease. "Guys, this feels wrong," I said. "Why haven't we run into anyone else yet?"

Shadi shrugged. "Maybe they're all asleep."

It was true that blood fiends tended to be nocturnal, but it still felt off. Wouldn't Bane have Sentinels set up at intervals?

Morales made a hand signal to move in. He and Shadi moved forward to check the area. Finally, I heard a whispered "Clear" from Shadi, followed soon by another from Morales. They jumped back down to join us.

"Okay, the area we believe to hold the stash is probably three hundred yards farther. That's probably where we'll find the guards. Be ready to go in hot and fast."

Morales gave the signal to head out. This section of the tunnel had several niches set into the walls, which meant each had to be cleared, making our progress slow.

Finally, up ahead, the light looked different as we approached another train platform.

"Cover me," Morales whispered. I crouched down by one wall and Shadi took the opposite. With each step he took, I scooted forward a bit. Behind us, Mez readied his potion bombs.

When we'd studied the blueprints, we discovered this platform was different from the other because it held a large room originally designed to be an electrical shed. We figured it was the most likely place for the stash since it had a door Bane could lock and guard.

"Clear." Once Morales called to us, we all climbed the platform.

Once again, my alarms started buzzing. "Guys, something's really wrong here." Where were all the Sentinels?

The door was maybe fifteen feet away. The area in front of it was covered in trash, just like the rest of the tunnels. I shined my light around and froze when it hit the ceiling. Over our heads, someone had spent some time creating a spray-painted masterpiece.

"Uh-oh."

"What?" Morales hissed. He was approaching the door but stopped when I spoke.

I pointed up and everyone stopped to look. "I think someone's trying to tell us something."

"It's a lizard eating a pig—so what?" Shadi said.

"That's a red dragon," I corrected. "The symbol of Bane's coven. Anyone want to take a wild guess at what the pig might represent?"

"That could have been done anytime." Morales narrowed his eyes as he studied it. "It's certainly not the first graffiti we've seen down here."

"Yes, but it's the first we've seen outside a stash room that is conspicuously free of guards," Mez said. "What if it's a message?"

Morales raised his gun and turned back toward the door. "Only one way to find out."

The wizard and I exchanged a tense look. Finally, he shrugged and pulled a potion bomb from his bandolier just in case. "Here goes nothing."

Since Morales had left the ram near the entrance of the

Arteries because of its weight, he had to open the door the old-fashioned way.

"Step back," he warned. Two seconds later, he raised his weapon and shot the lock. Sparks flashed off the metal door, which now sported jagged bullet holes. When no one fired back through the door or threw it open to engage, he started ramming the thing with his shoulder.

While he punished the door for existing, Shadi stood nearby with her rifle. Mez and I hung farther back, offering additional cover.

Soon the door surrendered and flew open. Morales dropped into a crouch and aimed his weapon into the dark room. Shadi went forward, shining her light inside. I couldn't see past either of them but moved ahead just in case things got spicy.

"What's that?" Morales called. "Get the lights!"

A split second later, Shadi flipped the switch and light spilled out of the room to create a pool on the platform.

"Shit!" Shadi called.

"Prospero, Mez—get in here!"

My heart started running before my feet did. The short distance separating us felt like miles instead of yards. When I skidded to a halt inside the room, Morales was squatting next to something. Shadi was in my way so I couldn't see what. There was no doubt we'd found where they'd kept the stash. The scent of ozone permeated the concrete and made my lungs feel clogged with dust.

"What's wrong?" Behind me, I heard Mez echo my question.

Morales didn't say anything, just looked at me with a grim expression that made my bowels feel watery. His finger pointed to the only item in the room—an empty, upturned crate. A piece of paper lay in the center.

"What's it say?"

Morales lifted it, read it, and then passed it over with a grim expression.

The words were written in dark red—blood, probably. "Behold, I send you forth as sheep in the midst of wolves."

"What the hell?" Mez asked.

"Not often you hear a wizard quote the Bible," Morales said, his jaw tight.

"How the fuck did he know we were coming?" I said.

"Let's figure that out once we get the hell out of here," Shadi said.

Morales punched the comm button on his vest. As soon as he finished filling in the commanders at the other end, shouted curses crackled into all of our ears.

"Goddamn it, Morales. Get your team out of there, STAT."

"Yes, sir," he said. I was glad he didn't argue. Lord only knew what other surprises Bane had stashed in those tunnels for us. We exited the room and gathered on the old platform to regroup.

But before we made it more than twenty feet, high-pitched howls shattered the silence. It was the kind of sound that made you believe in the existence of the devil. It was not the clicking sounds of Sentinels. It was the howls of Gray Wolf freaks. A lot of them, too, judging by the echoes.

My courage shriveled inside my skin. I could practically see the hackles rise on the back of Morales's neck. "What the fuck?" His tone wasn't frightened so much as pissed off.

In the silence, Shadi cocked her assault rifle with an ominous metallic crack. A smile spread across her dark face and for a moment I wondered whether the addicts were the ones who should worry.

I'd learned from experience that Gray Wolf users enjoyed human flesh, but they also fed off fear. They sipped it from the air like a fine wine, savoring the taste of terror. I couldn't count how many of them were howling from the tunnels. Hell, I couldn't even tell which tunnels they were coming from. But I knew we were outnumbered.

Morales shot me a look as he removed a second weapon from his hip holster. I didn't bother telling him that Mundane bullets were as effective on a pack of blood fiends as a pellet gun was against a herd of bulls. I trusted that he was smart enough to heed my warning about playing this carefully. In truth, my heart had started doing a tap dance against my ribs the minute I heard the first howl.

"Prospero?" Mez this time. He sounded less sure of himself than the other two, but I guess that was to be expected from someone who spent most of his time tinkering with beakers.

"Stay calm. They're trying to make us run." Wolves loved to play chase. "Hold your ground and they'll eventually come to us."

The howling went on for what felt like hours. There's this weird effect after you listen to feral beasts snarl at you long enough. At first it's easy to remind yourself that it's a trick, a ruse to scare you. But after a while, with the stink of shit and blood and the darkness and the shrill sound of their prey calls, it's easy to forget to be brave.

Despite my sweaty palms and the nagging stab at the base of my skull urging me to freak the fuck out, I planted my feet and focused on breathing slowly through my mouth. I could practically feel Morales's heart pounding against the walls. A fine sheen of sweat glistened on his forehead and his jaw clenched even as he hunkered into his fighting stance.

Finally, the menacing howls got too close and the first shadows moved into my line of sight. They were technically human, in that they had two arms, two legs, one head, etc. But the minute the potion hooked its claws in them it transformed the appendages—elongated them, curled them, sharpened them.

Fingers had become claws with long, yellowed nails caked with blood. Lips curled back to reveal canines, like daggers in the mouth. Ears grew and morphed into the highly advanced listening tubes of a predator. Backs bent to make running on all fours an option—the sound of claws scuttling against concrete was almost as spine-tingling as the howls. But what made my skin prickle were the glittering shards of yellow slashing through the darkness.

When I'd faced Harkins I learned firsthand how strong Gray Wolf made an addict. Now my team faced a whole pack of them.

"How many potion bombs do we have?" Morales asked.

"A few, but they're too close." Mez shook his head. "We can't risk one hitting us, too. I do have two knockout potions, though."

"Two won't get us very far." Morales punched a new cartridge into his rifle. "We shoot to kill."

Several more howls echoed from the darkness. My heart slammed against my ribs. One second we were surrounded by shadows and the stench of garbage. The next a group of monsters with fangs and claws and yellow eyes emerged from the dark like beasts straight out of hell.

They came at us hard. Chaos in motion. Leaping up off the tracks as if they'd been catapulted. We barely had time to point our weapons before the first wave attacked.

One landed almost on top of me. He came at me snarling, but my Glock was hot for action. The bullet ripped a path through his eye socket and made itself at home in his brain. His momentum carried him forward. Slammed me back against the concrete wall. The last gasp of breath escaped his mouth with the scent of blood and rot.

He collapsed to the ground in a twitching heap. But before I could catch my breath, three more monsters replaced him.

I shot one in the face. Pivoted. Used my right forearm to

ward off the snapping teeth of another. With my free hand, I removed the salt flare from my left side. Slammed it up under the asshole's chin and fired. The surface of his face exfoliated into one large wound. His screams pierced my eardrums and crawled inside my chest. I needed to finish him, but before I could, two strong hands grabbed my arms from behind.

I didn't have to think about my next move. On autopilot, I slammed my head back and punched my heel down into the soft instep of my attacker. The hands didn't ease up and no yelps of pain escaped him. But my scalp stung as if I'd hit a couple of teeth, so I knew I'd clocked him good.

I threw my weight forward, going limp. Slid out of his arms and swiveled so I landed on my back. The instant I made contact with the floor, I pulled the trigger. The bullet ripped through his chest, just to the left of his breastbone. The fiend shrieked in rage and lunged toward me. The second bullet finally brought him down after it tore through his esophagus. His weight landed on top of me like a sack of anvils. I kicked him off me and rolled.

Other gunshots cracked off the walls and pounded against my eardrums. I squinted through the dim light and the smoke to take stock. Morales and Shadi were fighting back-to-back, picking off any wolves who even looked in their direction. I could see Mez, but occasionally the air sizzled with the static of spent magic from one of his party favors.

It was hard to get a head count through the chaos, but I managed to identify at least a dozen deformed shapes outlined in the shadows. The potion patch had worn off, but my adrenaline was pounding like lightning through my veins.

A new figure ran at me from the tunnel. She wore a dress over her furry body that tented her thin frame like a muumuu. The floral catastrophe screamed Goodwill donation box.

I raised the Glock, only then realizing I'd lost count of my bullets. The woman ran at me so fast I didn't have the luxury of a tactical reload, so I just pointed the gun and prayed I had enough juice to bring her down.

The woman fell to her knees like a two-dollar whore. A dark-red splotch spread across the chest of the dress. Her hands clawed at the stain, as if she could scratch it away. When that didn't work, she pacified herself by sucking the blood from her fingertips. She looked so happy that I could only watch in horror, mesmerized by the unsettling image.

"Kate!" Morales shouted. My head jerked up. "Behind you!"

I swiveled, bringing up my gun as I went. A flash of pale skin and lips red with blood.

*Click. Click. Click.*

It was on the last click of the empty magazine that I recognized the face.

I dropped the gun as if it had burned me. My mind reeled. The sharp claws of fear scratched down my spine.

The potion had begun its work transforming the face into the twisted mask of rage. But there was no denying that I knew my attacker.

"Danny?" I whispered.

A flurry of questions and panicked thoughts scrambled through my brain. How had this happened? Had Bane gotten him before he reached school? Or did he lure him away? Oh God! Did Pen know Danny was missing?

What the fuck was I going to do?

Danny growled. Spittle bubbled from his lips. His eyes flashed hot red with bloodlust. Bloodlust forced upon him by a psychopath.

Bane. I was going to tear that motherfucker limb from limb for this horror.

The sounds of fighting rushed into my shocked mind, pushing out all the questions and replacing them with a shot of adrenaline. It was fight-or-flight time. But I knew if I ran, he'd only chase and we'd both end up dead.

The kid who had happily eaten breakfast with me that morning snarled and lunged.

Out of instinct, my arm came up to block the blow. "Morales!" Danny's hands went for my neck.

"What?" Morales yelled.

"Fuck!" I ducked a punch and delivered a jab of my own to Danny's ribs. He groaned and retaliated with a swipe to my neck with his claws. The skin there stung like acid and went cold as blood welled.

"Mez, go help Kate!" Morales called between grunts that indicated he had his hands full, too.

But the scent of blood was like lighting a match too close to gasoline. No longer content to try just to maim me, Danny went after my jugular like a shark attacking chum. He moved so fast I could barely keep up with defensive blows, much less cause any damage of my own.

"I'm coming, Prospero!" Mez called.

"Hurry!" I kicked at his shins and clawed at his face with my fingernails. Some horrified voice in my head whispered that I shouldn't be hitting back. That I should figure out how to defend myself against Danny without hurting him. But the practical side—the one that liked being alive—reminded me that if I didn't manage to fight him off I'd be dead and then the team would kill Danny.

The sound of running footsteps echoed from somewhere behind me. "Back off, asshole!" Mez shouted. I raised my head enough to glance at him. When I saw the Mundane gun in his hand, terror gripped my heart with a cold fist.

"No!" I screamed and swiveled to put myself between Danny and the gun.

"Prospero, get out of the way!"

Behind me, my brother realized I wasn't fighting him anymore. As I opened my mouth to explain to Mez, the attack came. Canines slammed into my neck like a serpent's strike.

I gasped and lurched forward.

"Goddamn it, Kate. I can't get a clear shot."

"No!" I yelled. "No bullets!"

The pain in my neck was indescribable—hot and sharp. Danny's weight on my back. The terrible sucking noises. Tracers dancing in the edges of my vision. Ice coating my skin.

"Danny—it's Danny." I swallowed against the taste of copper on my tongue. "Knock...out," I rasped. "Potion him."

Mez either didn't understand what I said or was too jacked up on adrenaline for it to register. "Drop to your knees."

"Potion, potion," I begged, my voice losing strength, "potion."

Little sparks danced in the periphery of my vision. My knees were weakening. If I didn't convince Mez to shoot Danny with the potion quickly, I was going to pass out and Lord help us all. "Morales!" I forced through my tight throat. "It's Danny!" I screamed the name with every last ounce of energy and air left in my body. "Danny!"

Just before I passed out, I saw grim-faced Morales grab something from Mez. The last thing I heard before I slipped into the black was the sound of a gun firing.

# Chapter Twenty-Six

R ed and blue pulsed everywhere. A high-pitched drone whirred through my head, but I couldn't tell if it was real or the result of the vacuum between my ears. For several minutes, the neon signs and buildings of the Cauldron blurred by, creating a dizzying kaleidoscope. After that, the scent of disinfectant and a wall of cold whiteness surrounded me.

The world passed in a blur of color and noise. Occasionally a familiar face would cross my field of vision, but my eyes couldn't focus long enough to establish context. Electricity must have zapped between my neurons, but none of those little packets of information registered anywhere on my motherboard.

Stinging pain on my neck. Promises it would pass. Needles and thread, trying to sew my jagged edges back together. But all the king's horses and all the king's men couldn't make me feel whole again.

Warm hand on my arm. A quiet voice whispering in my ear. My eyes burned. My ribs crushed my too-tight lungs. My heart a pulsing bruise inside my chest.

"Kate?" That voice again. I recognized it but didn't. Some part of my fractured mind realized I'd heard it before, but the tone sounded...off. Too careful. Worried.

"She's in shock." A woman's voice this time. "Anyone would be."

"He was going to kill her." A male voice, deep, shaken.

"Thank God you stepped in," another shaky male voice said. "I almost—"

"Hush now, you didn't."

The words washed over me as if I didn't exist at all.

The white void gave way to the shape of a man. He had dark hair and brown eyes. A leather jacket creaked as he knelt in front of me.

"Kate," he said, "the doctor needs to talk to you."

I heard the words. Each had a definition I understood. But it wasn't worth the effort to analyze the collection of vowels and consonants and turn them into actions. I wanted to stew in the blissful numbness. That liminal space between what came before and what would be. The place where I could pretend this was all just some sort of horrible dream.

DannyDannyDannyDannyDannyDanny...

I squeezed my eyes to shut out the memories that threatened to rush forward. My body rocked back and forth to ward off the intrusion of reality.

The sharp scent of ammonia hit my nose like a punch. I reared back, shocked out of my haze. I blinked and saw Pen standing over me with a vial in her hand.

My eyes snapped open and my brain snapped back into the matrix of reality. "What the fuck, Pen?" I supposed I should have been glad she hadn't slapped me, but the ammonia stench of *sal volatile* wasn't much more pleasant.

She crossed her arms and the frown between her brows was so deep, soldiers could set up residence in the trenches. "Enough, Kate. Pull yourself together." She raised a hand and pointed a finger toward the closed door next to the waiting area. "The doc needs your permission to provide treatment." She leaned down and got in my face. "So you're going to get off your skinny, white ass and make sure that boy gets the help he needs."

I stared up at her but it was like looking through a plate glass window. Beyond Pen, Mez and Morales stared in open-mouthed shock. Shadi leaned against the far wall looking as if she couldn't decide whether she was mad at Pen or respected the hell out of her. Gardner's expression was unreadable, but she didn't move to step in.

I witnessed all of these things as an observer more than as a participant. Which meant I also suddenly got this image of myself, slumped and surrendered on the chair, while my baby brother lay alone and broken in the next room.

"What's it going to be?" Pen arched a brow in challenge. "You going to sit here and feel sorry for yourself, or are you going to get up and do the damned thing?"

I cleared my throat, sat up straighter, and looked her in the eye. "Were the smelling salts really necessary?"

My best friend smiled and held out her hand to help me up. "Nope." She shot me a shit-eating grin that did little to disguise the dark circles under her eyes and worry brackets around her mouth.

The door to Danny's room was ten feet away, but it felt more like miles. I glanced uneasily at Pen. "Will you come with me?" I whispered. Everyone else suddenly pretended they had more important things to do or talk about.

Pen put her arm around my shoulders. "Try and stop me."

♦ ♦ ♦

The next couple of hours were a blur of medical jargon, sympathetic looks, and endless forms. Luckily, I was still officially on the BPD health insurance plan. Unfortunately, I'd signed up for the plan that had a sky-high deductible for any medical care that required the assistance of a medical wizard. At the time I thought I was being smart since I kept Danny away from magic. Guess the joke was on me.

"Katie?" Pen stuck her head in the door. The incessant beep of the heart monitor and the *hush-thrush* of the breathing machine were momentarily drowned out by voices from the hallway. She'd exited earlier to take a call from the principal at her school. The entire administration was scrambling to find out what had happened and cover their asses. I didn't blame the school. I didn't blame Pen, either—even though she seemed determined to assume some of the guilt.

I blamed Bane. Period.

"Katie?"

I looked up, thankful for the interruption. For the last half hour I'd been alone in the room with Danny. He was too quiet, too still, too…absent from the shell that lay on the bed like a sacrifice to the gods of Big Magic. Tubes and wires jutted from his mouth and nose, arms and chest. His face was calmer in repose, but the Gray Wolf was still in his system, leaving his features mangled and deformed. Combined with the medical equipment, he looked like a modern-day version of Frankenstein's monster.

Bane's monster.

My teeth clenched and a hot rush of blood coursed through my veins at that thought.

"Kate?" Pen again, more insistent.

"Yes?" I said, rising. I assumed she'd come to tell me she needed yet another set of forms filled out.

"Your friends are asking if they can come in."

"Which friends?"

She pursed her lips and cocked her head. "Your team. They've been here for hours."

"Oh right." I shook myself. "Yeah, okay."

"I'll give you a second to clean up." She winked at me.

Thankful to have something to do other than stare at my brother, I went to the sink. The small mirror over it told a sad tale of a woman who'd been through the shock of her life. Blood smeared her cheeks and chin. The dark circles under her eyes were a combo of lack of sleep and mascara tracks. A bandage glared harshly white on her neck.

I wet a towel and scrubbed my face. The rough nap of the fabric felt like burlap and the water was cold as a slap. When I finished, the skin was flushed, but all the blood was gone.

Another knock.

"Come," I called. The quick glance toward the bed was reflexive. I could have invited a brass band to play in the room and Danny wouldn't have stirred.

The door opened to reveal a solemn crew. Gardner came in first, naturally. Morales followed. Pen came in after him and leaned against the counter with her arms crossed. Her expression resembled a bulldog's, as if she was ready to kick their asses out if they upset me.

"Where are the others?"

"Shadi's helping the BPD." Morales shared a tense glance with Gardner. "Mez is back at the lab."

"Has the BPD been able to identify any of the other people who attacked us?" I said.

Gardner's expression went tense, like she'd hoped I would

have forgotten about that. "Not yet." Her tone was subdued. "They're hoping some of the fingerprints taken off the deceased will provide clues to their identities."

"What's taking them so long?" I demanded.

"Kate, listen, maybe we should talk about this later—" Morales began.

I swiped a hand through the air. "Later? You mean after Bane's gone totally underground and we lose all hope of finding him?"

"There are some complications," Gardner said. "The media got wind of the raid and Mayor Owens is crawling all over Eldritch's ass."

"Fuck the mayor!"

The words hung in the air like a black cloud.

"Kate." Gardner's voice was quiet but steely. "I understand your frustration, but there are procedures we have to follow. If we go after Bane through improper channels, we'll never make a case against him."

"Won't need to make a case if he's dead."

"Stop right there," she snapped. "Haven't there been enough casualties already?"

The word "casualties" made the eggshell veneer of calm begin to fracture. Danny wasn't a fucking casualty. He was just a kid who had become another tragedy in the war on magic.

Tears burned the edges of my lids. I pointed to Danny's gray face. "That bastard did this to him." My voice cracked. I cleared my throat and took a deep breath. If there was one thing I hated more than crying because I was sad, it was crying because I was angry. "You know it and I know it. And if you won't arrest him, then I will personally hunt him down and gladly do the time."

"Stop it." Gardner's expression didn't change, but the air around us tightened, hardened. "That won't fix Danny."

"Nothing will fix Danny," I whispered.

Her head tilted. "What? Is that what the doctor said?"

I swallowed the fist-sized lump in my throat. "He has to stay in the coma until an antipotion for Gray Wolf is found."

Morales cursed under his breath.

Gardner's face softened a fraction and she came forward into what probably counted as a comforting distance. "Let us worry about all this. If I know Mez, he's already two steps ahead and working on an antipotion. Shadi's handling the BPD and Morales and I will be working other avenues to track down Bane." She bent down so I was forced to look in her eyes for the vow she was about to deliver: "And we will find him."

I hesitated, but I knew she meant what she said. They might be federal agents, but they were still cops. And cops took care of their own. At least these cops did. The same couldn't be said for any of the BPD officers since none had even showed up at the hospital to show their support. My conscience rose at the uncharitable thought. Hadn't Gardner just said Shadi was out with the BPD looking for Bane? That was the kind of support I really needed. Finally, I nodded. "What can I do?"

"You've got your hands full here. Focus your energy on Danny and taking care of yourself. Leave the rest to us, okay?"

"If you need anything," Morales said, coming forward, "you call us. Seriously. Anything."

I looked up at him and a new wave of emotion rose up in my throat. This time, though, it wasn't despair threatening to drown me. It was gratitude and something like hope. "Thanks," I whispered.

Two big arms suddenly wrapped around me. I started to pull away, but the support was so appreciated, so needed, that I surrendered and accepted the comfort offered.

I held on for all I was worth. His muscled arms and shoulders seemed as though they could hold the weight of the world, which was good because my worries felt like just that.

Gardner cleared her throat. Morales pulled back reluctantly and looked me in the eye. "I mean it—anything."

I forced a weak smile and nodded.

He grabbed my hand and slipped something inside. "Mez left this for you."

I frowned and looked down. The item in my hand was a round leather amulet hanging from a braided leather cord. In the center, a small bubble of glass was filled with an iridescent green liquid. "What is it?"

"We call it the 'Oh Shit' amulet. Break the bubble if there's trouble and it will ward off magical attacks, as well as activate a GPS chip embedded in the disc."

I opened my mouth to argue, but Gardner spoke up. "If Bane comes after you we'll be able to track you down anywhere in the city."

"I don't—" I'd been in the process of rubbing my arms because I suddenly felt cold. The movement brushed a raw, reddened spot where I'd ripped off the patch.

"Save it, Prospero. I'm well aware of your aversion to using magic." Gardner crossed her arms, shooting my arm a pointed look. I didn't have the energy to feel betrayed that Morales had told her I took off the patch. My conscience reared up. Maybe if I hadn't pulled it off I could have fought harder, smarter. Maybe done something to prevent—

Gardner's voice cut through my self-recriminations like a blade. "Bane potioned your brother because he knew he was your Achilles' heel."

*Boom.*

Everyone went silent in the wake of that punch to the gut. I glanced at Pen, but she was suddenly very interested in the patterns on the flecked linoleum.

"He will come at you again," Gardner added, unnecessarily.

"Yeah," I snapped. "I got it. But if he does it'll be so fast I won't have time to activate the amulet."

"It might help, though," Pen said. I shot her a disgusted look for siding with them. She of all people understood why I didn't want anything to do with magic. Especially now that magic had turned my brother into a vegetable.

I placed a hand on the butt of the gun at my waist. "Not if I get to them first."

"You listen to me." Gardner's entire posture changed. It seemed as though she grew six inches. "If I catch you anywhere near Bane or his property, I'll personally arrest you for obstruction."

My mouth fell open.

"I won't have you risking your life or anyone else's over some personal vendetta," she snapped. "You let us worry about Bane. You keep yourself busy getting that boy the help he needs and watching your own ass." She grabbed the amulet Morales still held and thrust it at me. "Put this on and keep it on. If I catch you without it, I'll surgically implant a tracking device in your ass. Are we clear?"

If I clenched my teeth any harder, they'd shatter. "Crystal," I gritted out. She raised a brow, signaling she wouldn't leave until she watched me put on the damned thing. With a sigh, I threw it over my head. The disc was surprisingly lightweight, but on the skin it felt like a lead yoke.

"Good girl," Gardner said. The patronizing tone made me want to punch her, so I clenched my fists. "Now"—her tone lightened up—"we'll get out of your hair. I'll check in on you tomorrow."

She nodded at Morales, who snapped to attention and followed her out like a good little soldier. The instant the door shut behind them, I rounded on Pen.

"Can you believe that bitch?" Even I heard the petulance in my voice. I hated it, but I couldn't help but feel as if I deserved a little bit of self-pity, all things considered.

"Honestly?" Pen said, watching the door my boss just exited. "I think she's kind of awesome."

I sighed and dropped back in the chair. "Jesus, Pen."

My best friend came over and grabbed my hands, which felt icy in her warm palms. "We'll get him better." She opened her mouth to say more, but at that moment the door burst open and Hurricane Baba blew in.

"Oh, my poor, poor boy!" she wailed. After that, any thoughts of planning revenge or ignoring Gardner's instructions flew out the window as Pen and I tried to answer questions we didn't begin to know the right answers to.

# Chapter Twenty-Seven

Two days later, on my way to the hospital, I grabbed a box of glazed donuts for the nurses and a bucket of coffee for me. I only wished answers were as easy to come by as sugar and caffeine.

The night before Baba had shooed me out of the hospital to go home to shower and sleep.

"You smell like a foot and you look like shit," she'd said in her most loving tone. "I don't want to see you back here before dawn." After that she'd tried to press one of her special teas into my hands, and I escaped just so she wouldn't make me drink it.

Walking back into that silent house had been like entering a crime scene. Echoes of Danny permeated the place—his shoes on the floor, dirty laundry next to the hamper, his toothbrush by the sink.

When I arrived, there was an e-mail waiting for me from Eldritch. It contained an attached police report detailing the information the cops had gathered about how Bane captured Danny. According to his friend Aaron, they'd arrived at school around seven thirty. Aaron was in the band so he had to go set up for the assembly, which was scheduled right after the first bell. Best anyone could tell, Danny decided to run to the corner store to grab some junk food before school started. The last person who saw him was the convenience store clerk, who reported seeing a tall male with brown hair, about mid-thirties, talking to Danny in the parking lot.

I paused reading and removed the watch they'd found at the scene from my pocket. One of the cops who'd come by the hospital had brought it to me. They'd found it next to the curb where the store attendant saw Danny speaking to the stranger. I closed my fist around the cold metal and squeezed my eyes shut. So much for its bringing him luck. I swiped angrily at the tears I didn't want to indulge and shoved the watch back into my pocket where I didn't have to look at it.

By the time the first class had begun and Danny's teacher noticed he was absent he'd already been abducted. And by the time news of his absence had trickled to Pen and she'd begun leaving the frantic messages I found on my phone later, I had already been fighting Danny in the tunnels.

I'd closed the e-mail with a nagging sensation to go along with the weight in my chest. Why would Danny go somewhere with a stranger? He knew better than that. And the clerk hadn't reported a struggle between the two. It didn't add up.

To distract myself from my loneliness and the memories and the theories, I'd called Morales around midnight for an update. He'd groggily informed me that they'd identified some of the Gray Wolf addicts who'd attacked us.

"Shadi ID'd five of them as vagrants who hang out at one of the shelters downtown."

"Did she go there?"

"Of course."

"And?"

"And what, Kate?" He sighed. "Did she find Ramses Bane sitting on a cot waiting to be arrested?"

The conversation was pretty much over at that point.

It's not that I didn't trust Morales and the rest of the team to get Bane—well, that's not true. I didn't want anyone but me to deliver the swift kick of justice directly to Bane's ass. But I also realized that my hands were tied. As much as I hated to admit it, Gardner was right: Danny needed to be my priority.

He might be unconscious, but the doctor felt sure he could register some of what was happening around him. Even if he didn't remember everything—and Lord knew I hoped he forgot what happened in the tunnels—when he eventually woke up, I had a feeling he'd know deep down that he hadn't been alone. That had to count for something.

So, really, I had no choice but to put my faith in the team. Which meant I probably needed to add an apology to Morales to my to-do list for calling him an asshole before I'd hung up on him.

The nurses cheered when I dropped off the box of glazed donuts at the desk. Apparently the Cauldron had hosted a busy night of ODs, stabbings, and assorted other magic-related violence that kept the ER hopping. That meant the nurses in Danny's ward had had to step it up to cover all the staff who had been commandeered to handle triage.

"We didn't expect you until later," Rita, the shift supervisor, said with a yawn. "But we're sure glad you showed up when you did."

I smiled. Inside I longed to ask them what kinds of potions were involved, but I left them to enjoy their breakfast in peace.

265

Even if the cases were related to Gray Wolf, there wasn't much I could do with the knowledge besides harass Morales some more.

"I'll just go check on Danny," I said to the nurses.

"Oh! Mrs. Nowiki went down to grab some coffee and breakfast at the cafeteria about half an hour ago, but your other friend showed up not too long after."

I frowned at her, wondering if Morales or one of the task members stopped by. "What friend?"

"Let me check." She started rifling through stacks of files on the counter, looking for the visitor log. "One of the other nurses was on duty, so she wrote it down."

I waved a hand. "Don't worry about it. I'll go see for myself." I started to walk away, thinking it was probably Pen. It wasn't until I approached the room and saw that all the curtains were closed to the hallway that my gut told me to worry. I reached for the door at the same instant the nurse called down the hall.

"Oh, here it is," she called. "It's Mr. Volos—"

My heart plummeted ten stories. I threw open the door and ran inside.

"Hello, Kate."

My feet froze to the ground. For a moment, all I could do was stare. Volos stood on the far side of Danny's bed, holding my brother's hand as though he belonged there.

The instant my brain snapped out of it, my gun was in my hand and pointed at Volos's chest. "Get the fuck away from him."

His hands didn't tremor as they rose. "Easy there."

"I said get away from him." My voice was permafrost on the air.

Footsteps squeaked down the linoleum hallway. "Officer Prospero?" the head nurse called.

"Call security," I said quietly without taking my eyes off Volos.

"I thought you were security." Volos smiled. "Put down the gun. You know I wouldn't hurt either of you. In fact, I've come to offer my help."

I stared hard at his innocent expression for a full fifteen seconds. I knew better than to trust that poker face, but I was also extremely curious to hear how and why he was offering help. Finally, I looked over my shoulder. "Leave us."

The shuffling of reluctant feet followed. Volos and I stared at each other across my brother's silent form until we were again alone.

"What do you want?"

"Won't you lower the weapon?"

"No."

"Fair enough." The corners of his lips lifted. "But if you're going to shoot—" He unbuttoned the top few buttons of his shirt. The top of what looked like a stretchy black undershirt peeked out between the widened collars. "You're going to want to aim for my face."

I frowned at him. "What the fuck is that?"

"Bulletproof fabric."

It looked a lot like the same fabric that made up the patch Mez had given us to wear for the tunnel raid. "Why are you wearing it here?"

"Says the woman pointing a gun at me." He tapped it with his knuckles. At my narrowed eyes, he sighed. "Let's just say some of my former colleagues aren't exactly my biggest fans." He smiled tightly. "I'm sure you understand."

"What do you want?"

"To help you."

My eyes narrowed. "Why?"

He straightened himself as though my suspicion ruffled his feathers. "Recent events notwithstanding, we once were very close." He cleared his throat. "More to the point"—he glanced at Danny with a look bordering on warmth—"I have always had an affinity for the kid."

A heavy weight settled on my chest. It had been so long since I'd thought about the good times. Back before Mom died, when John and I were still in love. We used to take Danny to get ice cream from the cart on Canal Street. Once, when Danny dropped his cone in the gutter, John bought him two more to get him to stop crying.

I clenched my jaw against the memories. They were dangerous. *He* was dangerous. "Just say your piece and get out."

The skin around his eyes tightened. Volos wasn't used to being spoken to like that. From what I'd seen of this slick, new CEO persona, he commanded ultimate respect at all times.

He tilted his head. "Where's this hostility coming from? You know damned well I had nothing to do with this mess."

"Doesn't mean you're innocent or that I trust you."

"Trust... right. You know a lot about that."

"What's that supposed to mean?"

He ignored my question. "Let's put our past aside for the moment and focus on Danny. What Bane did was beyond a crime." He paused, letting it hang there just long enough to pique my interest. "I may have access to a remedy for your brother's ailment."

"He doesn't have an ailment." My stomach clenched like a fist. "He's brain-dead because of a fucking dirty potion."

He made a noncommittal gesture as if I were splitting hairs. "Regardless, it's clear conventional medicine and clean magic aren't the proper tools."

"Are you saying I should employ illegal dirty magic to cure

my brother when it was illegal dirty magic that harmed him in the first place?" It was so ridiculous that I laughed bitterly. "You've got balls, I'll give you that."

"What I am saying is that sometimes you have to fight dirty with more dirty." He raised his hands in a pleading gesture. "He's not going to recover without it, Kate. You know that."

"More to the point, what makes you so sure of that? Maybe you're in bed with Bane."

"That's your stupid stubborn pride talking." He smiled sadly. "You know I'm as much a target for Bane as you are."

"So if you didn't cook it, how could you possibly know where to get the antipotion?"

He watched me quietly for the span of three heartbeats. "I may be out of the dirty magic trade, but old training dies hard. Once I saw what Gray Wolf did to people, I decided to start gathering materials to see if I could work out an antipotion."

Something clicked. "Wait. Is that why you received the shipment of oil of rose quartz?"

He nodded. "That's also why I ordered the oil instead of distilling it myself. I knew it was only a matter of time until Bane made his big move."

I stared at him as a million questions and thoughts tripped over themselves in my head. I must have stayed quiet too long because he shifted uncomfortably. "So you figured it out?"

He grimaced. "It's not progressing as quickly as I'd hoped. I never had your talent for breaking down the recipes of existing potions." He let it hang there, like a hook with a juicy worm.

"Surely you have access to wizards who can help you—"

"No one I trust. If word gets to Bane that I'm working on an antipotion, he's bound to do something desperate."

"So if you don't have the antipotion to offer, what are you doing here?"

"I want you to help me cook it."

My stomach pitched south. "Fuck you."

"Kate," he said, coming toward me, "you know that between the two of us we'll figure out the cure for Danny."

I shook my head rapidly, as if I could knock his words free of my ears. "I can't."

He frowned. "I get it. You're a little rusty. It'll come back."

I held up my hands. "No, you don't get it. I don't cook anymore." I looked him in the eye. "Ever."

His mouth fell open. "You're joking."

I pointed at my brother, who looked like the poster boy for desperate cases. "Do you honestly think I would joke about something that could save his life?"

John's mouth snapped shut. "I don't—I had no idea you didn't cook at all."

I crossed my arms protectively and looked away from the mix of curiosity and concern in his blue gaze.

"Surely you'd make an exception here."

I shook my head. "Magic did this to him, John. I'm not going to multiply the crime by cooking dirty in some vain hope of curing him."

He ran a hand through his hair. "I—okay, I can maybe figure something out. It'll take some time, though, Kate."

I shook myself. "I didn't say I'd let you give him a potion whether I helped cook it or not."

"Why the hell not?"

"Because I don't think I could afford the price you'd ask in exchange."

"I don't want your fucking money."

I looked him hard in the eye. "It's not money I'm worried about. It's the inevitable favors."

His jaw hardened like I'd offended him. "What have I done

that you would think so little of me?" he asked quietly. "You left me, remember?"

I crossed my arms and glared at him.

"I don't want anything from you. I just want to help the kid." He sighed. "For his sake, I hope you'll put your pride aside sooner rather than later."

"Don't hold your breath."

He turned to look at my brother's pale, expressionless face. "Eventually you'll realize that even if you catch Bane, he'll never give up the formula for the antipotion. Or maybe Danny will take a turn for the worse. Or maybe the money for his care will run out."

I swallowed hard. It had run out before it began, hadn't it?

"Or you'll just run out of hope." He looked up then, straight into my eyes. "And when that happens, you'll have no choice."

I pointed a trembling hand toward the door. "Get out."

"Kate—"

"Get out!" I screamed. My weapon was in my hand again without me realizing I'd drawn it. "*Get out!*"

He held up his hands and scooted toward the door. Just outside, the nurses were running again along with a couple of security guards.

"I'll be waiting for your call." With that, he ducked past the security guards and nurses who had congregated at the door. The instant his blond head disappeared into the crowd, I sagged against the bed. I looked over at the gray face of my sixteen-year-old brother and felt the fragile facade I'd been maintaining shatter into a million pieces.

"What are we going to do, Danny?" I whispered. "What the fuck are we going to do?"

# Chapter Twenty-Eight

By noon, I was on my way to the gym. Heading there had been a decision motived by two factors.

First, Baba had returned with four women who looked old enough to be Methuselah's aunts. The group often got together for such activities as quilting, making scrapbooks, and casting revenge spells under the full moon. I guess after Baba told them what happened to Danny, they'd decided it was a good idea to sit vigil around him and chant to Hekate for a quick recovery.

I hadn't pointed out that some stupid chants weren't going to fix my brother, but I didn't argue with them about their plans. If chanting helped Baba feel less desperate about Danny's situation, I wouldn't stop her from finding the solace that I'd been unable to find. I had escaped as quickly as possible before they started drawing pentagrams from the salt packets they'd stolen from the hospital cafeteria.

The second reason I headed to the gym had been the conversation with Volos. After I'd calmed down a little, I realized he'd been right about one thing. The doctors at the hospital couldn't cure Danny. They could keep him alive and somewhat comfortable—if you considered a coma cozy. But they had no idea how to reverse a dirty magic potion that combined blood magic with alchemy. What I needed was a wizard who knew a thing or two about street magic and had access to samples of Gray Wolf to analyze. And the only person who fit that description besides John Volos was Mesmer.

Luckily, I found him working alone in his lab. When I reached the top step, he poked his head around the divider and his face morphed into a smile. "Kate!"

"Hey, man." I looked around at the empty gym. "Where is everyone?"

That day his dreads were back to their normal dark brown color, but his eyes were different. I squinted at them for a moment before I realized his irises were vibrant violet instead of the typical chocolate brown. He was also wearing eyeliner.

He sighed. "Morales and Shadi are working with the BPD to figure out where the hell Bane went. And Gardner is in Detroit trying to convince the ASAC not to pull the plug on the whole operation."

I reared back, eyes wide. "What's an ASAC and why would they pull the plug?"

"Assistant Special Agent in Charge, aka Gardner's boss," he explained. "And he's pissed because the mayor's raising hell about the clusterfuck in the tunnels."

"Shit," I said. "What a fucking mess."

"No shit, sister. What brings you in?"

I hesitated, trying to figure out the right tone to use for my request. "I need to talk to you about something, actually."

His brows rose in curiosity. "Oh?" He waved a gallant hand

toward the lab. "In that case, please step into my laboratory, madam." He pronounced it la-*bore*-atory, like someone from an old Frankenstein movie.

Once we were inside, my eyes automatically went to the shelf of beakers and Erlenmeyer flasks and burners. A mustard-yellow liquid boiled furiously in the largest of these and choked out a noxious rotten-egg scent. "What are you cooking?"

He shrugged. "It's a little something I'm trying out. A potion that changes colors when it's exposed to a person's personal scent profile. I'm calling it K9 for now because it works kind of the way a dog tracks scent in the field."

"Huh," I said, impressed. "You thinking it'll help track down Bane?"

He blew air from between his lips. "I have to get the formula figured out first. I tried it on a piece of pH paper yesterday and the stuff caught on fire."

"Ouch," I said. "Back to the drawing board, huh?"

He laughed. "Something like that. So," he prompted, "what were you going to ask me?"

I crossed my arms and leaned back against the counter. The move jostled a test tube, which rolled toward the edge like a convict hell-bent on escape. I caught it a split second before it could shatter on the floor. "Oops," I said with a self-conscious laugh. "Sorry about that."

Mez shot me a worried look. "Everything okay?" He came forward to take the tube from me. He showed me the label on the side. I'd almost dropped a tube filled with nitroglycerin. I felt myself pale. Damn, I really need to get my head in the game.

"All right," I said finally, "here's the deal: I'm starting to think that the chances of the docs finding a cure for Danny are zilch. Plus, now that you've told me the ASAC is thinking of pulling the team out, the hope of catching Bane and forcing him to give us the antipotion is nil."

He chewed on his bottom lip. "You don't know that."

I shot him a frank look that had him glancing down, almost as an apology for insulting my intelligence with platitudes. "So it comes down to finding the antipotion some other way."

Mez licked his front teeth and nodded. "So you figured you'd what—cook up an antipotion here?"

I shook my head. "Not exactly. It's been ten years since I cooked. But I figured"—I let it hang there for a second—"maybe you'd be able to help?" I cringed, bracing myself for rejection.

He sighed. "Look, Kate, I like you, but you're asking too much. First of all, I'm not allowed to use MEA resources for potions not directly related to an active case. But even if I was willing to bend that rule, if Gardner ever found out I was cooking dirty potions, she'd kick my ass out of the agency so fast my dreads would straighten out." He leaned back until I was forced to look up at him. "Why can't you do it?"

I raised my hands in a futile gesture. "I don't have a lab, for one thing, and it would take too much time and a lot more money than I can access to get one set up. Second, I haven't cooked in so long that I'm not even sure I'd be able to do any good."

He scoffed. "Magic is like sex. You really never forget."

"Regardless, it's not an option here."

"Isn't there someone else you can ask? Family or an old friend, maybe?"

That was precisely the problem. Not that I'd tell Mez about John's offer. "Not exactly."

He placed a hand on my arm. "Look, it's probably for the best. The only way to reverse a dirty potion like that is with something even dirtier. I know you're worried about Danny, but you're talking about breaking, like, ten federal statutes here. If Gardner or Eldritch found out you cooked dirty—even to help your brother—you'd be out of a job and probably thrown in Crowley. And then who would look after Danny?"

By the time he finished listing all the reasons it was a bad idea, I felt like a drowning woman with cinder blocks tied to every limb. "I can't just stand by while he dies, Mez," I whispered. He came forward to give me a hug. The scent of ozone and burnt cedar from the sticks he used to light the burners clung to his lab coat and dreads. The combo was oddly comforting.

"Stay strong, sister," he said. "All of us are pulling for you and the kid. Morales and Shadi are out pretty much twenty-four/seven trying to find Bane." He pulled back and made me look at him. "We will find him. Then we'll do whatever it takes to get the formula from Bane."

I snorted through the tears that sprung to my eyes. "Good luck with that."

"Are you kidding? Applying the thumbscrews is Morales's specialty. His old squad called him the Bull."

"Why?"

"Because I'm so stubborn I always win."

I turned toward the doorway to the lab. "Shit, Morales. We didn't hear you come in."

"I did," Mez said. I shot him a look.

"What you doing here, Cupcake?" His tone was casual, as was his posture, but I sensed a leashed energy inside.

"I came by to see how things are going."

"Could have just called," he said. Then he snapped his fingers as if he'd forgotten something. "Oh wait. I get it, you prefer to call people 'Asshole' to their faces."

My shoulders drooped. It's not that I didn't feel bad for hanging up on him the other day, but I wasn't really up for adding groveling to my to-do list that day. Before I could, though, Mez cleared his throat. "I, uh, guess I'll go...do something somewhere else." He shot me a weighted look, a reminder to heed his advice about the potion stuff and walked off.

When he was gone, Morales crossed his arms and shot me a challenging look.

I sighed because it was easier than cussing. "Look, I'm sorry I called you an asshole."

"And for hanging up on me?"

I nodded. "Yes, for that, too. I know you're doing your job, it's just"—I cleared the pride clogging my throat—"it's been torture to sit around and not be able to help you guys get Bane."

A speculative gleam lit up his brown eyes. "Who said you couldn't help us?"

I paused. "Gardner—"

"Said you couldn't go after Bane yourself. She didn't say anything about not helping us with the investigation."

A weight lifted off my shoulders. It hadn't occurred to me that while I was sitting around that hospital room I could be going over files or something, anything to help make progress. "What did you have in mind?"

He licked his bottom lip and squinted at me. "Remember when that snitch told you the potion was being sold out of that absinthe bar?"

"The Green Faerie—yeah?"

"We're scraping the bottom of the barrel as far as leads go. Any chance he's got a bead on Bane's location?"

I tilted my head and regarded him with mock doubt. "I don't know, Morales. Introducing you to my favorite snitch is a pretty big step."

"Like it or not, Cupcake, if we're able to nab Bane we'll be stuck together for a good long time."

"Hmm." I grimaced as if the prospect wasn't exactly what I'd been hoping for since I met Gardner in Eldritch's office. "All right. But keep your trap shut, okay? As it is I'm going to have to do some fast talking so he doesn't shut down the minute I bring a stranger onto his turf."

"I can live with that."

"Okay, let's go," I said. "Oh, and one thing?"

He raised his brows.

"Don't say anything about the diaper."

# Chapter Twenty-Nine

"Hey, lady."

One of Mary's massive paws rested protectively on Little Man's rounded belly. The homunculus's eyes were closed as he basked like a drowsy lizard in the afternoon sun. When his sister saw Morales walking up behind me, her other arm tightened protectively.

"Stranger," she whispered fiercely.

"Hi, Mary. This is my friend Drew." I smiled at her. "He's nice."

Her eyes narrowed at the holster peeking from beneath Morales's jacket. "Guns."

"Put your hands up," I said under my breath. He shot me an annoyed look but complied. "Drew's a police officer, too, Mary. He would never hurt Baby."

"Damn straight he won't," LM said with his eyes still closed. "Because I'd fuck his shit up."

Morales jerked and he openly gaped. "What the fuck?" he breathed.

Little Man's eyes snapped open and he speared the cop with a disgusted look. "What's wrong with your friend?" He shot Morales an evil, mostly toothless grin.

I waved a hand and forced a laugh. "Apparently he's never talked to a homunculus before."

Little Man leaned forward, using his tiny elbows for leverage against Mary's flat chest. He looked Morales up and down with eyes too wise for his infantile body. "I guess we're even, then, because I ain't never seen no beaner cop look as retarded as this one here."

Morales raised a bored brow. "I prefer 'spic,' asshole."

Little Man threw back his head and laughed. "Oh, I like this one, Prospero."

"I'm so relieved," Morales said in a monotone.

"Now that the pleasantries are done," I said, "I need some help."

Little Man raised a tiny hand and rubbed his thumb across the tops of his fingers.

Shit. Seeing how, according to the MEA and the BPD, we shouldn't even have been there, I didn't have access to petty cash to pay informants. I nudged Morales, figuring that, unlike me, he had more money than lint in his wallet. He shot me an annoyed look. "Nice."

"I'll buy you a beer later," I said.

He rolled his eyes and approached LM. As he walked he jerked the wallet out of his right back pocket.

When he reached LM, he handed him a ten. The homunculus gaped at the cop. "You trying to insult me?"

Morales sighed the sigh of the martyred and removed another ten from the wallet. "You better have a good singing voice."

"Throw in an extra twenty and I'll do a little dance." LM performed a slow hip thrust.

I threw up a little in my mouth. "We'll just settle for an address for Bane's safe house."

Mary stiffened as if she smelled trouble and LM's smile froze. "Why would you think I'd know something like that?"

"Because not much happens in the Cauldron without you knowing."

He chuckled. "Your high opinion of me makes me feel all warm and gooey, Prospero, but ain't *nobody* that connected."

"All right," I said, crossing my arms. "How much?"

Morales made a disgusted sound. I ignored him and stared down my tiny informant.

"I'll take all the money you got, but it still isn't going to get you the answer you want."

"Come on, LM, give me something. This is important."

"Always is with you." He looked at me for a moment with pursed lips. "Heard Hieronymus got collared."

"What'd you hear?"

"It was you, right?"

I flinched before I could stop myself. "Yeah."

He shook his head. "Is it true he snitched on Bane?"

"No," I lied.

LM digested that with a nod. "Heard Bane went after your kin as payback."

All he got in return was a nod. I was so not discussing Danny with him.

A low whistle escaped his rosebud mouth. "Good luck, girlie," Little Man said. "You'll need it."

"She won't need luck if we find Bane first," Morales said.

"You'll need plenty of luck for that, too, Macho."

Morales's eyes widened at his new nickname. I put a hand on his arm to remind him not to assault my CI. "So who would know where Bane is?"

"I admire your tenacity, but the only cats who'd know something like that are Bane and Harry." The homunculus shook his head. "You ask the Frost Prince about that?"

"We tried," Morales said. "But that creepy motherfucker's already got his deal signed and sealed. He won't give up jack shit anymore."

"C'mon, LM. Give me something," I said, my voice rising in frustration.

"Whaddaya want from me?" Little Man huffed out an offended breath.

"You don't know where Bane is or who could tell us." Morales snapped his fingers. "Give me my money back."

LM cringed. Mary's arms wrapped around her burden as she leaned forward to growl at Morales. My partner stepped back with his hands up. "Relax. I'm not going to hurt the little bastard. Just want my cash."

The homunculus patted Mary's arms. She relaxed but kept her eyes on Morales. "All right," LM said. "You're right. I don't know what you're asking. But I do know something you haven't asked about."

I pursed my lips, growing tired of this myself. "Spill it."

He rolled his eyes and settled back against Mary with his arms crossed. "You're no fun."

Morales and I both shot him cut-the-shit glares.

"All right, all right," he said finally. He leaned forward on the edge of his carrier. "Did you wonder how Bane knew about the early morning raid? How he had enough time to clear out?"

I glanced at Morales. All this time I figured Bane had just gotten spooked when he found out we nabbed Harry. "I bet you have a theory."

He shrugged. "I been hearing some rumbling about maybe Bane having a guy on the inside."

Morales frowned at him. "Inside where?"

LM's eyes sparked with excitement. "BPD."

"Bullshit," Morales snapped. But I put a hand on his arm.

Mary looked up. "No yell at Baby."

"Then tell *Baby* he needs to do better than spread rumors if he wants money," he snapped back.

I closed my eyes and prayed for a break that I knew was never going to come. By the time I reopened them, Mary was rocking back and forth on the bench.

"Shit, Macho," LM said, sounding frantic as he tried to pat his sister's arm. "Now you've upset her."

"Mary, it's okay," I said quickly. "He didn't mean to yell."

Mary's rocking became more frenzied. Her large hands came up to grip her oily hair and a high-pitched keening came from her slack jaw.

"Shhh," LM soothed. "It's okay, Mama. It's okay. Baby's here."

Morales shot me a worried look. "Prospero, maybe—"

"LM, is she okay?"

Two mean, black eyes looked up at me from the infant's face. "Get out of here," he gritted out between clenched gums. "Fuck off!"

Morales grabbed my arms and pulled me away. I went along but kept my eyes on them. By that time Mary's rocking was so violent, the legs of the bench squeaked in protest. Her hands tore large clumps of hair from her scalp. Little Man pulled something from his diaper. I couldn't make out what, but it looked like an ampoule. With his tiny hand, he stabbed the attached needle into her fleshy forearm. Two seconds later, the rocking and the keening stopped altogether.

I could have gone back and arrested them for using a potion on public property. LM and Mary weren't wizards, so there was no way they'd brewed that shit by themselves. But I didn't bother. I was too freaked out by the suddenness of Mary's episode and the gentle care LM took with her. Plus, I couldn't afford to lose my best snitch.

I dragged my eyes from the pitiful pair on the park bench. "You thinking what I'm thinking?"

"Yeah, I'm wondering which freak show you raided to find those snitches."

I rolled my eyes. "No, about the mole thing."

"Do you trust the homunculus enough to tell Eldritch he might have a crooked cop on his staff?"

I shook my head and met his eyes over the roof of the car. The strain of the last few days pressed down with a sensation that bore a striking resemblance to hopelessness. "Let's just go."

# Chapter Thirty

An hour later, Morales pulled up in front of my house. On the way, we'd called Gardner to tell her the bad news. Unfortunately, she had some of her own. The ASAC had given her and the team seventy-two hours to find Bane before he called them back to Detroit for reassignment. It was better than an immediate withdrawal, but it also added another layer of pressure. Especially since the entire team was showing the strain of burning it from both ends for the last few days.

As we pulled in, my phone buzzed to indicate an incoming text. It was from Pen, telling me I had the night off because she was at the hospital. "Shit," I whispered.

My original plan had been to spend the night at the hospital, but Pen had beaten me to it. I shot back a quick text thanking her, but inside I wanted to cry. Probably she thought she was doing me a big favor, but the idea of another night alone in that too-quiet house made me want to claw off my skin.

"Everything okay?" Morales asked, shooting me a look.

No, it wasn't. Not at all. "Yeah."

"Well, there's someone bothering me—well, there are lots of things, actually," Morales said, putting the car in Park. "But the main thing is, the potion itself. You said early on he had to have help cooking a potion with those alchemical elements, right?"

I nodded. "He could have recruited some wizard from the Votaries to help him."

He shook his head. "Or maybe we were too quick to clear Volos."

I froze. Considering I was hiding the Volos visit from Morales, the conversation had just taken a turn into dangerous waters. I searched Drew's face for some hint he knew I was withholding something, but his expression was curious, not accusing. "Look, I'm no Volos apologist, but that doesn't make any sense."

"Doesn't it?" he said, raising a brow. "What if they worked together and staged Marvin's murder to clear Volos of suspicion?"

"You're forgetting one thing," I said. "Volos is building that community center on Bane's turf and with the botched tunnel raid, they've had to postpone the project. What's in it for Volos to cooperate with Bane when Gray Wolf has done nothing but cause problems for him?"

Morales blew out a breath. "None of this adds up. Why would Bane go to such lengths over a stupid community center?"

Relieved to have the conversation centered on Bane again, I shrugged. "It's not really about the community center at all." I toyed with a frayed thread on my jeans. "It's about principles . . . and turf."

Morales snorted. "Spare me the street wisdom, Prospero. Sociopaths like Bane don't have principles."

"Sure they do," I said, looking up. "It's not conventional morality, but covens are guided by their own codes. The first of which being that a wizard's turf is sacred. Volos isn't just sending some guys to sell on the Sangs' corners. He's using the legitimacy he earned by lining the mayor's pockets to drive Bane out of his territory altogether. That's the ultimate insult."

He pursed his lips and seemed to think it over. "If that's true, then Volos knew exactly what he was doing."

"He knew." I nodded. "In fact, I'd bet he was counting on it."

"So do you think he's doing all this because he wanted Bane's territory for himself?"

I nodded at him. "Maybe. Maybe not. But he definitely knew his plan would piss off Bane."

"I just wish we had more time on this." He scrubbed a hand over his face. "Or that LM had a location for Bane so we could end this today."

"I think LM liked you," I said, trying to lighten the mood.

"Yeah, sure. Before you know it we'll be trolling the titty bars together." He shuddered at the thought. "I hear homunculi are real pussy magnets."

I choked on a laugh. My head filled with an image of Mary hunkered on a stool sipping a Shirley Temple while LM played wingman to Morales. Beside me, Morales's deep baritone echoed my own higher giggles. After the stress of the case, it was cathartic to laugh over something so ridiculous. Finally, I wiped the tears from my eyes and let out a contented sigh. "I needed that." I looked at him. "Thanks."

"I do what I can." He smiled genuinely. It hit me then that without really meaning to, I'd started to actually like the ass. "You want some company? I could come in for a while."

The words hung there in the air between us like a big neon question mark. His gaze was too frank to misunderstand his meaning. If he came in we'd probably share a few beers, some war stories, maybe a few more laughs. And then, we'd share a few pleasurable hours in my bed. A few merciful hours when I wouldn't have to worry about Danny or Bane or Volos or any of the hundred other problems weighing me down.

He waited patiently while I weighed my options. He hadn't made the suggestion from any sort of emotional place. It was almost as if he'd thrown it out there because having sex was what all guys and gals did together eventually.

No doubt he'd be a firecracker in the sack. And I wasn't worried about romantic complications. He was too practical for that, and I wasn't naive enough to let a couple of orgasms make me stupid over a man.

"I'm thinking it's better if you don't," I said finally.

Idiot! The voice in my head sounded disconcertingly like Baba's, which did nothing to spark my libido. But I knew the only reason I'd be inviting him in was because I was afraid to be alone, and I refused to let fear guide my actions.

"You sure about that?" He tilted his head in a way that I'm sure would have changed the minds of most women.

But I wasn't most women. "Yeah."

He looked surprised and disappointed, but also a little impressed that I'd somehow managed to resist his charms. "If you change your mind, I'm just a phone call away."

You had to give the guy points for persistence. "I'll keep that in mind." I opened the door and climbed out of his truck. "Have a good night, Morales."

Just before the door shut behind me, I heard him mutter, "Yeah, right."

He waited for me to get inside before his truck roared off into the dusk. I watched until the red lights disappeared, and then I went inside to face the silence.

◆ ◆ ◆

Twenty minutes later, I was drinking a beer at the table in the kitchen, wishing it were something stronger. The can was cold and wet in my hand. The clock ticked agonizingly slowly in the background.

My eyes were on the phone in front of me, willing it to ring. I'd already called Pen and chatted with her for a few minutes. But the strain of pretending I was keeping everything together became too much so I'd ended the call quickly.

The idea of calling Morales to come back flirted with my bad decision sensors. But before that thought could gather much steam, something sticking out from under the fridge caught my eye.

I pulled the item out and realized it was *The Alchemist's Handbook*. It had been there ever since Danny had thrown it at me. Jesus, that night felt as if it had been months ago instead of just a few days. I snatched it off the floor and sunk back into the chair. Heaving a big sigh, I opened the cover to a random page. Despite myself, a small smile tilted up the corner of my mouth. The chapter I'd landed on was called "Practical Tips for Cleansing Tools."

And just like that I was transported to a time fifteen years earlier when Uncle Abe was giving me yet another one of his lectures on the importance of cleaning my beakers and burners between batches. "A lazy wizard is a dead one, Katie-girl."

Back then I had definitely been lazy, but now? Laziness was a luxury I couldn't afford. In fact, I couldn't remember the last time I'd had the house to myself for a night to do nothing. I should appreciate the time, but instead all these fucking thoughts about Danny kept poking away at my brain.

Like, most of the time when I sat by Danny's bed, I wished

it had been me potioned instead of him. That's what I was supposed to feel, right? As if I'd gladly trade places so he could live a healthy, full life?

On the other hand—and I'd never admit this out loud—sometimes I was relieved it wasn't me. I tried not to even acknowledge that thought. It was more like a shameful itch at the back of my skull. If I'd been the one hurt, Danny would be dealing with the worry and the fear. And the thought of being hooked up to hoses and a bag to collect my urine made my spine shrivel.

And then there was the third kind of thoughts, the dark ones, when I really resented that it hadn't been me. Not out of any sense of nobility. Quite the opposite. Sometimes I wished I were the one always being taken care of and worried about for a change. Not the caretaker. Not the doer. Not the one spending every moment fighting. Not thinking, thinking, thinking all the fucking time. And that's why I never talked about it. Because the shame of that selfish train of thought made me want to put my revolver in my mouth and pull the trigger.

A rattle sounded as my phone danced on the table. I jumped out of my self-pity and scrambled to grab it. Some stupid part of me hoped it would be Morales trying to change my mind. I picked it up, not sure I'd say no this time, but when I saw whom it was from I cursed.

> The offer still stands. Don't let pride make your decision. Let me help Danny. —John

"Fucker," I said to the phone. I wanted to throw it, but with the mounting medical bills, and the extremely recent threats of unemployment, I didn't have enough money to replace it. Instead, I set it on the table with slow, deliberate movements.

I couldn't blame Volos for sending the text—actually, yes, I could—but for some reason the wording of it was what really got to me. Who texted with perfect grammar? I mean, really? He might as well have been engraving an invitation to a fucking ball. And how the hell had he gotten my phone number?

For lack of anything else to punish, I picked up the book again and began flipping pages. Every now and then I'd find hastily scrawled notes I'd left in the margins. That earnest girl, the one with nothing but potential ahead of her, felt like a stranger now. If I hadn't detoured her off her original path, she'd probably have had no problem coming up with the potion we needed to save Danny. Because that girl, despite all her faults, was talented. "My little miracle worker," Uncle Abe had called me.

Where was my miracle now?

I took another long swallow of beer. Miracles didn't happen for the wicked, no matter how righteous their current path. But then my conversation with Pen the other day when she told me about that little girl dying floated to the surface.

"You can't save them all," I'd said. And then she looked at me with a mixture of despair and resolve. "I have to try."

Shit, who was I kidding? The minute Volos had walked out of that room, a tiny voice in the back of my brain had begun whispering. I'd managed to ignore its words until now, but in the silence of that house, which already felt haunted by a boy who wasn't even dead yet, I listened to it.

*Maybe I can save him if I cook.*

I ran my hands through my hair. This was crazy. When Morales arrested Bane, he'd make the asshole give up a cure for Danny.

"Don't be naive," the voice whispered.

Bane had pulled Danny into his plans because he knew it

would handicap me. For some reason, he wanted me in pain. He'd gladly do a longer sentence for not offering up the antipotion if he knew I'd be suffering outside the cell.

So what was the alternative? Sit around, wringing my hands and hoping that my principles would keep me company after Danny died?

Principles were nice in concept. But in practice, they were real sons of bitches.

I set down my beer and followed my gut to the place where I knew I'd find what I needed. Down the stairs. Past the Mount Doom of laundry and into Danny's room. His scent—a combination of funky gym socks and the cologne I'd given him last Christmas—lingered in the air. I ignored the painful scent memories and soldiered on. Pushing aside an avalanche of clothes, sports equipment, and other tools of the American teenaged boy, I finally reached the door at the back of the closet.

I'm not sure why the previous owners had built the hidden space. I assumed it was for added storage since the original construction had no attic and they'd converted the basement into a bedroom. It was more of a small closet set behind another closet, but we called it "the attic" anyway. Probably they'd used it as a convenient space for old clothes and photos and precious memorabilia. But me? I used it as a dumping ground, a hiding space—a cemetery?—for all of the skeletons I didn't want to see anymore but couldn't bear to destroy from my old life.

The instant I wedged open the door, the musty scents of dried herbs and essential oils gone rancid hit my nose like a punch. The fist to my gut wasn't caused by the scents so much as the realization that part of me was eager to go digging through those boxes.

"Jesus, Kate," I said out loud. "Get a grip."

Cardboard boxes were shoved in haphazard piles along the walls. I groped for the string I knew was hanging from the ceiling and pulled. The single, bare lightbulb exploded with light too close to my eyes. Tracers and dust motes danced in my vision for a moment, playing tricks on my mind. I imagined I saw Uncle Abe's smirking, too-knowing face in the corner. I blinked and rubbed my lids to clear away the specters.

This room was where Danny had gone to find the potion manual and the old pictures of our mother. Evidence of his snooping was everywhere—from the torn lids on a few boxes to a sticky puddle of soda and the footprints he left in the dust.

"At least I don't have to worry about him turning into a criminal mastermind," I muttered to myself. The sarcasm felt forced and overly optimistic given the fact that at that moment my brother needed the help of machines and tubes to breathe, eat, and piss.

I swallowed the bile that rose at that thought and moved forward with a determination borne from denial. Going through those old boxes suddenly felt a lot less scary than contemplating the idea that my brother might never wake up from his nightmares.

The first box was a loser. Nothing but some old clothes. The acid-washed denim jacket I'd worn my entire fifteenth year after Volos told me I looked cool in it. Next came some old CDs from bands no kids today had ever heard of. Hell, they'd barely even heard of CDs.

The second box revealed I was getting warmer. Some old beakers and a few tools of the potion trade. But the third box presented the mother lode: a heavy marble mortar and pestle, an empty olive-wood saltcellar, and a ceremonial athame. I ran my thumb over the edge of the blade, which was dull and curled over as if it had simply lost the will to hold its edge.

Mama had given it to me for my twelfth birthday. At the time I thought it was the most precious thing in the entire world. The jeweled handle and shiny metal made it seem like a rare treasure. But looking now with adult eyes and the tarnish of maturity, I realized it was little more than cheap brass and aluminum, now browned and pitted from time. And as for the "precious jewels," they were little more than paste gems glued into the handle.

My fingers rubbed dust from my nose and brought with them the sour stink of the brass on skin. Much like the future Uncle Abe had promised me, the athame had proven little more than a glittering illusion. In reality the promises of power and happiness were worth less than that cheap brass knife.

I jerked myself out of those memories and threw the knife back in the box. A quick wipe of my hands on my jeans didn't dispel the scent, but it made me feel a little better. That was another benefit of being older: I realized my emotional connection wasn't to the cheap metal or the paste jewels, but to the woman who'd given the knife to me. Funny how I'd used it every day as a girl, but now it might as well have been an alien artifact.

I grabbed the box and stacked the other on top. The cubbyhole wasn't large enough for any potion work. I stopped and considered my options. Doing magic in our home seemed sacrilegious somehow—not to mention dangerous. That left one option: the old garage-turned-storage shed out back.

I headed that way, hefting the two boxes with me. After I'd dumped them outside the door, I went back in to grab a few more supplies: candles, matches, and a couple more beers because it was never a good idea to do dirty magic sober—blocked the flow of energy.

Naturally, I was aware that all my prep work was its own

form of procrastination. Truth was, it wasn't the early autumn chill that made my hands shake. But once I had everything hauled to the dusty, old shed, I couldn't put it off any longer. I pried open the double doors and was immediately assaulted by the scents of gasoline from the old lawn mower and fertilizer I'd bought for the flowers I'd never gotten around to planting.

I dragged in the boxes and set to work, clearing space on the old workbench. The small lantern from Danny's fifth-grade campout went on the shelf. The meager light wasn't much to brag about, but once I lit a few candles visibility would improve.

Next came the bag of ceremonial tools. Lots of wizards these days scoff at the old ways. They see the ceremonial traditions as little more than superstitious mumbo jumbo. I wasn't sure I disagreed, but the routines had always helped to relax me and get me into the right frame of mind for cooking up a potion. I wasn't sure they did much to help the magic work, but they sure made me feel better. Or they had—back when I did magic regularly.

After I made sure the doors were shut, I went back and prepared the initiating rituals. First, I lit four candles—one for each direction on the compass. Closing my eyes, I took a deep breath. My lungs hitched as if they were congested. I cleared my throat and tried again. This time the air flowed more smoothly into my lungs until my ribs expanded. On the exhale, I tried to release all my stress. I blew for a long time. Felt as though I could have exhaled for a year and I'd still have tension to spare.

The wind kicked up outside. Leaves scuttled across the lawn and pelted the side of the shed. Inside the garage, every noise was amplified, which did nothing to calm my jittery nerves. I did the inhale, exhale thing again.

It didn't help. So I took a swig of beer instead.

"All right," I said to the empty room. "Start with something easy."

I dug around in the box of equipment and pulled out a glass dish and a hot plate. I took a step back and chewed on my lip.

I knew I didn't begin to have the proper equipment to formulate a complex antipotion. Especially since getting it right would require my getting ahold of a sample of Gray Wolf and reading its energy to break down the components. Plus, many alchemical processes—even the down-and-dirty ones used on the street—took time.

My main goal that night was just to dip my toe back in those old, familiar waters to make sure I could handle it. The thought made my stomach quicken and my face flush. I licked my lips and tried to remind myself it was just this once—for Danny. If I failed no one had to know. In fact, even if I succeeded no one could know.

I had a bottle of vodka in the house and could probably scrounge up some herbs to make a basic Spagyric elixir, but distillation would take up to a week. And even then, after I'd filtered the solution through a pair of panty hose, it would have to sit an additional twenty-four hours before it was usable.

On the other hand, I found an old vial containing some sort of herbal extract. I opened the stopper and sniffed. The astringent scent of concentrated rosemary brought back memories of the cleansing bath salts I'd made for my mother one Christmas. Smiling at the memory, I decided I could manage a simple operation to make a "salt of salt" preparation of rosemary.

Salt of Salt requires a basic calcination procedure—basically, burning something down to white ash. I poured some of the thick, brown rosemary extract onto the dish. Next, I struck a match and touched it to the solution. The alcohol in the extract caught immediately, and soon the heat intensified the sharp pine scent inside the space. The mixture of infused alcohol and rosemary needles turned into a thick, black resin after a few moments. I took a small metal wand and stirred it, humming to myself as I worked.

As far as alchemical operations went, this was about as simple as they came. But, then, simple was exactly what I needed. The steps kept my hands busy and my mind quiet, and that alone was a blessing.

To speed things along, I lit the camp stove under the glass dish so it was burning from all sides. I sipped my beer as I kept one eye on the flames. If there had been a large quantity of extract, burning it down to ash might have taken hours or days even, but that night it took only about half an hour for the first round of heat to reduce the resin to a dark gray ash. I scraped the powder into my mortar and ground away at it for a few minutes with my pestle.

I repeated the heating and grinding two more times until the ashes were very light gray. Then the ashes went into a beaker with ten times its volume of water. Tap water worked just fine since I wasn't cooking clean. If I had been, only sterilized and distilled water would do. After all that, it was simply a matter of letting it boil down until all the liquid evaporated. The white crystals that remained were the Salt of Salt.

I turned on my stool to look at the salt in the light. The white crystals gleamed dully in the poorly lit garage. I smiled at it and laughed at myself. It had been so long since I worked with magic that I guess I'd expected my first time back to feel...earth-shattering. Or at least dramatic. Instead, there had been a pleasing boredom to the process.

Despite what movies suggest, magic isn't a flamboyant process. It's not flying lasers from fingertips or flashes of lightning or wands waved and chants shouted. Instead, it's a subtle art. Adepts don't force magic on items, we coax and harness their inherent energies. The process I had gone through that night drew the elemental salt from the rosemary. Purified it with fire to reach its essential energy. Some believed fire elevated that energy, too. All that was left was for me to decide what other energies to mix it with to create the magic I needed.

But then I remembered that the kind of magic I needed was more complex than playing with simple herbs in a toolshed. I needed a lab and equipment and high-quality ingredients. One of those miracles I'd thought about earlier wouldn't hurt, either.

Before I could get too worked up about that, though, I realized my back felt very warm. Too warm considering the night air was filled with early autumn's chill. I turned and cursed. Flames licked up the sides of the camp stove and were dancing dangerously close to the wooden walls of the shed. I jumped up, looking around for something with which to put out the fire. Since I'd dissolved all the water, the only liquid on hand was the last half of my last beer. The fire hissed at me but didn't surrender. Panic started to rise in my chest like heartburn. The edge of a cardboard box began to smolder. I whipped off my sweatshirt and started beating the box and the camp stove.

In the process of smothering the flames, my hand whacked the hot plate's glowing red element. "Mother of fuck!" At that point, panic fled as rage roared in. With my right hand—the unburned one—I grabbed the cord of the stove and ripped it out of the wall.

I try not to stew in self-pity often, but it was all too much. Boxes went flying and tools clanked and shattered to the ground. I kicked the mortar for good measure, which added a nice big toe contusion to my burn and the puncture wounds in my neck from when Danny attacked me. I'm not sure when the kicking turned into crying, but before I knew it I was on the floor in the smoky shed bawling like a child. Through the haze of tears, I looked down to see the rosemary salt crystals lying scattered among broken glass.

Pressing the heels of my palms to my eye sockets, I tried some deep breathing to get my emotions under control. A pity party wouldn't help Danny. I glanced down at the burn wound. An angry red blister slashed across my Ouroboros tattoo. I ran a finger along the snake design and remembered how proud I'd been the day I'd earned the right to get inked with the symbol of my coven. Within six months of that day, I'd walked away from magic completely.

Obviously, the fire had been a sign that I should have stayed away.

"I get it," I said to the universe. "But as long as you're sending signs, how about one to tell me what to do next?"

I waited for a good minute in the silence before I sighed, hauled myself off the ground, and cleaned up the mess. Unfortunately, the universe doesn't run on a human schedule. That's why it waited until the next morning to send its message.

# Chapter Thirty-One

When I dragged myself into Danny's room the next morning, I felt about ten types of shitty. Sleep hadn't been an option the night before, so I'd left the house at the ass crack of dawn. Unfortunately, no matter how fast I drove, I couldn't outrun my existing problems and even more waited for me in Danny's room.

I froze at the door. Machines beeped like maniacal robots. The doctor shouted orders like a general in battle. And the nurses' rubber-soled shoes squealed against the floors like stuck pigs.

"Kate!" Nurse Smith saw me and rushed over. She had something yellow—bile?—all over the front of her scrubs. She grabbed my arm and tugged me away from the door. Shock prevented me from fighting her.

Through the tangle of bodies surrounding my brother, I caught a glimpse of Danny's ghostly white skin and blue-tinged lips. The frothy spittle spilling onto his chin. The rag-doll reflexes as the nurses moved him and poked him with needles.

A single word dove from my brain straight down to the dark

pit of my stomach, where it cannonballed with all the force of a boulder: dying.

My soul shriveled within my skin.

"Kate, honey, I need you to listen to me," she was saying from far away. "He's gone into some sort of shock. Doc thinks it's withdrawal from the potion."

I blinked slowly. Nurse Smith, black void, Nurse Smith.

"We're getting him stabilized and then Dr. Henry will come talk to you, okay?" She shook my shoulders. "Do you understand?"

Inhale, exhale, inhale.

Nodding took great effort. "Withdrawal. Stabilized."

Don't lose it. Don't lose it. Don't lose it.

She smiled, but it was fake. She patted my arm, but I didn't feel it. "I'm going back in to help."

"Wait! Where's Pen?" I said, grabbing her before she could walk away.

"She left half an hour ago to run an errand. She'll be back soon. Why don't you go grab some coffee? Dr. Henry will be with you in a few moments."

Coffee? I turned slowly toward the direction of the coffeepot at the other end of the hall. Coffee couldn't scrub the image of my brother's blue lips from my eyes. It wouldn't calm me down—if I were any more numb I'd collapse. But getting coffee was movement. It was active.

So I marched down the hall. I grabbed the little white foam cup. I put the coffee pod in the machine and depressed the lever that injected a needle into the little plastic container of grounds. I punched the button that forced scalding water to churn against the bitter grounds. Then, abracadabra, a perfect cup of caffeinated alchemy. All that remained was for me to add the creamer or sweetener of my choice.

How sad that the only thing I controlled in my life fit into a six-ounce foam cup.

I stared at the steam rising from the dark surface. The white tendrils reminded me of a movie I saw once where a soul escaping a body was depicted by a puff of white smoke. I squeezed my eyes shut so hard that motes danced in my vision. They would have been beautiful if they hadn't been accompanied by stabbing pain.

"Kate?" A hand landed on my shoulder.

I willed my eyes open and turned to face whoever had interrupted my own private psychic breakdown. Luckily, it was Pen.

"Honey, what's going on?"

Gravity won the battle and I fell into her as if she was oblivion. She caught me and held on. "Shh."

I didn't cry because I didn't have the energy. But my limbs shook and I screamed inside my head so loud I was surprised no one in the hospital could hear my pain.

"Tell me what happened," Pen whispered.

I shook my head because if I opened my mouth the screams would escape.

Pen's chest expanded and contracted on a sigh. Then she was guiding me farther down the hall to the waiting room. All the chairs were empty but she took me to the ones the farthest from the doorway.

Once I was sure we were alone, I pulled away and told her what the nurse had said. And then I took a deep breath and confessed all my sins. Every one I'd committed since I'd taken over as Danny's guardian all the way to the huge fight we'd had about magic on his birthday. Maybe I was hoping that by the time I'd finished, Pen would give me a list of tasks to do to wipe the slate clean. Some degrading exercise that would teach me a lesson. Maybe once I'd completed the karmic chores, everything would go back to how it was before. Danny could return to being the goofy sixteen-year-old going on thirty, and I would go back to being the almost-thirty-year-old going on sixteen.

But that's not what happened. In real life, things don't go back to normal at the end of the half hour. Confessing your sins more often damns you than saves you. And no matter how much you wish it were otherwise, you can't just wish away the consequences to your shitty decisions.

Pen held me close and told me it was okay to be scared because she was, too. And then I held her back and we were scared together.

"Officer Prospero?" the nurse said from the doorway. "Dr. Henry will see you now."

I snapped my jaw shut and looked at Pen. She nodded even though I hadn't asked her out loud to come with me.

We rose together and she grabbed my hand for a quick squeeze. "It's going to be okay, Katie," she whispered.

My gratitude for her patient listening morphed into anger. I didn't need saccharine platitudes. I just needed someone to play straight with me for a change. Not use political maneuvering or double-talk or emotional blackmail. I just needed someone to cut the shit and be honest.

"Kate? Doc Henry's waiting."

For Doc Henry's sake, I hoped he wasn't planning on blowing sunshine up my ass. Because I was a woman on the edge and I wouldn't hesitate to pull him and everyone else over with me.

◆ ◆ ◆

The room that had been so chaotic an hour earlier was now silent as a funeral home. Which was fitting since I couldn't help but look at Danny's too-still form and feel as though I was looking at a corpse.

Especially when I saw that regret in the doctor's eyes.

I didn't speak to him. Instead, I crossed my arms, raised my brows, and braced myself.

"He's alive." He motioned to the chair next to Danny's bed. "But we need to talk."

I glanced at the bed to see if I could pinpoint the reason for his grave tone. The machines were beeping as usual, and—thank God—his chest rose and fell in an artificially rhythmic pattern. But it was hard not to see the damage the potion and the coma had done to him. His cheeks had hollowed into gaunt blades and his complexion was the color of wet cement. He basically had become a hollow shell that was alive only through the will of modern technology.

I tore my gaze from Danny and looked back at the doc to let him know I was ready to take the punches. Pen stood next to me and held my hand.

He clasped his fingers over the clipboard and held it in front of his waist like a shield. "There's really no good way to say this, Kate, and I'm damned sorry to be the one to do it."

Frost lined my stomach. "Jesus, what is it?"

"The potion we gave Danny to keep him in a coma is still working. The machines are doing their job keeping his respiration and fluid levels normal. He's young and relatively healthy, all things considered."

I tilted my head. "So what's the problem?"

He waved a hand toward the third, silent body in the room. "We're managing to keep him alive, but the dirty magic is eating him from the inside."

"But you said—"

He nodded. "The machines and potions we gave him are

working. But unless we find an antipotion, his body is going to consume itself to feed the bloodlust the potion created."

"What?" Pen said. "How is that possible?"

Doc rubbed the bridge of his nose and took a deep breath. "If there's no blood coming in, the blood magic in the potion turns to the host to get its fix."

I rolled up my sleeve. "Take my blood." They could take every fucking drop. I didn't care.

"That's not all." He shook his head. "The attack earlier was withdrawals. We've stabilized him for the time being, but he doesn't just need more blood, he also needs more of the potion. The blood magic needs more blood and the alchemical components need more potion to sustain themselves."

My mouth fell open.

"In my opinion, if he doesn't get more Gray Wolf soon, he'll die."

Pen reached blindly for a chair and fell into it. As soon as her ass hit cushion, she crossed herself. Her inconsistent Catholicism was one of the many idiosyncrasies that endeared her to me. Right then I wished I believed in some sort of religion, too. One that would explain to me why bad things happened to innocent people. One that explained why bad people got away with murder. One that offered salvation in exchange for adhering to a few simple rules.

But religion and me? We weren't on speaking terms. Which meant all I had to guide me was the seething rage and a bottomless pit of regret. I stood on the lip of that well and looked into the inky blackness. Ahead of me was the abyss—a future spent mourning. Cold memories to haunt my nightmares. Six feet of dirt and a mountain of guilt separating me from Danny for eternity.

A light rose from the abyss, and a voice in the back of my

mind whispered, *Are you ready to sell your soul to the devil to save him?*

"Yes," I whispered without reservation. There wasn't a choice. Not really. Not one I could live with that was easier than owing a debt to John Volos.

"Kate?" Pen said, turning toward me.

I shook myself out of the protective cocoon of shock. "Yeah?" I said, as if I hadn't just come to a decision that would change the course of all our lives forever.

"Did you hear what Dr. Henry said?"

I nodded but the movement was jerky. "I'll take care of it."

She went still. "What does that mean?"

I pulled my eyes away from Danny's emaciated form to look at the fear in my best friend's eyes. "It means I'll take care of it."

Pen shot a look at the Doc. "Excuse us for a moment." She grabbed my sleeve and hauled me toward the door. I went with her without argument. The instant I realized how close I was to losing Danny for good, every drop of fight evaporated.

"Explain yourself," she demanded. She had me backed up against a wall.

I couldn't tell her everything. To do so would admit to things I wasn't ready to admit to myself. So I simply whispered, "John said he could make the antipotion."

She reared back. "John *Volos*?" she hissed. "What the hell?"

"He came here the other day to offer it. I turned him away, but now?" I motioned toward the doctor. "I don't have the luxury of turning down help."

I fully expected her to launch into a lecture about healthy decisions and not compromising one's principles. Instead, my best friend nodded solemnly. "You think he's telling the truth? Can he really figure out the cure?"

"Do you think I'd even consider going to him if I doubted he was capable of this kind of magic?"

She chewed her bottom lip for a minute. She glanced back at the unconscious kid on the bed—the one she loved almost as much as I did. Then my friend, who fully understood the implications of what she was about to say, looked me in the eye and said, "Go."

# Chapter Thirty-Two

The text I sent to Volos read: We need to talk ASAP.

His reply was an address and instructions to meet him in one hour.

That gave me enough time to run home to grab a few things before I showed up for the meeting. The first thing I grabbed was my gun. It went into my shoulder holster. I stashed a salt flare in the holster at my ankle and a canister of salt-and-pepper spray in a jacket pocket. And, finally, I fingered the protection amulet Gardner had given me a few days earlier. I hadn't put it on again since the day she'd given it to me in Danny's room because it made my skin crawl with guilt. But considering I'd tried to cook the night before and was about to go meet a wizard to help him cook a dirty magic potion, my qualms about wearing a protection amulet were moot. The disc held a small bubble of glass in the center filled with a viscous green liquid. All I had to do was burst that bubble and an alarm would signal the team that I was in trouble and tell them where in the city to find me.

Once I had everything, I pulled out my phone and punched a couple of numbers. He picked up on the second ring. "Cupcake."

I smiled despite the nerves roiling in my gut like a nest of vipers. "What's up, Macho?"

"Ah, you know." I could hear the smile in his voice and the creak of a chair as he leaned back to put his boots up on the desk. "Madman's on the loose, the ASAC is breathing down our necks, and Eldritch is trying to blame the clusterfuck in the tunnels on Gardner, but beyond that I can't complain. How's Danny Boy?"

My chest tightened. "We had a bit of a scare this morning."

The tension crackled through the line. "Shit, Kate. Is he okay?"

I swallowed hard. "He will be." The words were as much a vow as an explanation.

"If there's anything I can do—you know that, right?"

I nodded even though he couldn't see me. Problem was, the one thing I needed help with, I had to do alone. If Morales knew I was calling him right before I headed out to help a known criminal brew a dirty magic potion, he'd be speeding over to arrest me. I forced a laugh. "I thought you saw me as a pain in the ass and wanted me off the team."

He chuckled low, the sound oddly intimate. "Oh, you're definitely a pain, but as it happens you're also not a total loss at this cop stuff."

"Flatterer." I sighed because I couldn't force myself to fake a laugh. "Anyway, I think it'll all be better soon."

"I hope so." In the background, I heard Gardner's voice echo through the gym. The shuffling sound that followed was probably Morales covering the receiver with his hand. A muffled response filtered through the earpiece. A second later he came back. "Hey, listen, I need to go. BPD just got a tip about a Bane sighting. Shadi and I are going to go check it out."

"Got it. Be careful, okay?"

He paused for a second and I imagined that maybe he caught something in my tone. But instead, he just said, "Don't worry about me, Cupcake. Just take care of yourself and the kid."

I hung up and went to do just that.

◆ ◆ ◆

The address Volos had sent ended up being the old Iron Hop Brewery building. The place closed back in the eighties and had remained abandoned since. The red bricks and old chimneys squatted on the banks of the river. This part of the riverbank hadn't benefited from Volos's plan to attract Mundane dollars into the Cauldron. Thus the area was decorated with trash and puddles of stagnant water and graffiti from the covens' Heralds instead of expensive multiuse real estate developments.

I parked down the road from the building and used a pair of binoculars to scope out the broken windows and boarded doors. There weren't any cars parked out front, which meant Volos either hadn't arrived or had parked elsewhere. His text had said to meet in an hour, which meant I still had ten minutes to case the joint.

I didn't see any lights on inside the warehouse, but it wasn't dark enough outside yet to tell for sure. The sun was setting on the far side of Babylon, where Lake Erie spread out like a freshwater sea. The splashes of reds and pinks might have been pretty to the naive eye, but to my jaded ones, they were just reflections of the pollution that tainted everything in this city.

Before long, a black sports car pulled through the gates and drove to the large bay door set into the facade of the building.

It wasn't a vehicle I'd seen before, but I definitely recognized John's profile through the window.

I was relieved to see he'd come alone. Part of me had been wondering if he'd bring that bitchy lawyer along, too, just to make my indentured servitude legally binding.

How do you know this isn't a trap? my practical inner voice challenged.

"Only one way to find out," I said aloud. I threw off the seat belt, checked the piece at my shoulder, and touched the amulet hidden inside my shirt for good luck. "Here goes nothing."

The street was so empty it might as well have had tumble-weeds blowing down the center. The algae stench of stagnant water mixed with the stink of trash from the landfill down the road. Most of the buildings in this part of town were warehouses and abandoned tenements. Inside they were like ant farms filled with potion junkies, hookers, and mentally ill homeless people who'd never touched a potion but had nowhere else to turn. Maybe I imagined the eyes glittering in the shadows like polished dimes, but I doubted it. Not much happened in the Cauldron without someone seeing it. Problem was, when shit went down, witnesses had a tendency to scatter like rats escaping from a sinking ship.

When I finally reached the building, I knocked on the metal door to the right of the larger bay. Not five seconds later, it opened and the void it left was filled with John Volos. He didn't smile or offer a greeting. He just grabbed my arm and pulled me inside before I could slap his hand away. Once he slammed and locked the door behind us, he jerked his head, saying, "This way."

Several things hit me at once. First, the air stank of wet concrete and stale urine. No doubt the walls had seen their share of vagrants exchanging all sorts of indignities for hits of a cheap buzz potion. The temperature was a good ten degrees cooler here than it had been outside, but my palms were sweating. The front of the warehouse was empty except for the car, which clicked as its engine cooled. "Hold on," I said, grabbing his shirtsleeve when he turned to walk away. "What the hell is this place?"

His jaw clenched with annoyance. "I just bought the building for a new business venture."

I raised a brow. "A legal venture?"

He shrugged.

I nodded. "Do you have the supplies in the car?"

He smiled like I'd made a joke. "Everything's already set up. Come on." He looked eager, like a kid who wanted to show off a forbidden treasure. I shook off the thought as soon as it arrived. John wasn't the mischievous teenager I used to worship anymore. He was a man with an addiction to power.

"Kate?" he called, sounding impatient. I jerked my head up to see him standing twenty feet away next to a set of stairs. I jumped into motion. The sooner we could get this done, the sooner I could get as far away as possible from the confusing feelings that rose up every time I was around him.

The stairs curved up to the second story and dumped us at the edge of what used to be the brewing floor. Huge metal-encased windows on three of the walls provided late afternoon light. The sun I'd watched earlier was now positioned perfectly to send a warm glow into the old building, making the decay and ruin look almost otherworldly.

"We still have a lot of work to do just to get the place cleared out," he said, almost apologetically.

"So you're going to what—gut the joint and turn it into a mall or lofts?"

His lips twitched at my jaded tone. "Nope. This will be a pet project. A new hobby."

I raised my brows.

"A few years ago I found an old alchemist's grimoire at an estate sale. Inside were the most wonderful recipes for spirits and liqueurs. And then it hit me: Alchemists basically invented distillation, so why not start an artisanal alchemist liqueur company?"

I blinked at him. "Really?"

His smiled wobbled. "Yeah, why?"

I shook my head at his injured tone. "Nothing, it's just—" I searched for words that wouldn't insult him more.

"You figured if I was involved it would be something under-handed and possibly illegal?"

I chewed on my lip. "Something like that."

"Kate, you're the last person I'd pretend to be a saint with. But I honestly do try to mostly stay on the right side of the law these days."

I shrugged because I was withholding judgment on that. "So alchemical liqueur, huh? It's kind of a cool idea, I guess."

He shook his head at me. "You've grown too jaded in the last ten years."

And he'd gotten too…everything. I crossed my arms and looked away from his knowing gaze. "Are we going to do this or what?"

His openness of a few moments prior evaporated and his smile froze. "Of course." He held out a gallant hand for me to precede him. "The lab is just through there." He pointed to an arched doorway at the far corner of the cavernous room. As we walked, we skirted around the huge holes where the brewing vats used to rest. Judging from the darkness below, the floor we were on was over a boiler room or storage basement.

John led me through a bricked archway to a room that prob-ably had been a testing room where quality assurance techs made sure the batches were up to the brewery's standards. But now, it had been completely transformed into an alchemy lab that would make most wizards greener than a youth-potion addict. "Holy shit," I breathed, walking in.

Large copper distilling vats had been set up along one wall. Under the massive warehouse windows, a dozen barrels and even more boxes with shipping stamps from Canada and Europe sat patiently, waiting to be opened and turned into elixirs. I noted that several of the barrels were marked as containing rose quartz oil. Guess that explained the mysterious shipping manifests Shadi had found.

I turned from the windows toward the worktables that had been set up along the wall opposite the distilling vats. Long coils jutted from glass flasks like alien antennae. This was no slapdash operation. Volos hadn't gotten my call and hastily put all these things in place. I turned to look at him. "How long have you had this set up?"

"A few weeks. I'd originally intended to use it to refine the recipes for the products we'll eventually make here, but once Gray Wolf came into the picture, I decided to start working on an antipotion."

I narrowed my eyes. "When did you start working on it?"

"The day after you killed that MEA snitch."

My eyes widened. "How did you find out about it so quickly?"

His lips lifted at the corners. "Is that really what you want to ask me?"

I held his gaze to show him his pointed question didn't embarrass me. "What's in this for you?"

He nodded, like that was the question he'd been expecting. "It's the best way I know how to ensure Bane's plans don't interfere with mine."

"That's not what I meant," I said.

"I know." He crossed his arms. "You're wondering what I want from you."

I tipped my chin down.

"I don't know yet."

In the silence that followed that admission, I felt a lot of conflicting emotions. One, I was surprised he'd actually admitted to being unsure about something. Second, the fact he couldn't say he didn't want anything worried the shit out of me. And third, I was both intrigued and terrified to wait for the moment when he finally figured out the answer.

I cleared my throat and looked toward the cold beakers. "How far have you gotten with the antipotion?"

His gaze burned into me for a few moments while he obviously debated whether to let me change the subject. Finally, he sighed. "I've already thrown out a couple of batches. I think I'm close with the most recent sample, but there's something I'm missing in the original potion."

"Can I see that one?"

He nodded and grabbed a couple of test tubes from a small fridge. "There's a sample of Gray Wolf, too." I jerked my gaze toward him. How in the hell had he gotten his hands on the potion when the MEA couldn't? He shrugged. "How else was I supposed to figure out the recipe?"

I rolled my eyes. Raising the vials, I examined the one labeled GRAY WOLF. "You don't look like much for a potion that's been causing so much trouble," I said to it. I shook the glass and the liquid inside sloshed around like oil.

"What do you know about it?"

"It's a mix of blood magic and alchemy, but you knew that. Antimony is a core ingredient." He urged me toward the worktable, where a notebook was laid open with writing in his bold hand. He pointed to a line. "But what's really interesting

315

is that instead of human blood, Bane used wolf blood." My brows rose. "And, I could be wrong, but I also detected Van Helmont's Alkahest, also derived from a wolf."

My expression morphed into a sour grimace. "Gross." Van Helmont's Alkahest was a fancy term for piss salt. Yeah, that's right, salt derived from urine. "Guess it's a good thing the potion isn't administered orally."

"The thing is, I can't get over the feeling that if we could read the alchemical signature we'd know what's missing in the antipotion."

He was referring to the energy fingerprints wizards left on the potions they created. Typically they didn't tell you the ingredients as much as the identity of the wizard who cooked it, but sometimes wizards used signature ingredients. If we could figure out which alchemist had helped Bane, we might be able to find the key to breaking the potion.

And by "we," he meant me.

John was a talented wizard, but his strength lay more in the energies of transformation than those that allowed one to read magic. That was my specialty. The only problem was that reading a potion's energy sometimes meant seeing other things— like bad omens.

My palms were already sweating. But first, I decided to see if he was right about his prototype not working. I grabbed a small beaker off the shelf.

"You're going to want to be careful," John said.

Ignoring his unnecessary warning, I flipped the top off the vial of Gray Wolf and sniffed. The acrid stink of copper and sickly sweet burnt brown sugar of heroin and the chemical bite of drain cleaner singed my nose hairs.

I grabbed a beaker and poured a quarter of the potion— only a couple of teaspoons, really—into a glass beaker. My eyes started to water from the fumes. I reared back to escape the stink. "Grab me a pair of goggles and a mask, will ya?"

While he did as instructed, I opened the stopper on the sample of antipotion. The liquid inside was a gray-brown color—like brackish water. Its scent was reminiscent of dirty feet and rotten meat, but it was still a pleasant change from the Gray Wolf's horrible odors. John returned and I made quick work of donning the goggles and mask.

I took a small pipette from the counter and sucked up a little bit of the antipotion. Behind me, John scooted back a couple of inches. I glanced at him over my shoulder. The goggles made him wobbly, as if I were watching him through water. "Just in case," he said.

With a grimace I turned back to the beaker. If this were truly dangerous, he would have already run from the room. I blew out a breath. "Here goes nothing."

The instant the first drop of antipotion hit the Gray Wolf, a puff of smoke curled up from the surface. A split second later, the consistency of the oily liquid morphed into a sort of greasy, smoking solid. I touched the edges of the beaker and found it seriously hot to the touch. And all that was before the clump burst into a small column of flame. "Huh," I said. "That's not good."

We weren't in any immediate danger in the lab since it was such a small sample. But it wasn't hard to imagine what injecting the antipotion into the vein of a Gray Wolf addict would do to their body.

"Well," I said, "I'd say that's pretty much a fail."

The corner of his mouth came up. "Told you. Now what?" He said it too casually. We both knew exactly what came next. He just didn't want to risk saying it out loud and spooking me. I kind of hated him for knowing how to manage me like that.

I'd watched too many people die from potions. Seen people burn from the inside. Seen flesh and bone collapse as a body consumed its own cells. Neither fate was one I wanted for my brother.

Which meant it was time to get down to the business of magic.

"I need a heat source, a Florence boiling flask, water, and glass stirring rods." I continued to list as Volos gathered equipment. Finally I finished, "Oh, and gloves and a beer, if you have any."

While he went to collect everything, I stared at the potions and tried not to look as if I was screwing up my courage.

"I think this is all of it," he said, setting the last of the items down. I grabbed the beer he'd pulled from the fridge and smiled at it. I typically bought the cheapest lager I could find, but this was an expensive brew from Germany. "Good to go?"

I pulled my mask down, twisted the top off the bottle, took a long pull, and exhaled loudly. The fancy lab and equipment I could live without, but I could definitely get used to the fancy beer. "Let's get to it. How much Gray Wolf you got?"

"Two more vials, but that's the only sample of antipotion."

After I replaced my mask, I poured about half of the Gray Wolf into a boiling flask and set that over a Bunsen burner. While that started to simmer, I used a pipette to place a few drops of Gray Wolf on a glass slide. A quick look through the microscope didn't provide any clues. I hadn't really expected it to, though.

Truth was, I was just trying to ease my way into the magic by using more scientific methods. Luckily, Volos had made sure his lab was filled with all sorts of expensive equipment. It was ironic since, back in the day, we'd cooked in kitchens and bathrooms with whatever supplies we could beg, borrow, or steal. That's why dirty magic was sometimes called "bathtub alchemy." It's also one of the reasons dirty magic is considered dirty—the cooks weren't in sanitized labs with sterile equipment and controlled ingredients. Though Volos's lab was clean, the work we were doing was definitely dirty.

I lit a match and held it to a piece of paper coated with a drop of Gray Wolf. The paper didn't blacken at all. Instead, the ashes were snow-white immediately. That was the antimony's fingerprint at work.

I took a step back and chewed on my lip. The best way to break down a potion was to experience it with all five senses. I had sight and smell covered. When the potion started to bubble in earnest on the hot plate, the components didn't make any odd squeaks or crackles—so hearing didn't tell me much. Taste was out of the question since it would require me to ingest some of the dangerous brew. Not to mention the wolf urine.

Instead, I took a little between my fingers and found the texture oddly thick and oily. I raised it to my nose and sniffed again. Rubbing it had warmed the potion to body temperature, which brought out a new texture and scent.

"Petroleum jelly," I said, almost to myself. From the corner of my eye, I saw John watching me with a small smile hovering on his lips. "What?" I sounded defensive even to my own ears.

He shrugged. "Nothing. It's just great to see you at work again."

Hairs prickled on the back of my neck. I wasn't sure if it was being this close to magic after so long, or an actual sense of foreboding. Either way, I pulled my eyes from his and went back to work.

Clean magic always required the use of organic—read: expensive—essential oils. They were more stable and potent, but their prohibitive cost made them a rarity in street potions. Therefore, the covens tended to rely on cheap petroleum jelly and mineral oils to serve as the bases for their potions. Problem was, when applied topically, they also tended to clog pores and prevent the skin from releasing toxins. When they were absorbed by the body, they also could keep vitamins from being metabolized properly. That's why so many potion addicts had horrible acne and lesions.

"Do you have a pencil or something?"

A split second later, a legal pad and an expensive-looking fountain pen appeared in front of me. I didn't comment that I would have preferred a simple pencil. While John watched over my shoulder, I listed all the ingredients I'd identified so far. Tapping the pen on the tabletop, I realized nothing I'd listed was especially interesting or unique. Granted, the way the components were combined was sometimes more important than the chemicals themselves. But in order for these things to do what I'd seen Gray Wolf do, it would take some seriously dark energy.

"Where's your list?" I asked, looking up. He grabbed a file folder from a leather satchel he'd brought with him and flipped through to a page with a list written in his bold cursive. Comparing the two, I realized his correlated with what I'd seen so far, but then I saw something different.

I looked up. "Dragon's blood? You're sure?"

"That was a guess," he said. "It can have psychoactive effects."

"But this is also a blood potion," I said. "Dragon's blood would make the wolf's blood coagulate."

He frowned. "Willow's bark or cat's claw would prevent that."

"That doesn't seem right." I shook my head. "We're missing something."

I checked the beaker and was pleased to see the potion reducing quickly. Hopefully once it thickened enough I could dry it and analyze it in powder form.

"Kate?" he said quietly.

I turned my head to the side to look at him through the veil of my hair.

"You're stalling."

I stretched and worked the kinks out of my neck. As I did, I caught the time on a clock he'd installed over the distilling apparatus. Two hours had passed. I glanced quickly toward the large windows and was shocked to see it was already full night. At some point while I'd worked, John had turned on the large lights overhead. With some embarrassment, I realized that I'd been enjoying myself so much I hadn't even noticed the time passing.

"I'm not stalling," I said. "I'm trying to be thorough. Magic isn't the answer to everything, John." The beaker was hot, so I used the cuff of my shirt to pick it up. I tipped it over to spread it out on a drying sheet.

"Messing with those beakers isn't going to cure Danny. Time's a-wasting, Kate."

Something hot burst in my stomach. Guilt. But also fear and definitely a lot of resentment. "None of this would have happened if you hadn't decided to build on Bane's turf." When in doubt, turn your anger on someone else. So much easier than facing your own role in the problem.

He crossed his arms. "You really want to play the blame game or are you going to make shit happen?"

I wanted to rage at him. I wanted to punish him for bringing me here. I wanted to walk away.

Unfortunately he was right. I could resist reality or I could accept that I just had to do the damn thing, as Pen was fond of saying. "Fine," I snapped. "Do you have a divining bowl?" I almost prayed he didn't.

He smiled. "Of course." He reached to a top shelf and pulled down the most beautiful divining bowl I'd ever seen. The porcelain was so fine it was practically transparent. Once again I was struck with how far we were from the days working in my mom's kitchen, reading potions in the chipped coffee mugs she stole from the Blue Plate Diner. "Like it?" he asked, mistaking my look for admiration. "Bought it at auction last year. It's from Jingdezhen. The alchemist who fired the porcelain named it the 'Bowl of Illumination.'"

I sighed and shrugged. "It's fine."

He frowned like I'd insulted his manhood. Jesus, what happened to the 'hood rat who once gave me wilted dandelions as a romantic token?

"Grab me another ampoule," I said. His frown deepened, as if his patience with my bossing him around was losing its novelty.

He set the new vial next to my hand. "What else do you need?"

"Lights out, complete silence, and some privacy."

His left eye twitched like he was trying to decide if he should argue with me about the privacy part. Apparently my own look told him that this was one area where I wouldn't budge. I wasn't about to let him stare at me like a voyeur while I stumbled my way through serious magic for the first time in a decade.

"Suit yourself." He turned on his heel and marched toward the archway that led to the old factory floor. "There's matches and candles in the drawer to your left," he called over his shoulder. A second later the overhead lights extinguished, leaving me alone in the pitch black. Through the large windows to my right, I saw lights from the Mundane part of town glowing cheerfully across the river.

With a sigh, I removed the gloves and scrubbed my damp palms on my thighs. My hands fumbled with the drawer, but soon a small flame licked the darkness. I blew out a long, centering breath. Showtime.

I poured the entire vial in the divining bowl. The potion's rusty color looked like old blood against the pristine white. I took a step back and closed my eyes. Drew in air through the nose, expanding my ribs. A pause. Exhaled slowly, yet audibly, through the mouth. Repeat twice. Imagined circling myself with an aura of golden, protective light since reading dirty magic opened one up to all sorts of negative energies. Once I felt as though I'd cleansed and protected myself, I opened my eyes and began.

Stepping up to the table, I raised the bowl and swirled it widdershins three times. I raised my left hand and held it over the liquid. The potion's energy reached toward mine like metal shavings toward a magnet. I touched the dark light of its aura gingerly at first. A tingle skipped up my arm.

Next, I swirled my left hand up, gathering the energy into a ball and balancing it on my fingertips. It glowed as if someone had flipped on a black light. Inside the center of the ball was a poison green core. Its energy rolled through me like thunder.

"Who made you?" I whispered.

The core began to shift and morph. At first it looked like a blob of mercury rolling in space. But then, slowly, it turned into the shape of a wolf. The symbolism for that was obvious given the purpose of Gray Wolf. Squinting, I pulled my hand closer for a better look. The wolf morphed into the shape of a cat with its hackles high. The symbol of a deceitful acquaintance. That wasn't much of a shock. That cat became a dragon—the symbol of Bane's coven. So far, so good.

I held my breath and tried to will the magic to reveal itself faster, but magic had its own agenda. The dragon's fire spread out to form a protective barrier around it, but from the resulting smoke a new creature emerged. The monster had the head and feet of a rooster but the tail of a serpent. It was a basilisk.

Like a flashbulb, the mysterious wizard's identity appeared behind my eyes. My stomach pitched and rolled into icy waters.

The rooster reared back its head and let forth balls of flame and a high-pitched hiss. The dragon exploded, leaving behind a bag of gold. Then the basilisk transformed into a green, crowned serpent, which curled around the gold and began to swallow its own tail.

The symbols came so fast and furious and the messages they delivered were so troubling, I felt shaky and my skin was clammy with sweat.

But the magic wasn't done telling me its story. The image shifted and a second snake appeared. The two serpents braided over each other until they started swallowing each other's tails, creating a sort of infinity symbol. In the next instant, a sun, moon, and six-pointed star rose behind the entwined snakes. On a gut level, I knew this last image had nothing to do with who created the potion. It was a portent, a warning.

I released the energy so fast I doubled over as if I'd been punched. Gasping, I sucked in air and steadied myself with a hand on the table. The magic might have dispersed, but the images still haunted me.

The basilisk. It could be only one person. The worst possible foe.

Abraxas Prospero.

Now, in addition to the symbols, questions swirled through my head as if it were a centrifuge. How in the hell did Abe get involved in Bane's plans? And more important, *why?* What did he have to gain? Because Abraxas Prospero never did anything without expecting a personal boon.

And then I remembered how the investigation had played

out. How all signs seemed to point at Volos's being responsible for Gray Wolf. When it became clear Bane was involved I figured he'd tried to frame John because he'd dared go after the Sangs' turf. But now I realized that if Abe was involved, the motive had been much simpler than a turf war.

Abe wanted revenge. He'd tried to frame John for Gray Wolf to make him pay for betraying him.

"Goddamn it," I whispered.

The lights flashed on overhead, disorienting me even more. I tried to pull myself upright despite feeling like a wrung-out dishrag, but suddenly two strong arms came around to support my weight. My senses filled with the sharp bite of ozone and the woodsy fragrance of John's aftershave.

He cursed under his breath as he caught me. "Kate? What's wrong?"

I licked my lips and blinked rapidly as vision came rushing back. John's frown was blurry at first, but a relief from the static. But then an image of the basilisk superimposed itself over that face. Fear raced through me, along with a need for action.

I pushed away from John and stumbled toward the shelves. My eyes scanned the bottles for the ingredient I needed.

"Kate?" John stood directly behind me. I could feel his worry. "What did you see?"

"No time," I snapped. "Where's the green vitriol?"

"Just tell me—"

I rounded on him, my fear manifesting as anger I directed at him. "Did you know?" I demanded, my voice rising.

He squinted and tilted his head. "Know what?"

I paused because I was suddenly afraid. Almost as if saying the name would somehow summon the devil into that brewery. I shook my head and kept combing through the cabinets.

He grabbed my arms and forced me to look at him. "What?" He shook me a little, as if he was trying to rattle sense into my brain. "Tell me."

I told myself to tread lightly. His reaction to my next words would determine how this would play out. "It was Uncle Abe."

It appeared in his eyes first, the rage. Then his confused expression tightened, contracted as the dominoes of evidence fell in his mind. "That's not possible."

His left hand was wrapped around my left wrist. I looked down at his-and-hers Ouroboros tattoos. Dragging my eyes from the image, which was too disturbingly reminiscent of the vision I'd just had, I looked him in the eye. "You know it is very possible."

He shook me again. "Are you absolutely certain it was him?"

Was I? It had been so long since I'd read magic I couldn't blame him for his distrust. Some symbols were open to interpretation, but some were as sharp and bright as a honed knife's blade. "Yeah," I said, swallowing bile. "I'm sure."

John dropped his arms and stepped back. He shook his head in denial. Easier to fool himself than to accept how well and truly screwed he'd be if I was right. Because if Abe was calling the shots behind Bane the whole time, we'd been playing a child's game without realizing we were really fighting a war.

Anger flared in my gut. "Thanks for dragging me into this bullshit, by the way."

His eyes flared. "I didn't drag you into anything, Kate. You're conveniently forgetting that you wouldn't have gotten involved in this at all if you hadn't killed that MEA snitch or talked your way onto the case."

I shook my head even though he was right. It hurt too much to accept that my own ambitions had started the chain reaction that led to Danny's getting hurt and my having to cook to save

him. Being angry at John was so much easier than turning that
weapon on myself.

"Whatever," I said. "It really doesn't matter how either of us
ended up in the middle of this. This big question is, How did
Abe pull this off and what's his endgame?"

He stared at me hard for a second, as if he couldn't decide
whether to let me off that easily, but in the end he played along.
"Let's face it: The warden at Crowley probably can't take a shit
without Abe's permission."

I couldn't argue with that. "And the endgame?"

"Knowing Abe there's no way we'll ever see that coming. Better
to focus on using what we know now to finish the antipotion."

I nodded and blew out a deep breath. "Where's the green
vitriol?"

He frowned. "For what?"

"That wasn't dragon's blood in the Gray Wolf. It was cinnabar."

"Shit. Of course." He let out a breath. The basilisk wasn't
just a nickname for Abe, it was also a symbol for cinnabar,
which is why Abe used it in most of his alchemical potions.
"How did I miss that?"

I shrugged. "Because he wanted us to miss it. He put in extra
quicksilver to help disguise it, probably." I moved a few bottles
around looking for what I needed.

"Green vitriol is over there." He sounded weary. "Might be a
good idea to add some extra sulfur, too, just to balance it out."

I looked up and over at the cabinet he pointed toward. This
one had locked doors. Not surprising. High-quality green vitriol was expensive and difficult to lay hands on since the government regulated its sale. "The key?"

He removed it from his pocket and tossed it over. "There's
not much."

"I only need a little. Enough for a cure for Danny." I pulled down the small vial filled with green crystals. I poured a quarter gram into an unglazed earthenware container.

"Kate?"

I ignored him. So far I'd been doing a fairly decent job of convincing myself not to freak out about Abe's involvement. Keeping my hands busy helped, and so did just plain old denial. But fear was curling around the edges of the wall I'd erected, like poisonous smoke. As much as I tried to convince myself that I could just get the cure for Danny and then go on with my life, the truth was I was now tangled up in Uncle Abe's web as sure as Volos was.

John got tired of waiting for me to respond. "I'm sorry."

I shoved the green vitriol into the furnace. The heat from the flames was intense and made my skin burn. I wanted to pretend I hadn't heard him. I didn't want his apology. I didn't want our shared predicament to forge any sort of intimacy. "Forget about it," I said finally. I turned before I continued, "I'm just here to help Danny. Don't expect me to help you fight him, John. I can't afford to get involved any more than I am."

He watched me for a moment. My gaze skittered from the disappointment in his eyes. Finally, he nodded curtly. "You think that's going to work?"

"I sure as hell hope so," I said. "Otherwise we'll be screwed."

A laugh echoed through the lab. Low, mean, and very unexpected. We both swung around to see Ramses Bane himself standing by the doorway. "Oh, I'd say you're both a little more than screwed."

# Chapter Thirty-Three

My gun was in my hand before Bane finished his sentence. "Stay where you are."

Those doll eyes were dancing with humor and his lips were twisted into a sick pretender of a smile. "Does that mean I'm not invited to your little magic party?" His tongue darted out to lick his pale lips, like a predator tasting blood on the air. "Put down the gun, please." He had one of his own pointed at us.

It was the first time I'd seen him since he'd forced my brother to use a potion that almost killed him. Maybe still would. Hatred boiled up in my stomach, and my fingers itched to scratch his eyes out. But I couldn't let him see how angry I was because he'd use it to his advantage. No, I had to play it nice and cool, even if I felt anything but. "My team is already on their way here, Bane."

While I spoke, I slid the vial of antipotion up my left shirtsleeve. If Bane got ahold of it, we'd have to create a new batch from scratch, which would delay my ability to get it to Danny. Although, honestly, hiding it was a mere formality. I'd tear Bane apart with my bare hands if he tried to take it.

"Don't be silly. Your team isn't coming for you at all."

"Yes, they are," I said. "You've got maybe two minutes."

He laughed too confidently. "Nope."

"What makes you so sure?"

"Because I've been watching you, Katherine." At my curse, he chuckled. "That dreadful car of yours isn't exactly difficult to spot."

John's hand came up to grab my arm in warning. "What do you want, Bane?" he demanded.

Bane threw back his bald head and laughed. "Don't pretend you don't know." He glanced toward the end of the aisle. "Michael, come help your friend get more comfortable."

From the shadows behind the coven leader, Officer Michael Hanson entered the room with a gun raised high. "Drop the weapon, Prospero."

Rage threatened to boil out of every pore in my body. "If it's all the same to you, I'm more comfortable with the gun," I quipped, but the tremor in my voice gave me away.

Bane's lips quirked at my bravado. Hanson made quick work of divesting me of the Glock and the S&P spray from the pocket of my jacket. He didn't take the amulet tucked into my bra, though. Or the salt flare at my ankle. Rookie fucking mistake.

But there was no way for me to activate the amulet with Bane watching me like a hawk staring down some juicy carrion, and they were both positioned to put a bullet through my brain before I got anywhere near my ankle.

A smile spread over his cherry Kool-Aid lips. Now that Hanson had his own weapon and mine pointed at us, Bane put his weapon in his waistband and removed something from his jacket pocket. He held it up for us to see that it was a vial. He popped open the top of the ampoule and brought the potion to his nose for a sniff. "Mmmm," he murmured. "This is something new I cooked up. A youth potion." He glanced at me and winked. "None of us are getting any younger, are we?"

With deliberate movements, he darted the tip of his tongue out for a taste. "Coppery." He closed his eyes and tasted again. "Sweet. That's the goji berry, I think. Oh, and there's the turmeric and chili." He opened his eyes and licked his lips. "Spicy."

He tipped back the vial and drank the rest of the potion. His eyes rolled back and his whole body shuddered.

An unsettling giggle escaped him. "My tongue is numb." He leaned forward and whispered, "It's the cocaine. I add it for energy." He placed a pale finger in front of his lips, as if it was our little secret.

"You're a lunatic." Volos's tone was calm but had a cadence that was engineered to make the listener feel like an idiot.

"Careful, boy. I've skinned men for less insult." Bane sniffed. "Tell me honestly, Kate. How is dear Danny doing?"

I saw red. Hot, bloody red. If I'd been able to burn him alive with my eyes, I would have charred him to the bone. "I'm going to kill you."

"Not if I kill you first," he sing-songed.

"How do you think you're going to pull that off?" John asked. "The minute they find our bodies they'll know it was you."

"That's right," I said quickly. "You think the cops circled the wagons after you hurt Danny? Wait until you see what they do after you murder a cop."

Bane snorted. "Methinks the city will be more torn up to lose the mayor's new toy. Tell me, John, is it true Owens is a power bottom?"

I glanced up and saw John's face had hardened into a bored expression, but his eyes glowed with heat.

"All right," Bane continued, "I can respect that you don't want to kiss ass and tell. Regardless, you're more valuable than Prospero to this town."

A scornful laugh escaped Volos. "And you're nothing more than a tunnel rat. You'll die in the gutter where you belong."

"Careful," Hanson warned, stepping forward. "You might be good at magic, but you're not immune to lead poisoning."

"Back off, you fucking traitor!" I yelled.

His gun swiveled in my direction. He didn't look angry or as if he anticipated making me bleed. Instead, he almost appeared resigned.

Bane clicked his tongue. "Oh, Katherine. Why the harsh language? Poor Michael here is as much a pawn in this game as you, I'm afraid."

"What?" I demanded.

"Go ahead," Bane said with an indulgent smile. "Tell her."

Hanson's jaw tightened. "He got some...pictures that he's going to send to Eldritch if I don't help him."

I tilted my head. "What kind of pictures?"

Bane giggled. "Poor Michael has a taste for magical pussy, don't you, Mikey? It was a simple matter of having my dear cousin take a few snapshots during his last visit to her temple."

His cousin was Aphrodite Johnson, the leader of the sex magic coven—the Os. Last I'd heard Bane and Aphrodite had been on the outs over some sort of debt she owed him. Probably he had used that to convince her to help him with Hanson, too.

"You asshole," I said. "Why not just kill him?" I stabbed a finger in Bane's direction.

Hanson's face morphed into an offended mask. "I'm not a murderer, Prospero."

My mouth fell open. "What the fuck do you think he's planning to do to us?"

"Oh, I'm not going to kill you." Bane paused and let that sink in. Let that spark of hope grab a little oxygen and flare before he stomped it out. "John is."

Something cold exploded in my heart. It felt a lot like fear. My brain scrambled, looking for angles and escape routes.

"Why would I do that?" Volos sounded a lot less freaked-out than I felt. But then he moved a fraction closer. I wasn't sure whether the move was designed to reassure me—or him.

Bane shrugged. "Because once I dose you with Gray Wolf you won't be able to stop yourself from tasting her tender flesh."

All the blood drained from my face. Even the marrow in my bones felt cold.

"Oh no," Bane said with a giggle. "You both look so upset. Does this mean you're fucking again?"

Over the years, I'd had perps say all sorts of things to try to distract and unsettle me. Bane had just misfired by a long shot. I shook off the specter of John's getting potioned and focused on getting us both out of there before it could happen. "Yeah. We're fucking." My tone was flat and dry as an Arizona highway. "You figured us out."

Volos cleared his throat. "Might I suggest we come to some sort of compromise?"

Bane and I both looked at him. John's posture was casual and his tone was formal, but the steel in his eyes made him look every inch a man capable of wreaking revenge of biblical proportions. If I hadn't wanted to kill Bane so much myself, I would have felt bad for him.

"No compromises," Bane said.

Bane raised his gun as casually as a man checking the time. With dawning horror, I watched him squeeze the trigger. An instant later, the bullet punched a large, red hole in the center of Michael Hanson's chest.

The cop's eyes widened in surprise. The betrayal had only just begun to register on his face when blood seeped from his lips. And then, just as quickly, the light dimmed in his traitor's eyes. His body collapsed into the steel worktable. Glass beakers shattered across the floor along with his blood.

Regardless of whether Hanson was coerced or aiding Bane willingly, watching a fellow cop get murdered so easily, so coldly by that psychopath made my blood run icy-hot. Suddenly it felt a lot less as if we'd make it out of there alive.

"Now, where were we?" Bane asked, his tone bored. "Oh yes. I was going to start the game." He moved, as if to get the Gray Wolf from a pocket.

"Why did Abe get involved in this?" John asked quickly, desperately.

Bane looked up with a slow smile. "Simple: He wanted revenge."

"Why?" We needed to keep him talking. I shifted ever so slowly toward my right, hoping maybe I could reach some sort of makeshift weapon from the supplies.

"If he hadn't testified against Abe, then none of this would have happened." Bane pointed the gun at Volos. "You should have kept your fucking mouth shut."

My eyes jerked toward John. He looked resigned. "So trying to frame John was Abe's idea?" I asked.

"No! I went to him once this asshole announced plans to take over my turf." Bane was panting with anger now. "Abe made the potion, sure, but it was my idea. I was finally going to earn the markers to take over the Cauldron. Just had to take Volos out of the picture."

"How did Danny figure into this?" I asked, my voice hard and low.

"Payback for arresting Hieronymus and blackmailing him

334

into betraying his daddy." Bane shrugged. "Plus I needed to get you out of the game. Figured the kid would either kill you or you'd just walk away. But as usual you were too stubborn to know what was good for you."

"Jesus, Bane." I pushed aside the baiting words as it all clicked together. Bane had failed to take out Volos. He'd failed to hold onto his turf in the Cauldron. And he'd gone after Danny—Abe's own blood—to try to fix his fuckups. "Do you have any idea what Abe's going to do to you once he finds out you screwed up everything? You won't survive a day in Crowley."

I hated Bane more than anyone, but the threat of Abraxas's vengeance was enough to make me pity him. Failure not only wasn't an option—it was a crime punishable by extreme pain and a slow death.

"I won't be going to Crowley." He sounded so sure of himself. And that's when it hit me: Bane was screwed only if this last-ditch effort didn't work. Abe might be pissed the original plan failed, but if Bane could pull off a scheme to make Volos hit the evening news as a werewolf cop-killer, well, even Abe couldn't stay mad too long. Especially if the cameras just happened to catch the BPD shooting Volos dead. "Abe won't be able to stay mad at me. Especially when he finds I took out Volos and his traitor niece."

I frowned. "Abe gave me his blessing when I left."

"He figured you'd come running back for help, but then you had to go and become a fucking cop." He shook his head, as if he was cursing his dumb luck. "When I found out that asshole MEA snitch attacked you, I tried to clear you so you'd stay away from the case. But then you had to go and get yourself assigned to the task force. Always sticking your nose where it's not wanted. And you!" Bane stared at Volos with wild eyes.

"The Sangs should have ruled the Cauldron after Abraxas went to prison. Instead, you decided to get in bed with the government and steal our corners and tunnels from us." He pulled a second gun out of his rear waistband with his left hand.

Hearing Bane admit his motives out loud made me sick to my stomach. All of this—all the dead bodies, the violence, Danny's coma—had been over a stupid dirt lot and personal vendetta.

My eyes zeroed in on the weapon in his hand. From a distance it appeared to be a typical semiautomatic. But closer, I realized it was a modified tranquilizer gun.

The next minute of my life passed in both fast-forward and slow motion at once.

Bane fell into a crouch. The gun swiveled toward Volos. A loud pop sounded. A red blur zoomed through the air. Volos jerked backward, his hand coming up to his throat. He slammed into the table, flipped backward over it, and landed with a loud crack that sounded suspiciously like skull against concrete.

I yelped and started forward, but from the corner of my eye I saw movement from Bane as he reached for a Mundane gun. Instinct drove me to tuck and roll. The gun barked. Searing pain in my right calf. My ribs slammed into the floor with blunt force. The momentum pushed me out of the line of fire and behind the overturned table.

Volos lay maybe eight feet away. His face was alarmingly pale and sweat plastered his shirt to his chest. His breaths came in shallow pants and the veins in his neck were pulsing rapidly.

I grabbed the salt flare from my ankle holster. Breathing heavily, I cursed myself for not bringing more Mundane firepower.

"Kate," Volos rasped. I looked over in time to see a small

pistol glide across the floor toward me. In a smooth movement, I grabbed it and swiveled upward to deliver two shots. Then I fell behind an overturned table. I quickly stashed the salt flare back in the ankle holster and checked the ammo in the pistol. Just a couple of bullets left. I sent one in Bane's direction.

A satisfying yelp sounded from across the room. "Fucking bitch!"

Judging from the echoing sound of scrambling footsteps, he'd retreated back to the factory floor. Probably he'd want to find a nice hiding spot from which to watch the hunt once John turned.

Sucking down my fear, I surged up and ran full tilt toward the archway. My breath rasped in and out of my sandpaper lungs. My heart churned to keep the blood pumping through my taxed veins. With my back to the wall, I crouched down and went left—away from the large holes I'd seen earlier. I tried to get my adrenaline under control as I moved. Cool heads saved more lives than hot firearms.

There was no doubt in my mind that the tranq dart was filled with Gray Wolf. That meant I had only a few moments before Volos hulked out with a serious case of bloodlust.

From the corner of my ear, I heard a sound. Bane. Judging from the small whimper, I'd clipped him somewhere painful. But not painful enough. No amount of pain would be enough for that bastard now.

A wet noise, like gagging. "Kate," John groaned thickly. "Run!"

Oh shit. Fear rippled across my skin.

Before I could react, though, Volos's warning was followed by a low, guttural moan.

Lightning zinged through my limbs. My muscles yearned to run, but Bane still had a gun somewhere in the dark. The best

I could do for the moment was take shelter behind a low, crumbling wall. Shit, Kate, think!

First things first—backup.

I pulled off the amulet and looked at the little bubble on the front. The iridescent, green liquid sparkled dully in the dark.

I hesitated. I'd gone without using magic for a decade, but now, because of my involvement in the MEA, I was knee-deep in it. What the hell had this case done to my convictions?

A growl echoed, closer now, making my spine crackle with fear. Volos wouldn't stop until he consumed me, and even if I managed to escape him, Bane wanted my blood, too. I put a lot of faith in my wits and my gun, but I wasn't a fucking idiot.

I cracked the vial and lifted it to my lips. All the while, I promised myself that if I survived that night, I'd go back to never touching the stuff again. The liquid tasted bitter on my tongue and the texture was effervescent like those rock candies kids loved. The amulet didn't light up. No sirens sounded. No immediate sign at all that the bat signal even worked. Morales had said they were going to be on Bane's tail that night. Obviously he'd given them the slip. Had they closed up for the night? Was anyone even monitoring the alert system? "Please work," I whispered.

"Kate," Bane taunted. The echoes made distances hard to determine, but I guessed he was probably about halfway through the room, hauled up behind the old crates. "Can't you imagine the newspaper headline: 'Cop Killed By Wizard Ex-Lover'? The reporters at the *Babylon Register* are going to cum all over themselves." His giggle echoed through the space, making hairs stand on the back of my neck. "Better run before the potion does its work."

He was referring to Volos, but the one I'd just ingested was working, too. Already the pain in my injured leg was less severe.

My breathing calmed and I felt a kick of energy as the potion heightened my stamina.

Another bullet whizzed by. Too close. I scooted back along the wall to see if I could get a bead on Volos's location. But where he'd been before, I saw nothing but tile floor and a pile of green sick.

I looked out across the factory floor and froze. A hulking shadow was moving away from me.

On one hand, I should have felt relieved that I was not his first target. On the other, I now had both a psychotic wizard and a werewolf between me and freedom.

My heart sprinted in my chest. Shit, shit, shit. I had to figure out how to get out of the place with the antipotion so I could save Danny.

Time to think. Obviously I had two choices. The first involved my waiting for the team to respond and hoping they arrived before Volos found me or I ran out of ammo.

Second option: I could try to lead Volos toward Bane and let the beast rid the Cauldron of a major criminal element.

Another option hit me like a bolt of lightning to the synapses.

I could finish the antipotion. Short of putting a bullet in John's brain, finishing the cure was the only way to ensure we both made it out alive.

A feral roar came from within the labyrinth of garbage on the brew floor. I couldn't pinpoint where he was exactly, but I had a bad feeling he knew exactly where I was. The blood trail from my calf wound alone would be like a beacon to his predatory instincts.

"It's too bad it had to come to this, Katherine!" Bane yelled, his tone bordering on hysterical. Where the hell was he hiding that he felt confident enough to yell?

I rose into a crouch and started making my way toward the

lab. If I could lock myself inside, maybe I could survive long enough to finish the antipotion. Or for backup to arrive.

A loud crash exploded from the darkness. I twisted around and fell on my ass with a gun pointed toward that direction. When no buck-toothed monsters emerged from the shadowed trash piles, I rose and ran toward the lab. My harsh breaths worked my ribs painfully and my heartbeat pounded in my head.

"Where are you going, Katherine?" Bane giggled nervously.

I was only half listening because I had bigger problems. If the terrifying noises behind me were anything to go by, my movements had earned me the attention of a very large, pissed off, and hungry Volos. Adrenaline and Mez's speed potion made my movements fast but imprecise.

I slammed the large door and my fingers fumbled with the bolts. I'd finally slid one home when a very heavy body slammed against the panel. Claws scraped wood. Rage-filled howls promised pain. The next bolt closed more easily. For good measure, I took advantage of the added strength I'd gained from Mez's potion and adrenaline to shove a large filing cabinet in place as well.

Satisfied I'd done all I could to barricade the door, I ran across the room to the furnace. Using my shirtsleeve, I flipped the latch to open it. Searing heat slammed into my skin. Squinting into the red-hot mouth, I tried to see if the green vitriol was ready. "Shit." I couldn't see anything.

Wasting precious seconds, I scrambled to find an insulated mitt among the shards of glass and overturned tables and stools. While I slid it on my left hand, the banging continued at the door. The snarls of an angry werewolf crept into my head and haunted the parts of my brain responsible for remaining calm. My boots slid on broken glass as I struggled back to the furnace.

Even with the mitt, the heat permeated the material and made my palm sweat. Or maybe that was nerves. Either way, carrying the vessel back to the counter was an uneasy feat.

The crack of splintering wood lit a new fire under my ass. I removed the vial of John's test antipotion from my sleeve and set it in a bracket. The green vitriol had burned into a white ash, as I'd hoped. But the tricky part was still to come, and judging from the creaks and groans that door was giving I didn't have near enough time.

I poured the ash into a mortar and gave it a very quick grind to ensure all the crystals had pulverized. Luckily, the chaos earlier hadn't harmed any of the cabinets, so it only took a couple of seconds to find a brown bottle labeled SULFUR.

People always think sulfur smells like rotten eggs in any form, but that's not true. Heated sulfur releases chemical compounds that stink like rotten eggs and gunpowder residue, but not the pure form. I didn't have time to heat the sulfur correctly, so I poured it in the still-smoking pot I'd pulled from the furnace along with the calcined vitriol. The container wasn't hot enough to melt the crystalline powder, so I'd need additional heat to activate the magic.

On top of the sulfur and ash mixture, I poured the rest of the prototype antipotion John had made. I caught my breath as they met and mixed in the pot. This was my best and only chance to save John and Danny.

Sweat beaded on my forehead and my hands were slippery as I lit a match from the book John had given me earlier. I touched the small flame to the concoction. It caught fire immediately. The melting sulfur turned from yellow to red, giving the mixture a bloody cast. The stink was noxious so I breathed through my mouth—panted, really.

A loud crack echoed through the room, reaching right into my gut and twisting. Time to make some magic happen.

Up until now, I'd been doing basic alchemical processes. But now, it was time to bring magic into the mix. By manipulating a substance's energy, an Adept can take toxic materials and combine them in such a way that they may be ingested to create desired outcomes. If a Mundane mixed a paste of vitriol and sulfur and then tried to ingest it, he'd vomit profusely and probably die. But once magic was in the mix, the melding of compounds and intention morphed the ingredients into something...*other*.

I blocked out the angry pounding and scratching at the lab door and closed my eyes. My heart thumped in my ears and red veins glowed dully behind my lids. Starting at the top of my head, I scanned down my body, trying to relax each limb and part as I went. Another loud crash behind me. Trying to ignore the sounds, I willed my cells to vibrate at the proper frequency. This wasn't just a matter of my thinking magical thoughts, I actually had to manifest the energy and infuse it into the ingredients.

Opening my eyes, I focused my energy at the flames licking the air above the elixir. At first, the fire was the typical red and orange. I raised my left hand above the mixture and focused every cell in my body on activating the antipotion. I'm not a praying woman, but I did a little of that, too. My hands shook and my stomach roiled as the energy flowed through me. It had been so long since I'd played with these energies that I had trouble regulating my body's reaction.

The flames slowly turned blue. A split second later, the mixture swirled and morphed from grayish to brilliant green, indicating I'd transformed Volos's failed sample into a viable antipotion. I let out a little whoop of victory. But the only way to ensure the elixir worked properly would be to apply it directly to a sample of Gray Wolf.

The werewolf outside decided he'd waited long enough.

The world exploded into a storm of wood shards, black fur, and the heat of angry animal. Volos's once-familiar and handsome face was now the image of rage personified: snapping fangs, red-rimmed eyes that glowed with hunger.

"Fuck!" The panic switch flipped on and with it the instinct honed by training that turned that panic into fuel. While the beast stalked in and commenced with his intimidation display, I scrambled through drawers looking for a syringe. I didn't exactly love the idea of having to get close enough to him to prick him with the needle. But judging from the way he was stalking me, I wouldn't have much of a choice about getting close and personal.

Panicked, I grabbed a syringe, threw off the wrapper, and shoved the cap between my teeth. Then I jabbed the needle into the vial in a smooth motion. I'd just managed to pull back the stopper when the attack hit.

One second I was hunched over the vial, working feverishly. The next white-hot pain erupted in my shoulder. If I'd been wearing my leather jacket, the slice wouldn't have caused much damage. But I'd shucked the coat earlier and was left clad in a thin T-shirt that shredded like paper under the sharp assault.

The hit knocked me to the side. I grasped the syringe in my left hand and curled it protectively against my chest as I fell. I didn't stay down long because that was just begging for death. Shoving the cap back onto the needle, I dug in my feet and sprinted toward the door.

An offended roar told me Volos was done playing around.

Strong—so fucking strong. Even with Mez's potion in my veins, it took every ounce of strength in my body to fight off the blows. I tried to grab the salt flare from my ankle, but his fist slammed into my face and I was suddenly too busy trying to stay conscious.

He grabbed me by my hair and threw me out of the room and into the larger brewing space. Judging from the intense pain of impact, my body slammed into a concrete pillar. If it hadn't been for Mez's potion, I probably would have died right then. I was either very lucky or extremely unlucky I did not die. But before I could decide which side of that question I fell on, the weight of the enraged werewolf slammed down on me again.

The bone structure that used to be my face morphed into a matrix of pain. I could see only through my left eye and what it registered terrified me so much I wanted to squeeze it closed again. Saliva dripped from the canines he aimed at my throat. Only adrenaline and fear combined with the elbow wedged between us stood between me and death.

On the periphery of my vision, just beyond the monstrous visage looming over me, I saw Bane had come closer to watch the scene. The violence excited him so much, he was rubbing his crotch like a perv at a nudie show. I hated to disappoint the sick bastard, but he wasn't going to have a happy ending.

There are certain times in your life when you have to surrender to reality. When I'd gone to meet John that night, I'd had a plan: Get the antipotion, help my brother, and save the day like a comic book hero.

But this wasn't a comic book and I sure as shit wasn't Wonder Woman. My only means of survival was the antipotion in my left hand. The only way to save Danny's life now was to ensure that John Volos lived.

My right arm was losing strength fast. With my left hand,

I tried to uncap the needle without pricking myself with the antipotion. Hot breath on my neck, stinging scratches on my shoulders, rage-growls echoing in my ears. My fingers fumbled to spin the plunger into stabbing position.

Sharp points scraped my neck. It felt as though he'd gained fifty pounds. The weight and the struggle and the fear were weakening me. Time to move—or die.

I threw my weight right. He didn't budge but a few centimeters, but it was enough to swing my left hand up. I stabbed the needle into his jugular and punched the plunger. He reared back and his eyes widened on a roar. A split second later, the yellowed pupils rolled back in their sockets.

Panting as though I'd just run a marathon, I dislodged his weight and dragged myself out of grabbing range. He fell back onto the concrete, panting.

I watched in shock from the dirty floor as the doubts bubbled up. What if I'd been wrong about the green vitriol? What if my not using magic for so many years had dampened its power? What if Uncle Abe booby-trapped Gray Wolf so antipotions sped up death?

John's body convulsed like I'd applied jumper cables to his limbs. Saliva bubbled from his mouth. His hands clenched into fists and his body bowed up off the floor. He froze at the top of the arc and a scream ripped from his chest.

My brain flashed back to another untested potion. The one that killed my mother. Had I just killed John, too?

The trembling began in my limbs. I told myself it was Mez's potion wearing off, but in my gut I knew it was fear. I couldn't carry the debt of his death, too. Especially since John's demise would also doom Danny.

Oh God, Danny. My stomach roiled at the thought of a future without that kid around to drive me crazy.

Volos gasped and listed to his side away from me. A racking cough shook him as his body tried to rid itself of the dirty magic. A split second later, the vomiting began. His rib cage heaved with each retch as his body tried to dispel the toxic Gray Wolf from his system.

Finally, I could breathe again. The vomit was proof the green vitriol was working. As far as signs of hope go, it was pretty gross, but I'd take it because it meant I didn't have to add John's name to the roster of people I'd murdered.

Thank Christ.

I rose to go check on him, but a clapping sound behind me made the hairs on my neck prickle. Bane had hoped to see me lying battered and bleeding out on the floor. Instead, I was swaying but on my own two feet over the prone body of his assassin by proxy.

The ironic applause stopped as he got a good look at my face. His hands fumbled for the gun in his waistband. The barrel got caught in his belt, which gave me an opening to leap toward Hanson's gun, which had been kicked that direction during my scuffle with the beast.

I dove at the same moment Bane pulled off his first shot. It pinged off a metal shelf somewhere behind me and ricocheted to the concrete.

"Might as well give up now, Bane. Volos won't be killing anyone today."

"Shut up, bitch. I'll just kill you both."

I swallowed the fear that clogged my throat. He sounded crazy enough to deliver on the promise. "If you kill us, how are you going to pin this on Volos?"

"Won't matter as long as he's dead."

I decided to keep him talking. "You know, I never bought

that you came up with the formula on your own. Figures you had to have Uncle Abe help you. He's gonna be so pissed when he finds out you fucked up this bad."

"Be quiet! I'm thinking."

"You know what I think? I think that by the time your own son finishes singing to the BPD, you're going to spend a nice, long time in Crowley." I pointed the gun right between his doll eyes. "Unless if I kill you first."

"I said fucking shut up!" He whimpered like an injured animal. He stalked Volos's still form. He raised his head and I saw the red rimming his eyes. "I'm dead anyway. You're right. Abe's going to kill me the minute they put me in Crowley."

He smiled wildly and brought the gun closer to Volos's head. I didn't want to kill Bane. I mean, yes, I wanted to kill him, but it seemed like the easy way out for him. Suicide by cop.

I stepped forward. "Back off, Bane."

"Stop or I'll shoot him right fucking now," Bane said.

Time to make my move. "I'll save you the time." I swung the gun toward Volos's back.

"What—" Bane shouted.

I squeezed the trigger twice. Bane's shouts were lost in the explosions. Volos's body jerked with each hit. After the shots echoed off the walls, he went completely still.

"What the fuck?" Bane yelled.

I shrugged. "You wanted him dead, right?" I tossed the emptied gun aside and removed the one from my ankle holster.

His eyes were saucer-huge. "You crazy bitch."

"Fuckin' A." It was finally my turn to smile. The move made my face throb, but it was worth it.

Bane threw down the gun and raised his hands. "I want to see my attorney!"

Deep down where the root of my humanity resided, something snapped. It released something dark and acid into my veins. The taste of metal on my tongue and my vision went static tinged with red. The fact he thought it could be that easy. That he could cause so much destruction and pain and just raise his hands and be protected by the law. Why did he get that when the innocent did not?

I thought of my brother lying unconscious in a hospital bed. Depending on tubes and bags to keep him alive. I thought about Marvin's body bleeding out on the sidewalk in front of Volos Towers. I thought about Ferris Harkins, who thought he was helping the MEA, only to get shot down because he'd been potioned by a real monster.

I stalked forward, my gun pointed at his forehead as if it were a bull's-eye. He took a cautious step back, another. His eyes narrowed when I didn't lower my weapon. "Read me my rights, Officer."

I blinked rapidly through the rage blurring my vision. Sweat coated my forehead and my hands trembled with staunched anger. "You have no rights." Another step forward.

He shuffled back some more. "Read me my rights!"

"You gave them up the minute you came after my family." My voice was cold and low. Another confident step forward.

"But"—his tone went from demanding to cajoling—"we are family. Uncle Abe's my cousin. That makes us what?"

"Enemies." I laughed bitterly. "How convenient that you could ignore shared blood when you stuck a needle full of poison in Danny's jugular." I tightened my hand on the gun. "Give the devil my regards."

*Boom!*

A loud, drawn-out scream followed. But it was drowned out by the cacophony of doors being kicked in and running boot heels. Smoke filled the place and chaos reigned as what seemed like hundreds of bodies spilled into the space. In reality, it was the MEA team combined with a handful of BPD officers. Light flared inside the warehouse, forcing me to blink.

"Kate!" Morales called. He barreled out of the smoke and ran toward me. I blinked at the cavalry in confusion. He slowed and took in the scene.

He placed his left palm over my trembling hands and forced me to lower the hot gun. I didn't fight him but I also couldn't help wishing he'd come in thirty seconds later.

"Help!" A pitiful shout rose from the hole, followed by a raspy cough.

Morales frowned and edged to the perimeter of the large hole in the floor. He glanced down for a long moment. When he looked up at me, he looked puzzled. "What happened here?"

"The crazy bitch tried to murder me!" Bane's voice filtered up from the story below.

Morales raised a brow at me.

My hands were shaking as I pointed to the gun he'd taken from me. "Salt flare."

Then Morales turned and walked over to the prone form of John Volos. "Did you shoot him with the flare, too?"

"Nope." I shook my head. "I shot him with real bullets." Quickly, I added, "But I knew he had on an antiballistics shirt."

Gardner had been walking up behind Morales when I spoke. "How'd you know he was wearing it?" she asked.

"I saw it peeking out from under his shirt when he attacked me." I didn't tell them about Volos showing it to me at the hospital. Doing so now would only raise more suspicion since I hadn't mentioned John's visit to anyone.

"Why did he attack you?" Gardner continued with her questions. I didn't like that interrogator's mask she was wearing.

I sighed. "Because Bane potioned him with Gray Wolf." Both their eyes flew to Volos's still form.

A groan sounded from the ground. The three of us skidded over to see what was up with John. He was pale and sweating, but at least the tufts of hair had receded and his face had morphed back into its normal shape. His eyes blinked open and closed several times and he coughed.

"Mr. Volos? Are you okay?"

He managed a nod. "Kate," he gasped, "saved me."

Gardner's suspicious gaze flew to mine. "What I want to know is why you were here in the first place."

I paused, my mind going totally blank. Mental and physical exhaustion had shut down the part of my brain that allowed me to bullshit off the top of my head. I could not think of one good reason for me to be in that brewery that wouldn't get me kicked off the team.

"I called her," John said into the silence that followed Gardner's question. "I figured out the antipotion for Gray Wolf and I wanted to give her a sample to save Danny."

I squinted at him. It wasn't as if I was in any position to take credit for figuring out the antipotion, but I resented how his covering for me painted him as a real fucking hero.

"That true, Kate?" Morales asked.

I nodded. "I guess Bane had been tailing me."

Gardner sucked on her teeth for a moment, as if she expected me to suddenly break down and admit to some sort of major crime. I just stared at her with a look fueled by adrenaline crash and shock.

"All right," she said finally. "Morales, get medics to help Mr. Volos. Have them check out Kate, too, while you're at it." When I opened my mouth to protest, she snapped, "Don't.

That potion Mez put in the amulet will wear off soon and then you'll wish you were dead."

A commotion came from over near the lab. The uniforms had found Hanson's body. Shadi came running toward us, dressed in combat boots, jeans, and a black turtleneck. "What happened there?" she demanded.

Already the mood in the place was shifting now that the cops knew one of their own had died. Expectant gazes zeroed in on me as I debated telling the truth. Gardner must have seen something in my face because she suddenly stepped in. "We'll discuss it once you've had medical attention," she said to me. "Call Eldritch," she said quietly to Shadi.

Then she turned to the room at large and yelled, "Focus on getting the job done! We can mourn once we get the evidence to make the case."

They accepted this with solemn nods and got back to work.

Morales had been scanning the scene while she talked. As Gardner went off to oversee Hanson's body, he turned to me. "Back up—why did you shoot Volos if you dosed him with antipotion?"

"After I'd saved him, Bane was going to shoot him. I knew he had on the shirt, so I shot him instead to distract Bane."

He blinked. "You shot Volos because you knew he wore a bulletproof shirt and it would save his life?"

I was basically upright only because of shock, so all I could manage was a clipped nod.

Morales ran a hand through his hair and blew out a long breath. "You're a piece of work, Cupcake."

"She's a bitch is what she is," Bane called from the gurney where the medics were strapping him down. His face and arms were covered in bright red, oozing wounds from the salt shrapnel. There was a neck brace around his throat and the way he was groaning and moaning, he'd probably ruptured some discs or something in his back. Good.

"Get him the fuck out of here!" Morales yelled at the medics. They nodded and started to haul him out.

I turned to see where Volos was, but yet another commotion came from the stairway. A flurry of red hair appeared over the crest of the steps. The lawyer. She cried out when she saw the medics loading John onto his own gurney. I looked away because the scene she was making over him embarrassed me. I was glad Volos survived and all, but considering how many people had given their lives in this case, it felt . . . wrong to dote over the precious wealthy man who was alive only because he could afford expensive magical defense gear that the city wouldn't buy for any of the cops in that room.

"Miss Turner," Morales said, "we'll need to question Mr. Volos."

"Not tonight you won't. He's going to the hospital. Only once he's had a chance to receive the treatment he needs will we even consider making a statement."

A muscle in Morales's jaw clicked. I could practically hear him cussing at her for her haughty attitude in his head. "Understood, ma'am. You still have my card?" She nodded dismissively, which I took for a no. "Here's another just in case."

"We're ready," the medic said to Jade.

"Come on, John." She turned and started marching toward the stairs as if she was ready to fight her way out of there. Unfortunately the effect was ruined when the gurney he was on slowly started to rattle and squeak across the dirty concrete floor.

"Hold on," Volos said to the wiz-medic. "Kate?"

"John! Let's go," she called from the stairs.

He grimaced but didn't respond to her. His eyes searched

mine, pleading with me to approach him. With a sigh that hurt way more than it should have, I placed a hand over my ribs and limped over. I bent over to hear him, but not so close as to invite heartfelt bullshit. "Thanks," he said, his breathing rapid. "I know this could have turned out ten other ways that didn't involve me breathing."

I bit my lip to hide the smile. "Don't think about it."

"I will, though."

Before those words could sink in, he reached up and grabbed my neck to pull me closer. I'm sure to those who watched us it looked like a tender moment. But what really happened was he pressed his lips next to my ear. "Don't tell them about Abe." His hold relaxed and I pulled back to glare into his cool, blue gaze. "I'll get the antipotion to you within twenty-four hours."

In other words, he'd send the new dose of antipotion for Danny once he was sure I hadn't told the BPD and Gardner about Uncle Abe's involvement during the debriefing.

I gritted my teeth to keep in the angry words that were clawing at my tongue. If I didn't know better, I'd think the asshole had manipulated the entire situation just to put me in this corner. Of course, no one was that powerful. Not even the amazing John Volos. Still, my resentment burned like acid in my chest.

"Kate?" he said quietly.

I swallowed hard and nodded because I couldn't force myself to utter the words out loud in front of the people he wanted me to lie to in exchange for my brother's life.

John nodded back to let me know we understood each other. Then he motioned to the medic and glided away.

And I was left there, dumbfounded, wondering how after I saved his life—twice!—John Volos had just managed to get the upper hand again.

# Chapter Thirty-Four

Jeez, Kate," Danny said, swatting my hand away. "I'm fine."

I pulled my hand back and fisted it to keep from touching him again.

"Get used to it, kid," Pen said from the doorway of Danny's bedroom.

He rolled his eyes. "I'm telling you, I feel pretty awesome."

Honestly, he looked great. He was still a little thin, but his color was high and his eyes had the sparkle of mischief in them again. All signs of the Gray Wolf infection were gone, so only the memories remained like the echoes of a nightmare. Oh, and the track marks on his body from all the IVs and potions he'd received in the hospital to keep him alive.

"I don't know what was in that stuff John sent, but I feel awesome."

I gritted my teeth. Every time he or Pen praised Volos for saving Danny's life, I wanted to scream that I'd been the one who'd figured out the formula. But doing so would be an admission of working dirty magic, which would only damn me.

As promised, the antipotion arrived by special courier exactly twenty-four hours after the debriefing that proved my bullshit was convincing as ever.

The cure arrived with the following note:

> *Inject in jugular. Plenty of fluids and rest. Everything will be as it should.*
>
> —*J*

I'd waited until all the nurses and doctors had left the room. Then I stared at the liquid inside for a good long while. On some strange level, when this case had started, the last outcome I would have guessed was John Volos's saving the day. Yet there we were. I might have figured out the formula, but he'd been the one to get the saving dose to Danny. Irony was a major bitch.

Finally, I injected the neon green liquid into Danny's jugular. Unlike John, whose reaction to the antipotion had been unpleasant but manageable because he hadn't had the Gray Wolf in his system long, my brother's recovery was... Well. Let's just say that after several days under its hold, his body had some issues with the cure.

The doctor had helped Danny through the transformation as much as he could. Mostly he offered generous doses of pain-killer and barred the media from the hospital so Danny could recover in privacy. Every nurse on the floor knew we'd given Danny a dirty magic potion, but none of them said one word about it. They all seemed just as relieved as we were to see him finally free from Gray Wolf's claws. However, the official medical records reported that the recovery was due to the patient's youthful immune system and a cocktail of very clean magic potions.

After a final battery of tests, Doc declared Danny recovered and released him to my care. It had been two days since we'd been home and I'd begun to stop bracing for side effects. But it appeared that in the end, despite the serious tarnish on his armor, Volos had turned out to be the big hero.

Asshole.

"You feel awesome, huh?" Pen asked my brother with a raised brow. "Guess that means you're ready to head back to school?"

A sudden, very fake coughing fit greeted the comment. "Maybe I could rest a few more days," he rasped. "Just to be sure."

I laughed. "If you think that's best."

He stifled a yawn.

"All right, my friend," I said. "You stay here and rest. We'll be in the kitchen if you need us."

He nodded but his eyelids were already getting heavy.

Pen and I went to the kitchen, where Baba was cooking something at the stove. Pen made a beeline for the fridge and removed three beers.

"How's the patient?" Baba asked, stirring a large pot of something that smelled pleasantly of browned meat, tomatoes, and cheese. "Polish soul food," as she called it.

"He'll live." I lowered myself into a chair, cringing at the pain in my leg. Bane's bullet had scored a nasty trough into my thigh. I'd live, but the doc was pretty sure I'd have a permanent scar to remind me of that fucked-up day.

"He really does seem completely cured," Baba said. "It's a miracle."

I nodded. "Yeah, he's all good, I think."

"I hate to admit it," Pen said, "but it looks like Volos really came through for you guys."

The idea of anyone praising Volos made me feel all itchy, but I couldn't tell her the truth. I'd told her the same revisionist tale I'd told Gardner, so she had no idea I'd cooked magic, not once but twice. I just couldn't stomach the get-back-on-the-wagon speech that admission would require. Or risk her accidentally saying something about it to the team. So instead of agreeing with Pen's praise of John, I just took a long swallow of beer to wash down the acrid taste of resentment.

"So, is Agent Hottie coming by today?" Baba asked too casually.

"No, *Drew* has some meeting with Gardner."

Baba's hopeful expression fell, but Pen's brows rose. "About the task force?"

I shook my head. "No idea."

Baba tapped the wooden spoon on the lip of the pot. "Maybe I should make some Sexy Juice for him, eh? Maybe his *schwanz* needs a little encouragement." She arced the spoon upward to illustrate her point.

"Absolutely not," I said in my best and-that's-final tone. "And since when do you speak Yiddish?"

She pursed her lips and shrugged. "Gladys at the senior center's been teaching me so I can make the moves on the widower Goldman."

I shook my head at her. "Just promise me you won't give Morales any of your witch's brews, okay? And for that matter, please don't bring any more over here. I appreciate that you're trying to help, but I really prefer for my home to be free from magic."

Baba's face went pale. Across the table, Pen froze with the beer at her lips and her eyes were wide as if she expected the old woman to have a heart attack or a conniption fit. Instead, Baba cleared her throat, slowly removed her "Witches Do It

Magically" apron, and flipped the burner off with a resolute click.

My conscience reared up in the face of her strained dignity. "Baba—"

She raised a gnarled finger. "Shh," she said. "Baba understands. You think you're too good for my low magic."

I rose. "No, it's not that. It's just"—I sighed—"I don't trust myself around any magic."

The words tumbled out before I'd realized I was going to say them. And in the wake of the confession, the two women both went utterly still and silent. My cheeks flamed and recriminations echoed through my head. Why had I said such a stupid thing out loud? Did I want them to figure out what I'd done in that brewery?

"Kate," Pen said, "that was really brave of you." Her tone didn't hold any judgment. Maybe I even detected a hint of pride, as if she'd been waiting for me to make that breakthrough for years.

"You're a moron," Baba said.

I pulled back in shock. "Excuse me?"

She waved a hand, finally getting animated. "You two with your recovery meetings and your 'one day at a time.'" She made a disgusted sound. "You sound like children afraid of shadows. Magic is a gift from God. A divine tool given to us to make life easier. But you act like it's your master. That's *farkakte*!"

I blinked at her. I didn't speak Yiddish, but I got the idea. "No offense, Baba, but those homespun poultices and tinctures you brew are nothing like dirty magic. You can't begin to understand the power it holds over people."

Baba made another disgusted noise and waved a hand through the air. "People allow things to have power over them. You want to get your head right, girlie?" She snapped her fingers together as if she were grabbing something from the air. "You gotta snatch that power back!"

I crossed my arms. Arguing with Baba was like trying to herd drunken cats. "Regardless, I'd appreciate it if you'd respect my decision not to bring magic into my home."

She sniffed and looked away. "Suit yourself," she said in a tone that implied a silent *idiot* at the end of the sentence. "Now if you'll excuse me, I need to get home before the girls arrive for our book club meeting." With that, she made an incredibly hasty and elegant exit for a woman who walked with the assistance of a cane.

Once she was gone, Pen and I stared at each other, dumbfounded. "You're going to have to apologize."

I shook my head. Even though I felt justified in my request, I knew I could have handled it better. If nothing else, I'd make it up to her somehow just to assuage my stinging conscience. I dropped back in my chair and took a long pull from my warming beer. "I'll add it to my to-do list."

"Speaking of, any word from Eldritch?"

I shook my head. "Not since the debriefing. I guess he and Gardner have been pretty busy helping Stone prepare the case against Bane."

She sighed. "Still, sucks for them to leave you in limbo like that."

"I'm kind of enjoying limbo."

She toasted me with her bottle. "Nice that it took almost being killed to force you to slow down."

I shrugged. "Whatever works."

She toyed with the label of her beer. "I got some news."

I leaned forward, glad to talk about something other than my issues for a change. "Spill it, sister."

"Detective Duffy called last night. They formally charged that mom with supplying illegal potions to a minor."

"That's fantastic, Pen!"

She nodded. "They need me to testify in court, but Duffy thinks it's a slam dunk."

"I'm glad."

"Sometimes we do win, Kate."

I nodded and smiled. "Sometimes." I wasn't sure whether I considered the fight with Bane a full victory, though. I didn't trust the system enough to believe he'd receive the punishment he deserved. And even if he got the life sentence he'd earned, there was no guarantee that he'd survive long inside once Uncle Abe realized how badly he'd botched up the plan. Although, frankly, I wouldn't put it past Abe to torture Bane for a few years before he finally did him in.

And then there was the whole issue that my deal with Volos meant Uncle Abe would escape any sort of legal punishment for his role in the whole fiasco. I assumed Volos had some plan to make the old man pay for what he did, but I hadn't worked up the energy to talk to him to find out.

"Have you made any decisions about what you're going to do?" Pen asked quietly.

I sighed and shook my head. "You mean once Eldritch calls to tell me I'm off the task force?"

"*If* he does," she corrected.

"He will," I said. She hadn't seen the conviction in his eyes when he'd kicked Morales and me out of the station. "Shit, I don't know, Pen. I can't go back to patrol. That much is sure." I played with the beer cap. "But what the hell else am I qualified to do?"

She smiled. "Lots of things."

I tilted my head and shot her a don't-blow-sunshine-up-my-ass glare. "Get real, Pen. I've had two jobs in my life besides cop: potion cooker and waitress. I quit the first one and got fired from the other. Not exactly a sparkling résumé."

"You could go back to school."

I snorted. "With what money?"

She sighed like she'd lost her patience. "Guess you should just give up then."

I grimaced at her. "That's helpful."

"Look, you know as well as I do you could do just about anything you set your mind to. But you ask me, you haven't made other plans because you don't want to be anything but a cop."

Was that true? I wasn't sure anymore. I knew I used to want to be one. I'd loved it while it lasted. But the job came at too high a cost. "Sure," I said, my voice dripping in sarcasm, "I'd love to keep getting shot and having psychopaths go after Danny."

She didn't say anything, but I could tell by her look she was just letting me vent my spleen.

"Besides, maybe it's time to grow up and settle down. Get a nice, safe job behind a desk. One that doesn't require me to carry a gun. Like, I don't know, a secretary or something."

She looked up quickly. I thought she was about to say something insightful. But then the first giggle escaped.

I crossed my arms and leaned back to glare at her. "Shut up."

The laughter increased until tears formed in her eyes. "I'm sorry," she gasped through the giggles. "But that's the funniest thing you've ever said. You'd be a terrible secretary."

I flipped her the bird and chugged the rest of my beer. "I'm serious, Pen. I'm tired of the bullshit politics." I pointed toward the phone. "Do you have any idea how many times I've had to tell those fucking reporters that Mike Hanson was a hero?"

Even though I'd told Eldritch and Gardner the truth about Hanson's involvement, they had decided it was best not to muddy the waters by making his betrayal public. Therefore, the media had been told he'd died helping me take down Bane. Since the shoot-out at the brewery, I'd received several phone calls from reporters, and every time I uttered the word "hero" in the same sentence as Hanson's name it tasted like a shit sandwich. But Babylon was already healing from too many wounds for me to make it worse by telling the truth. Plus, I was already lying about so many things I figured one more couldn't damn me any more than I already was.

"So Hanson gets a hero's funeral and I can't even get anyone to tell me if I have a fucking job?"

She set down her beer. "I know. Trust me. But maybe you should wait to hear from Eldritch and Gardner before you decide to move to the suburbs and spend your days filing and getting coffee for some mid-level manager."

I chewed on my lip and watched the clock tick. Every minute that passed without a phone call felt like a year.

# Chapter Thirty-Five

Two days later, I stood outside the police station, looking up at the seal of the city of Babylon. The sun sparkled off the symbol of a large gate guarded by a roaring lion. For some reason, it called to mind the day I'd earned the badge that bore the same insignia.

Back then, I was a starry-eyed recruit, fueled by a craving for justice and the conviction that I was finally one of the good guys. That I could make a real difference. I imagined myself as that lion, guarding the innocent from the bad guys.

But now, less than five years later, I stood in front of the building where I graduated waiting to hear if I still had a job. The stars had dimmed and the conviction was wavering. I didn't feel like a lion anymore so much as a kicked dog. The only thing that hadn't changed since that day was the desire for justice.

But that had to count for something, right?

I sucked in a deep breath, stuck my shoulders back, and marched through the doors to hear the verdict on my future.

My bravado lasted only as long as it took me to cross the threshold.

Every officer I passed wore a black ribbon across their badge. To them it was a way to honor their fallen comrade, Mike Hanson. To me, it was a reminder of a system that favored politics over truth.

Eldritch greeted me near the sergeant's desk. He made a big presentation of giving me a hug. "Welcome!" he said in a forced tone that made me want to turn around and leave. But before I could, he urged me toward his office while smiling for the troops and claiming I was the woman of the hour.

Once we reached the office, some of his joviality dimmed but he remained friendly.

"Sit, sit," he said, waving to the chair. He sat on the edge of the desk near me and sighed. "First, how's Danny?"

"He's good." I smiled. "Ornery."

"Excellent!" Eldritch slapped his knee. "One thing I'll say for you Prosperos: You're all fighters."

I nodded to accept the backhanded compliment. "We got the casserole from Francine. Thank her for me." I'd thrown it out in the garbage the day it arrived. Why did everyone send casseroles in times of crisis? Why didn't anyone ever send brownies and Jack Daniel's?

"Ah, it was nothing." He chuffed out a breath. "Anything you two need, just call."

I need to know if I have a job, I thought. "Thanks."

An awkward pause followed. The kind that happens when the pleasantries are done with and it's time to get to the uncomfortable business but no one wants to be the asshole.

Just when I was about to start squirming, the door opened and Gardner rushed in. "Sorry I'm late," she panted. "Had to meet with Stone about the Bane case."

I rounded to look at her. "H-hey." Last I'd heard she was on her way to Detroit to give her regional director an update on the drama at the warehouse. "I didn't know you were back in town."

"Got in yesterday." She waved a hand. "How's the kid?"

"He's good. What's up with Bane?"

"Nothing you should worry over." She shook her head and my heart sank. "What did I miss?"

"Nothing yet."

She nodded and sighed. "Good. I didn't want to miss seeing her reaction."

My face contracted into a deep frown. "What?"

Eldritch crossed his arms. "Well, first, you've formally been cleared of the shooting incident."

I nodded impatiently. Eldritch practically vibrated with excitement. Gardner was more subdued, but I sensed tension from her. Not bad tension, just . . . expectation, maybe.

"With everything going on with Danny, we've put through paperwork to retroactively pay you for the time you were suspended plus an extra two weeks of paid personal leave."

My brows shot up. "Wow, that's great." Now maybe I wouldn't go bankrupt paying off the hospital. Plus it gave me another five days to nurse Danny until I . . . did whatever came next. I looked at them both expectantly, waiting for them to fill in the blanks.

"Once that leave is up, you have a choice to make. You can either return to your old post at the BPD patrol division." Eldritch glanced at Gardner and nodded.

She smiled. "Or you can represent the BPD on the MEA task force full-time." My mouth fell open, but she held up a hand. "With a promotion to the rank of detective."

All the blood rushed from my head. "Holy shit!"

Gardner cracked a smile. "Is that a yes?"

I shook my head.

Her face fell. "It's a no?"

I sucked in a deep breath to collect my scattered thoughts. I'd walked in prepared to get fired and then move away to give Danny—and me—a more stable life. But the instant they'd mentioned a promotion, things suddenly didn't seem too cut-and-dried. "I don't know. I thought the mayor revoked permission for the task force to operate here."

"He changed his mind after you brought down one of the city's most dangerous coven leaders," Eldritch said, all magnanimous.

"So the team is back in play for good?"

"Well, I wouldn't say for good. But for the foreseeable future, yes. Captain Eldritch has also been generous enough to convince the chief to grant us a few additional officers for the team."

"That's great," I said. "And you're sure you want me on it?"

"What's the problem, Prospero?" She tilted her head. "I thought you'd be thrilled."

"Forgive me, but I expected to be reprimanded, not given a promotion." After I'd admitted to going to see Volos without telling anyone, I'd been read the riot act.

Eldritch cleared his throat. "We all said a lot of things in the heat of this investigation that we didn't mean. But the bottom line is you brought in the guy, and you deserve to be rewarded for all your hard work and sacrifice." The words were nice, but they rang hollow. More likely, the promotion was to keep me happy so I never went to the media about the Hanson situation.

I looked Gardner in the eyes. "Are you being forced to take me?"

"Absolutely not." She didn't flinch or look away. "Has anything I've done given you the impression I'd let the mayor or anyone else force me to take a team member who didn't have the chops?"

I snorted. "I guess not."

"You're dedicated to the job, more knowledgeable about the Cauldron than the rest of the team combined, and show the promise to be a great detective."

My cheeks heated and I couldn't stop the corners of my mouth from turning up at the praise.

"You're also stubborn." She shook her head. "And unpredictable. I thought you'd be jumping at this. Eldritch says you've been angling for detective for a couple of years."

"I have."

"So what's the problem?" Eldritch's tone was annoyed, as if he was worried he'd be forced to take me back on his staff.

"I just—" I swallowed. "I've just had a lot of shit going on. But you're right. I thought this was everything I wanted—the promotion, the spot on the task force. But after Danny was hurt—" I paused and swallowed the unexpected emotion that suddenly clogged my throat. For a made-up excuse, my body was sure reacting to my words as if they were the truth. "After Danny got hurt, I started wondering if maybe I should be a cop at all."

Eldritch made an awkward huffing sound, like he was completely unprepared to deal with this much emotion. Gardner, however, tilted her head. "That's bullshit."

I reared back in shock. "Excuse me?"

"I get that your brother's situation was scary. It would be for any of us. But I saw you, Kate. You didn't act like a woman who doubted whether she needed to be in the justice business." She chuckled. "You didn't hide from the pain. You turned into a pit bull. Maybe you're telling yourself you long for a nice, safe, easy life, but I think you know you'll never be happy with a civilian job."

The words were tiny daggers piercing my half-formed plan for a normal life. My ideas about moving to the 'burbs and getting a desk job had been a form of self-defense. I'd expected to walk in that office and find out I was officially relieved of duty. Instead, they offered me everything I thought I wanted. And it scared the hell out of me. What if I wasn't good enough? What if I let everyone down? What if Danny got hurt again? What if I did and he was left alone?

"Kate?" Eldritch snapped.

I sucked on my teeth for a moment. Out of nowhere, his words from earlier echoed in my brain. "You Prosperos: You're all fighters."

He was right. But I didn't learn how to be a fighter from Uncle Abe or his wizard pals who swaggered around the Cauldron like kings. Instead, I'd learned how to be strong from my mother. A humble woman who worked two jobs to support her kids. A proud woman who never got a fair shake but didn't complain about it. A complicated woman who always told me she wanted Danny and me to have a better life than she had. A beautiful woman who died too early because I didn't understand then that selling potions wasn't the path to a better life.

In the days following Danny's recovery, I'd tried to convince myself that a simple existence in a cookie-cutter house with a boring job was better. But deep down I knew the truth. A better life was one where I got to be that lion standing in front of the gates.

"Kate," Gardner prompted, "what's it going to be?"

I lifted my head and looked Gardner in the eye. "When do I start?"

# Chapter Thirty-Six

The stage stood in the center of what used to be the barren lot in front of the Arteries. Not ten feet from where I'd put a bullet into Ferris Harkins's face, John Volos smiled like a politician as he addressed the crowd gathered to celebrate the ground-breaking of the community center.

Danny and I stood in the back, near the street carnival Volos had hired. Morales was with us, watching with his arms crossed. Behind us, calliope music and the occasional screams provided the sound track to Volos's speech.

"Today is a new day not just for the citizens of the Cauldron, but for the entire city of Babylon. For too long, we've allowed criminals to rule these streets and prevent us from providing adequate services to the future of this city—our children."

A smattering of applause rippled through the crowd. On my left, Danny stared up at his savior with wide, worshipful eyes. As far as the kid was concerned, any tarnish on Volos's armor had been polished away the moment he rescued Danny. I tried to tamp down the spark of jealousy it caused, but just once I wished my brother would look at me with that kind of admiration.

"It is my hope that the Cauldron Community Center will be a safe place for kids to go after school to learn a new hobby or practice a new sport or just hang out in an environment that fosters creativity and confidence. Every child deserves to grow up feeling safe—especially those who have been marginalized by circumstances beyond their control. For too long the Adepts of this city have been treated as second-class citizens."

The Mundanes in the crowd shifted uneasily, but the Adepts burst into a round of enthusiastic cheering.

"Fortunately, Mayor Owens agrees that it's time to start healing the rift that magic created in our community. In fact, he and I met just yesterday to discuss plans to build a free clinic in the Cauldron. The clinic will help those ravaged by addiction by offering discount antipotions, which will be provided by Volos Labs and subsidized by the City of Babylon. Our hope is that by next summer, we will be able to put a dent in the dirty magic problem in this city by addressing the demand side of the equation."

I snorted. Yeah, they'd be putting a dent in the magic problem by putting extra coin in Volos's pockets. Was there any opportunity he couldn't find a way to profit from?

John glanced back toward the end of the stage where the mayor and Captain Eldritch sat. "The Volos Corporation is also donating $100,000 to the joint BPD/MEA task force to help address the supply side of the equation."

Morales nudged me with his elbow. I grimaced up at him. I hated the idea we'd be using Volos's money to fund our operations, but since the task force was already on thin ice with the mayor, refusing the donation wasn't exactly an option.

Eldritch came forward to accept a check from Volos. The

men shook hands and smiled politely for the cameras. I thought it was interesting Gardner hadn't been invited onstage, too. Instead she stood to the side, looking unimpressed by either the spectacle or Volos's generosity.

"I've heard enough. Let's go ride some rides." I tugged on Danny's shirtsleeve. "You coming?" I asked Morales.

"Will you buy me some cotton candy?" He shot me an amused look.

"No." I smiled. "But I'll let you buy me a beer."

He held my gaze, his eyes sparkling with something that made me nervous. "Deal."

◆ ◆ ◆

The inevitable happened an hour later. I sat alone on a bench with a rapidly warming beer in my hand. The sun was warm on my face and the leaves were turning colors in the distance. Danny and Morales were somewhere high up above me on a ride that appeared to exist solely to induce nausea in its riders. I was smiling when the shadow fell over me.

"Having a good time?" Volos's voice was warm like the sun, and just as likely to burn.

"Yeah." I squinted at him. "I was going to call you."

"Liar." The corner of his lip lifted. "How's the kid?"

"Better." I shoved my hands in the pockets of my worn jeans and shrugged. "Thank you."

He watched me for a moment, as if he was trying to figure out if I was thanking him for asking or for saving Danny's life. Either way, he nodded. "Any side effects?"

"Low-grade fever for a couple days, but that's cleared up." I shook my head. "Nightmares, too, but I'm not sure if that's a side effect of the potion or the ordeal."

He nodded too quickly, as if he'd experienced the same

problem. Instead of thinking about that because it might make me feel bad for him, I soldiered on. "But his appetite's normal and he's bitching a lot, which is a good sign."

"If anything changes, be sure to let me know."

"Of course." I looked away because now was the time to offer my heartfelt gratitude. But I couldn't do it.

Volos cleared his throat. "Thank you, by the way."

I jerked my head up. "For what?"

His color was high and he couldn't quite meet my eyes. He rubbed his chest in an unconscious gesture. "For shooting me." His lips lifted in irony.

"My pleasure." I smiled to let him know I meant it. "I mean, don't get me wrong, I'm glad you survived and all because of Danny, but I kind of enjoyed it."

"I guess I deserve that." He sat next to me on the bench. I scooted over. He looked at me with a raised brow. "If you'd been able to, you would have killed me when I was freaking on that potion, wouldn't you?"

I looked away quickly as the memory of his snarling face flashed behind my eyes. "No, but only because it would have meant Danny died."

He was quiet for a moment. "I'm sorry you had to go through that."

"Whatever. I did what I had to do."

"Regardless, I know what it cost you."

I clenched my jaw and said the words I'd been fighting. "Thank you for saving Danny. I wasn't sure you'd send the antipotion."

"I'm not all bad, Kate. Maybe one day you'll accept that." He rested an elbow on the back of the bench. Tipped his head back and watched the tracers of light from the rides overhead for a moment before answering. "You didn't tell them about Abe."

I turned toward him fully. "I didn't have a choice, did I?"

"Sure you did. You just didn't like the alternative." He turned his head to look at me. "Besides, you know I would have sent that antipotion anyway. I wouldn't screw the kid over like that."

I glanced away. Maybe deep down I had known, but I didn't want to admit that Volos was capable of that much humanity. It was too confusing. "No, I didn't."

"I have a theory."

"Oh?"

"I think you didn't tell them because you're curious to find out what I'm going to do to Abe."

I licked my suddenly dry lips. "That's ridiculous. I'm a cop, John."

"A detective now, right? Congratulations, by the way."

I grimaced because I wasn't about to let him wriggle out of this conversation with flattery. "Cut the shit. What are you planning?"

"What makes you think I'm going to do anything?" At my don't-bullshit-a-bullshitter look, he shrugged. "I can't tell you that, *detective*. But rest assured, Uncle Abe's going to experience a reckoning."

I looked down at my hands. A sort of shameful excitement filled my midsection at the idea of John's exacting vengeance on Abe. I told myself the feeling was a normal reaction for someone who'd almost lost a loved one because of a bad man's actions. But something deeper inside me whispered that I'd just plain enjoy watching that bastard burn.

Still, as a cop, I couldn't exactly condone a citizen's targeting another citizen for murder. Even if I thought the target deserved it. "If he dies, I'll have no choice but to report that you've threatened him."

"I'd actually love to see you try to fast-talk your way through that discussion." His lips quirked. "But you can relax, Kate. Having Abe killed isn't on my agenda. It's far too easy a punishment for the crimes he's committed against me and people I care about."

*People I care about.* I cleared my throat, trying to exorcise the spike of pleasure that comment conjured, but it didn't do any good.

John brushed my arm in an almost caress that could easily be written off as an accident. "Forget Abe for the moment. There's something else we need to discuss. A favor."

I didn't want to talk about Abe anymore, but I knew we'd have to eventually. But I also knew pressing him would only earn me a brick wall of silence. "What is it?"

He crossed his arms, as if he was uneasy. "I need you to be my trump card."

I didn't bite. Just raised my brows and tried to look bored by his flair for drama.

"It won't be long before the MEA task force turns its microscope on me. I need you to warn me when that happens."

"Why, Mr. Volos, I thought you were a legitimate businessman." I raised my brows. "A pillar of the community." I batted my eyelashes like a Southern belle and used my best sweet-tea voice. "Why on earth would the MEA investigate you?"

"Cute." His lips stretched into a tight line. "I'm not interested in playing coy here, Kate. The bottom line is that if you want to keep your job on the task force you'll tell me what I need to know."

*Boom.*

There it was. The other shoe I'd foolishly convinced myself would never come just dropped like an anvil into my lap.

The ride Danny and Morales had been on stopped and people started weaving out of the gate like drunks from a bar. Eventually I saw Morales's dark head looming over the group. His lips were spread into a wide smile as he teased a very green-looking Danny.

I crossed my arms over the raging bile in my stomach. "What do you mean, keep my job on the task force?"

I kept my eyes on the pair exiting the ride. When Morales's eyes landed on me sitting next to Volos, he jerked and started over. I shook my head. The last thing I needed was for him to add his gas to the already highly flammable situation. He nodded and steered Danny in the other direction, toward another ride.

Apparently, Volos saw Morales spot us, too. "What do you think your new partner would do if he found out that you lied about the reason you were at the brewery that night? Or that you willingly performed illegal magic? Or that you intentionally omitted information about your uncle's involvement in the case?"

Our eyes met and held. Electricity zinged between us. Unlike a decade earlier when that look would have resulted in a passionate kiss and a roll in the sack, this time the energy made me want to put a gun in his face and finish the job I'd started back in that warehouse. His bulletproof magic wouldn't stop a shot to the forehead.

I snorted. "Your word against mine."

"Wrong. Your word against the security footage of you reading Gray Wolf's energy signature in my lab."

"You fucking filmed me?" All around the bench, passersby jerked their gazes in the direction of my raised voice. I cringed and slid down a little. "Your video also shows you helping me."

"No. It doesn't, actually." He crossed an ankle over his knee, all casual, as if he weren't a shark circling everything I held sacred. "Don't look at me like that. I'd prefer not to have to do this, but it's unavoidable."

"Like hell," I hissed. "Is this some sort of sick revenge for leaving you?"

He tilted his head and shot me a disappointed look. "Kate, please, we're not children. I understand your anger. I know you must hate me."

I nodded eagerly, which earned me another censoring grimace.

"But the ends will eventually justify these unavoidable means. I'm sure of it." He smiled reassuringly, as one would to a child who didn't know how to see through the bullshit. "In the meantime, I just need you to warn me if the MEA decides to dig in my sandbox."

"This isn't a fucking game." The words were delivered in a diamond-hard tone I'd never heard come from my mouth before. Guess I'd been saving it for a special occasion.

John chuckled. "When are you going to learn? Magic is always a game. What was it Uncle Abe used to say?" He cocked his head and quoted the man he'd just threatened a couple of minutes earlier: "You either cook or you get burned."

Considering the rage smoldering in the center of my chest, I had a pretty good idea which category I fell into.

My left hand lifted before I made a conscious decision to slap him. His hand caught my palm before it made contact. "I'm sorry." Raised my fingertips to his mouth. Planted a kiss there while he stared into my angry gaze.

I ripped my hand away and cradled it to my chest. "Get the fuck away from me."

He smiled tightly. Paused and regarded me with a look I

couldn't identify. I just knew it scared me a little. But finally, he nodded. "All right, I'll go." He glanced down at his watch. "But I'll be talking to you real soon, Kate."

In shock, I watched him walk away. But before I'd taken two breaths, I realized I couldn't sit on that bench and wait for Morales and Danny to come find me in that state.

I stood and walked away on wooden legs. Away from the grating racket of the carnival. Past the clearing where the community center would stand next year. Toward the gate that used to lead down into the Arteries.

Since the raid, the mayor had had every entrance to the tunnels sealed shut with cinder blocks. I placed a hand over the red paint that spelled the words KEEP OUT. Behind me, the screams of joy from the carnival-goers mixed with the noise from the freeway and the melancholy horns of the riverboats.

I climbed up a grassy rise to the top of the road that ran over the old tunnels. From this higher vantage point, I could see most of the Cauldron.

I looked around. Really looked. The sun was setting in the distance over Lake Erie. That massive body of water was filled with mutated fish, dumped chemicals, and more bodies than the Babylon Eternal Rest Cemetery on Highway 52.

Closer, a tenement down the road was lit up like a faerie dwelling, but no mythical faerie-tale creatures lived in there. Instead, its walls were thin prisons that barely contained the despair of its residents. Magic was the least of their worries. Instead, poverty, addiction, and abuse were more abundant than clean water, fresh produce, and a decent education.

I wasn't sure how long I looked around at the fetid landscape before the sounds of sirens echoed in the distance. Before the mom walking by with her toddler screamed and knocked the kid upside the head because he tripped. Before the gaunt, blond junkie stumbled out of the alley and offered the teenaged Adept who worked that corner a blow job in exchange for a diet potion.

Eventually I watched the immorality play long enough that my shoulders slumped and what was left of my optimism seeped out like a leaky balloon.

The future John Volos had promised the citizens of the Cauldron was a mirage. All those families who gathered to listen to his pretty words wanted to believe he was offering them a dream come true. Instead it was more like a hallucination fueled by dirty magic and his own ambitions. Ambitions he'd see realized no matter whom he had to fuck over in the process.

I pulled my gaze from the urban landscape to see Morales climbing the hill toward me.

"Where's Danny?" I asked, suddenly afraid for him to be alone.

"He's throwing baseballs at a clown with Pen and Shadi."

I nodded and sighed, my gaze on the lights of the midway.

"What did Volos have to say?" He fell in next to me, his eyes scanning the horizon.

I shrugged but wouldn't meet his eyes. "Just wanted to know how Danny was doing."

He turned to look at me, a brow raised in challenge. "Sure that's all? You didn't look too happy." I could tell by the tightness of his tone and the anger in his eyes that he'd seen me try to hit Volos and what happened after.

But telling Morales about the conversation wasn't an option. So I just shrugged.

Morales let me have my silence for a few moments. When he finally spoke again, it was on the heels of a sigh. "You know, I didn't really like this town when I first got here."

I glanced at him. Wondering at the pensive tone and the rapid change in subject. "Oh yeah?"

He nodded and looked at me from the corner of his eyes. "But now I'm glad I'll be sticking around for a while. This place is a mess. All sorts of fucked-up history and complicated issues to navigate."

I snorted. "Yeah, sounds like you're thrilled."

He laughed. "But the Cauldron's also got lots of secrets. Makes me want to understand what makes it tick." He turned toward me fully. "And there's good here, too." He nodded toward the carnival. "Those people? Their dreams are worth fighting for."

"You think?" I swallowed.

"Yeah, I do." He nodded. "Even if it means we're the ones who have to take on the bad guys to make it happen."

I sucked a deep breath into my lungs. It smelled like ozone and car exhaust, but there was also the smell of fried fair foods and the crisp, smoky promise of autumn. I blinked and instead of looking at the bad, I tried to focus on the good. The lights of the carnival. The children skipping through the midway. The tired, indulgent smiles of the parents. The way the sunset's reds and oranges and purples shifted over the surface of the lake like a kaleidoscope's colors. The pale crescent moon overhead cupping the evening's first stars in its embrace.

"Maybe you're right."

"Of course I am." He nudged me with his shoulder. "You've only just begun to see the resources the MEA can bring down on the bad guys. Now that we've taken down Bane and gotten the mayor some positive press, the ASAC will throw funds our way. Plus we're getting some more warm bodies for the team. The covens won't know what hit 'em."

Across the field, past the stage, I saw a group of four people headed toward us. I recognized Mez's dreads immediately, tonight back to their dark brown color. Pen picked her way gracefully over the ruts and grass. Shadi strutted with her arm around Danny's shoulders.

Danny. Seeing him smile and laugh was like a balm to soothe my ragged edges.

"Here comes trouble," Drew said, sounding amused.

I looked up at him. "You really believe we can make a difference?"

The corner of his mouth lifted. "You bet your ass, Cupcake."

I just prayed I'd have a chance to prove him right before Volos made good on his threats. Because one thing was sure, I'd quit the team before I helped him slither his way out of an investigation. I might not be a saint, but I sure as hell wasn't a traitor to the badge like Mike Hanson.

By that time, the others finally reached our perch high on the hill. I looked around at the faces of my team and my little family. Morales was right. There were lots of things worth fighting for in the Cauldron.

Across the clearing, at the edge of the carnival, I spied a long, black limousine with taillights that glowed like a blood fiend's eyes in the Arteries. John Volos emerged from a tent and walked purposefully toward the waiting car. He reached the door but paused before ducking inside. Turning to look over his shoulder, his eyes scanned the carnival, the busy lot, the street. But his gaze never landed on the source of his discomfort.

Get used to looking over your shoulder, I said silently as I imagined an invisible target on his forehead. Because I'll be watching you.

Finally, he gave up his search and ducked into the car. A few seconds later, the limo pulled away, and Babylon's favorite son disappeared into the Cauldron's protective embrace.

"Kate?" Danny called. "You okay?"

I forced a smile and put an arm around my kid brother. "Yeah, I'm good."

Or I will be, I silently amended. A quickening began in my middle and expanded outward, heating my limbs and hardening my resolve.

Volos may have won this battle, but I would win the war.

# Acknowledgments

The writing experts say you should write what you know. As it happens, *Dirty Magic* is about some things I knew all too well, but also a lot of technical things I hadn't a clue about when the idea knocked me upside the head. But I do now, thanks to the following people.

The Plano, Texas, Police Department and the Plano Citizens' Police Academy were invaluable resources. During the twelve-week crash course in being a cop, I got to handle illicit substances, learn how to defuse bombs, and drive police cars at high speeds. Thanks especially to Sergeant Lindy Privet and Officer Mark Dawson for your senses of humor and patience.

A special shout-out to Officer Chris "Laser" Turner, who hosted me for an eight-hour ride-along. He answered all my ridiculous questions honestly and with a great sense of humor. When I told him I was a writer, his immediate response was to request that if he appeared in the book he get a cool nickname, "Like 'Laser,'" he said. Done. I also owe him for the idea of "tactical wizards." Awesome.

Thanks to Lee Lofland and all the officers, agents, and experts who taught at the 2012 Writers' Police Academy in Guilford County, North Carolina. I will definitely be back, and I recommend this event to anyone who wants to write about characters in law enforcement.

I have huge gratitude, as always, for Devi Pillai at Orbit for pushing me to take my writing further. Thank you, Lauren Panepinto, for the gorgeous cover. The rest of the Orbit team is pretty amazing as well, including Tim Holman, Alex Lencicki, Ellen Wright, Susan Barnes, and all the unsung heroes in sales and marketing.

Thanks to my fabulous agent, Rebecca Strauss, who makes sure I don't set my hair on fire and also seems to like my writing despite the fact it freaks her out (don't mention Little Man to her). You rock, lady!

No author makes it very far without a gang of fellow writers with whom to commiserate, gossip, and laugh. Huge thanks to Liliana Hart, Mark Henry, Nicole Peeler, Suzanne McLeod, and the League of Reluctant Adults.

When I was young, my mother was a bookstore manager by day and a cop at night. When she wasn't driving me to play-dates, she was winning shooting competitions. Needless to say, her input, advice, and encouragement were invaluable as I wrote this book. Thanks for being my first superhero, Mom.

Speaking of my mom, I am lucky enough to come from families filled with uppity broads. Thank you, ladies, for inspiring me to live with passion, love fiercely, and laugh loudly and often.

Thanks to Spawn for making me laugh every day and reminding me not to take anything too seriously, except for how much I love him.

My husband is pretty much the most patient man on earth, as well as my biggest supporter. Without his reminding me that I always threaten to quit writing when I'm on deadline, I would have given up a long time ago. Or worse, never tried to begin with. ILYNTB.

Thank you to the makers of fine coffee, dark chocolate, good bourbon, and delicious cheeses. Your creations are the fuel this writer uses to turn ideas into words.

*Acknowledgments*

But most of all, thank you, gentle reader, for spending time in this made-up world with these crazy characters. All I ever wanted was to tell stories, and because you're willing to listen, I'm living out my dream. Infinite thanks for that blessing and privilege.

# extras

orbit

# meet the author

*copyright On Location Portraiture*

Raised in Texas, *USA Today* best-seller JAYE WELLS grew up reading everything she could get her hands on. Her penchant for daydreaming was often noted by frustrated teachers. She embarked on a series of random career paths, including stints working for a motivational speaker and at an art museum. Jaye eventually realized that while she loved writing, she found facts boring. So she left all that behind to indulge her overactive imagination and make up stuff for a living. Besides writing, she enjoys travel, art, history, and researching weird and arcane subjects. She lives in Texas with her saintly husband and devilish son. Find out more about Jaye Wells at www.jayewells.com.

# interview

*What inspired the world of Babylon and the Cauldron?*
So many influences go into building a world from scratch.
I knew from the beginning that I wanted a magical slum in
this city. The name "Cauldron" came to me pretty early on
and I built from there. Around the same time, I'd seen a gallery of photographs based on abandoned buildings in Rust
Belt towns. Old churches, factories, and mansions just left
behind to rot. The images were haunting and pretty powerful and encouraged me to do more research. What I learned
inspired me to create a sort of amalgam based on Rust Belt
cities, which became Babylon, Ohio. It's heavily influenced
by Cleveland, but I borrowed elements from other towns to
flesh it out.

It was great fun to take a known idea—the Rust Belt—
and twist it a bit to show the ways the corrupting influence
of dirty magic might have contributed to the cultural and
economic problems in a place. The Cauldron is not always
pleasant— you wouldn't necessarily plan a vacation there—
but there are flashes of spirit and beauty in the gritty landscape. The more I wrote about the city's magical slum, the
more I realized it had become a character of its own.

# extras

*Why mix potions and cops? What drew you to the premise?*
My husband and I had just watched the fantastic TV series
*The Wire*. Since I'm a fantasy author, it's usually only a matter of time before my imagination takes an idea and inserts
a wizard, demon, or faerie. So I thought, what if instead of
gangs of drug dealers, they were fighting covens of wizards
who deal magic? Bam! There was the idea. The process of
building the world and characters was much more complex a
process, but that was the genesis.

I also knew I wanted the magic to be concrete. Instead of
waving wands and zapping people, I needed my wizards to
sell tangible magic in the forms of potions, amulets, patches,
etc. All that basically led me in the direction of alchemy and
the idea of clean-versus-dirty magic.

It's impossible to ignore that writing about covens of
potion-dealing wizards is a not-very-subtle metaphor for
drug dealing. For sure, there are a lot of parallels and I don't
shy away from exploring the effects of addiction on the characters who inhabit this world. I definitely tried not to pick
a side on what is really a very complex cultural, moral, and
economic issue, but I think in some ways the issues are easier
to explore and discuss through metaphor. Overall, though, I
was drawn to combining cops and potions because it's really
fun and full of juicy conflicts.

*Who was the hardest character to write? And your favorite?*
I'm not sure anyone was particularly hard to write. This
world and its characters were very vivid for me from the
beginning. However, since I write in first person, Kate was
probably the most work since it's all in her voice.

My favorite character to write was Little Man (and by
extension his sister, Mary). The first time I showed a Little

Man–and–Mary scene to my agent she got totally creeped out, but I love that little bastard. He embodies everything I love about creating characters who are products of the world that created them.

***Kate is essentially a single parent on top of being a cop, an Adept, and a former coven member. What made you add that extra dimension?***

When I was a kid, from the ages of about three until five or six, my mother was in the police reserves in our town. During the day, she managed a bookstore, and at night she busted perps. Awesome, right? At that same time, she was also a newly divorced mom. Obviously that was all a pretty big influence on my life and, ultimately, my work. When some of your earliest memories are of field trips to the bookstore followed by a visit to the gun range, it sticks with you.

What's funny is I didn't even make those connections when I started the book. I was just kind of happily writing along, not questioning the choices I was making for Kate, including the addition of Danny, her younger brother. Then I was chatting with my mom one day and mentioned that I was working on this new book. It wasn't until I wrote what it's like to face down an armed perp in a dark alley that the connection hit me. While I didn't base Kate on my mother directly, those experiences strongly influenced the choices I made for the character.

So, yes, there is definitely a reason for making Kate a single mom. I'm fascinated by and in awe of women who manage to juggle the rigors of a career in a male-dominated field with the demands of a family. In addition, I wanted Kate to have the responsibility of Danny to keep her connected and grounded. He reminds her that there is still innocence in the world, even though she spends her day seeing the worst of humanity.

**How much research did you have to do to make the world feel so believable?**

One of the coolest discoveries I've made about being an author is that I'm willing to do all sorts of crazy things in service of my stories that I'd never do for just myself. For example, in order to understand cops, I signed up for a local police academy my city hosts for its citizens. For twelve weeks, I got to hold weapons, get up close with gallon bags of marijuana and vials of meth, and drive cop cars at high speeds. It was freaking amazing.

The program also gave us the chance to go on a ride-along with an officer. I spent eight hours on a deep-night shift with Officer Chris Turner, and that experience was invaluable because he was candid in answering all my nosy questions. I also went to North Carolina for the Writers' Police Academy. For three days, I took classes from ATF, DEA, sheriffs, EMS, and cops who worked in jails. I learned how to cuff people, interrogate suspects, and search cars for narcotics. So, basically, I'm just like a cop now, except without a gun, badge, powers of arrest, or bravery.

But learning how to think like a cop was only part of the challenge. I also had to read every book I could get my hands on about alchemy. In order to make the potions and magic in Kate's world seem believable, I needed a working knowledge of alchemical processes and symbolism. Naturally, I get to take some license with the magic, but I do want everything to have the ring of truth.

There were times when I was reading *Anatomy of the Psyche* by Edward F. Edinger, which is a Jungian text about the psychological implications of alchemical symbols, during the day, and then spending my night at Citizens' Police Academy learning how to defuse bombs. I officially have the coolest job ever.

**_Is there one thing about either the world or the characters of_ Dirty Magic _that you loved but couldn't fit into the book?_**
Ack, there's so much. The case Kate worked on in _Dirty Magic_ made it difficult to get too far into the other covens, and I had to keep Uncle Abe in the background to an extent. But that's the beauty of writing series. I get plenty of books to really dig deep into the world and the characters' backgrounds. There are lots more surprises in store for readers.

**_What is next for Kate and MEA?_**
The second book, _Cursed Moon_, will focus on the effects of a powerful Blue Moon on the Cauldron. It's a time when magic is heightened and secrets are revealed. We'll finally get to meet Aphrodite Jones, who is the leader of the sex magic coven, and I'm pretty sure it won't be too long before Kate has to deal with Uncle Abe. There's a lot more trouble cooking in the Cauldron.

# introducing

If you enjoyed
DIRTY MAGIC,
look out for

## STRANGE FATES

*by Marlene Perez*

*Brooding, leather-jacket-wearing Nyx Fortuna looks like a twentysomething and has for centuries now. As the son of the forgotten fourth Fate, Lady Fortuna, he has been hunted his entire life by the three Sisters of Fate who murdered his mother.*

*Fed up and out for revenge, Nyx comes to Minneapolis following a tip that his aunts have set up a business there. His goal: bring down his mother's killers and retrieve the thread of fate that has trapped him in the body of a twenty-year-old unable to age or die.*

*But when a chance meeting with the mysterious, dangerous, and very mortal Elizabeth Abernathy throws off his plans, he must reconcile his humanity and his immortality.*

*Fortuna audax iuvat—*
Fortune favors the bold

# Chapter One

The dank bathroom smelled, the stench thinly disguised by a lonely pine-scented air freshener that had probably been there since the club first opened.

I'd been at the bar nursing a beer since six, waiting for somebody who had information I needed. After I figured out my guy wasn't going to show, I'd drowned my disappointment with several shots of the Red Dragon's cheap whiskey, and now I was paying for it.

I started to push open the stall door, but a couple stumbled in, obviously looking for more privacy. The Red Dragon men's loo wasn't my idea of a romantic interlude, but whatever rocked their boats. I peered through the crack in the door to make sure they were decent.

The guy, a hipster-looking dude with a supercilious attitude, said something I didn't catch, but I heard the girl loud and clear.

She was tall and curvy, with ice-blond hair, the rare shade of white blond that nowadays almost always came out of a bottle. Her eyes were probably blue, I speculated.

A glimpse of her heart-shaped face propelled me forward, but I forgot the door in front of me and banged my shin in the process.

"There's someone in here," she said.

I took another peek. God, she was gorgeous, but I'd met

plenty of gorgeous girls. The spark of mischief in her eyes called to me. I'd bet the last hundred in my wallet that trouble followed her like a cat after cream. I wanted to get to know a girl like that.

Apparently, so did her date. "It's just some drunk," the guy said. "He won't even know we're here."

"I changed my mind," she said. "Let me go."

The guy smacked his lips a couple of times, which grossed me out no end. It was a good thing my stomach was empty, especially when I heard his sales pitch.

"C'mon, baby," he said. "You know you want to." Charming.

The girl pushed him away. "I said no, Brad."

"And I said yes," Brad replied.

I stepped out of the stall, unwilling to be witness to Brad's borderline attempted date rape any longer. Besides, I kind of liked the idea of playing knight errant for a change.

"She's not interested," I said. I crossed to the sink, washed my hands, and splashed cold water on my face. There was something about the girl that bothered me, but I couldn't get a fix on it.

When Brad looked away, the girl kneed him in the groin so hard he fell on the floor, gasping.

Evidently, no knight in shining armor was needed. I liked her even more. I stepped over Brad's prone form and extended my hand to the girl. "Hi, I'm Nyx."

She took it and a tingle went through my hand and a few other places. I was wrong. Her eyes were green, not blue. Even better.

"I'm Meadow," she said. The lilting sound of her voice sent the vibrations through me again.

"Hippie mom?" I asked.

"No, lunatic," she told me.

It must have been clear I wasn't following, so she elaborated.

"Lunatic mom, not hippie mom. My mom's way too young to be part of the peace generation. She did go through a grunge phase, though."

I ignored Brad's bitching and moaning and concentrated on Meadow. "Wanna get out of here?"

You'd be surprised how many times that line actually has worked, but I wasn't really counting on it to work on Meadow. Despite the fact that she'd been playing grab-ass with a creep like Brad, she seemed intelligent enough.

She smiled at me. "I don't think so."

"Listen, Nyx," Brad blustered from the floor. "Meadow is mine."

I raised an eyebrow. "She doesn't seem to think so."

"Wanna dance?" She gave me a smile so dazzling that my head spun.

I nodded and grabbed her hand and we exited the bathroom, ignoring Brad as we went.

The music hit my bloodstream as potently as any alcohol. I lost myself to the rhythm as Meadow swayed in front of me. Heads turned to enjoy the view. I couldn't blame them.

The tap on my shoulder wasn't completely unexpected. I knew Brad would come looking for us eventually. His hurt pride wouldn't allow him to slink off, no matter how much the kick to the balls had made him want to.

I took my time turning around. Brad would probably take a swing the minute I did and he didn't disappoint me. Mortals were so predictable.

I ducked and his fist slammed into the dancer behind me.

Dancer-dude shoved a burly-looking guy, who flew into a couple making out. That guy moved his girlfriend out of the way and shoved the burly guy. Burly guy flew into a group of girls and they shoved him back into the crowd. Burly guy bounced around like the ball in a giant pinball machine. Pretty soon there were punches being thrown wherever I looked. Two girls rolled around on the floor, pulling each other's hair. That's when it became a serious bar fight.

I looked around for Meadow but couldn't see her in the brawling crowd. I finally spotted her as she made her way to the bar, but then I lost sight of her when Brad took another swing at me. That punch connected to my jaw. I bit my tongue hard, and blood spurted into my mouth.

I grinned at him and hit him in the gut. I was no longer a tearstained child, drenched in my mother's blood. Blood didn't frighten me any longer. Time had hardened me. I wasn't just a survivor. I was a fighter. There was a knife hidden in my boot, but I didn't need it to fight a mortal.

Someone slammed into me and I lost my balance, but I was holding my own. I'd learned to fight a long time ago and I'd learned to fight dirty. Things were going well, too well, it turned out. Someone behind me hit me over the head with what felt like an anvil, but was probably just a barstool. I went limp as the world exploded behind my eyes. I shook it off and tried to stand, but that douche bag Brad put a knife in my heart.

And I'm not exaggerating the excellence of his aim. His blow went straight to my heart. It should have been a killing blow, but instead it felt like my heart was being squeezed by a giant fist. I stood there staring at him like an idiot as my blood dripped onto the floor. My aunts always said that I'd come to a bad end, but that was more of a promise than a prophecy.

"Was she worth dying over?" Brad stood over me. "I guess you'll never know." Ah, there it was. Although luck was always on my left shoulder, calamity kept her company on the right.

The world wasn't any better or any worse today than it was two hundred years ago. Mortals still killed each other in the name of their god, money, or sex.

Some things never changed.

"That hurt," I finally said, right before I passed out.

I bet you're wondering what kind of phony asshole I was or if I was crazy or high or both. I have been those things at one time or another, but that was the old me. The new me was one thing and that is truthful. I couldn't die, no matter how much I wanted to.

When I came to, I heard Meadow and Brad talking—arguing actually. I opened my eyes and saw two of everything, so I closed my eyes while I listened to their conversation.

"We can't just leave him," Meadow protested.

"I'm outta here," Brad said. "My dad will kill me if this hits the papers."

"I'm staying," Meadow said.

"Suit yourself," Brad said. "It's your life, what you have left of it."

If I ever saw that Brad guy again, I was going to curse him with an STD he'd never forget. I passed out again.

When I came to again, I was on the floor, but there was a guy taking my pulse.

"I'm an EMT," he said. I detected a slight slur to his words. He'd been drinking.

"Sure you are," I said.

"I'm off-duty," he said. Like I'd let a drunk corpse chaser work on me.

Meadow was kneeling there beside me, but there was only one of her this time. She was holding my other hand.

I sat up and almost gave the EMT a coronary. Brad was gone, which wasn't surprising. There were a bunch of people standing around me, but they didn't concern me. Meadow and the EMT had hopefully blocked me from the crowd's curious eyes—and if not, the dark bar and substantial amounts of alcohol that had been consumed would do the rest.

My jacket was on but my shirt had been ripped open, probably to get to the wound, but I didn't care about that. My rib cage ached and my jeans were smeared with blood. I touched a hand to my chest to make sure my mother's chain was there. It was made of such fine silver that most of the time I forgot I even had it on. I relaxed a fraction when I felt its weight, like a breath, light and warm, at the back of my neck.

"Your wound," the EMT said. "It's gone." I'd been skewered like a pig and would have another scar to add to my collection, but he didn't see that. I'd used a little magic to convince him otherwise.

"My jacket must have taken the worst of it," I lied quickly.

"Yeah, his motorcycle jacket is practically in tatters," Meadow said. "But he's barely scratched." It hurt to look into her green eyes. I realized what was familiar about her. She looked just like Amalie, but Amalie had been dead for a hundred years. I shook off the feeling of déjà vu.

I liked a girl who knew how to ad-lib. She had to see the gaping hole in my chest. I didn't have the strength to glamour both of them. I was intrigued by the matter-of-fact way she was handling my near-death. If I were a normal guy, that is. There was no way she could have known about me.

"It's not a motorcycle jacket," I replied. "It's a World War Two fighter pilot jacket." There were healing amulets sewn into it. I needed the amulets before I passed out from the pain.

"I'll take him home," she said. "He'll be fine."

"Meadow's right," I said. Her momentary lack of recognition of the name confirmed what I'd already suspected. Meadow was definitely not her real name. Probably something she told losers like Brad.

"A scratch?" The EMT was dumbfounded. "But there's blood all over the floor, all over him, all over everything."

"Yeah, I bleed a lot," I said.

"He's a hemophiliac," Meadow said. For a minute, I thought she'd oversold it, but the EMT bought it. The crowd dispersed after they all realized there was nothing exciting to see.

I scrambled to my feet and grabbed my jacket. "It's been fun, but I've gotta go." The sharp pain to my heart reminded me how stupid it had been to make a sudden movement, but I needed to make my exit before the cops got there. Or someone much much worse.

On the way out, I didn't see any surveillance cameras, which was a relief and another reason I gave holes like the Red Dragon my business.

The street was deserted, but it wouldn't stay that way long. Bar fights brought the cops, usually with sirens blaring, so I took it as a good sign that it was quiet.

I looked younger than my driver's license indicated, but that was to throw off the Wyrd Sisters or anyone else they sent looking for me. They'd managed to garner quite a bit of information about me, including the fact that I liked a lager now and then. My current driver's license said I was twenty-five, but I wasn't sure it would stand up to official scrutiny.

I'd grabbed a handful of cocktail napkins, but I had a feeling they wouldn't be nearly enough to stem the blood flowing down my chest. Though I'd made it out of the bar without any problems, the girl caught up with me two blocks away.

"Wait up," she called out. I kept walking, hunched over from the pain.

The original goal of the night was to meet my contact and get wasted, but now I just wanted to get the hell out of Dodge. Or Minneapolis. At least long enough to lick my wounds. I'd need every bit of strength for what I had planned. Meadow, or whatever her real name was, stayed close on my heels.

"I don't know how to say this politely," I said. "But get lost." A strange girl who looked like my dead ex? That smelled like trouble.

I kept one hand firmly on my wound and tried not to think about how my blood was slowly soaking a cheap bar napkin. It had started to snow and I blew on my other hand to try to warm it. Minneapolis was cold as Hades, but I didn't think my aunts would expect me here.

"I know a safe place," she said, panting a little as she caught up with me. "You're fast. It took me a few blocks to find you."

I swayed and stumbled and she grabbed me to help me stay upright. I moved away from her. "I can walk on my own," I croaked.

"Suit yourself."

We walked in silence for a moment.

She was so close that our arms brushed and I could smell her fresh citrusy scent. It didn't seem like her. I had expected her perfume to be something that suggested smooth whiskey and rumpled sheets.

"My car's this way," she said.

I wasn't sure I could trust her, but I was definitely attracted to her. It had been a long time since I'd felt anything that strongly. I shook my head to clear it.

It was the floral barrette that decided it for me. It looked like it belonged on a third-grader. I went along with her, even though my instinct warned me against it. I could pick up my Caddy in the morning. I'd made sure no one would spot it and if anyone tried to touch it, they'd regret it.

"What makes you think I need a safe place to stay?"

"The fact that you only had fifty dollars, no credit card, fake ID," she replied. She handed me my worn leather wallet.

I shot her a look. "I had a hundred in my wallet, not fifty."

405

"I wasn't going to keep it," she said, offended. "I wanted to see if Nyx was your real name."

I hesitated. She was cute, more than cute really, and I barely had enough money on me for a bus ticket out of there.

"So what's your real name?" I asked.

"What gave it away?"

I'd surprised her. Good. "You aren't as clever as you think you are," I said. What gave it away was that she waited a beat too long before she answered to Meadow. "What's the con?"

"It's not a con," she replied. "I'll explain in the car."

The distant wail of sirens made my decision easy. The scenery would be better with Meadow than where the cops would take me. I seriously doubted I'd find out her real name. I didn't really blame her. Names had power.

For instance, Nyx wasn't my real name, either, but I had taken it after the last time Gaston had found me, and I'd grown fond of it. I'd found myself reaching for that name more than any other, giving it out as easily as normal people did their given names. Regular Joes handed out their true names like verbal party favors instead of what they really were, secrets they should guard with their lives.

We came alongside a cherry-red Lexus with a license plate that read ZOOM-ZMM.

Meadow opened the passenger door and gestured for me to get in. I slid in cautiously.

"*I* don't give people phony names," I told her. A lie, but she didn't have to know that. "You were Meadow earlier. What's your story?"

She shrugged. "My name is Elizabeth. My real name." She looked me up and down. "You should see a doctor."

"No doctors," I said. She didn't seem surprised. Was she a poor little rich girl who picked up criminals for kicks? Not that

I was a criminal, but I wasn't the kind of boy you brought home to meet the folks, either.

"I'll take you to the cottage." She started the car and pulled out without bothering to look in the mirror. I winced, but it didn't slow her down. She gripped the wheel tightly, and I noticed her long slender fingers had nails that were bitten to the quick.

She drove without fear, taking the turns on the icy road with cavalier abandon. I didn't find it appealing, especially after she took a speed bump at fifty and my head went all fuzzy.

"Elizabeth, do you mind slowing down?" I said. I didn't believe that she'd given me her real name this time, either, but I liked the name Elizabeth.

She didn't answer, but she did slow down. When she turned a corner, though, jarring pain radiated out from my heart to my head. That was the last thing I remembered before I passed out.

VISIT THE ORBIT BLOG AT

# www.orbitbooks.net

FEATURING

## BREAKING NEWS
## FORTHCOMING RELEASES
## LINKS TO AUTHOR SITES
## EXCLUSIVE INTERVIEWS
## EARLY EXTRACTS

### AND COMMENTARY FROM OUR EDITORS

WITH REGULAR UPDATES FROM OUR TEAM,
ORBITBOOKS.NET IS YOUR SOURCE
FOR ALL THINGS ORBITAL.

WHILE YOU'RE THERE, JOIN OUR E-MAIL LIST
TO RECEIVE INFORMATION ON SPECIAL OFFERS,
GIVEAWAYS, AND MORE.

# imagine. explore. engage.